# HOLDER OF THE HORSES

Lisa Slater

Holder of the Horses

2019

This book is fiction; a product of the author's imagination. Any resemblance to persons, living or dead, is coincidental.

All rights reserved.

Copyright © 2019 by Lisa Slater

Book Design by Lisa Slater

Requests for permission to make copies of any part of the book can be submitted to:

Lisa Slater; infolisaauthor@yahoo.com

*Thank you, to my family and friends who have bestowed upon me their love and encouragement. Also, to my wonderful editor Max Van Zile, with Editing for Authors, who shines his light upon my pages.*

*Most of all, thank you to my husband who lifts me up onto his shoulders so that I can see further than I could ever see on my own. And my two sons, who are the joy of my heart. I love you.*

# HOLDER OF THE HORSES

## CHAPTER ONE

Twenty-year-old Jonny Sandgren leaned a slender shoulder into the large sliding door of his family's wooden barn as he watched the sun begin to rise over the beautiful land of eastern Montana. Lifting a mug of hot coffee to his sun-darkened face, he sipped at the bitter black liquid, contemplating the blood that had dripped into the making of this ranch—completely unopposed to adding his own. And therein lay the problem, the single element on which he and his mom disagreed most.

Unlike many twenty-year-old boys, Jonny knew exactly what he was destined to do. He was born to follow in his family's footsteps. Those large dimpled footfalls in the ground were compressed in the shape of a cowboy boot. Which, non-coincidentally, was exactly what Jonny intended to leave in his wake.

Despite the Spanish blood from his dad's side, and the Blackfoot blood from his grandmother, his blond hair with sun-bleached ends blew with the morning breeze. The fact couldn't be argued, he was the spitting image of his fair-skinned mom and her mother, who he called "Grams". Like Grams in her youth, he was a little too trim for his age, but handsome as heck—or so he was told.

Jonny watched the horizon, mesmerized as always, while the sun slowly emerged from its great exertion of providing light and warmth to the other side of the world. It never failed to impress him—enlighten him, really—that the sun never rested, nor slumbered. And if the sun didn't waste precious energy idly laying around, then neither should he. He took another sip of coffee, recalling the pieces of the Morris Ranch's history that he knew.

He knew it started with his great-great-grandfather, Charleston Morris. Naturally, Charleston had left the first and deepest footprints in the ground of the ranch's past. Following him was Jonny's grandpa, Sonny Morris, who'd married Amara Duncan: "Grams." The marks Sonny had left on the soil were spoken of with great love, and he was considered a family legend. Unfortunately, Grams only told the stories as they were triggered by events or memories. And never were they delivered in order, nor complete. Jonny often suspected it was because the stories were multifaceted, legends and truths folded together. His mom said it was because she was too old to keep them straight. Nonetheless, the only thing he loved more than working the ranch during the golden splendor of the day—either end, sunrise or sunset—was listening to Grams tell her stories.

Jonny stretched his shoulders as the sunlight glistened across the dew, then slapped a gloved hand against his leather chaps, turning to his mom, Charlie, inside the barn. "Where's Grams?" he asked. "I thought she wanted to help us move the herd today."

Charlie was organizing her things to fit perfectly as a puzzle of objects into the leather saddlebag hanging from her dark bay gelding, Wallow. A white Stetson cowgirl hat sat over her soft, blonde, shoulder-length hair, which swayed lightly as she turned her head to look at him. "Resting in her bed, hopefully," she answered. "Not only has she not ridden in years, she hasn't been feeling well. I really don't know what the stubborn woman was thinking, telling you she wanted to help."

Jonny likened watching his mom pack her saddlebag to art: "Charlie Art." The rest of the world would probably classify it as evidence of obsessive-compulsive disorder. But it wasn't. That's just how some folks are. Either way, it was something he had watched her do thousands of times, and had become involuntarily accustomed to—like breathing. Due to her unfailing process, Charlie always had a tool for every job: a snack for every rider, a first-aid kit putting the most respectable doctor's office to shame, a fold-up saw, a fold-up hammer, bag balm, and what seemed like a million other things. The list of "might need" was extensive, and had grown over the years.

Although it was agreed that Charlie was always overpacked and overprepared, she was never underappreciated. She was the glue keeping the ranch together. The older Jonny got, the more he recognized and valued the way her organized dexterity was being steadily woven into the fabric of his own identity as a man. He could almost sit back and watch her meticulous prudency mimicking itself in him. The exception being that he had packed his own saddlebag over an hour ago, and had filled it with only necessary tools, such as duct tape, a bundle of hay string, and a knife. He left out a snack for every rider, including plenty of frozen Starburst candies for himself. And where his mom's horse was still being packed like a mule in the middle of the barn aisle, his sorrel gelding, Nails, stood ready and waiting outside.

Jonny took another long sip from his coffee, looked out from under his raised eyebrows, and warned Charlie, "Grams said she wanted to come."

"Grams shouldn't be gallivanting around on the back of a horse, Jonny. She's eighty-nine years old," she defended, then dropped her saddlebag's leather flap into place. "Stop encouraging her, will you?"

Jonny's dad, Billy Sandgren, stepped into the barn, his gleaming black horse in tow. "Grams will do what Grams thinks she ought to do," Billy said as he wrapped the lead to his horse's halter around a pole. "As for me, I snuck out of the house quiet as a church mouse." He winked at Charlie. "As requested."

Charlie grinned at him appreciatively.

Billy had a handsome Spanish face, dark-skinned with jet black hair. Many of Jonny's female friends had told him they thought his dad looked like Antonio Velazquez, though Jonny would add "with a well-fed gut" for good measure and a laugh. All laughs aside, what Jonny admired most about his dad was his honest sense of humor, and the fact that he was one hell of a cowboy. A superior set of qualities Jonny aspired to live up to.

"Oh, almost forgot," Billy said, tossing Charlie a banana. "You're always taking care of everyone except yourself!" He turned to grab his saddle.

"I meant to grab something on my way out," Charlie defended.

Saddle in his arms, Billy bent and kissed the top of Charlie's cowgirl hat. "Only your hands were full of snacks for everyone else."

"Just trying to keep my husband happy."

Billy's cowboy boot lifted from the ground and bumped Charlie's rear with a soft thud. "You already do."

"Cut it out!" said Jonny. "That's a visual I don't want to relive when I close my eyes at night. I'm going to run to the house. I think I forgot something." He almost made it out the barn door before Billy stopped him.

"Oh no you don't. You are *not* going to go wake Grams."

Jonny crossed his arms argumentatively. "If we leave her, there will be hell to pay."

"So, we'll pay—when we get back. Right now, let her rest. She's done her fair share of work."

Jonny shook his head, considering whether or not it was in his best interest to continue advocating for Grams. He'd warned them twice as it was. Suddenly, a shadow moved at the back of the barn, and Grams wobbled into the light, a grooming bucket swinging from the deformed fingers of her right hand, and her cowgirl hat adorned with a white feather dangling from her left.

"Calm down, Jonny," she grumbled as she shuffled, snail-paced, across the compacted dirt. "I've been here all along. I snuck out of the house and fled like a fugitive to my own barn, right after you."

Jonny knew in Grams' younger days she had been a tiny beauty, with golden-blonde hair flowing past her waist, and fire in her veins all the way to her toes. As Grams told it, Grandpa Sonny had met her, fallen in love, and brought her here to the ranch. And here she still was. The difference was, now her waist had less definition, her skin was as dry and crumpled as an old newspaper, and her body had begun failing her one piece at a time. Her hair was still long, of course, but it had been gray for as long as Jonny could remember. Charlie brushed it and pulled it back into a thick braid for her every morning, apparently a ritual they had begun years ago. One thing had not changed, however—the fire in her veins still ran all the way to her toes.

Frowning at Charlie, Grams limped past her surprised and disapproving daughter. When she reached Jonny, she offered up a wide, toothy smile, making it extremely clear that he was her favorite, today.

Placing a wrinkled hand upon his shoulder, she said, "Thank you for catching my horse for me and putting him in the back stall. Would you hold him while I climb on? I'm not the ballerina I once was."

Jonny nodded and set his coffee mug on a post. "You were a ballerina, Grams?" he asked as he strolled to retrieve her horse from the shadowy stall in the back. "You never told me that."

"Of course not," Grams spat. "But at least I could bend at the hip before. Now I can't bend at the waist either. Or the elbow. Or the knee." She continued grumbling while the rest of them mentally turned down their nonexistent hearing aids.

Heading for the horse, Jonny had to carefully pass his fuming mother, giving her a wide berth as she glared a hole in the side of his head. "You two conspired against me?"

As he made it down the aisle, Jonny could feel a new hole in the back of his head developing. Resisting the temptation to pet the hair down over the burning hole, he kept his eye on the prize: the back stall. Once he reached it, he could dip out of view and out of range.

"No," Grams answered. Jonny heard her hang the grooming bucket on a hook against the wooden plank wall. Her hat, too. "You tried—unsuccessfully, I might add—to conspire against *me*."

"Amara," Billy interrupted gently, securing his rope to his saddle and patting his big black horse. "Why the sudden urge to ride?"

"Sudden urge?" Grams asked, placing her fragile fists on her hips. "There's nothing sudden about it. I haven't ridden in years."

"Exactly my point," Billy interjected. "It's too risky. I know you want—"

"And I'd say I'm long overdue," Grams cut Billy short. "Think I can't do the job anymore? Need I remind you who won the last bet? Who was able to walk right up to the agitated red roan broodmare?"

Billy sighed. "You."

Grams nodded, looking like a bobblehead that had been left out in the sun, the plastic crinkling and wrinkling. "That's right. I'm the one who helped bring her foal into this world. That's because she knows," Grams said, tapping her crooked finger on her head.

"Knows what?" Billy asked.

"She knows I pay the bills."

Billy chuckled. "We just don't want to see you get hurt."

"I've never been hurt a day in my life!" Grams said. Her chin lifted in boastful pride.

"What about last summer when the heifer pinned you against the railing?" Charlie asked.

"A sore rib," Grams answered.

"Was it five years ago now that the gray mare kicked you in the head?" Billy asked.

Grams lifted her frail shoulders. "I think it's been longer than five years, but it was just a headache. I didn't even go to the hospital."

"You should have," Charlie said.

Having returned with Grams' chestnut mare, Jonny joined in, "What about the time your horse spooked and dumped you onto the barbed wire fence?"

Grams glared at him. "I got a scratch. I could say just as much for the rest of you. Now stop flapping your lips and grab me a headstall off the wall. The one with the silver shanks," she said, pointing.

"Yes, Ma'am," said Jonny, grabbing the requested headstall.

"Only the rest of us aren't eighty-nine years old," Charlie continued the debate.

The argument was far from over, and Jonny feared it would never be. Standing toe to toe were the two most stubborn women he had ever met.

"No, no, no," Grams said. "Take the leather reins off, Jonny." Pulling a set of rough, textured brown and black reins from around the waist of her jeans, she handed them to him with a satisfied smile. "I use these. Your Great-Gramps made them with his own hands, using horsehair."

Jonny smiled and nodded. "You remembered to bring them from the house."

"Of course I did," Grams retorted spiritedly.

"Mom," Charlie cut in, pulling her attention back.

Tenderly, Grams laid her hand on Charlie's shoulder. "I'm riding with my grandson, Charlie. I won't be stopped." She took a deep breath, allowing the admission to linger. Releasing the breath, she conceded with great sadness, "I won't ask to ride again."

"You mean, you won't *demand* to ride again," said Charlie. Grams nodded gravely in agreement. Charlie hung her head, clearly feeling no typical winning spirit. "All right," she finally said. Turning to Jonny, she gave the order. "Give her a leg up."

After trading out the leather reins for the horsehair, Jonny softly slipped the headstall over the head of Grams' chestnut mare and smoothed down the forelock.

This was to be the last ride for both horse and rider. The mare had been a faithful partner—also long past her prime—and deserved a good rest. Jonny flung the reins over the horse's dainty, aged head. As he did, for just a flash, he experienced a strange sensation. Some sort of stirring in the air. It was one of those moments which caused a person to pause and look up, expecting to see something. But as soon as the something is confronted, it vanishes, sensation and all, leaving no realization to be understood, and a doubt there was ever anything to begin with.

The old mare didn't even blink as Jonny positioned himself next to her shoulder. Standing as still as the mountains, the mare waited for her long-standing friend to climb onto her back. Grams nodded, just once, in approval, as she carefully placed her tiny leather boot in Jonny's woven hands, and he lifted her carefully up onto the mare.

Why they all stopped what they were doing and held their breath, Jonny didn't know. Had they expected her to topple over? Or break her brittle bones just sitting in the saddle? Heaven knew the saddle was darn near older than the dirt they were standing on. Theoretically, it should have crumbled years ago, but Grams wouldn't let the old thing die. Jonny was suspicious that Grams had put more money into the historical saddle over the years than anything else on the property. One day, he would retire the poor sack of leather and situate it affectionately next to her favorite chair. There, he could gaze upon it, remember, and tell her stories. If he could ever get them straight.

"Jonny," Grams said, pointing to her dirty cowgirl hat with the white feather stuck in it. "Hand me my war bonnet." He did, and she plopped it on her head, pulling it down snugly. She sat tall in her saddle, as tall as she could with a hunched back, ready to ride.

Surprisingly, she didn't look out of place: not too old, nor too delicate. With her hat on her head, she looked like a textbook picture of what every cowgirl fantasized about being. The difference was that Grams wasn't fantasizing. No, the tough woman had lived every day of a harsh, demanding life. There was a story for every scar and a scar for every story—though not all were visible. Jonny knew Grams wasn't perfect, but in his eyes, she was perfectly proud. She had been born a cowgirl, and a cowgirl she would always be.

As Jonny swung his long leg over the back of Nails, Grams winked at him. He smiled, glad she was riding with him, but terribly disappointed that it was to be her last time. Grams had taught him so much more than just the job. She had taught him how to play while *doing* the job. She had taught him how to find, and possess, the joys and freedoms of tending to land and animals. She taught him to love the dirt and the wind, and to take pride in the pain. When they worked together, it was more than work, it was ranching.

Today's chores consisted of checking fences (always checking fences), checking in on the herd of yearlings, and moving the broodmares closer to the house for foaling. Just like Grams, his favorite chore was moving the herds, especially the horses. There was just something liberating about riding alongside a herd of horses.

Tipping his hat, Jonny whooped, and Grams tipped her hat and whooped in reply. Jonny laughed. Maybe, just maybe, he had fire running through his veins too.

Outside, they began to work on the fence, and Jonny pulled two strands of broken wire together on a section of collapsed fence with a loud grunt. Unbothered by the tedious, never-ending chore of fixing fence—presumably created by either a herd of horse-sized elk, or a family group of mule deer—Jonny felt fortunate to be working on land that belonged to his family. The air was crisp and clean, and the early spring sunshine reignited life all around him.

From the back of her horse, Grams dutifully handed him tools on request, and kept both their horses occupied with chunks of carrot from her saddlebag.

"Grams, you're going to spoil my horse," Jonny protested, as he spliced two strands of wire together.

"Pish posh," Grams retorted, as she shoved another chunk of carrot into Nails' greedy mouth. "It didn't ruin you when I snuck *you* cookies at bedtime."

Jonny laughed. "Maybe it did. Maybe I would be a devoted dietarian today if I hadn't been spoiled by you and your sugar. Ever think of that?"

"Let's not forget the red meat," Grams volunteered.

"Yeah, there went my chance at being a vegetarian too," Jonny said, straining to pull the next broken lines close enough to clamp on his wire stretcher. "I could be enjoying a tofu and veggie burger in an air-conditioned country club, practicing my golf clap right now."

Grams tapped the fingers of her right hand quietly against the palm of her dry left palm. "What a torturous, boring noise," she mumbled. "Really, if a person has a reason to cheer, then they ought to make more of a commotion of it. For example, when my grandson uncorks a bronc, I'm going to wake the snakes. Isn't that right?" Jonny nodded in encouragement, so she continued. "And when my daughter and son-in-law bring in the herd, you won't see me standing at the gate quietly murmuring, 'Aw, what a beautiful sight this is.' And you sure as heck won't catch me eating a tofu burger! Make me a hamburger! A burger raised on my family's grass, suckled on the tit of our fine heifer and bred by my family's first choice bull. And don't forget to smother it with butter."

Laughing, Jonny fastened the broken lines to the stretcher and ratcheted it until they were close enough to splice. "Grams, you sure have a way of making me hungry. It's not even lunchtime yet."

"Ask your mom for something. I saw her saddlebag; the poor pitiful seams were screaming. No one warned them she was coming. Otherwise, the thread would have slithered out and ran off a long time ago." Grams thought about that. "I suppose thread can't run without legs, though. Can it?" Not bothering to wait for a reply, she gazed up at the sun. "Is it just me, or is the sun moving more quickly?" she asked. "Speaking of which, I'm pretty sure I fixed this section of fence before, but twice as fast. Are you getting old, or am I getting impatient?"

"Well, then, get down here and show me how it's done, impatient woman."

"I would, I would," Grams assured him. "But if I got off, you would have to give me a leg up again. Subsequently, you would throw out your back, old man. Then where would we be?"

"Good point," Jonny said, smiling as he fastened the last strands of wire together. "Stay up there and supervise. You're good at that."

"Yes, I believe I will. I have to keep my eye on you." Grams squinted skeptically at him. "Boys your age tend to forget that idle hands are the devil's playground."

"Preach on, sister." Jonny handed Grams the wire stretcher and mounted his horse. "Let's finish this fence line and work our way to the broodmares. Mom and Dad can manage getting the herd collected and moving without us. We can take our time."

"Take our time?" Grams asked, disgusted. "Is that how you remember riding with me?"

"Not a single day of my life."

Grams clucked to her horse, which took off at comfortable lope. "Keep up, slowpoke." Her body jerked, stiff from age, but she refused to stop.

Jonny called, "Hold up, Grams! Wait."

Grams ignored him, riding haphazardly away.

"Does this mean you're getting the next gate?" Jonny hollered as he kicked Nails into a lope to follow her.

"Not a chance," he heard her voice call through the breeze.

After the fences had been checked and mended on all the lines assigned for today, they rode through the yearling pasture. Pulling their horses to a stop at the top of a knoll, they looked out over the land where the yearlings munched and played. The two gelding elders, strategically placed in the herd of yearlings to keep order like crosswalk guards, paid little heed to the rambunctious youngsters, unless a colt took it upon himself to flout or make a nuisance of himself. Jonny could tell his mom and dad had already been through the area by the shod hoofprints and overturned grass edges, so he and Grams continued on.

When they caught up to where his parents had prepared the herd of broodmares for the move, they slowed. His mom and dad sat on their own horses, across the herd in the distance. Glancing at Grams, Jonny noticed she suddenly appeared old and weary— even more than usual. Her crinkled cheeks were flushed from the wind, but the rest of her face was bedsheet-pale. "Grams," he said as he sidestepped his horse closer to hers, "I think it's time to take you home."

"Not yet," Grams said, shaking her head.

Jonny wasn't convinced. He glanced at his mom. If she happened to get any closer, she would certainly see Grams' deteriorating condition and stop the foolishness immediately.

Charlie, having spotted them, waved, and Jonny and Grams both lifted a hand in return. While dutifully observing the herd, Jonny spoke from the side of his mouth. "You don't look well. You know Mom will skin me alive for not taking better care of you."

Grams reached out and touched his knee. "You have taken fine care of me," she reassured him. "I am a blessed woman. Thank you for riding with me."

"Will this really be your last ride?" Jonny asked, afraid to hear the honest answer.

Grams patted his knee, consoling him, as if he were ten years old and had fallen from his bike: there, there. Then she took a deep breath of the fresh air and closed her eyes. A moment later, she opened them. "I'm too old to take the lead. You best take my spot up front."

The lead position was typically filled by the boss, or the highest-ranking rider of the group. The lead position is a place of high esteem, distinction, and duty. The lead rider isn't just trusted to blaze the safest and easiest route, they guide the herd through hazards, indicate danger, and become the pivotal rider in turning and holding the horses in times of rest, watering, and settling. On any normal day, that would have been Billy. But with Grams present, as far as ownership and respect, the lead was granted to her. Today, however, she decided to bestow the honor on Jonny. Pleased, he obediently took off at a lope, not wishing to disappoint.

Shortly after, Grams sent a loud, shrill whistle over the herd's heads, catching Charlie and Billy's attention. When they looked, she drew a circle above her head with her crooked fingers pointing to the heavens. Round 'em up!

Jonny could see the smiles on his parents' faces, and agreed with their sentiments. It felt darn good having Grams taking the reins again. Both Charlie and Billy kicked their horses into a trot and took separate positions on either side of the herd. Grams urged her sweet horse on and began pushing the herd forward, slow and steady.

Today was not about running and whooping with everyone's hair on fire, nor was it about checking off this chore in order to move on to the next. Today was about something more. Something indefinable and inexpressible. An old traditional feel to a new and changing breeze. Today the familiar chore, done a thousand times before, felt surreal, as Grams' fingers embraced her horsehair reins and her slumped shoulders moved along with the movement of her steady horse. The pair, horse and rider, were tired but ceaseless. They knew their job, and neither would quit until it was finished.

The Bible says there's a time for everything.

It was time to bring the herd home.

# CHAPTER TWO

"Good boy, Wallow," said Charlie, patting her dark bay horse as she quietly set out the next morning to check the health of the stock, her rifle and saddlebag strapped securely to her saddle. "I know you'd rather be sleeping in. We all make sacrifices."

Wallow walked briskly over the hard roads and waited like a gentleman at each gate as Charlie dismounted and mounted again and again. Together, they patiently moseyed through the herds, checking each and every animal they came across for signs of injury or illness. It was a skill her Great-Gramps, Charleston Morris, had taught her. For a man that had been as old as dirt by the time she knew him, he had an unflappable sense of tolerance and kindness for her when she was a child. Instead of losing patience with her inexhaustible horror at ranch life, he'd waited until she had been soothed (usually by a parent), and then he would teach her how to care for the animals she loved. That was part of ranch life too, he told her.

It had been a good year thus far. They hadn't lost but a handful of animals to the all-too-common natural hazards of weather, predators, and sickness. Charlie would consider it a lucky year, although she knew it wasn't *all* luck, but enduring, determined work. Her sleepless hours were worth it. With livestock came deadstock. It was the single largest reason she struggled with the life she had been handed. She hated death.

Ranching was the family business. Although it wouldn't have been her first choice, it was, in the end, her choice. And as Gramps had taught her, she embraced it and made it better with her organization and tenderness. The others wouldn't admit it outright, but they appreciated her extra effort, enabling them to cowboy more and worry less. It was teamwork in motion, the way a family ranch was meant to be.

Charlie smiled at a calf suckling at his mother's tit, his tiny tail swishing happily back and forth. The cow watched her and Wallow warily as they passed peacefully by. Just as they prepared to continue on, a soft bellow sounded from behind a straggly tree stretching its arms out in every direction, clinging to the world with its dead leafless branches. The bellow was not that of a bothered cow calling to its naughty calf who had wandered too far, or that of a provoked cow warning the herd of an approaching threat. It was a low bellow of inescapable anguish.

Charlie trotted hastily towards the sound.

As soon as she came around the tree, she pulled up on the reins, slowing Wallow's heavy hooves, not wishing to startle the anguished cow and push it into further distress. She was here to help the cow, not make its situation worse. But when Charlie's eyes landed on the source of the anguished bellow, she knew liberating it was impossible. The cow had become so entangled in the barbed wire fencing that, with her struggling, she had ripped her lovely brown hide clean off her bones. One leg was strung up awkwardly, obviously broken. The cow's miserable head rested on the ground, her white eyes bulging and rolling, her pasty white tongue draping over her jaw.

Charlie sighed sorrowfully, and stepped from her saddle. As soon as the toe of her boot touched the grass, her legs felt as if they had been poured with concrete. They did not want to help her do what needed to be done. After all, it had been her fault. The fence had a hole the cow had tried to get through. Standing by Wallow, she told herself that she should have checked this pasture last week. A dozen things she could have done better flooded through her mind, filling her heart with bitterness and remorse.

As Charlie reached up with her sweaty hand to retrieve her rifle, her palm rested on the butt instead, and a memory she had carefully buried came back to her.

\*\*

*Charlie Morris' scrawny six-year-old hind end hit the thick blanket of cold snow with a thud. The evil red pony she had previously been sitting on kicked out its back foot in triumph and trotted off. Sitting there, rump in the snow, tears welled up behind her stubborn glare. She tried to sniff them away, but they collected nonetheless, like tiny pools just above her bottom eyelids.*

*"Get up, Charlie!" Amara called. "Catch him before he takes off!"*

*Her mother Amara, young and slender, was sitting on Jake, a black gelding which Charlie thought looked more like a giant black sheep since his winter coat had grown in. Amara was dressed from head to toe in thick winter clothing, a scarf wrapped around her blonde head, hat on top, another scarf around her neck, and a long brown jacket long enough to cover the tops of her thighs. Her gloved finger pointed at the red pony.*

*"Pops is your ride home! You best catch him!"*

*Charlie looked at her mommy, knowing her tears were not only showing but that they would soon frost over and be stuck. Pops had slowed to a walk and would be making his way home between fits of digging, in hopes of finding hidden grass beneath the cover of winter's blinding whiteness.*

*"I don't want to ride Pops!" Charlie cried, lugging herself and the heavy winter clothing she wore out of the loose, dry snow that had swallowed her feet. She didn't dust the snow off her rear, because she just didn't care if it was there or not. The tears were pouring down now. They weren't supposed to, the little traitors. They were giving away her displeasure at being dumped, but she couldn't stop them. Her hind end hurt. Her britches were wet. And now she was cold.*

*"Charlie, baby, if you don't get back on Pops, you'll be walking. In the snow. All the way home. Come on. Get back on. At least the snow caught you, right? You're not hurt?"*

*Charlie shook her head and sniffed, half-heartedly dusting her hind end and starting towards Pops. Pops was pawing angrily at the snow, but he must have noticed her anyhow because he stepped away, turning his fluffy red butt to her. Charlie glared. "Stupid pony." With every step she took, Pops matched her, almost print for print. "Pops," she growled. "Stop it!"*

*Pops pinned his short, hairy ears.*

*Amara appeared on the other side of Pops, leaned down, and grabbed his reins. "Stop it, Pops," she reprimanded him. "Come on, Charlie! Hop on, baby. We're almost done checking for early newborns."*

*"I don't want to ride him, Mommy. He's a bad pony."* Charlie stood next to Pops, staring at the empty saddle. It was going to remain empty. Not because she wouldn't get in it, but because he would keep bucking her off. *"Stupid pony,"* she grumbled.

Pops ignored her.

*"Alright, alright,"* Amara finally conceded, stepping from her horse and joining Charlie in the snow. She kneeled down and smiled. *"Would you like to ride Jake?"* she asked gently.

Charlie nodded. *"What will you ride, Mommy?"*

Amara stood up, placing a single gloved hand on Pops' fluffy butt. *"What? You don't think I can handle him?"* Pops' brown eye looked at her. Charlie giggled. No, she was pretty sure Mommy could handle Pops, but it would be a guaranteed funny. Amara put her fists on her hips and nodded, a smirk covering her face. *"Challenge accepted,"* she said staunchly.

With that, she set Charlie onto Jake's warm back and proceeded to climb aboard Pops. She was too big for the pony, her legs dangling like long strings. At first, Pops ignored her, but when she picked up the reins and stuck a heel in his rib, he lost sight of the little grass nub he had been betting was just beyond that last layer of the snow. His hairy belly expanded as he held his breath, then everything exploded.

Short, fluffy red legs popped up in every direction. Amara spurred Pops, who snorted and tossed his head. Too quick for a lazy pony, Amara caught his nose and sent him in a tight circle. They went around and around, digging up a track in the snow. They circled so much that Charlie started to feel dizzy watching them. Every time Pops lifted a hoof, Amara spurred him to hurry his pace. Faster and faster they went. Amara laughed, Pops snorted, and Charlie watched, rather entertained.

After a short while, Charlie realized her hind end hurt a little. She set her elbow on the saddle horn and her chin on the back of her gloved hand. She had watched with interest, but now she was starting to wonder when it would be over. She was getting bored watching Mommy and Pops turning and turning, and she yawned.

Jake yawned too, grateful for the break from hoofing his way through the snow. But the more they stood, the more the sweat under his thick coat chilled. Jake began to get impatient too, and dipped his head, bumping the reins to get Charlie's attention.

"Mommy, are you done?" Charlie whined.

"Do you see?" Amara asked, her breath hitting the late winter air, looking like thick clouds of smoke, inviting Charlie's attention to the task. Pops was swinging his back end around and around. "Disengage his back feet. Put them to work. And then…" Amara released Pops and sat very still. "There. Just how Daddy showed us. Right?"

"Yes, Mommy."

"Would you like to lead the way?" Amara asked, fixing her coat around her.

"Yes, Mommy!" Charlie answered brightly, as she straightened her back, sitting tall in the saddle. She got to ride Jake and lead. That made her very special. Just as Charlie moved her short legs to nudge Jake forward, she heard a loud bang fill and shake the icy air. Her head jerked towards the sound as the echo bounced off the far hills. Amara turned too.

"It's alright, Charlie—"

*Amara had tried to comfort her daughter, but it was no use. No use at all. Charlie kicked Jake as hard as she could, and the horse picked up his heavy feet and started loping slowly through the thick snow, heaving his giant body up and over, up and over.*

*"No, Charlie!" Amara called after her. "Stop!"*

*Another rifle shot filled Charlie's ears and reported softly, as if it were whispering, "You're too late." The deed had been done. Charlie kicked Jake again, refusing to believe it. Daddy and Gramps were growing bigger the closer she got. She knew Mommy was behind her, making slow progress with Pops, trying to get after her, but it was no use. Charlie's heart just couldn't take it. She had to stop them.*

*"Daddy!" Charlie called. "Stop!"*

*Sonny glanced up, rifle still in his arm, pointing at a large lump on the ground. His radiant blue eyes shone out from a handsome, stubble-covered face, and a few strands of his blond hair peeked out from under a brown cowboy hat.*

*"Please! Stop shooting her, Daddy!" Charlie cried desperately. Jake was glad to rest, and Charlie flew off his back, landing on her rear again. The fall was farther than she had expected, but she landed in soft, deep snow. "Please, Daddy..." she begged as she struggled desperately toward him through the snow.*

*"Charlie, what are you doing?" Sonny handed his rifle to Gramps and hunkered down to catch her in his big arms. "You know better than to run off from Mommy like that."*

*Charlie peeked over her daddy's broad shoulder and saw Gramps' aged face staring at her. It was a face she loved, but today it held no compassion for what she had done. He was not happy with her. She knew it* was wrong to run up on them while they were shooting a rifle, and it was wrong not to listen to Mommy, too. She wanted to explain it to Gramps, she couldn't help it, but no such excuse would be enough.

Never minding the trouble she was in, Charlie looked at the cow lying on the snow. The cow was dead. Charlie buried her face in Sonny's coat and sobbed. "Why, Daddy?" Her sobs were muffled by his powerful shoulder, snot and tears leaving a wet mark there.

Sonny held her tightly against him. He didn't care about any snotty wet marks. "I'm sorry, my little one," he whispered into her ear.

But his gentle apology didn't help. The cow's thick tongue still hung from its gaping mouth, haunting Charlie's tender heart. Although she squeezed her eyes shut tightly, the image wouldn't be rid of. She cried, trying desperately to will it not true. But she couldn't will it away with wishes and tears.

At the sound of Pops' tiny hooves joining the group, Charlie felt Daddy's arms loosen from around her and set her down. With her back to the dead cow, Daddy pointed her to Gramps. "Go with Gramps now. I'll catch up with you."

Gramps held out his hand, and she took it. With his other hand, he collected the brown and black horsehair reins he always used and pulled his horse along behind. Mommy softly placed Pops' reins into her gloved fingers. A few steps away, Gramps carefully blocked Charlie's view of the dead cow and helped her mount onto Pops. Headed for home, she felt colder than she had earlier.

"Charlie," she heard Sonny's voice break the bitter silence when he caught up to ride alongside her. "I know you love the cows, but you must never run up on anyone when they're shooting, ever again. Do you understand?"

"But—"

Sonny held up a hand to silence her as Gramps pulled ahead. "That was very dangerous. For everyone. I will not entertain an argument on this, Charlie," he said sternly. A tear slid down her cheek at his harsh reprimand. Sonny was never harsh.

After a long minute or two, his voice softened. "Would an answer to your question help you to understand?"

Charlie wasn't quite certain it would. She felt, with all the conviction a tiny body could feel, that life wasn't to be taken senselessly. A six-year-old little girl putting such big feelings into little words was a hopeless feat, so she simply nodded.

Charlie watched Gramps' hunched shoulders sway over his visibly stiff spine as he poked ahead of them, pretending he couldn't hear. Mommy said Gramps always heard more than he let on. But true to his dependable character, he slowly led her further and further away from the nightmare behind them—while remaining just within earshot of the conversation.

"Nothing lives forever." Sonny pointed to a giant old tree that had fallen over, piled high with snow. "We all are born, serve our purpose, and then die."

"What was the tree's purpose?" Charlie asked, distracted by its dead and straggly limbs.

"The tree provided food and shelter, for us and other animals. Even in its death, it continues to house bugs and shelter tiny animals." Charlie thought about that as Daddy continued in the smooth and masculine voice she found comforting. "People and animals die too."

"Not you, or Mommy, or Gramps though."

Gramps' head nodded up and down. "Me too," he called over his shoulder.

"No, Gramps!" Charlie whined. Gramps wouldn't die, like a cow. He was going to stay right here with her, forever. Right alongside her, Mommy, and Daddy.

"Hush, Charlie," Gramps reprimanded. Whining grated on his nerves. "Grandma Lizzy is waiting for me. And I've been taking my sweet time about it. I'm sure she's growing impatient."

Charlie fell quiet, thinking.

Grandma was already in heaven. She had never met Grandma Lizzy. Would she recognize Grandma when she got there? It would be nice to know someone was waiting in heaven for her, too. "Will you wait for me, Gramps, like Grandma waits for you?" Charlie asked. "I'm scared I won't know anyone, or where I should go."

"With bells on," Gramps answered in his raspy voice.

"You too, Daddy?"

"Me too."

"Pinky promise not to forget?"

"Pinky promise," Sonny assured her, and he stuck a gloved pinky out towards her. "You just promise to take your sweet time about getting there, like old Gramps is doing."

"We all will," Charlie agreed, smiling as she grasped his pinky with her own. Charlie watched Pops' ears flick this way and that before she asked, "Did the cow go to the other side?"

"Would it be heaven if she didn't?"

Charlie thought carefully. The things she liked most about life were the animals. "No," she answered.

"Well then, you know she did. Wouldn't be heaven without her, now would it?"

Feeling the fresh sting of the cow's death, Charlie asked, "Why did you shoot her, Daddy?"

"I have an important job, Charlie. Do you know what it is the animals ask of those who care for them?"

"To feed them?"

Sonny's head bobbed in agreement. "We also mend them when they're hurt or sick. What else?" he asked, pushing her to think harder.

Charlie thought and thought. The cold air was numbing her brain. Finally, she was able to offer another answer. "Protect them?"

"From what?"

Charlie scratched her nose with her thick glove. "Other animals, like mountain lions and wolves."

"Yes." His head bobbed encouragingly again. "And?"

Charlie thought some more. Was she supposed to know the answer? Was her brain too frozen to conjure something up, or did she truly have no idea? She was fairly certain she didn't know, and wondered if Daddy or Gramps was going to tell her. Or was this one of those times they weren't going to tell, and let her stew over it instead? They often told her that she'd figure it out on her own, even if it took a few years. Charlie hated when they told her that. There were questions she had asked that she still had no answers to. Some of them, she'd plum forgotten what they even were. Gramps had said once, "I suspect you'll remember the question when the answer presents itself." Well, that didn't make her feel at all better.

Charlie growled under her breath, frustrated.

Luckily, this time Gramps bailed her out. "The animals, sometimes they get themselves into a bad predicament," he said. "In those times, they expect us to protect them from something truly awful."

"What?" Charlie asked, her eyes wide with fear. She wasn't aware of anything so truly awful that wasn't a mountain lion or a wolf.

"Suffering."

Blinking away the fog that clouds over a person's eyes when cold air blows on them too long, Charlie thought about the word. Suffering. Suffering from what? From who? What kind of suffering? How had Daddy known the cow was…suffering?

Gramps bailed her out again. "The cow Sonny shot, she was starving." There was a long pause, as if Gramps was deciding whether he ought to say more. "She ventured away from the herd, and from the feed." He decidedly left it at that. Charlie guessed there may be more, but if he thought she couldn't handle it, he was right. She didn't want to know any more.

"She wasn't going to make it," Sonny said. "She was suffering."

When Daddy looked at her, she nodded that she understood. Her understanding was limited, and wasn't entirely accurate, but it was enough for today. Maybe, when she wasn't feeling this raw gnawing in her tummy, she would inquire further.

"That," Daddy stressed, "is when we're called to do our best." He looked forward again and spoke so softly that Charlie could barely hear him. "It won't feel like your best," he explained, as his horse stepped through the thick snow. "But whether you are called to mend a cow, or you are called to end a cow, do your best. Alright, my little one?"

"Alright, Daddy."

\*\*

Charlie stood with her hand on the butt of her rifle, looking into the eyes of the miserable cow, strung up by wire and waiting to die. She was suffering. The cow looked at Charlie, and a calm seemed to sweep over both of them. Even the breeze stilled.

Charlie lifted her rifle from its dark leather scabbard. Clutching it by its hard wood stock, she carried it a few feet in front of her horse and pointed the long barrel at the center of the cow's skull, lining up the front and rear sights. She would do her best, so when she pulled the trigger, the cow wouldn't feel another thing in this world.

The butt of her rifle kicked against her shoulder and the shot rang in her ears, even long after it was over. Little singing birds scattered like brittle leaves in a windstorm, quickly as their feathered wings could carry them. Hating death, Charlie lowered the rifle. The cow's suffering had ended, and she had done her best. Though she agreed with her daddy, it didn't feel like it.

## CHAPTER THREE

That evening, Charlie handed Jonny a large bowl, filled to the brim with steaming chicken and dumplings from the extra-large crockpot. Jonny took it, eyes and mouth watering, then disappeared into the living room. She heard the familiar plop of his rear hitting the leather couch, across from the fireplace. It wasn't lit this time of year, but it was still the focal point of the log-and-beam living room.

Billy was next in line. He cradled his empty bowl in his hands as if it were a toad about to wiggle free and hop off. As she ladled hot supper into it, he gazed in, grinning from ear to delighted ear. Then he followed his son around the beautiful arched corner, where the logs had been expertly cut and sanded. Without looking, Charlie knew her husband would lower himself next to Jonny on the middle cushion of the dark leather couch.

Grams was already seated in the matching leather reclining chair, closest to the fireplace. She'd always said she'd liked the warmth: the warmth of family which had gathered around it over the years. Charleston Morris had built it for his wife, Lizzy, years ago. Grams propped her feet up on the ottoman with a colorful quilt thrown over her lap, grinning tiredly at Charlie as Charlie carefully brought her a small bowl of hot supper. When her hands reached out for it, they were shaking. Charlie helped guide it all the way to Grams' lap, for fear she was too weak to hold it steady.

"You overdid it yesterday," Charlie observed, regret flooding her heart. She knew better than to let Grams go. It had been a moment of weakness. "You're unwell now. I can see it."

"I'm fit as a fiddle," Grams replied. "An old fiddle," she mumbled under her breath.

"She knows, babe," Billy said, mildly requesting that the fact not be brought up again.

"Why don't we all eat at the table?" Charlie suggested. She didn't want Grams spilling her supper all over her fuzzy pajamas and embarrassing herself.

"No, no, no," Grams grumbled. "I want to sit by the fireplace."

"Mom, it's not even lit."

"I don't care." Grams fluttered her fingers and took hold of the silver spoon sticking out of her bowl, ignoring Charlie's pressing stare.

What was worse? Leaving her mom behind at the house, when all the woman wanted—and had left in the world—was to go see her ranch? Or take her mom along and cause her failing health to break down twice as fast? Worried now more than ever, Charlie retraced her steps to the kitchen to fetch her own bowl of chicken and dumplings.

Why had Charlie been assigned the curse of being the protective worrier of the family? How she envied the peace the others had, letting her worry and fret for them. It wasn't their fault, of course. Worrying was just what she did. No reason for everyone to worry and fret when she did enough of it for all of them. Still, she often wondered where she'd acquired the habit. No one else that she knew of in the family was such an extreme worrier. Where had she contracted such an annoying, dogged determination to imagine the absolute worse-case scenario for every situation in full and vivid detail? As often as the question plagued her, she said nothing of it. It was just another silly thing she wouldn't tell her family. Ranch life gave everyone enough to consider already, there was no sense in adding more.

She had to give Billy credit. Without him, the concerns and fears associated with a family-operated ranch would have been too great. Ranching was an uneasy venture through a dark, forested path, with bottomless holes and fatal traps hiding just beneath the thin grass covering. Because of such nervous beliefs, Charlie wasn't really made for ranching. Yet she sucked it up, because that's what a heart does for those it loves.

In return, Billy pulled more than his fair share, willingly transferring every ounce of weight Charlie would allow from her gentle shoulders to his strong, broad ones. Without a doubt, it was he who made ranch life a passable route for her. Charlie may have been a rancher's daughter, knowing the ropes, even accepting the ropes—but they weren't *her* ropes. She had only taken them because they came attached to the man she loved. Billy was the rancher, through and through.

Hot supper in hand, Charlie found her spot on the couch next to her husband and allowed the worn cushions to swallow her up. The poor couch had been sat on so many times that the stuffing inside the leather casing had given way, like a sinkhole. Charlie didn't mind. She liked the feeling of being hugged as it enveloped her.

Billy smiled at her, setting down his empty bowl, scooping her up, and pulling her close to his side. "Thank you for dinner," he said.

Billy had proved his loyalty to her over the years by eating every meal she had experimented with. Grams had been zero help in the learning-to-cook category, not that Charlie blamed her. Grams never had time to learn to cook, and it was unanimously agreed upon that no one wanted to risk her trying. Gramps hadn't been much help, either; the extent of his labor was opening a can.

"Thank you, Mom," Jonny added, scraping his bowl, catching every last morsel.

Charlie grinned tiredly at him as she scooped up the soup and trickled it over the dumpling in the middle of her bowl. "You're very welcome."

"What's on your mind?" Grams asked Charlie, her voice weak. The rest of her was weak too, she had barely moved the spoon in her bowl.

Charlie forced a bland smile. "I'm just tired."

"Ranch work never was your first love," Grams said. "That was Billy." She winked at him. "All of a sudden I couldn't keep you out of the barn. He's been flexing his muscles, posing dramatically, and capturing your little heart ever since."

Charlie smiled softly. It was true.

"Billy," Grams directed, steering the conversation towards the course of her choosing. "Don't you think it's time to hire a replacement hand? We never replaced old what's-his-name when he left."

"That's because Jonny came home about the same time," said Billy. "He's been a big help. I guess I took him for granted and forgot."

Jonny became visibly interested in this new course of the conversation, sitting up in his seat.

Grams nodded. "Charlie has been working too hard," she said, pointing toward the front door. "There's so much to do in here. Plus, she's taken over all my chores. What little housework she allows me to do is only to pacify me."

"That's not true, Mom!"

"Oh, pish posh, I'm not as helpful as I once was, I know that. You're having to work in here *and* out there. It's too much to ask of you." Charlie opened her mouth to argue, but she was cut off by Grams' merciless voice. "Add to that, if Jonny goes back to college, then where will we be?" True to form, Grams didn't wait for an answer. "Therefore," she said, accenting the "therefore" as if she were making a royal declaration, "we need to hire another hand."

"First off," Charlie replied, "it's not *if* Jonny goes back to college. It's *when*. Secondly, I enjoy working the ranch. Not all aspects of it, but being alongside my husband, very much. And third, you're still the woman of the house."

"Pish posh. I'm not the woman of the house. I'm a mascot. Like an old dog laying on a porch, drooling on my paws as I nap. Charlie, you can still work next to Billy as you see fit. But not like you've been doing. I see your happiness melting away. I never should have let it go on so long. I'm sorry."

"Mom, it's my job," she argued. "Besides, I'm happy."

Grams pointed to a large, dust-covered, baby blue box sitting on a shelf to the left of the fireplace. "When was the last time you sat down and wrote a story?"

Charlie glanced at the box. She couldn't remember the last time she had taken the time to sit down and write. Writing short children's books used to be her passion. But lately—using "lately" very loosely—she simply hadn't been able to afford the time.

"You should stop dragging your feet and get those stories published," Grams demanded. "You've put them on the backburner too long as it is."

"I agree," Billy joined in. "But Grams, do you realize that if Jonny leaves, and Charlie starts writing again, we won't be short one hand, we'll be short two?"

Grams leisurely stirred the chicken soup around and around in her bowl, glancing at Jonny curiously. "Three, really," she said. "Jonny does the work of two— easily. Haven't you noticed your workload decrease dramatically, Billy?"

Billy glanced at his son proudly and nodded. Charlie sighed heavily. She knew where this was going just as plainly as Jonny did, which was clear from his thrilled expression. And she didn't like it.

Jonny sensed his opportunity and jumped aboard. "This is all *if* I leave," he said. "What about keeping me on? If I stay, you may not need to hire anyone."

"Why does everyone keep using this word 'if?'" Charlie asked tightly. "You're going back."

"I don't have to," Jonny reasoned, setting his dinner bowl aside. Grams shook her head at Jonny's wording, frowning into her uneaten bowl of soup. "What I mean is, I can finish most of my college right here, without leaving," he corrected. "I can do both." Grams nodded approvingly.

Charlie glared at her mom. Grams' focus was conveniently and inflexibly settled upon the dumpling she was ripping into shreds. Charlie wished the woman would quit playing with it and eat it already.

"This is where I want to be." Jonny pushed forward, scooting to the edge of his chair, barely resting any weight on it at all. "I can finish college, just like I agreed.

But this is where I want to be. Home. Working the ranch."

"This will always be your home, Jonny," Charlie said. "But you have a future to find."

"This *is* my future," Jonny maintained. He clasped his hands over his knees, squeezing them forcefully. "I've always been a part of this ranch, and I'm proud of that. I want to stay. I want to carry on our family legacy."

"Legacy..." Charlie muttered. She had never quite seen it that way.

"He's an agriculture genius," Grams offered calmly, still digging annoyingly at her dumpling, trying to play off nonchalance. Charlie wasn't buying it. "With a college education, I bet Jonny could improve the breeding program, developing sturdier, healthier stock. I bet he could even think up some new strategies to make better use of the land we have. All of us old farts, we're workers. None of us are developers of ideas, like Jonny."

One side of Billy's mouth curved upward in a slight smile as he said, "It's been nice having him here. I have to be honest, Jonny has been saving my back, both figuratively and physically. It's in his blood, Charlie. There's no getting around it, he belongs here—if this is where he wants to be."

"It is!" Jonny beamed.

Charlie sympathized—she really did—and she admired her son's strong allegiance to the ranch. In spite of this, she glared at her mom. Feeble or not, the dogged woman was still razor sharp, putting these ideas in everyone's heads. A part of Charlie knew there was a possibility the three of them were right, but she wanted Jonny to have opportunities outside the ranch. The ability to follow his (unrealized) aspirations.

All Jonny had known was the ranch. How else was he going to know what was out there if he didn't go and experience it? She was certain that if he did, he wouldn't choose to come back. If only she could convince him.

Charlie felt a spark of rare anger building inside her. The people who lived here, died here. It was hard work. It took your all—and then it took some more. No one knew that raw throbbing detail better than Grams. Why was she pushing this so hard? Charlie suppressed the desire to stomp her feet in the obnoxious fit of a three-year-old. Instead, she shook her head at them, unconvinced and unwilling to yield.

"I'm sorry," she said. It was the most decent thing she could think of.

\*\*

When bedtime came around, Grams dawdled even more than she usually did as Charlie and Billy headed to the master bedroom to recharge for tomorrow's chores. As was the custom when Jonny was home, she wandered to the kitchen to meet him for a secret cookie-eating fest. But not before making a pit stop in her room. There was something important she had to do. She'd been planning it for years.

Jonny was already waist-deep in the wall of cupboards, digging for their secret stash of cookies, when Grams shuffled in, a blue book in her hand. "To the left," she said. "Your mom came in when I was trying to hide them, so I just kind of tossed."

"Ah-ha!" Jonny backed out of the cupboard, a package of oatmeal raisin cookies clutched in his raised hand like a trophy. "Here they are!"

"Good boy. Now open it up."

Jonny did, and offered her the first cookie. Unable to resist, she plucked one out. Nibbling at the cookie half-heartedly, she sat next to him at the built-in bar over the cupboards separating the kitchen from the living room.

"Agricultural genius, huh?" There was an amused gleam in his eye as he stuffed an entire cookie into his mouth and reached for another.

"Don't let it go to your head."

"Did you mean it, though?" he asked, stuffing the second cookie in before the first was even gone. Amara didn't lecture him on slowing down so he didn't choke. She wasn't one to correct cookie eating manners, and besides, he was too scrawny as it was.

Grams pretended to mull the question over. "Sure, sure," she said unconvincingly, and took a nibble of the cookie between her two fingers. A few crumbs fell on the counter.

"If you eat any slower, you'll get just the one cookie," Jonny advised, nodding his head to the nibbled treat in her fingers. "I'm not going to wait on you. I *will* eat the rest."

Grams took another nibble, not really tasting it. Her stomach didn't want the cookie any more than it wanted Charlie's delightful chicken and dumpling stew. It was all she could do just to stay upright on the tiny, torturous wooden circle called a stool. Yesterday's ride had been hard, and she could admit—to herself only, of course—that it had been too much. But it had been necessary. Now, the next step.

"What's that?" Jonny asked around a mouthful of oatmeal cookie, pointing to the blue homemade book she held on her lap. He had fallen right into her trap.

"It's the book I wrote. Well, it's *kind* of a book..." Her voice trailed off. Looking down, she patted the heavy, cardstock-covered book, tied together with twine. "It's not good, like Charlie's stories, but it's my contribution to the family legacy."

"Like Great-Great-Gramps' horsehair reins?" he asked, his face scrunching up.

"Yeah. In a way."

"And you made it yourself? I mean, you wrote it yourself?"

"Yes. Both. I made it and wrote it."

"So it's homemade."

"Yes..." She looked at him, her head listing to one side. "Are you falling into a cookie coma? You're not usually this dense."

"Very funny," said Jonny. Grams watched him wade through his thoughts, until he finally worked up the courage to ask, "Is this a thing, then?"

"Is what a thing?"

"Homemade stuff. Does everyone have to make something? What did my dad make? Or is he exempt?"

Amara smirked despite her growing discomfort. Living in an age-racked body stunk. It snuck up on a person, like a soundless slithering snake, and proceeded to interrupt every thought, every conversation, every single thing you tried to do.

"Is this a deciding factor?" she asked.

After thinking over his life decision for all of two seconds, he shrugged. "No, I guess not. Maybe, by the time I'm old and full of tricks like you, I'll have picked up knitting."

"I don't knit."

He shrugged and popped in another cookie. "You might."

She held her book out to him. "Anyway, here." Jonny stared at it, as if taking it gave some sort of unspoken consent that he had accepted the challenge of carrying on the tradition of crafting something homemade. "I'm too old and impatient to continue handing this to you," Grams complained, wiggling the book like a worm on a line. "Are you taking it or not?"

Hesitantly, he reached out with his crumb-covered fingers and took the book from her. He held it very carefully, as if it were going to fall apart in his hands.

"Oh, for heaven's sake, it's not going to deteriorate," said Amara. "It's not as old as I am."

He looked at her, then grinned. "When did you write it then?"

She looked at the book in her grandson's hands. Finally it was where it belonged. Even still, she felt a sad sense of separation. "I started writing it after you were born," she answered. Jonny nodded, having heard her words, although understanding wouldn't come until later.

"Good night," she said, slinking carefully off her stool.

Jonny watched Grams shuffle painfully from the kitchen, and he knew his mom was right. Permitting Grams to ride had been too much. It was all she could do to sit there and pretend to be interested in their secret cookie-eating fest after not having eaten dinner either. Jonny stared at the oatmeal halfmoon Grams had left on the counter. Yet she had come and met him, like she had always done since he was old enough to chew. Only this time, she had brought some sort of handmade book.

Curious, he turned the book over in his hands, checking out the same plain blue cover on the back. It was at that moment he realized that this book was the entire reason Grams had forced herself to stagger into the kitchen. She hadn't cared about the cookies. What was important was giving him the book.

"I almost forgot," Grams said from behind, startling him. Her crinkled, innocent face peeked around the log corner. "Tell your dad I said, 'It's time to keep your promise.' Can you do that for me, Jonny?"

"Keep what promise?"

"He'll know," she said, and disappeared again.

"Sure, Grams," he said, knowing she moved slow enough that she was still within earshot.

Alone again, he grabbed the package of oatmeal cookies, held them captive under his arm, and carried the book into the living room. Flopping down on the couch in his usual fashion, he flipped the book over so he could start at the front—usually the best place to begin. The handwritten title was worn and smudged from being handled. Removing a cookie from the package and stuffing it into his mouth, he began to read.

## CHAPTER FOUR

### HOLDER OF THE HORSE
### (68 Years Earlier)

Amara Duncan stepped daintily from the back-passenger door of her friend's small red Honda in a grocery store parking lot in Lovell, Wyoming. Her college girlfriends scrambled out of the front. Feeling tired and overheated, she wiped at her face with both hands. She didn't have to worry about smudging her makeup, since she wore none, refusing to smother her face with fake pigments and unrealistically dark lashes. If she had been meant to have green, chunky eyelids, she felt confident she would have been born with them. All the childish boys—mistakenly crediting themselves as men—didn't look twice at her. If one so happened to speak to her, she had zero intention of being fake. Take her or leave her just the way she was. They usually left in a hurry, in hot pursuit of girls touting all sorts of fake things, an exterior appearance assembled for the sake of interior confidence. Plugs and padded bras may be just the thing for some, but not for twenty-one-year old Amara.

Her long blonde hair, extending well past her waist in gentle waves of gold, floated and danced in the afternoon breeze. Closing her eyes, she opened her arms, welcoming the glorious cooling relief on her sweaty skin. Her friend's car had no air conditioning, and it was miserable, causing Amara to heavily regret having decided to wear a long-sleeved white lacy dress. In the store, the dress had seemed to have lightweight material and sheer arms, but in the small, sweltering car, the dress was simply warm and sticky.

Amara had envisioned the dress in the perfect pictures of this trip she'd created in her fantasies. She would be posing elegantly in an innocent white country dress, the breeze gracefully lifting the length around her legs. On her feet, she would wear her freshly purchased red cowgirl boots for the splash of color. Adding to the majesty of the picture, she would be touching a wild mustang. It was a marvelously grand plan. The adventure of a lifetime. But it didn't happen.

Instead, she had slipped on the fence at the Wild Mustang Center as she tried to climb over it, hitting first her shin and then her chin. The wild mustang nearest her reared up and ran off, taking the entire herd with him, away from the other spectators. A member of the center's staff came and greeted her with a stern reprimand, accompanied her quickly through the gift store line, and escorted her off the premises. It was embarrassing, but mostly just disappointing. She had planned her entire part of the trip around that one moment, and it was ruined.

Amara's dark hazel eyes took in the small town of Lovell from the grocery store parking lot. From where she stood, there wasn't much, mostly time-worn buildings. But the surrounding hills: what a magnificent sight! To be there, in those hills, rather than here, standing in a parking lot, waiting on her college friends. Carefully placing the matching large white lacy hat on her head to protect her pale skin from the harsh sun, she squinted at the landscape looming behind the town. Her friends had started scampering off towards the store for refreshments.

"Come on, Amara!" they called to her.

"I'll be right there," Amara shouted back, ducking back into the car to rummage through the backseat, which was packed full of belongings and souvenirs. Where was her purse? It had been here before she had fallen asleep during the drive from the Mustang Center.

Frustrated that her purse was flat-out refusing to present itself, she pulled the black stuffed horse she had purchased at the Wild Mustang Center out of the car by its two back ankles. After all of her careful research, planning, and saving, the stupid fake stuffed horse was the only horse she had been allowed to touch. She stared into its brown glassy eyes, not feeling the love. In fact, all she felt was disappointment.

"You ought to know I don't care for fake things," Amara confessed, disenchanted. "And you're a fake horse. It's the worst kind of fake. A sham." The soulless brown eyes revealed no hard feelings over her admission.

Slamming the car door, she whipped around and started to stomp quickly towards the shade of a nearby tree, not paying attention. Something collided into her. Stunned, she blinked, staring straight into the chest of a man. She had to pull her eyes further towards the sky to see his face. When she did, the handsome face looking back at her stopped her heart. He couldn't have been more than twenty-five, but his hard body (and she knew it was hard from having collided with it) filled the thighs of his jeans, and his shoulders filled his white button-up shirt. Dirty blond hair peeked from underneath his white straw cowboy hat, and light blue eyes sparkled against his sun-darkened skin, putting clear waters all over the world to perfect shame. It occurred to her that she should say something. But like the fruitless search for her purse moments ago, nothing presented itself. So she stood there, stupefied.

"Hi there," the cowboy said, tipping his hat, not bothering to step around her.

Maybe he was a figment of her imagination derived from heat and disillusionment. She hadn't actually woken up in a grocery store parking lot, she was still dreaming. No way something so handsome would be standing in a parking lot, speaking to her. She knew just how to test the theory.

"I don't wear makeup," she said, resisting the urge to stand on her tippy toes. The man's height alone made her feel about eight years old, not to mention the presence of the damn fake horse in her hands. Quickly, she hid it behind her back.

He crossed his arms, his thick forearms pressing against one another. "Is that a fact?" he asked, seemingly amused.

Amara crossed her arms too, the horse hanging from where her fingers were wrapped tightly around its neck. "It happens to be," she said defiantly. "What do you think of that?"

He laughed.

Amara blinked. Before her still stood a man with about a week's worth of light brown stubble on his face, still not retreating. How could she continue tolerating this ruggedly attractive hallucination currently making an extremely formidable—yet striking—wall?

He shrugged. "I guess I don't think much about it."

Amara gasped. "Is it really your place to decide?"

"Nope," he said, pursing his lips. "I could care less if you wear makeup or not. You don't appear to need it, though," he added, cocking his leg and shifting his weight. Was he making himself comfortable? Why was he making himself comfortable? Did he intend to stay there, casting a shadow like a tree all day?

Amara glared. "When, then, does a girl qualify to *need* makeup?"

This appeared to stump him briefly. He shrugged again. "I guess they don't ever *need* makeup," he answered. "I'm a guy, I don't know why they wear it. Why don't you tell me?"

Amara felt her mouth open, and a puff of air escaped. Cocking her own knee now, she placed her fist, which was still tightly wrapped around her horse's neck, on her small hip. "I don't know," she admitted, letting an acknowledging smile break free.

"Well, I guess that makes two of us," he said, extending his hand. "My name is Sonny Morris."

Hesitantly, Amara took his hand. His palm enveloped her entire hand, and traveled up her arm a short way. "Amara," she said.

"You have a nice-looking horse there," Sonny said, gesturing to her stuffed companion.

"He's fake," Amara grumbled.

"I see that," said Sonny with a smile. "What's its name?"

"I haven't named him," Amara said, shrugging. "I don't think I will. He's my consolation purchase. They wouldn't let me touch the wild version, so…" She held up her black stuffed horse. "This is what I got."

"Who's *they*?" Sonny asked, squinting. "And did you *try* to touch a wild horse?"

"Well, yeah!" Amara exclaimed exuberantly. "I planned this entire portion of the trip around touching a mustang at the Wild Mustang Center. All I've ever wanted was to touch a horse. Only, when I was finally right there, the horse was right there, I climbed the fence and reached out…" Amara stretched out her hand, showing him how close she'd been. "Well, let's just say I kind of got kicked out."

"You climbed the fence?"

"Yes." A light breeze ruffled her hair, and she shoved it back. "Apparently they don't permit touching."

"No, not usually." Sonny gestured to her consolation prize again. "Not exactly untamed and *wild,* is he?"

"No. About the only thing he's good for is a pillow. And I fully intend to spend the majority of my time, and the remainder of the trip, drooling on him. I got to do what I wanted—or had the opportunity, anyway. Now it's my friends' turn to do what *they* want."

"May I?" Sonny held a hand out, asking for the horse.

"Have at it," Amara said, handing it over.

To Amara's surprise, Sonny pressed his coarse face against the stuffed animal and closed his eyes. Amara felt her heart stop for the second time since she'd met him. She nearly had to punch herself to get it started again. When Sonny opened his eyes, they immediately fixed on hers. For a moment, she wondered if she ought to call for a defibrillator.

Sonny handed the horse back. "Soft. It should do the trick," he said, endorsing the animal as a pillow with a stunning smile. Something about the way he gazed at her hinted that he was hesitating, possibly weighing the odds of a stake race somewhere. Then he asked, "Does it have to be wild?"

"Does what have to be wild?"

"The horse you want to touch."

Amara's unmanageable hair blew in the wind, and she tucked it behind her ear. It blew right back out, so she decided to let it fly. Like her, it wanted to be wild. Who was she to stifle it? Amara dropped her eyes, taking Sonny in from hat to boot, and naughtily wondered: how wild might he be under that collected exterior?

"I've dreamt of touching a real horse since... well, before my mom told me I never would," Amara answered. "No, it doesn't have to be wild. I just had this unrealistic picture in my head of me touching a mustang."

Sonny smiled so infectiously that she had to smile back. "My Gramps and I raise quarter horses in eastern Montana. Have you been to Montana?"

"I have not," Amara said, hugging her horse, unsure why she felt nervous all of a sudden.

"You're nearly there."

From the corner of her eye, Amara saw her girlfriends tracking their way toward her. They were giggling, whispering, and pointing. She knew it was Sonny they were giddy over. She felt her cheeks flush, her insides burning. Was she jealous that his attention was sure to turn to the more attractive Jeanie? Or was it pleasure? After all, it had been her he was speaking to, not Jeanie.

"Are your horses better than this?" Amara asked, holding up her fuzzy horse for scrutiny.

Sonny smiled, rubbing his chin. "I don't know, that's a hard one. Yours doesn't eat, poop, or destroy property. Then again," he said, raising his eyebrows at her. "Mine are real." Sonny couldn't have known the power such a simple statement could have in her book.

"He's real," said Amara, petting the horse's fake black mane, pretending to console it. "You can see him, can't you?"

Sonny leaned in, closing the distance between their faces. In a smooth, deep voice, he asked, "But can you ride him?" Amara felt a warm shift inside, leaving her legs feeling weak and wobbly.

"And who's this?" asked Jeanie, her brunette friend, grabbing Amara's left elbow. Her other friend Rosalynn attached herself to Amara's right, smiling sheepishly from under a head full of curly red hair. Rosalynn always reminded Amara of a red-headed Shirley Temple, but without the bubbly flair for singing.

Her friends' presence snapped Amara into a full recovery. Motioning to her new friend, she said, "This is Sonny. Apparently he raises horses in Montana."

"I'm Jeanie," said Jeanie, thrusting out her hand. Sonny took it and smiled back. "Shy fry, hiding on the other side, is Rosalynn."

"It's nice to meet you both," Sonny said, acknowledging both of them but looking back at Amara.

Jeanie lost her smile and turned to Amara. "More horses?" Turning back to Sonny, she said, "I'm sorry. I don't mean to be rude. It's just, we're on a limited time schedule. I know what Amara is about to ask, but Rosalynn and I are up next for the weekend's event list, and we're headed to a casino." Jeanie added, in her favorite syrupy persuasion voice—which usually ended her up in someone's bed for the evening— "You're welcome to join us."

Amara could feel Rosalynn reach around her and give Jeanie a firm bop on the back.

Sonny removed the cowboy hat from his head, revealing a head full of slightly messy, dirty blond hair. "I'm afraid I can't. I have to get home. I'm expected to get the flatbed back this afternoon."

"Flatbed?" Jeanie asked, confused.

Sonny stuck his hat back into place. "Delivered a load of hay to some folks," he answered, as if it made for a clear explanation.

Jeanie stared at him emptily. Sonny either didn't notice or didn't care, because he quickly switched his focus back to Amara, catching her in the act of crushing the black horse against her deflated heart. She had just met him, and her chances at getting to know him were already over. Such an anticlimax.

"I know how much you're looking forward to drooling on that horse for the remainder of your trip," Sonny said to Amara only, "but the offer is still on the table. There's a clean, vacant house below the main house you could stay in while your friends visit the casino." If Amara was reading him right, his expression looked cautiously hopeful.

Amara looked to Jeanie and Rosalynn. A little for guidance, a little for a secret treaty. They would have to come pick her up, but more importantly, they would have to keep it a secret. Amara's parents could not know. Jeanie shrugged, uninterested, and Rosalynn smiled. "Go ahead, Amara."

"Will it be too much to come pick me up?" Amara asked.

"Are you—" Jeanie started to speak, but Rosalynn interrupted.

"Not at all. Just call us."

"I'll pitch in extra gas money," Amara volunteered, before the shell-shock from the fact that she seemed to be going through with this kicked in.

After retrieving her things from the back of Jeanie's Honda, she stood on the sidewalk next to a perfect stranger as she watched Jeanie and Rosalynn walk away. At the last second, Jeanie muttered to Rosalynn, "I hope he's not a murderer." Rosalynn stopped short, her hand frozen on the handle of the passenger door. "I'm kidding," said Jeanie with a laugh, slamming the door. "Get in!"

## CHAPTER FIVE

Amara sat in the taxi cab she had insisted on taking to the address Sonny Morris had provided her—which she'd subsequently gave to Rosalynn before leaving town. Taking a cab was expensive, but an appropriate thing for an intelligent, independent young woman to do. Alright, so an intelligent young woman probably wouldn't have accepted an invitation to a stranger's home in another state, but at least the cab ride was a step above riding with said handsome stranger—even though he had waited with her for her cab. They had sat together, swinging their legs, on the long, empty wooden trailer attached to his dirty ranch pickup. Her ulcer-lined mom would have approved of Sonny's chivalrous manners, or so Amara told herself.

Who was she kidding? Her mom would never approve of this spontaneous, solitary escapade. She had barely agreed to the girl's trip—if you call crossed arms and a scowl an agreement. Thus, Amara thought, she had no intentions of telling her.

For miles, since Amara woke from her nap, she hadn't seen anything but the glorious splendor of color and land blending together as they raced past, but suddenly the cab slowed and turned. The driver inched up to the only gate she could recall seeing all day. A lone, orange-barked ponderosa pine leaned over the entry, gracing what appeared to be a small gravesite with the gift of shade and shelter. The thinly built, balding driver exited the vehicle, opened the gate, moved the car, and closed the gate behind them.

"Have we arrived?" Amara asked. The bald head nodded. "Why didn't you leave the gate open? Won't you come back this way?"

"This is cattle country, Miss. If you open a gate, you close it."

"Are you familiar with this place?" she asked.

"This is Morris Ranch."

"Do you know anything about them?"

"Charleston Morris is the kind of man other folks either esteem to impress, or esteem to become."

"So I'm not coming here to be murdered, then?"

His bald head bobbled as they drove over the gravel road. "Shouldn't you have asked me that question earlier? Oh, that's right, you were too busy sawing logs."

"The logs needed sawing," Amara answered defensively.

"Not that you were losing any sleep over it, but no, you're not likely to be murdered." He hesitated, then added, chuckling to himself, "Unless you're a short-horned steer. In which case I suggest you pay me to take you right back where you came from."

"Not a steer," Amara admitted needlessly. "Do you know Sonny Morris?"

"Mr. Morris' grandson helps him, I think," the man answered, without any further explanation.

"Do you know anything about him?"

The driver shrugged. "I'm not invited to thanksgiving dinner or nothing."

Amara turned her focus out the window. "Oh. My. Gosh. Have you ever seen anything so beautiful?"

The driver must have assumed the question was rhetorical, because he didn't answer.

Promptly rolling her window down as far as it would go, she peered out, mesmerized. The pasture grasses were speckled with blue and yellow flowers and dappled with wild shrubbery. The hillsides were covered, like tiny quilt blankets, with thick patches of Douglas fir trees, and in the distance, gentle rolling slopes led up to the Pryor Mountains, home of the wild mustangs. Her heart fluttered excitedly.

The road slowly guided them down into the marvelous folds of the land. Intently watching out her window, Amara observed and appreciated every detail. Magnificent trees jutted from the ground, declaring their superiority. Amara thought she glimpsed the sparkling of a small creek slithering beneath the surface of the dry ground, and right beside it, a deer lifted its head. Straight away, she spotted three more nibbling at the short grass tops. She sucked her breath in, and on her tongue she savored the taste of sage from the air.

The cab rattled and vibrated as it rolled across a cattle guard. All around, standing under trees, hiding behind shrubs, and lying on the ground, she spied cows. Some glanced her way, while others dozed, as if they were frankly discounting the importance of her existence among them. They were a different color than she was used to seeing in farm fields and on the covers of books: mostly red and white mixed together, like a kaleidoscope. She loved them instantly. She loved their remote aloofness, their lack of concern with the rest of the world—their undisturbed freedom.

As they continued over a rise, a gigantic wooden barn seemed to majestically materialize from the floor of the world they were entering. Beyond it, trees dotted the view and leisurely revealed a large ranch house made from traditionally hand-cut and stacked logs. The fencing, chutes, and corrals—even machinery—were noticed second, almost as an afterthought. Functional, but not the main focus. Not a distraction, as was widely common in property with late additions. Whoever had designed this piece of heaven had been a gifted artist, with a talent for foresight of what would be necessary without insulting the first inhabitant: nature. It remained a distinct feature of the property.

A handsomely built man stepped from the front door of the log home, a coffee mug in hand, as the cab rolled up. Amara recognized him: Sonny Morris. He sipped casually from his mug as he leaned against a fat log holding up the small deck attached to the upper loft room above his head, which served nicely as a porch cover. Sonny smiled and moseyed to meet the cab driver, handing him a paper bill and pointing to a small road curving around the large log house.

"Just down that way," Amara heard Sonny say. "It's unlocked."

Obnoxiously, Amara threw open the car door. She needed to affirm her self-reliance. Clambering noisily from the backseat, she hit her head first, then her knee. The heel of her left boot temporarily tangled with the floorboard mat. Finally, unjumbled from the hold of the cab, Amara plunked her hands on her hips with staunch conviction. "I'm paying the driver," she announced.

The taxi took off around the corner, leaving her standing there in the dust.

Sonny turned to her, shrugging. "If you can catch him."

"Well, where's he going?" she asked, exasperated. "He has my things."

"Dropping them at the small house," Sonny answered. "I can take you down there now. I just thought I'd introduce you to Gramps first."

"Gramps?" *He must be referring to Mr. Morris,* Amara thought, looking down at her wrinkled white dress. "If he doesn't mind that I'm a mess."

"Follow me, then," Sonny said, turning towards the house.

"Lead away."

As she entered through the front door, the first thing she noticed was all the natural wood and stone everywhere. The logs that made up the house on the outside were the same ones visible on the inside, displaying their stunningly warm beauty. There would be no hollow spaces within the walls in need of fiberglass blanket insulation. The logs themselves were all the home needed as a protective barrier. Even amid the spacious floor plan and the cool, decorative stone tones, the home managed to possess a cozy, friendly ambiance.

Both the exterior log walls and the interior sheetrock walls were adorned tastefully with authentic pictures of actual working cowboys and cowgirls. Upon closer inspection, Amara could easily make out Sonny in a few of them. Scattered meticulously, hanging between the pictures, were retired pieces of equipment for exhibition. The sum of the impression was grace with a rustic flair.

"Amara," Sonny said, as she leaned in close to a pair of rusty but flamboyant spurs to study the engravings more closely.

Glancing up, she saw he was leaning against a beautiful archway of logs, cut and sanded to perfection. Somehow, she had walked right by without seeing it, having been too taken by the memories and history in the living room.

The log archway granted a rather splendid invitation to the kitchen. Just to the right of the archway, a breakfast bar made of stones (matching the fireplace) separated the dining area and front door from the kitchen. Joining Sonny, Amara spotted Mr. Morris straightaway. Leaning against the kitchen sink stood an old, weathered cowboy with thick gray hair and a long, narrow mustache. He had a coffee mug in his hand, and he was watching her, amused. Apparently he had been surveying her the entire time. First through the kitchen window, and again while she shamelessly explored his beautiful home. He smiled, his long mustache lifting at both ends.

"Gramps, this is Amara Duncan," said Sonny. "Amara, this is Charleston Morris, my gramps."

"Howdy," Charleston said, tipping his head and extending his free hand. Amara inserted her hand into his. It felt rough and warm, like his voice. "So you're the pretty long-haired lady who tried to touch a wild mustang."

"Word travels fast," she said, returning his smile. Had Sonny described her as pretty, or had Charleston inserted a charming compliment on his own? "Come to find out, they frown at any attempt to climb in with them."

Charleston's eyebrows rose and fell as he scratched his chin. "Crying shame. Might have been a good way to die." Until Sonny's response, Amara wasn't sure if Charleston was serious or heckling her.

"Gramps, don't encourage her," Sonny lectured.

"I'm not encouraging her. I'm just thinking about adding it to my bucket list."

"You don't have a bucket list."

"I do now."

"Oh no, *do* encourage me," Amara said, smiling now. She may have just found her people in this world. People like her, daring and free—how she wished to be, anyway. "All my life I've been slowly dying from boredom. If I'm going to die, I sure don't want it to be from boredom," she explained. "I want..." Amara searched the kitchen walls, lined with cupboard doors, for her explanation.

"Adventure," Charleston suggested.

"Yes!" said Amara. "Adventure, and—"

"Freedom," said Charleston, smoothing his mustache with his scrawny fingers.

"Yes!" Amara announced, astonished. How had he known exactly what she had always been searching for? Something her mom had never been able to recognize.

Charleston plonked his coffee mug on the counter. The coffee swished violently inside. "Then you came to the right place," he declared. "Adventure and freedom are all we have around here. Some folks call it work. I call it—"

"Living," said Amara.

Charleston smiled, the corners of his mustache twitching. "You interested?"

"Gramps," Sonny attempted to cut in.

"Absolutely," Amara answered. Sonny sighed, and his shoulders slumped. He was being overthrown.

Charleston tossed his coffee mug into the sink. It was too late in the day for coffee anyway. "Saddle up then," he told her. "Sonny will take you out to get your feet wet before the sun goes down. You start tomorrow at dawn."

"Gramps!" Sonny spoke more loudly this time. Charleston glanced at him. "She's a guest, not an applicant," Sonny explained irritably. This got Charleston's attention, though he still appeared defiantly ho-hum about it, staring at Sonny as if he'd never heard such a jug of nonsense.

"It's true," Amara confirmed in regret. "I'm only here for a day or two."

"You arrived in a taxi," said Charleston.

"My friends will come to pick me up."

"Well, then, there's no time to waste," Charleston remarked, rubbing his hands together. "Where's your stuff?"

"I had the driver take her luggage to the ranch hand house," Sonny answered. "I told you she would be staying there, Gramps. Would you stop behaving like your gears aren't whirling the proper directions?"

"My gears *are* whirling in the proper directions," Charleston replied. "I'm not talking about her clothes. I'm talking about her saddle, her chaps, her rope..." Sonny rolled his eyes.

Amara shook her head. "Sorry, I have none of that."

"Humph," Charleston grunted. "No matter. Sonny, go fetch Lizzy's saddle from my room. Amara can use my wife's stuff. She won't complain, she's dead." Sonny didn't budge. "The day is nearly gone," Charleston explained unnecessarily. "Amara needs to meet her mount before tomorrow. Get a wiggle on."

Sonny turned to Amara, studying her with those light blue eyes. "You don't have to ride tonight. You don't even have to go up to the barn and meet any of the horses," he said, leaving the decision up to her.

She smiled up at him. He seemed even taller when confined to the kitchen. "I wouldn't mind getting to meet them, or even ride one," she admitted, hoping she wasn't inconveniencing his evening plans.

"Okay," he agreed, a half-smile lifting one corner of his mouth. Then he departed from the kitchen.

"Do you have guests often?" Amara asked Charleston, making conversation.

Charleston grabbed a clean coffee mug from a cupboard and handed it to her. "Help yourself to some coffee," he said, then leaned back against the sink, crossing his long, skinny legs at the ankles. "Nope," he answered. "Not much for guests." His mustache shifted side to side as he chewed on some sort of nonexistent bit in his mouth.

"Juice?" Amara asked. Charleston nodded toward the refrigerator, so she helped herself, pulling out a carton of orange juice. She poured a few swallows into the cup. "Family gatherings?"

"Nope. Can't say we do. How about yourself?"

"The same," Amara admitted, placing the orange juice back into the refrigerator. "I'm not sure if the extended family can't stand us, or if we simply don't have any."

About that time, Sonny returned with a saddle under one arm and chaps draped over the other. "Well," he said, smiling at her, "let's go see some horses." He threw a glare at Charleston. "Since Gramps refuses to acknowledge that our guest is, in fact, a guest and not a recruit, and is certain it can't wait until morning."

Amara tossed the orange juice down her throat and placed the mug carefully on the counter. "Thank you," she said to Charleston, and rushed to follow Sonny toward the front door. When she spun around, she had to admit the view was nice. She trailed behind him all the way to his pickup.

When they got there, Sonny heaved Lizzy's things into the truck bed. "Hop in. I'll take you down to the house you'll be staying in first, so you can change."

He waited in the pickup while Amara jumped out at the much older, much smaller house. It was wood too, but made of overlapping wooden boards instead of logs. It had a front porch, much lower to the ground, with four-by-four posts holding up the porch cover. It was not magnificent, but it was certainly charming. A tree line and a gentle rolling hill separated it from the main house, so it was also private.

Inside, just like in the main house, the small living room was located straight ahead with no particular dining area, although there was a square, primitive wooden table crowded by four wooden chairs. A couch was pushed up against the wall, which Amara assumed separated the living room from the master bedroom. When she closed the front door, she nearly tripped over her luggage. As she caught herself, she glimpsed the tiny kitchen space on her right. There was no separation from the living room.

Amara quickly ran her luggage to the master bedroom and tossed it all on the clean, quilt-covered bed. Pulling out a pair of jeans and a sweater, she yanked off her torturous white dress and redressed. Hurriedly, not wanting to keep Sonny waiting, she crammed her feet back into her red boots and rushed back out the front door. Opening the passenger door, she leapt in, more excited than she had ever been. "Ready," she said, beaming.

After the two got back in Sonny's pickup, he drove them back up the slope and around the bend, and pulled in front of the beautiful structure with double-sided sliding doors that passed for a common horse barn.

Amara could already smell the fresh wood shavings and stacks of hay. Taking a long whiff, she smiled. It smelled like home. No home she'd ever been raised in, of course, but the home of her soul. The home she'd been longing for.

It was darn near unbelievable. What her mom had insisted was a delusional fantasy was taking form right before her eyes. Ever since she was a young girl, she had been fantasizing about this day—the day she would prove her mom wrong. She would touch, even ride, a horse, despite all of her mom's denunciations. At the first chance available to her to plan something for herself—her college break trip with her two friends—Amara had planned out what she'd hoped would quench her soul's thirst. All she wanted was a single picture, proof that she had been unrestricted and adventurous and free, just once. In the face of having failed in her carefully planned temporary independence, she collided with Sonny. Literally.

He'd been watching her daydream, and once again seemed amused by something about her. "What?" Amara asked.

"Just wondering if you need a set of paints."

"I don't paint."

"Can we get out, then?"

"Of course!"

Sonny slapped the vacant seat between them twice and then swung open his door. "Let's go catch your horse, cowgirl," he said, and stepped out of the cab.

Amara fumbled with the door handle, then met Sonny at the back. Greedily, she grabbed the saddle he had tucked under his arm and started pulling. "I can do it," she told him. He finally let go, but it didn't stop him from laughing at her as she hobbled behind him.

Once they were inside the barn, Sonny pointed her to a pole. "Put it there," he said, flicking on the lights. She did, grateful to relieve her spindly arms of the extra weight, and looked around.

The floor was made of hard, raked dirt, naturally depositing a thin layer of dust upon every surface. To her right was a large area, stuffed to the brim with sixty-pound hay bales. Roughly thirty feet further was a large feed room. The aisle wall that made the feed room was adorned with numerous hooks, along with pieces of leather horse tack and equipment. To her left was an open area for tying horses, lined with saddle racks. Then a line of horse stalls continued on both sides. Amara couldn't help but notice that all the stalls were empty.

"Where are the horses?" she asked.

"The horses," Sonny said, digging for a particular saddle pad from a stack of seemingly perfectly good ones, "are in the pasture, just out the back door there." He pointed down the aisle. "Gramps and I believe in leaving the horses out as often as possible. Outside is better for a horse. Summer weather is courteous enough to accommodate us."

"I see," she said. "How courteous."

If she wasn't mistaken, his eyes sparkled as he watched her checking out the leather bridles on the wall. Each one had a different type of metal bit, which went into the horse's mouth. But all she really cared about was getting out the back door to the horses. After what seemed like hours, he finally found the pad he was evidently looking for, flopping it over Lizzy's saddle. "Ready?" he asked, walking over to where she stood.

Reaching around her, he grabbed a halter off the wall. "Or should I postpone a little longer? See if you pop?"

Amara's eyes widened in disbelief and she swung around, her fists promptly jabbing into her hips. "You have an ornery side!"

He smiled, pleased with himself.

"Yes, I'm ready," she answered.

Sonny strolled past her, towards the back gate, and she bounded after him, unable to contain her excitement. His legs carried him much more swiftly than hers carried her. It was no matter. Behind him, the view was always nice, and she didn't mind keeping up.

Swinging open the back door, three horse heads popped up and stared at them like deer. Two of the horses were dappled gray, like marbles, with long black manes and tails. The third horse was orange-red with white speckling, like an Easter egg or a sponge-painted wall. All six ears were pricked with curiosity.

"That one there," Sonny said, pointing to the closest gray horse, "is Gramps' mare, JoJo. She's the mother of my gelding." He pointed to the second gray mare behind JoJo. "His name is Nick of Time, because he was born right before one of the worst storms we've ever seen. I just call him Nick. True to JoJo's rock-solid nerve, she had laid down outside in her paddock instead of in the barn. When we found her, she was too far along to move her." Sonny stretched his chin up towards the sky, and Amara almost expected to see the fierce storm approaching. "It wasn't very late yet, but the clouds were black as night. Lightning was illuminating the entire sky, as if it were setting off fireworks to celebrate Nick's arrival." Sonny rubbed a hand over his thick forearm. "Every hair on my body stood on end. It was an eerie feeling."

"I've never experienced anything like that," said Amara, watching the horses. Nick was meandering closer to see if they had brought anything with them to munch on. "Were you scared?"

"I've never been so scared. Gramps and I, we kept a wary eye on the sky the entire time. I don't know what we would have done, had we been hit, but we watched over our shoulders all the same. Anyway, as soon as Nick hit the ground, so did the tall tree which used to stand there." Sonny pointed into the field. Amara could make out a large divot in the ground where a tree had once stood, and had since been burned out and grazed over.

"Was JoJo scared?" Amara asked.

"Nah," Sonny replied. "JoJo is either the most fearless horse there has ever been, or she's just plain stupid."

JoJo had gone back to pulling grass out of the ground with her teeth, while Nick continued making his way over. The third horse persisted in staring, waiting to see whether Nick did, indeed, receive something to munch for his effort, or if the energy of walking over had proven wasted. Sonny walked ahead, closing the distance. When he and Nick reached each other, Sonny held out his hand, and Nick chomped something down from his palm while Sonny rubbed his forehead. Amara followed Sonny's lead, joining him in rubbing Nick's head.

Now the third horse was on its way. If treats were being handed out, he was coming. As they waited on the Easter-speckled horse, Sonny held his hand out to Amara, just as he had for Nick. When he opened his fingers, she saw a white gumdrop sitting there. Amused and starved, she took it and popped it into her mouth.

"Mmm. Peppermint."

Sonny laughed. "That was for the horse!"

"Oh!" Amara's face suddenly felt like it was swelling up, heat pouring from her cheeks.

Nick knew who had been in possession of his gumdrop, and he reached over to smell her fingers with his long neck and tickly nose whiskers. A wonderful feeling of untainted joy flashed through Amara, then escaped in the form of laughter. Never had she expected to experience such pure happiness. She had tried to imagine what touching a horse would feel like, but those fantasies came nowhere close to the real thing.

Nick's hair was short like a cow, but soft like a rabbit. She ran her fingers through his thin black mane. Looking up at Sonny, she knew she was beaming senselessly, childlike, but she didn't care.

Sonny squinted at her. "Have you always known you loved horses?" he asked. "Or is this a new revelation?"

"I've always known," Amara answered. "But I see now that I didn't in fact know why—until today."

Sonny went from smiling down at her to focusing on something over her shoulder. "And here's Moses," he said.

Amara turned her head, and there was Moses' huge orange nose, searching her face with tickly whiskers and blinking with long eyelashes over gentle brown eyes.

"He smells peppermint on your breath."

"Oh, do you?" Amara giggled, reaching out and touching his short, fluffy red forelock, above his forehead and between his ears. Dragging her fingers softly between his eyes, over the hard contour of his long nose, she made her way to his velvety soft nostrils. The nostrils flared, hunting for his treat. Just as Amara was about to apologize for having eaten his gumdrop, she felt Sonny's warm hand wrap around her loosely hanging fingers.

His quiet touch sparked a small shock of adrenaline, her heartbeat skyrocketing in her chest. Tenderly, he opened her fingers with his. Amara thought for an incredible moment that he was going to hold her hand, but then she felt two small lumps drop into her palm.

"Oh. Thank you," she said, hoping he couldn't see her blushing. Quickly she turned towards Moses, hiding her face—he wasn't going to tattle. But to seal the deal of secrecy, Amara presented him with two little white gumdrops. "How did Moses get his name?" she asked Sonny to distract herself.

"Funny you should ask," Sonny said.

"Is it? Why?"

"We breed quarter horses, so naturally, quarter horses are what we keep and ride. But..." Sonny's blue eyes sparkled. "One day one of the bands of wild mustangs ventured onto the ranch. They had gotten into our eastmost pasture with our steers. They eat a lot of grass, so we drove them off. All but one—a mare. She was lying in the grass. As we rode closer, we realized the mare was dead. Only she wasn't alone. A tiny brown foal stood over her, waiting for her to wake.

"Gramps was not a fan, but I couldn't leave him there. It just happened to be that we had a broodmare who had just lost her own foal. It was worth a try." Amara nodded on cue. "Are you familiar with the story of Moses from the Bible?" She nodded again. "I scooped him up and took him home. We weren't his people, but we raised him as our own." Sonny placed an affectionate hand on Moses' forehead. "He's very special."

"He's a mustang!" Amara declared happily. It was Sonny's turn to nod.

"You got to touch your mustang after all," he said proudly. Turning his attention to the docile Moses, his expression was warm and compassionate. When his eyes flitted to hers and he smiled, she felt like her insides were melting, threatening to give her away by oozing embarrassingly from the pores of her body.

"Do you want to ride him?" Sonny asked.

Amara blinked twice. "Absolutely!" she answered, positively glowing. She should probably divulge that she had never ridden before, but then again, Sonny already knew that, and maybe he would interpret such integrity as uncertainty. She was definitely certain. She had never been so certain in all her life.

After Moses had been saddled and Amara had been briefed on a few important basics, Sonny stood to the side and waved his arm for her to climb up. Every breath she had ever taken had led up to this moment. Without hesitation, Amara placed her foot into the stirrup, as she had seen done on television so many times, and somewhat awkwardly pulled herself up, swinging her right leg over Moses' back. Moses stood as if his feet were in thick sludge, waiting for her to ask something of him.

"Give his neck a pat—and breathe," said Sonny. "He's a good boy. He'll take care of you."

Amara patted Moses' thick, muscular neck—and breathed. The sweet smell of horse floated into her nostrils and through her entire body, baptizing her in the glorious name of freedom and adventure. When she bumped her heels against his sides, the way Sonny had instructed, Moses began walking. In no time, he had given her the confidence to trot—giggling like a giddy child—then to lope in wide, lazy circles. Arms spread like wings, Amara tipped her head back, letting the wind whip her long blonde hair like a flag behind her. Freedom, sweet, glorious freedom!

In the back of her mind, Amara knew Sonny was faithfully watching over her from where he had perched himself on the fence. But unlike her parents, Sonny didn't evaluate, disapprove, or rush her to finish the experience. He seemed absolutely content to wait. Once in a while, Amara waved at him from her place on the wind, and he would smile his gorgeous smile—the smile that made her heart pound like a bass drum.

Amara rode Moses around and around in the field until the sun went down and stars began to appear. The dark figure perched on the fence made it known that Sonny was still there. However, when she could no longer see him or the fences, she stopped riding. She could barely make out Moses' neck right in front of her.

"Sonny?"

"Yes?" his voice answered from somewhere behind her.

Turning her horse around, she nudged Moses toward Sonny's reassuring voice. "Are you still on the fence?"

"Yes," he said with a chuckle. "I'm right where you left me. Are you done riding?"

"I think so. Moses is tired." Sonny laughed, and she readjusted her direction, like a game of Marco Polo. "Can you see us?" she asked. "I can't see anything."

"I can see you," Sonny assured her. There was a scuffle of pants slipping from a wood rail. "Hang on, I'm coming for you."

"Okay." Moses and Amara walked in blind faith toward Sonny, until Moses stopped in his tracks. "What is it, Moses?" Amara asked nervously.

"It's me," she heard Sonny answer. Slowly, his face materialized from the dark at her left knee. Immediately, her nerves quietened, and she realized with startling clarity that she was suddenly in very real danger of falling—and it had nothing to do with horses.

## CHAPTER SIX

The next morning, dressed in jeans and a lacy pink tank top, Amara stepped onto her small, private front porch. Pitter-pattering with only white socks on her feet, she tossed herself in the old rocking chair next to the front door. The chair creaked and crackled as she applied a thick layer of sunscreen to her skin. Then she collected her long blonde hair at the base of her neck, wrapped a black hair band around and around, feeding the long tail through until it was as tight as her mother's sense of humor.

Her heart leapt the moment she saw Sonny's silhouette riding down the hill in the distance. He was riding a horse that looked like Nick, and towing another one that looked to be Moses. On a horse he looked even taller, his white cowboy hat rising and falling with his easy motions. The closer he got, the faster her heart beat.

Amara snatched her red boots from against the wall where she had left them the night before. Hurriedly, she shoved her feet into them and wiggled her toes. They were new, and entirely too clean for her to pretend they were anything but an eccentric splash of color for the preposterous cowgirl picture she had visualized. But now that she was here, she was determined to break them in—like real boots. After today, she would be able to boast they were indeed her cowgirl boots.

Hearing the clippity-clop of Nick and Moses growing louder, Amara leapt to her feet, borrowing the straw hat someone had left hanging on a peg above her head. She was pretty sure it was intended as a decoration, but it would do the job nicely.

"Morning," Sonny greeted as he rode up.

Amara twirled around. Damn, he looked fabulous, arranging his rear and legs in the saddle and tipping his hat politely. Nick shifted his hooves and sighed.

"If you haven't had too much riding," said Sonny, "I thought you might like to check the heifers with me. It's a fairly easy ride."

Amara smiled, shoving the borrowed hat down on her head. Lifting a hand to her face, shielding her eyes from the morning sun, she asked, "Heifers?"

"Young cows," he answered, without even the slightest hint of ridicule in his tone.

"I expect I can handle it," Amara said, stepping from the porch. Moses was wearing Lizzy's saddle again, and she ran a hand over its beautiful slick seat. "Why doesn't Mr. Morris display this saddle in the living room, with the other things?"

Sonny touched the coiled rope hanging from a tie on his saddle and bumped it casually against his leg. "Too personal for Gramps, I guess," he answered. "Grandma Lizzy's things have been off limits since her passing. Until yesterday."

Amara recognized what a tremendous honor she had been given, being allowed to put Lizzy's saddle to use again. "Question," she said, lifting her foot to the stirrup. "What's an old cow called?"

Sonny laughed.

Grunting loudly, Amara stretched her leg, and it cramped up and began aching. Grimacing against the searing pain, she continued stretching, still trying to get her foot in the stirrup. Almost…

"Sore today?" said Sonny, resting his elbow on the horn of his saddle in amusement.

"Yeah, a little."

Preparing to step off his horse, Sonny asked, "Can I help you?"

Amara put a hand up. "Nope. I can do this," she said determinedly, as she grabbed one stirrup with her toe and grasped the saddle with both hands. Pulling with all her might, she finally made it. "Got it!" she said, dropping heavily into the saddle. Copying Sonny, she gathered her reins. There seemed to be a lot of extra rein in her lap compared to him. Shrugging, she smiled. "I'm ready. Let's go check those girls."

"Now you're getting it," he said, including a wink.

An hour later, she and Sonny had located the herd. Half of the heifers were lazily eating; the other half were dozing in the sun. Sonny counted each head and jotted the number down in a small notebook he pulled from his shirt pocket.

"I know what to get you for Christmas," Amara said, rubbing her hands over her already pink shoulders.

"For Christmas?" Sonny asked, grinning sideways at her.

Amara squared her chin proudly, pretending to look over the heifers. "I'll get you a pocket protector." She leaned over and poked the spot on his shirt where the tip of his pen rested at the bottom of his pocket. "I wouldn't want your fancy shirt getting ink stains. Besides, what more could a man who carries a notebook and pen in his shirt pocket want?"

"Well, if you're getting me a pocket protector, then I'm getting you a pair of suitable boots."

Amara's mouth dropped open. "What's wrong with these?" she asked, holding a red boot out for him to take a closer look. "Are you prejudiced against red?"

"No," Sonny said, lifting his hat just enough to scratch his head with the interior of the crown, and then replacing it. "It's just that they're ugly."

"They're not ugly!"

He shrugged. "There's no way you'll be able to keep up with me wearing those."

"I can keep up with you wearing three-inch high heels, Sonny Morris."

"Really?" His eyes sparkled at her challenge.

She threw her long ponytail over her shoulder. "Yeah."

Without warning, Sonny kicked Nick's sides and began pulling away at a three-beat lope, Nick happily flinging his tail behind him. "Where did you go, high-heel wearer?" Sonny called over his shoulder.

"I don't wear high heels!" Amara hollered defensively at his shrinking outline. "Amateurs," she told Moses, bumping his sides. Moses gladly offered a gentle three-beat pace. They were keeping up, a small ways back, but not making progress.

"I'm leaving you in the dust!" Sonny taunted. "I think I changed my mind. I'm getting you high heels for Christmas."

Dust from Nick's feet floated into Amara's eyes and nostrils. She squinted and blinked feverishly, tucking her chin, attempting to escape the tiny pestering particles. "I don't like being in the back, Moses. Do you? What do you say we change the scenery?"

Moses bobbed his head with each stride, and Amara interpreted that as an agreement. Plastering a broad smile to her face, she squeezed Moses' round sides with her calves, and the horse seemed to smile too as he jolted forward and began eating up the ground between him and Nick. Oh yeah, she and Moses had this in the bag. The look on Sonny's face as she and Moses flew by was worth every cent she had paid for her overpriced, red, city version of country boots.

She let Moses keep pulling, loving every minute of the warm, dust-free wind wiping across her face and whistling in her ears. The grass blades blurred and the trees whizzed by. She could hear Moses' hooves pounding against the ground. His raw power asked no questions, took no notes, required no follow-up quizzes. He didn't lecture her like a child. He didn't demand that she repeat his every notion as if it were her own. No, Moses just ran. He ran for the joy of running, taking her with him, allowing her to borrow his carefree strength. She could stay here, in this moment, forever.

"Let's never stop," Amara told Moses, his ears flicking. "Let's keep going until we reach the end of the Earth." Moses seemed to agree.

"Amara! Stop!" Sonny called anxiously from behind.

Why he sounded worried, Amara didn't know, but the tone in his voice stripped away her smile and alerted her to pull on Moses' reins. It was a good thing she did.

Three strides later, she was still pulling Moses up when his nose dove towards the ground, yanking the reins from her hands. Amara felt herself fall forward, out of position. It felt as though Moses's legs were crumbling out from underneath. That was when she saw the deep, sweeping ditch, hidden by tall grass. It had eaten them up. The horse's heavy body fell like a slow-motion picture, tossing Amara to the ground. Moses' enormous, bulky ribs landed on her right leg, pinning her. She felt her shoulder hit first, followed by a tweak in her knee. Her head bumped the ground, where she stayed until Moses lifted his weight off her trapped leg. As soon as she was free, she pulled her legs from Moses. He jumped to his feet, shaking his long neck, startled to have found himself suddenly lying on the ground.

Sonny was upon them in an instant, leaping from his horse in one amazing, gigantic bound. Even in a panic, he was stunning. He sprung across the ditch and dropped to his knees next to her, his face drenched with worry. She was trying desperately not to laugh. Clearly he had no idea how attractive he was bending over her the way he was, looking over her nonexistent injuries.

"Are you hurt?" he asked. "I'm sorry. I never should have encouraged you to run."

"I'm fine," Amara assured him, dusting the dirt from her bare shoulder. It was tender—very tender—but not hurt. "Really," she stressed with a smile. He kept touching parts of her legs and ankles, testing for himself. "Ouch," Amara complained as he gently squeezed her right ankle. "That hurt a bit. Is Moses alright?"

"Moses is fine," Sonny said, still palpating her ankle. "Well, it's not broken. That's good." He released the pressure. "It's just a sprain. Where were you two headed, anyway?"

"To the end of the earth," Amara said, lifting her face to the sun and closing her eyes. When she opened them again, she saw amusement on Sonny's face.

"I know somewhere you might like," he said. "It's where I go when *I'm* looking for the end of the earth. It may help your ankle, too. Would you like to see it? Or would you like me to take you home?"

"I didn't come here to go home," Amara replied.

"Can you still trust Moses?"

Amara crossed her arms over her chest. "Of course I trust Moses. It wasn't his fault. I shouldn't have been so careless." Extending her arm for Sonny to pull her up, she said, "I would like to see your end of the earth."

Sonny grasped her hand and tugged, but as soon as she put weight on her ankle, it burned something terrible. "Do you think Moses could come closer?" she said, wincing in pain. "I don't think I can hop that far."

The next thing she knew, Sonny had swept her off her feet, his strong arms intimately wrapped around her body. At first, self-conscious, she giggled like a child, but when the brim of Sonny's hat lightly bumped the brim of hers, she felt something completely different—a tender burning deep inside. Swallowing, she did her best to bury it. It was unreasonable for such a simple, light touch to create such an intense reaction. But she couldn't bury the feeling.

She felt the fingers of his right hand wrap around her ribs, and the fingers of his left hand grip her thigh. Her cheeks were flushed again. Then his blue eyes caught, and held, her gaze. For a moment, she thought he might kiss her. She could admit she wanted him to kiss her. And he was thinking about it, she was pretty sure.

Then, without warning, he stopped abruptly, and she felt herself being swung upward. Her rear was met by Moses' back. "Here we are," he said. She was forced to scramble awkwardly up.

"That was easy—for me," Amara said with a laugh.

"One thing is for certain," Sonny said, retreating to his own mount. "I won't be nicknaming you 'featherweight.'"

After Sonny mounted, Amara allowed him to lead the way, at a controlled walk this time. They passed through a gate and crossed a small creek, at last coming upon a cool, peaceful pond. A few birds fluttered off as both horses dropped their noses to take in the welcome refreshment.

"Hang on," Sonny told Amara as she prepared to dismount. He slipped from Nick's back as slick as a slide, then positioned himself at Moses' side. "Alright. Slide off." She obliged, and he carried her to the bank, setting her in the long grass.

There was no need to instruct her from there. She happily removed her boots and dropped both feet into the cool water. Sonny was following suit, kicking off his boots and ditching his hat, which he handed to her for safekeeping. To her utter disbelief, he didn't stop there.

As Amara was placing his hat in the grass to her left, he yanked off his socks, then pulled his shirt over his head, tossing it to the ground. Her eyebrows lifted as he tugged his pants to his ankles, revealing strong muscular legs and a pair of underwear, the definition leaving very little to the imagination. Stepping on his pants, he freed each foot. When he glanced down at her, she looked away. Not quickly enough, though—he had seen her gawking, and she had seen his appreciative grin.

Never had a man undressed so casually in front of her before. Truth be told, never had a man undressed in front of her, period. How did he manage to move so confidently, so leisurely? Though resolving not to stare, she could sense his masculine presence only an arm's length away. Waiting stiff as a board as he worked up the nerve to jump in, she tried to not steal quick glimpses—not that he seemed to mind. She assumed that once he plunged into the pond, she would experience a sense of relief, but as the splash hit her and the wake rose to wet the bottom of her pants, relief was not what she experienced.

Sonny surfaced and stood up, the water rippling down his toned body. His hips were defined and white where his jeans normally covered them. Pushing the hair from his face, he opened his gorgeous blue eyes. Amara felt an involuntary warmth spread over her when his eyes locked with hers.

"Jump in!" he called out.

Moses and Nick were slowly working their way around the pond's edge, nibbling and ripping the grass with their teeth. Pretending to be enamored with them, she answered, "No, I don't think so."

"Worried about your makeup?" he teased, knowing full well she didn't wear any.

"You're a funny guy, aren't you?"

Seemingly unperturbed, Sonny waded to the edge of the pond, drew himself out, and sat in the grass on her right, exhaling a contented sigh. "You're missing out," he said, the sun beating down on his tanned skin.

The little water droplets began evaporating from his body, one by one. And as soon as he laid back, placing his arms behind his head, Amara stole a quick peek. Discovering that his eyes were closed, she surveyed him more leisurely, her gaze gliding up and down, taking him in. Guilt should have been kicking in, but it wasn't. She forced herself to turn away and focus on her bare feet, just beneath the surface. A few seconds ticked by before she broke. "Sonny," she snapped.

He opened his eyes. "Yeah?"

"Could you possibly get dressed?"

Sitting up, he leaned over and took a quick look at her feet dangling in the water. "Does your ankle feel better?"

She pulled her feet out, propping her heels on the grass bank to dry. "Yes."

"Alright then, break's over." Looking around, he spotted his hat and reached behind her with his left arm, his warm, bare body leaning in to press against her. He plucked his cowboy hat from the grass as Amara focused on breathing at a steady pace, truly unsure whether or not she was succeeding. He smelled like ivory soap, ponderosa pine, and masculinity.

"Would you please stop that?" she asked.

"Stop what?"

"*That,*" she said, gesturing to his body with her hand.

Sonny laughed, rolling onto the balls of his feet and standing up. "You're a funny girl, aren't you?" he asked, mimicking her tone. "Sorry for making you uncomfortable."

"I'm not uncomfortable," she said defensively. Amara pulled a sock over her wet toes, strongly trying to ignore him looming next to her, pulling on his jeans. "I'm not a child."

"I have eyes," he said, as he zipped the front of his pants.

Eyelashes fluttering, she paused, her sock dangling from her foot like an elephant's trunk. Was his comment a compliment? Or did she only wish to believe it was? Her makeup-less face, plain figure, and unattractively independent attitude frightened off most boys.

"Better?" Sonny asked, pulling his shirt over his head and placing his hat on his head.

Amara glanced at him as he plopped onto the grass next to her, joining her in replacing his socks and boots. "Yes," she lied. He may have been fully dressed, but his secret was out in her mind.

"Ready to ride?"

"Absolutely."

"Shall we head back? Or do you want to see more?"

"More," Amara replied, grinning sheepishly. Sonny rose to his feet and offered her a hand. Never before had she wanted to take a man's hand the way she wanted to take his at that very moment—so she did.

Later, while their horses trudged up a gentle slope, Sonny said, "I'm sure it's just ahead," for the second time in ten minutes.

"Are we lost?" she asked.

"No, we're not lost."

"Are we still on the ranch?"

"Yes, we're still on the ranch." His back straightened and his face brightened. "Here they are!"

"They?"

Almost in unison, both Amara and Moses lifted their heads, eyes widening. Immediately their energy and passion returned. In the green carpeted valley below, unbound horses speckled the panoramic landscape. Not a fence was in sight. If it hadn't been for the comforting, ripping sounds of Moses grabbing a bite to eat, the dreamlike stillness would have seemed an illusion, an artificial cloth drape quite impressively mimicking perfection. But for the first time in her life, it was indeed real—not a calendar or a picture in a magazine. There was a herd of roaming horses before her, a horse underneath her, and a stunningly attractive man beside her. She could die a happy woman, right now. But given the choice, she'd rather live.

Holder of the Horses

The benefit to climbing to the top of the gentle slope was that a refreshing breeze had found them. It brushed across her back, touched her cheeks, and wisped up Moses' mane. Catching their scent in the wind, the horses below lifted their heads, pointing their noses right at them. Having decided there was no threat, most of them turned away and returned to their afternoon nibbling.

Amara could feel Sonny watching her when she started counting the glistening, muscular bodies. Bouncing her finger from horse to horse, she hesitated as they wandered peacefully about in search of longer, greener, tastier grass. Eventually, she lost track. As she started her counting over, two of the horses entered into a mild scuffle over a particular grass patch, disrupting the herd. Half a dozen horses scattered, mixing with the ones she hadn't counted yet. Sighing heavily, she started counting from the beginning—again—when something Amara couldn't see, hear, or smell alerted the entire herd. She watched in surprise as a single gold-colored horse with cream-colored hair caused the herd to shift about four hundred yards down the valley. As the horses settled, they reconfirmed their ranks by taking the top priority grass spots. Dropping her counting hand to her lap, Amara gave up.

Sonny had his notebook out and ready. "How many did you count?"

"I don't know," she replied, admitting defeat. "I kept losing track." Sonny jotted a number down in his notebook anyway. When she leaned over, trying to take a peek at the page, he flipped it shut and stuffed it back in his shirt pocket. "What did you write?"

"Thirty-three."

"How did you—"

"Got to count faster," he said, adding a wink.

"Alright," Amara said. She considered herself coachable, so she began counting again, faster. Her finger was bouncing along when a movement in the sky caught her attention. "Wow! A bald eagle!"

The eagle was soaring above them, gliding effortlessly, his gigantic wings stretching out on both sides as if he were floating on the surface of an invisible barrier. His distinctive white head bent at the neck, looking this way and that, surveying for the tiniest movements rustling beneath bushes and breezeless grass blades. Amara threw up her hands, realizing again that she had lost count. "I concede."

"It takes practice," Sonny acknowledged. "Gramps was frustrated that I couldn't count a herd for years." He shrugged. "Of course, I was four."

"Somehow that doesn't make me feel much better. I just can't figure why," said Amara. Sonny chuckled. "May I ask about your Grandma Lizzy?"

Glancing at Grandma Lizzy's saddle, then back to the herd, Sonny answered, "She was gentle and kind. Don't get me wrong, she could wallop my ass when the circumstances called for it, but all in all, she was a very warm woman. Gramps bought her that saddle so she could accompany him around the ranch, so they could be together."

"Were they together a lot?"

"All the time."

"Were they happy?"

Sonny smiled, remembering. "Very happy." Pausing, he sighed. "Gramps misses her more than he would miss his own heart, if it were removed."

"What a beautiful thing, to be in love—truly in love—not just tolerant, or obligated." A mental picture of her parents' marriage popped into Amara's mind. "Truthfully, I can see how any marriage would require a certain amount of tolerance, but my parents are rarely ever together. It seems better that way—for them, at least. They're out of sorts with one another a lot. But they do love each other." Amara amended. "I just don't see them craving one another the way your grandparents seemed to. What a beautiful thing they had. I want something like that someday." Surprised that she had just caught herself telling Sonny something so private, she clamped her mouth shut, pressing her lips together. She was comfortable with him. Too comfortable. "Where are your parents? Do they live nearby?" she asked, hoping to remove the spotlight from herself.

"No," he said, shrugging. "Wherever they are, they're not likely together."

"Wherever they are? Do you not know?"

"My dad is what Gramps calls a crumb drifter."

"A crumb drifter? What does that mean?"

"A crumb is a worthless person."

"Oh."

"He knocked up my mother, brought her here to the ranch, then true to his character, he drifted on—without us."

Too horrified for words, Amara just listened.

"Took less than a year for him to duck out. Couldn't take another minute of feeling stuck. My mother—her name is Sue—managed to stick out a couple more years, needing the support of my grandparents. But even she couldn't take being isolated here for long."

"Where did you go?"

"I didn't go anywhere," he said in a voice which hinted at past bitterness. Then he grinned weakly. "I'm glad she left me. She hasn't kept in touch with any of us since the day she left. If she had taken me, I would have lost contact with the only people who actually loved me. I don't care where my parents went. This is my home, and I'm glad to be here."

"You don't see either of them?"

"John comes poking around every few years, asking for money."

She couldn't miss the fact that Sonny had called his dad John. It said a lot. "Has he ever tried to take you with him when he leaves?"

"Heck no!" Sonny answered vehemently. "He ignores me and I ignore him. I assume we share the same viewpoint; we remind each other of something we wish didn't exist."

"Have you ever tried to find your mom?"

"After she kissed my forehead goodbye, all I wanted was for her to come back," he said. "She didn't." Sonny squirmed in his saddle a little, suggesting discomfort. "She moved on. So I did too."

"I'm sorry."

"Lots of kids have parents who are hellbound drifters. I was the lucky one, not being dragged along with them. I couldn't have asked to be raised by better grandparents." Dropping the subject, he asked, "Shall we get going?"

Amara nodded, turning Moses to follow Nick. Carefully, they plodded along the top of the hill, making their way down into a gulley then back up the other side. Amara felt her rear scooting sorely in the saddle. She tried to find a way to sit on the hard leather seat that would wear her rear differently. Apparently, there was none. She gritted her teeth and kept on keeping on. As the day—and her rear—wore on, Sonny safely guided her back to the ranch. As they pulled their horses up outside Amara's guest house, she breathed a sigh of relief.

"I took you too far," said Sonny, who had noticed her weariness. "I'm sorry."

"It wasn't too far," said Amara. "It was the best day I've ever had. I wouldn't've changed a thing."

As she scrambled down from Moses' back, for a moment, she felt like the cowgirl her soul had always longed to be. After all, she had just dismounted a horse for the second day in a row. Making it better, on the evening breeze floated a strong scent of pine. If she could have paused time, she would have chosen to pause it right then, so she could relish the sensation a little longer. As time would have it, the breeze died down.

"Thank you for inviting me here," she said, handing Sonny one of Moses' reins. "Are you sure I shouldn't be helping you put Moses away? Charleston will be disappointed in me for my first day of work. I don't believe I've worked at all."

When Sonny smiled, his rugged face warmed her insides. "Don't worry about Moses or Gramps. They'll both be fine. You know," he said, toying with Moses' rein. "It's tradition that we feed our help supper. Would you like to join us?"

Amara smiled. "I would love to. I noticed my kitchen was stocked with a few things. I'll bring something."

Transferring both horses' reins to his left hand, Sonny asked, "Pick you up in an hour?"

"Alright," she said, happy to be able to see him again. And Mr. Morris too, of course.

Sonny turned Nick around, Moses followed, and the three of them rode up the hill towards the main house. She watched them trotting away, well aware that her stomach was being overtaken by fluttering butterflies. After they had disappeared around the trees, she willed herself to glance at her dusty clothes and smell under her arm. She wrinkled her nose; she'd better hustle and make good use of the hour. Quickly retreating, she snatched her boots from her feet, one at a time, hopping as she went.

Ten minutes later, she was showered and smelled of soap and lotion. She pulled on a clean pair of shorts and a fuzzy pink sweater. In the long mirror on the bathroom door, she gently teased a brush through her hair. She ought to feel out of place in this cozy old house, having lived in the city with white walls all her life. But she didn't. Strangely, it felt like home. It suited her. More so, Sonny suited her. Her stomach turned just thinking it.

Tossing the hairbrush onto the couch behind her, she frowned, reprimanding herself. No. Sonny couldn't suit her. She was leaving Montana and going back to college—to her controlled life.

Like her own mom had done so often when she was younger, Amara yanked her hair into a tight braid, starting at the top of her head and working her way all the way to the tip. When it was done, she nodded. There, controlled again. No stray hairs or dreamy thoughts. Determined, she gathered her red boots from where they had been strewn in her hurry, poking her feet back in. They were dirty boots this time, she thought, and smiled proudly.

Returning to the mirror to check out her clashing pink sweater and dirty red boots (her mom would be horrified), she saw her sunburnt skin reflected back at her. It was becoming the color of her boots. Playfully, rebelliously, she kicked her left boot and tapped the heel against the floor. The image of herself smiled back at her.

What was wrong with enjoying simple things? It hadn't escaped her attention: folks that had less seemed happier. They enjoyed the small things, like a silly dance in the mirror, more than a fancy car in the driveway. Someone could steal the car, but no one could steal the dance.

Across the street from the house in which she had grown up, she clearly remembered observing two different people—two different lifestyles. The first was a widow who always wore a smile. Her house was the least upkept on the block, to everyone's dismay, yet she loved her roses. Oh, how she loved her roses! She would sit in her wooden swing, hung by her late husband years ago, and stare at them for hours, visiting politely with her little brown mutt dog—who also always happened to be wearing a smile.

The second was a handsome middle-aged man, who lived in the biggest, nicest home on the block. Everything about him was perfect. His house, his shiny silver car, his grass, his six children, and his beautiful wife. Yet Amara had never seen him smile. Not even once. She had rarely even seen him utter a word to his children as he rushed by them in the yard on his way to work. Their disappointed faces followed him, learning (wrongly) what was to be worshiped in life.

Amara made her way into the tiny kitchen. It was much in need of a remodel; all the appliances were twenty years outdated. But it was no matter, she could still warm the instant coffee she had found in the cupboard come morning. Taking a quick inventory of the cupboard's contents, she found flour, sugar, and a few baking necessities. The problem was, she couldn't bake. Her mouth contorting into a crooked, lemon-sucking pucker, she continued looking around the kitchen for more ideas. If only she had taken cooking classes. But following in her mom's footsteps, there wasn't time for learning to cook when one is destined for a degree in success.

Amara huffed. "Success" was such a loose term.

Transitioning to the refrigerator, she found milk, butter, and eggs. She slung the door shut. What could she bring to supper? Then she spotted it. A bowl of fruit. There was an assortment of apples, grapes, and an entire pineapple. A fruit salad! Surely she could do that. Turned out that when your idea of having fruit salad meant a trip to the store, the easiest part of making it was retrieving the bowl from a shelf.

The apples wobbled and rolled as she tried to cut away the shiny red skin. It came off in itty bitty chunks, and when she tried dicing it, little black seeds littered the counter. Trying to hurry, she cut herself twice slicing the grapes in half. But the pineapple was the worst opponent of all. She stared at it. It stared right back. Dare she whittle it? She had no idea how to whittle a pineapple. But a decision had to be made. She shrugged and boldly inserted the tip of her knife into the hard, spiny shell. One piece at a time, the yellow flesh inside was revealed. It was extremely tough, not to mention time-consuming. But if there was a better way, she didn't know what it was.

## CHAPTER SEVEN

Sonny was walking back from putting up Nick and Moses at about the same time that Gramps pulled up in his pickup. Both cowboys beat their britches as they stepped up onto the porch, sending puffs of dust and hay fragments into the air. The dust hovered and fell. Together, they kicked off their boots.

Gramps looked up at Sonny from under his dusty straw hat. "What are you doing?"

Sonny removed his hat, running a dirty hand through his equally dirty hair. "Going in the house," he answered. Since when did going in the house require an explanation?

"Where's Amara?"

"At her house," Sonny replied impatiently.

"What's she doing there?" Gramps frowned. "She ought to be up here, with us, for supper." When Gramps opened the front door, Sonny tried to follow him in. Gramps stopped him, blocking the doorway. "Uh-uh, go get her. You know we feed our hands."

"She's not a hand," said Sonny, despite having used the same excuse to invite her to supper earlier.

"Humph." Gramps was having none of it. In his stubborn old mind, Amara had worked today, and she would be fed.

Shaking his head, Sonny pulled his boots back on and took a stroll down the hill, hands in his jean pockets. He walked slowly, hoping Amara wouldn't be unhappy that he would be showing up earlier then he had originally told her. Gramps just could not be reasoned with. When he set his bony foot down, there was no persuading him otherwise. Sonny hated seeing Gramps get his hopes up. Amara would be headed home as soon as her friends had spent all their money at the casino. She was only a guest. She had always been only a guest.

The closer to the old ranch house Sonny got, the more his stomach twisted. Why was he nervous? He had spent the entire day with Amara. He hadn't been nervous showing her around the ranch. But then he'd been in his element. Somehow, walking down to the house felt different. It felt personal.

Supper was a meal, not a date, he told himself. Especially with Gramps right there, insisting Amara rise at dawn and accept a position on the payroll. Speaking of which, what had gotten into Gramps? What was with unretiring Grandma Lizzy's saddle? Sure, Sonny liked Amara…alright, he liked her a lot. He'd liked her from the first moment he saw her, the wind whipping her long blonde tresses around her like angel's wings. He liked her contagious free spirit and her danger-defying attitude. She even pulled her own stunts, then got up and laughed about it. He'd never met a girl like her before.

Stepping onto the wooden porch, his heart suddenly beating faster, he set his knuckles to the door. Taking a calming breath, he tapped.

"Come in!" he heard her yell.

Feeling as though he were trespassing, he turned the knob and slowly moved into the same house he'd entered a thousand times. But this time was different. This time it wasn't a group of smelly working men playing cards, it was Amara, a tiny pretty thing. He hesitated, doorknob still in his hand, uncertain if he should stay in the open doorway and keep a respectable aura—or just strut on in as if he owned the joint, as if he wasn't at all uncomfortable.

"You're early," Amara said, her voice coming from the kitchen. He peeked around the door, not expecting to see what he saw. His eyes widened. There had been some sort of fruit massacre! The counter and half the floor was covered in fruit debris. Both innards and skins of apples, grapes, and pineapples were everywhere. It was like a grenade had detonated inside the fruit bowl he had filled for her, and this was all that was left. If it had been anything other than fruit, he may have puked.

"How's it going?" Sonny asked, cautiously shutting the door.

She smiled brightly. "Fine!" Then she glanced around, realizing that her fruit massacre had been discovered. Kicking a few pieces of pineapple behind her, she sheepishly explained, "Uh...making an attempt at fruit salad."

"Oh," was all Sonny could think to say, raising his eyebrows. What else could he say? Besides, she kind of looked adorable standing there, bashful, in her ugly pink-hair sweater and the same red boots he'd made fun of earlier. Even so, it took a surprising amount of willpower to keep his eyes from returning to the decimated fruit remains scattered about. Whatever had ensued here, he was determined to turn a blind eye.

He watched her take a bag of flour from the top shelf and carry it over to the bowl into which she had thrown the surviving fruit—if a person could call them *surviving*. *Carnage* seemed more fitting. She grabbed a spoon from the drawer and stuck it in the flour bag, pulling out a large heap. With wide eyes, Sonny grasped her plan; she was headed for the fruit with the flour. It only took him a single bound to make it across the tiny kitchen space to stop her. As he grabbed her wrist, a puff of flour sprinkling the counter, she looked up at him in surprise.

"What?" she asked. He released her immediately, his fingers barely brushing her forearm. "I take it flour does not go in fruit salad?" said Amara, her head cocking playfully.

"No, it really shouldn't."

"Then perhaps you can help me. What makes the creamy dressing in a fruit salad?"

Giving her a sideways grin, he answered, "Cream."

"What kind of cream? Sour cream? Cream cheese?"

"You really don't cook, do you?" he asked, then opened the refrigerator door, pulled out a paper carton, and pointed to it. "Cream." He pulled down a small bowl from the cupboard and handed her the carton. "Pour about a cup into here."

She opened the carton and began pouring. When she reached two cups and was still pouring, he stopped her. Next, he gave her a hand blender from the bottom cupboard. She took it, staring at him like a crippled owl in the road.

He laughed at her adorably helpless face. "When I was a boy, Grandma Lizzy always made the pie, and my job was whipping the cream." He stood to the side. "It's easy, just turn it on and mix."

Amara flipped the switch. The motor purred to life, whizzing at full blast. Then, cautiously, she stuck the beaters into the thick white liquid so they just barely touched the surface. Cream began spitting everywhere. Panicked that she had done something wrong, she yanked the beaters back out and held them out to him, waving them around. "Fix it!" she cried, while the motor roared and the beaters continued sending cream all over the kitchen—and Sonny's face.

Squinting and dodging, Sonny again secured Amara's wrist in an effort to keep her from waving the blender around. Nearly blind, he reached for the off switch with his other hand, hoping he didn't lose a finger in the process. When the white sputtering slowed, he looked at her. Her arm was outstretched, holding the blender, and her eyes squeezed shut tightly. As they slowly opened, her cream splattered face contorted into an expression of combined horror and surprise. Then, all at once, she burst into a fit of laughter, pointing and hooting.

"Having a good time, are you?"

"Yeah!"

"Well, look at you," he said, feeling rather entertained as he grabbed a kitchen towel and wiped off his face.

Looking at her own sweater, she frowned. "Oh, I hope it'll wash! My mom so despised this sweater."

His eyes narrowed in confusion. "Yeah...I'm not sure how you meant that. But I think I agree with your mom on this one."

"What?" she asked, raising her eyebrows. "You don't like my sweater?"

"It's ugly, and doesn't really fit you."

Tugging at the bottom hem, she frowned. "It fits."

"Take it off," Sonny directed. He began unbuttoning his shirt.

"What?"

"Take it off," he repeated, undoing the last button of his shirt, and pulling his arms out of the sleeves.

"You have a shirt on under that," she said, sounding somewhat relieved.

"Well, yeah. Don't you?"

Amara cleared her throat, daintily. "Of course I do."

When he lifted his eyebrows expectantly, she pulled her arms into the center of the sweater and yanked the entire mass of pink wool over her head. For a brief moment, her face was covered, her torso revealed. Damn, she was hot, her stomach smooth and slender with a perfect little belly button winking out at him. Sonny didn't check himself from looking at her exposed figure quickly enough, and she caught him with a steady gaze. He could have apologized, but he didn't. He'd just play it off instead, leave her wondering.

The corners of her lips turned up, knowingly, as she stood there in a short-sleeve purple t-shirt. If she was waiting on an apology, she wouldn't be getting one. You can't yank off your shirt right in front of a guy and expect him *not* to check you out. It was natural. In fact, even a girl would have checked her out to compare notes.

Chill bumps appeared on Amara's arms, so Sonny wrapped his shirt around her shoulders. With a little effort, she stuffed her hands in. On her, his sleeves looked like they belonged on an ape, dangling loose at her sides. Like a parent, he gently rolled each sleeve all the way up to her wrist, then handed her the towel to wipe off the worst of the cream splattering. His face had gotten the brunt, so his shirt wasn't too bad.

He stepped back and smiled. "Better."

"Looks better on me than you, doesn't it?" she teased, not expecting his next response.

He crossed his arms over his chest. "We agree. Let's finish whipping the cream and get up to the house. I'm starved."

She nodded, returning to the messy kitchen counter. "Alright, kitchen master. Teach on."

Sonny laughed and stepped in behind her, placing his right hand over hers. His arms around her waist, he guided her to set the beaters on the very bottom of the bowl. Switching the blender on and gradually increasing the motor's speed, one click at a time, they both watched as the cream began swirling in the bowl. With his body pressed against her backside, Sonny piloted her hand in small, smooth circles. She didn't fight his close proximity. In fact, she seemed to welcome it.

Together, they stood over the kitchen counter, watching the cream wrinkle and fall, wrinkle and fall, neither of them saying anything. Perhaps they were afraid to break the spell. They simply watched, staying in the moment for as long as it lasted, mesmerized. When the cream began forming peaks, no longer falling, Sonny considered letting the blender continue to spin. The cream would be ruined, becoming butter, but it would've bought him a few seconds longer having her in his arms.

Regrettably, he resisted the temptation and switched the motor off. Amara waited patiently, still wrapped in his long arms, as he tapped the beaters lightly on the side of the bowl. The majority of the whipping cream that had collected in the metal wires fell back into the bowl. The whipping cream was done, so he was forced to move away.

"Now what?" Amara asked, her vibrant hazel eyes locked on him.

"You can add vanilla," he told her, permitting himself to take notice of her small pink lips. What would happen if he discarded his gentlemanly role as host and kissed her? Just once? Yesterday, when he had first met Amara, her face had been exquisitely pale and delicate. This evening, however, the paleness had been replaced by the genuine glow of sun-pinked cheeks. He approved; the bright color better represented her playful personality. Either way, it didn't take a magnifying glass to see that Amara was striking and gorgeous.

Whatever had compelled her not to comply with traditional feminine behavior to a male stranger was beyond his limited understanding of the female race, but in doing so, she had instantly fascinated him. Where others might have been repelled by her fiery spirit, he found himself amused, charmed, even riveted. Her every thought, her every move, was like an adventure waiting to happen. The anticipation had him hanging on a cliff.

"Vanilla?" Amara inquired, still waiting. "Do I have vanilla?"

Unable to take the suspense any longer, Sonny leaned in, starting his own little adventure. Softly, he touched his lips to Amara's. If she was surprised, she didn't show it. Her soft, malleable lips received him with warmth. With the sweetness of her in his mouth, he realized that one kiss was never going to be enough. The chemicals that had been sizzling quietly between them all day ignited and set them both on fire. Now that he had started down this path, there was no guarantee there would be an end to it. And with her impending departure, he should have taken it into consideration before he kissed her.

## CHAPTER EIGHT

The next morning, Amara woke to a knocking at the front door of her little guest house. Simply opening her eyes, she could tell the sun hadn't even cracked over the edge of the horizon yet. Only the subtle gray promise of a new day slipped through the lacy curtains. Maybe whoever it was would go away. It would be enjoyable to lie on the crisp white sheets a little longer, wrapped in the handsewn quilt, reminiscing about yesterday's amazing kiss with Sonny—but the knocking persisted.

Sadly, she kicked her feet from their warm cocoon, abandoned the fluffy embrace of the bed, and made her way to the door. Who on earth could be here at this hour, and in the middle of nowhere, no less? It was a little early for her late-sleeping college girlfriends. Plus, they hadn't said they would arrive today. Since her hair was frizzing out of its braid, and her breath could scare off a bear, she hoped it wasn't Sonny. Wiping the fog from her eyes, she unlocked the door, opened it a slit, and peeked out.

Charleston's gray mustache and big cowboy hat greeted her. He was holding out a coffee mug. "Morning," he said.

"Um...morning," Amara replied in confusion, politely opening the door and taking the mug from him. "Thank you. Is everything all right?"

"Course. Course." Charleston nodded, his hat bobbing. "It's dawn," he said, examining her pajamas and undone hair. "You don't look ready."

"Ready for what?" Amara asked, taking a sip of the hot coffee. Maybe it would help combat her bear-repelling breath.

Charleston glanced at his pickup. He had left it idling. "Morning chores."

Amara smiled. Apparently, the day *had* started. Truth be told, it felt strangely splendid to feel like her presence was appreciated. She opened the door. "Come in," she said. "I'll be ready in five minutes."

His mustache curled up, and he stepped inside. Glancing around, he said, "Well, I'll be. Looks a lot nicer in here than it usually does. Smells better too."

"What does it normally look like?" Amara asked, setting her coffee on the wood box in front of the couch that served as a coffee table, and trotting towards her bedroom to throw on clothes in which she could do chores.

"Messier," Charleston answered from the living room. He looked around, evidently noticing the bareness. "I guess you haven't really moved in yet."

Amara spotted Sonny's button-up shirt, which she had worn home after dinner, hanging from the arm of the small wooden chair by the closet door. A warm feeling bubbled in her stomach. "No, I didn't bring much," she agreed, stuffing her legs into a pair of jeans.

"Well, you can have it sent, I suppose."

Amara laughed, yanking a red shirt from its hanger. "You know I'm not staying, right, Charleston?" she asked as she pulled the shirt on. Picking up Sonny's shirt, she pressed it to her nose. It still smelled like him.

Not wanting to appear smitten, she hung it back on the chair. She'd return it to him later.

When Amara stepped into the living area, she saw Charleston sitting on the couch, his long legs crossed. His head was resting against the back of the couch, eyes closed, cowboy hat on his knee, and her black stuffed horse stretched across his lap. She didn't believe he was actually asleep, it was just his way of passing over her question. She smirked. He wasn't so hard to peg. As she was quickly brushing her teeth, and then her hair, Charleston spoke up.

"Moving the nursery today. They've eaten the pasture they're in down to the nubs."

"Is that so?" Amara asked. She stuck her head out of the bathroom as she smothered it with sunscreen. "What nursery?"

"The mares and their foals."

"Oh."

The wood floor creaked as Amara exited the bathroom, switching off the light. She pulled at the bottom of her t-shirt. Charleston heard her coming and rose to his feet, gently propping her stuffed horse back into a sitting position on the couch. One of the things she liked about both Charleston and Sonny was their patience in answering questions. They seemed to be at peace with the fact that she didn't know all of the answers—any of the answers, really—but they were willing to teach her. It was nice, being treated like a valued member of the crew, even though she hadn't earned the right. It was refreshing to not have to earn it. Respect had been willingly gifted to her.

Amara grabbed her coffee. "I'm ready."

"You didn't eat anything."

"I'll be fine. I don't eat breakfast."

Stomping into the kitchen, Charleston poked around and came back with a sack of peanuts. "Allergic?"

"No, but peanuts for breakfast?" she asked skeptically.

With the peanuts tucked under his arm, he grunted as he left, "Who cares, you don't eat breakfast."

Soon they were driving through the ranch in Charleston's pickup, and eventually, he pulled up to an enormous hay barn with no walls, only a roof. "Crawl up there," he directed, pointing about halfway up the stack of bales, where large sections of hay were missing. "Then throw some bales down to the bed here. Try to aim them so I don't have to restack, will ya?"

Amara hopped down from the dusty bench seat, approached the stack, and looked up. These bales were much larger than the ones in the horse barn. These were more like four-hundred-pound blocks. Just one could crush her, let alone the whole pile, if it were to topple over. She could do this, she told herself. She wasn't sure she wanted to, but she could.

"You're not afraid of heights, are ya?" he asked, detecting her reluctance.

"No," she answered. "I'm afraid of the fall." Even still, she stuck her foot in a small crevice where two bales butted up against each other and grabbed hold of the strings of the bale above her head. She could do this. No problem.

Charleston chuckled. "Get down from there. You've proved your fortitude. We're going to use the forklift."

Amara jumped down, placing her hands on her hips. "Nice, Mr. Morris. Where's Sonny today?"

"Miss him already?" he asked, then, before she had the chance to answer, he turned his back to her to start up the forklift. "Doing morning chores, like you," he answered. "You'll see him later."

After Charleston loaded the flatbed with the ginormous hay bales, he signaled for her to pile back into the cab. Scooting into the passenger seat, she slammed the groaning, stiff door. Oh boy, could she relate, feeling stiff herself from yesterday's ride. She rolled down her window, letting in the fresh morning air. It was crisp on her face and sent goosebumps down her arms, but she wouldn't have traded the clean scent for anything.

Charleston reached behind the seat, pulling up a wrinkled, long-sleeved, flannel shirt. "Here," he said, handing it to her. She opened it up, checking the size. "It's Sonny's," said Charleston, likely assuming she was disgusted at the thought of wearing a dirty shirt belonging to anyone other than Sonny.

At the mention of Sonny's name, her insides warmed. She swung the shirt around her back, slid her arms into the sleeves, and covertly breathed in his scent. Again the faint hint of soap, pine, and hay. She buttoned the shirt with what she hoped was a casual display of indifference.

Pasture after pasture, Charleston had her drop hay off the back of the bed as they drove along. Two invigorating hours later, he ripped open the peanut bag, grabbing a handful and handing it to Amara. She accepted the nuts appreciatively, understanding now why breakfast was considered an important meal around here.

"You've got a few minutes to chomp on those," Charleston told her. "We're headed back to the barn."

"Have we fed everyone?" Amara asked, surprised she hadn't seen a single horse. Dropping the bag of peanuts between her legs, she began cracking them open, throwing the broken shells out the window.

"We fed half," Charleston answered. "It makes it easier to have two feeding routes. Sonny is feeding the other half."

When they arrived back, Amara noticed Sonny's pickup parked outside the barn, and the barn lights were on. After the kiss last night, she hoped things hadn't become too awkward between them. Ever since Charleston had come to pick her up, she had feared that Sonny hadn't felt comfortable showing her around anymore, or thought it was best to distance himself because he'd lost interest in her. So after Charleston parked the hay trailer, she waited and walked with him, rather than running ahead and looking for Sonny. Then she assisted Charleston with filling the water troughs. By the time they stepped into the barn, the sun was shining right through the big doors, illuminating the interior with warm yellow hues. As she expected, Sonny was inside. His back was to them, and he was grooming Nick with a wood-handled brush, sweeping the brush across Nick's back in long, smooth motions.

"Amara," Charleston said, tapping her shoulder with the heel of his palm, "Moses is in the third stall down. Why don't you get him ready for a ride?"

Sonny's head snapped to attention when he heard Charleston. He turned just as she walked by. "I didn't know you were up," he said, sounding surprised.

"Why shouldn't I be?" Amara asked, removing the brush from his hand as she marched calmly by.

Charleston dipped a scoop into a large bin of grain and took it to the wooden grain box in JoJo's stall. The sound of horse teeth grinding oats filled the barn.

"She was up at dawn, feeding," Charleston said in her defense.

"I wonder where she got that idea, Gramps," Sonny said.

"I brought her coffee."

"Gramps, you can't just barge in on her like that. She's a guest."

"I didn't barge in, and she didn't mind. It was dawn," Charleston reasoned, as if it were a good enough explanation.

"She doesn't work for you."

"She might," Charleston maintained.

Sonny growled in frustration. "Did you ask her if she *minded* being woken up at dawn?"

Amara was ignoring them as she gently brushed Moses' soft hair. His coat was already clean, but he deserved to have it brushed until he shone brilliantly—or until the two cowboys quit squabbling and helped her saddle him. Still as a statue, Moses soaked up the extra attention.

"Amara!" Charleston hollered through the wall. "Did you mind being woken up at dawn and helping me with chores?"

She could hear a saddle being tossed over a horse's back and some jingling. A horse's hoof pawed the compacted dirt floor.

"Not at all," Amara replied. "Could someone help me with putting on a saddle, please?"

"Don't look at me like that," came Charleston's gruff voice. "I like having someone around besides you."

Sonny appeared at Moses' stall door, and she was startled, not expecting him so quickly. "Morning," he said, propping an elbow against the wood frame, looking sexy as hell in his worn jeans and green long-sleeved shirt.

"Do you have a problem with me helping?" Amara asked.

"Nope," he answered, checking her out. "Nice shirt."

"I'm sorry I borrowed it. I was cold, and it was behind the seat," she said unemotionally.

"I gave it to her," Charleston's voice said through the wall.

Sonny twisted his lips, thinking. "Are you upset with me, Amara?"

"No, but you're chewing Charleston out pretty good for bringing me along. I *wanted* to come along."

Sonny lifted his weight from the wall. "Do you feel awkward that I kissed you last night?"

"No...but I'm afraid you do," she said, lowering her eyes. "I thought maybe Charleston came and got me because you didn't want to see me."

"I *do* want to see you. I couldn't wait to see you. I was...oh, never mind." He grabbed her around the waist, pulled her close, and closed his lips over hers.

The stubble on his face roughed her skin, but there wasn't a single part of her wishing it would stop. Everything was quiet except the blood pounding in her ears and Moses nudging her back pocket. When Sonny's lips pulled away, she breathed in deeply.

"Where did that come from?" she asked, breathless.

"Still think I might feel awkward about kissing you?"

"No," she said, shaking her head. Suddenly, she felt four eyes staring at her. Behind Sonny, Charleston and JoJo's faces were peering in curiously. Sonny, following her gaze, raised his eyebrows at the interfering spectators.

"Told you she didn't mind," said Charleston. He walked away, and JoJo followed. A loud thump on the opposite side of the wall made Amara jump. "Come on, we've got work to do," said Charleston's crusty voice. As if on cue, the roar of an engine and the crunching of gravel resonated through the wooden walls of the grand barn. "Reinforcements are here."

## CHAPTER NINE

An unbroken blue sky stretched over the Morris Ranch, seemingly surrounding the six horseback riders. Charleston and Sonny rode side by side on their nearly matching dappled gray mounts, rocking easily in their saddles, their lanky legs dangling around their horses' round sides. With each step, the muscles in the horses' hind ends flexed and worked, the men's broad backs matching the motion in perfect accord.

The three other riders that had pulled in with a trailer full of already-saddled horses consisted of a husband and wife team, Rod and Anita Sandgren, and their son, William Sandgren. William and Sonny were clearly best friends. The Sandgrens all had beautiful tanned complexions and thick dark hair. They rode three stout buckskin horses of various shades of golden tones and long black manes, all with calm, ho-hum demeanors. Each horse bore an identification freeze brand on the left side of its neck, declaring not only their registration status with the government, but their strong symbolic heritage—the Pryor Mountain Mustang.

A light breeze, like a foal's first breath, blew across the grasses. Placing her fingers to the cowboy hat she had borrowed again, Amara could feel her stomach tighten and relax as she shifted with Moses' side-to-side swaying walk. A smooth peace settled on her heart. When Sonny swiveled at the waist and looked over his shoulder at her, the sun flashing off the white of his hat, her heart flitted like a bird's wings. She hadn't realized she was giving him a smile until he returned it to her.

"Alright," said Charleston, directing his attention to the entire group. "Rod and Anita, flank to the left, through the low ground." Anita nodded, causing her dark braided hair to sway. "Sonny will flank to the right, along the crest. Amara, they'll all be pushing horses out to you and William. Stay behind and push the herd forward, collectively. Slow and easy. We don't run pregnant mares or foals."

William turned to her, tipping his black flat-brimmed hat in acknowledgment. Amara grinned at him, hoping she was hiding her disappointment that she wouldn't be riding with Sonny well enough.

Directions handed out, the riders spurred their horses on. It was time to work. Charleston peeled off sharply to the right. Rod and his beautiful wife Anita took to the left, visiting quietly with one another. William, carrying the same weightlifter-thick shape as his father, stayed in the center. Amara followed his lead.

Prior to riding off to his assignment, Sonny allowed Nick to nuzzle up to Moses' neck, and squeezed close to Amara in the process. He seemed unbothered about the riding arrangements. Indisputably, the more experienced riders had been assigned to bigger jobs, while she and William took the drag position. Time would tell if William was new to this, or if it was just her—she highly doubted he was. He looked just as comfortable on a horse as Sonny did, walking assuredly ahead, leaving her and Sonny to ride together for the moment.

"You're about to see something very beautiful. Something like you've never seen before," said Sonny.

Amara giggled. "More? I've never seen so much beauty. How will I contain it all?"

Sonny's eyes glistened. While she found his tranquility to be infectious, she deeply coveted it in herself. If the two were described as shapes, he would be a sphere, with easy-flowing consistent corners, while she would be more like a star, abruptly sharp at her points with unbending lines.

Nick stretched out his neck, nipping off the top of a plant.

"You can't contain it," Sonny cautioned playfully. "If you could, I would be selling it by the bottle."

She bit her lip. Part of what made this place what it was, was him, and he couldn't sell himself in a bottle—she wasn't about to tell him as much. Still, he was right. She wanted to soak it all up and store it in her memory, so she could tap back into it when she was home. She hadn't been successful in the endeavor, though, because each new sensation always replaced the last, starting over with each new experience. It was like turning pages, only when each page turned, it faded a little. She couldn't go back in the story and experience things just as she had the first time. Life looked and felt different when she attempted to view it in reverse.

Dreading the moment she would have to leave the ranch, her chest tightened with anxiety. Her time with Sonny would be like waking from a dream, forgetting how real it had been—the experience waning into the glaring light of the present.

"I have to try," Amara confessed, despite the task's impossibility, and even its consequences.

"Let's go, then."

At first, Amara felt entirely excited. Then, without warning, a strange uneasy intuition settled on her, soaking through her pores and swelling up in her chest like a balloon on the verge of popping. Immediately after, however, it was gone. Vanished into thin air.

She blinked, and a herd of horses came into view. It was as if God had stood back after having completed Montana, then adoringly sprinkled mares and foals over the earth as a final touch of perfection. Most of the kindly mares grazed and swished their tails, watching over slumbering foals, while other mares dozed themselves, only half-aware that frolicking foals were tripping over them. From time to time, a grazing mare would pin her ears at a pair of playmates who tussled too close, tangling in the legs of the adults.

While Sonny sat slightly slumped in his saddle, Amara straightened her back to sit even taller, not wanting to miss a single thing. After indulging in the view, she closed her eyes and inhaled, trying to imbibe the aroma. As Sonny had warned, no matter how hard she tried, she simply couldn't bottle it up and take it with her. And if she could turn it into a tantalizing perfume, the boys at college certainly wouldn't appreciate it. She could think of one extremely tantalizing man who already wore it quite nicely. Having been nearly immersed in it his whole life, he seemed to have absorbed the vanilla-scented pine through his skin, the fragrance infusing itself into his blood, becoming part of him.

"Amara!" Sonny's voice dislodged her from her daydream. Looking at him, she noticed he had rolled the cuffs of his long blue sleeves halfway up his forearm. The muscles connecting his elbow to his hand twitched as his fingers played with Nick's leather reins. "Are you sleeping?" he teased.

"Just cataloging."

He shook his head, chuckling. "This is before you," he said, gesturing to the scattered horses and their foals, "and you have your eyes closed."

"I'm trying to remember them."

He smiled at her. Maybe he understood. Maybe he didn't. But he seemed sincere when he said, "I've never met anyone like you."

A shrill whistle pierced through the serene song of the natural life around them. Charleston appeared on the opposite side of the herd pushing two mares: one with a dark coat, mane, and tail, and the other with a burning red coat with matching mane and tail. One of them was mother to the brown foal ambling between them. He had picked up the stragglers from the trees beyond, and urged them to join the main group.

Rod and Anita slowly came into view from the left, making their way toward each other. The mares glanced up at the invasive guests and began ushering their young toward what was to become the center of the caravan. William had taken his place at the back and held the converging herd from leaking backward, while Charleston whistled again, firmly reprimanding Sonny for being out of position.

"I guess I missed my cue." Sonny kicked Nick and started galloping away. "Don't go Calamity Jane on me!" he hollered over his shoulder, skirting the right side of the herd.

Amara swept her hair from her face, only for it to return on the breeze. "Who's Calamity Jane?"

William took a break from encouraging the herd, swiveling in his saddle to face her. His horse continued the job of moving forward without his full concentration. "She was an eighteen-hundreds woman of the wild west!" he hollered.

"Calamity doesn't sound like a very complimentary label for a woman."

"Well, it wasn't...but it was. She was one of the mavericks of her time."

"William, you make no sense." She trotted Moses to catch up to William so he didn't have to keep hanging off the side of his saddle.

He raised his thick eyebrows at her. "They say Calamity Jane had an affair with Wild Bill Hickok."

"Who is *they*?"

He nodded, drawing her attention to the herd, where two foals were biting at one another. "Western stories, little lady," he drawled. "We cowpokes know our stuff. Especially the dirty stuff." He winked.

William was a superb rider, like he had been born on a horse; he moved as easily as most people breathed. She tried mimicking his graceful movements, the easy way he stalked up behind a lazy mare or how he seemed to suck closer to his horse the quicker the horse's feet moved. His thick dark eyebrows raised over his brown eyes as he spoke to the horses in front of him. Since she couldn't make out most of what he said, she felt like she was watching a silent movie, a piece of history unraveling before her. She didn't have to hear the words to understand their meaning. William was a horseman.

Charleston had taken the lead position at the front of the herd, acting as a guide. Dust seemed to swell from every crevice of the ground into large puffs, obscuring the perfect outlines of the horses' thick and colorful bodies as they plodded along. Occasionally, a mare or two would assess the attentiveness of the two riders in the back and meander out of the flow, stepping off the imaginary pathway.

William laughed a lot, and he made Amara laugh a lot, comically showing her how to bring dawdlers back to the program without generating excitement in the rest of the herd. God must have granted ranchers a special gift of gentleness. Amara liked William immediately. Together, the two kept the herd going.

When a sand-colored buckskin and her pint-sized vanilla ice cream-colored foal veered abruptly toward a clump of thirsty scrubby trees, away from the herd, William gestured with one arm. It was Amara's turn to put her lessons into practice. Calmly steering Moses toward the outside of the voyaging pair, the mare proceeded to test her ability to dodge the bruhaha and go back to her grazing. Pint-size trotted beside her, not paying mind to the trailing horse and rider the least bit, only his mother. Amara glanced at William for guidance, and he signaled her to keep after them.

Moses offered an easy trot, and he and Amara began closing the short distance between them and the mare's intended escape route. Amara's already extremely sore rear end bumped against the hard seat as she urged Moses on. Moses advanced on the stubborn mare, paying her no attention when she arched her neck and pinned her ears to the back of her head. Her plan thwarted, she made no further struggle. Amara whooped victoriously as mare and foal gave up on their escape plan and rejoined the herd. William returned the excited whoop.

"That could have gone much worse," he said after she rejoined him.

"Worse?" Amara asked. "What could have happened?"

"Oh, not much. You could have just sent her galloping off into the afternoon glare with the entire herd on her tail."

Amara's eyes bulged. "You allowed me to nearly scatter the entire herd? Charleston would have killed me! Are you out of your mind?" The wind caught her waist-length ponytail and sent it fluttering over her shoulder.

William laughed heartedly. "Take a breath, Calamity, you were nowhere near scattering the herd. I've never seen a person take to riding so quickly. Are you sure you've never ridden?"

"Cross my heart," Amara said, allowing her eyes to drift to the right, where Sonny was sitting comfortably on Nick. She wished she still had the camera from her childhood so she could keep this picture forever on something more tangible and reliable than her memory.

"So you two met in a parking lot, huh?" William asked as he slapped his hands together. "That's a romantic story to tell your kids."

"Well, fortunately, I don't have kids."

"But you will," William said confidently, as if he were some sort of fortune teller. Amara glared sideways at him. "Oh, come on," he said, "I see the way you keep dribbling down your chin every time you look at him."

"I do not! It's not like that."

"It's not like that for who?" William asked, nodding his head in Sonny's direction.

Sonny had turned his horse, ever so slightly, and was clearly checking on her. Satisfied, he zipped Nick back around and continued down the unmarked trail to wherever it was Charleston was leading them all.

"How well do you know him?" Amara asked William.

"Well enough to know he doesn't invite girls to his house," William said, shooting her the only stern expression she had seen on his face all day. "And isn't that Grandma Lizzy's?" he asked, studying the saddle she was sitting on.

Amara ran her fingers across the engraved leather pommel surrounding the base of the horn. "Yes, it's beautiful, isn't it?"

William nodded knowingly. "You should know, no one other than Grandma Lizzy has ever ridden in that saddle. I haven't even seen it since she passed. Didn't even know if they still had it. I don't know what you've done, but you seem to have smitten both Charleston and Sonny."

"I haven't done anything," Amara protested.

"Be careful not to hurt them, Amara," said William. "I've never seen them like this before."

And just like that, the joy she'd been experiencing from this amazing day plunged without warning, draining like an unclogged toilet. Hurting Sonny and Charleston was the last thing she wanted to do. William went back to work, dropping the conversation. In a matter of minutes, his usually jovial demeanor returned. Amara dug her chin in and rode alongside him, taking it stride by stride, trying not to lose herself in his upsetting words.

As the sun beat down on her shoulders, Amara's stomach started grumbling. Thank goodness Charleston had grabbed those peanuts. It felt like days since she had eaten them. No wonder he ignored her senseless stand on not eating breakfast.

Charleston's whistle broke the leisurely silence. It was hard to make out from her position at the rear, but it appeared that the current of streaming heads was changing. Charleston, Sonny, Rod, and Anita all moved in sync, surrounding the herd. It became clear the horses could no longer move forward, so they gushed out at the sides. Amara wasn't sure what she was supposed to do but stay near William and keep the herd from turning back. The herd began pooling out to the boundaries, where the six riders had them barricaded. Amara thought it odd they didn't turn back towards her and William until the obstruction came into view.

Before her lay a shimmering pond of water, nestled in the low of the ground. Having dribbled down off of the small rises of land surrounding the area during the melting spring snow and rain, it had become a sheltered retreat. The reflection of the sky and tiny dotting white clouds were mirrored in its perfect stillness—until the first nose dropped to touch it. Afterward, the water rippled, and the ripple swelled larger and larger until it reached the grassy edges and dissolved. From that moment on, the sun flickered on the surface as each nose touched the water. Some drank deeply, while others pawed and splashed. A notably red mare, with a striking blonde mane and tail, kept kicking off the bratty, insolent mares, making room for the parched foals.

Charleston rested both arms across the horn of his saddle, watching his living treasures with pride. His thin back arched as he slumped, completely at ease with his place in life. From this distance, his age was camouflaged by his attractive shape and stoic demeanor. Sonny was a darn near perfect representation of Charleston, only it was painfully obvious that this stronger built cowboy was younger and more desirable—at least to her. If she were an avid fisher, then to her Sonny was like a shiny lure, sitting on his horse with his hat blocking the sun from his rugged face.

She thought about William's warning. Was she supposed to resist the lure? Nothing in her wanted to resist. But she supposed she ought to, with her leaving and all. Maybe it would have been better if Sonny *had* lost interest in her.

For now, the only clear thing was that the horses were being allowed to drink and rest. Amara was wishing she had the good judgment to have brought along water for herself when Sonny and William casually traded places. She smiled as Sonny rode up to her, holding out a bottle of half frozen, half melted water. She took it gratefully, drinking only a couple gulps.

When she tried to hand it back, he shook his head. "Keep it. I brought two. When you're done, I'll put it back in my saddlebag so you don't have to carry it."

"Thank you." Greedily, she drank more this time, the cold water sliding down her parched throat.

As the herd began to settle, no longer contending for water or calling for their young to get back in sight, Amara noted how exceedingly serene the panorama was. If her mom could see her now, she'd have a fit, Amara reminded herself. Mom would not approve. Her father? Also no. Her friends?

Unexpectedly, a realization dawned on her. No one truly knew, or cared, about what she wanted. Rosalynn was the closest to meeting the bill, but she wasn't an intimate friend, she was just sweet. Everyone seemed obsessed with picayune concerns that didn't interest Amara at all, such as appearance of both the physical and financial fashions. Amara sought neither.

Closing her eyes, Amara mentally sopped up every sun ray landing on her skin. She loved the warmth almost as much as she loved cold, blustery snow days. While snow kept most folks indoors, Amara used to take to the streets on frosty remote walks, marveling at the novelty of a fresh, virtuous realm in which she could be alone with her thoughts and free from her dreary day-to-day duties. The only exception was if any neighboring children daringly donned jackets and mittens for a snowball fight. If this were the case, she would promptly engage in the beloved sport, whether she knew the children or not. Children were not so coldly opposed to quick-made friendships, like most adults.

"Sleeping again?" Sonny's voice fetched her from her daydream once more, transporting her back to the sublimely picturesque present. He was standing next to Moses' left shoulder, like he had been when he rescued her from the dark. Nick was resting behind him, eyes and lips drooping. Sonny's dismounts were far quieter than her ungraceful scrambles. "What would you do if everyone up and took off with the herd, leaving you sitting here with your eyes closed?" he asked.

"Moses would tell me," she answered, bending over at the waist to pat Moses' thick neck. Moses was staring off at the herd. At least one of them was paying attention. When Amara looked up, the brim of her hat just barely missed hitting Sonny's. They were eye to eye. Ignoring the sudden rush of adrenaline, she asked, "*Would* you leave me?"

"Not a chance," he replied, without even a hint of hesitation. She believed him. His attention was momentarily diverted, checking on the mares, making sure they were still abiding by the unspoken rules and staying within the set parameters. Unable to pull her own gaze away, she noticed how effectively his well-kept facial hair accented his handsome, sharp profile. Re-meeting her gaze, he asked, "What about you? When do you leave?"

Her heart sunk. "The girls should be coming back for me any day. My phone has lousy service, but I'm assuming it's enough for them to get through, once they try." From the look of Sonny's serious eyes flicking across her face, William may have been a better fortune teller than she liked to admit. She didn't want to go.

Sonny handed her an apple and a Snickers bar. "Something to hold you over until supper," he said. "I would have made sure you had packed a lunch, but Gramps decided to take matters into his own hands. And he only had one thing on his mind."

"What's that?"

"Turning you into his employee."

Amara laughed. "To his credit, he did make sure I had some peanuts." She took the apple and candy bar, and then wondered aloud, "Wait, is this your lunch?"

Sonny shrugged. "It's just a snack. I'm not hungry."

"I'll split it with you," said Amara, kicking her foot free from the right stirrup and sliding clumsily down from Moses' back.

After carefully opening the plastic wrap from the warm, slightly melted bar of chocolate goodness, stomach growling, she held it out for Sonny to take the first bite. It was the least she could do after everything he had done for her. His large hand enveloped hers and pulled it to his mouth, his white teeth cut off a small chunk, then he tenderly guided the chocolate to her lips. Feeling abnormally shy, she took a nibble. They continued dividing the bar, taking turns nibbling off small bites. Amara watched Sonny suck the last morsel of chocolate from the plastic wrapper—the only thing separating her fingers from his mouth. The red apple clutched in her hand was forgotten and dropped to the ground with a thud.

Powerless to resist, Amara put her hands around Sonny's neck, pulling his face down to meet hers. Without permission, she touched her lips to his. Sonny didn't require an extended invitation. He grabbed around her waist and leaned them both gently into Moses, kissing her deep and long, melting her insides like the chocolate dissolving from their fiery tongues. If it weren't for Moses supporting them, keeping them upright, they might have tumbled to the grass right there.

## CHAPTER TEN

Later that evening, after a hearty supper of Charleston's chicken noodle soup from a jumbo-sized can and a loaf of French bread taken from the freezer, Amara felt her body give up the ghost. Too tired to care about how it looked to others, she laid her head on Sonny's shoulder. In the haze of her exhaustion, she could hear Charleston telling a story; something about a foal having ventured too far into the pond and getting stuck. As he described the story in great detail, with Sonny interposing now and again, the only thing registering inside Amara's skull was how lulling their voices were, how they soothed every beat and bushed nerve.

Without permission, her eyes fell closed. That's alright, she could rest them for a time and rejoin the conversation. Or so she remembered thinking.

The next thing she knew, her body was being lowered onto an impossibly comfortable bed. Warm arms, once wrapped around her, fell away. She shivered. With great sleepy effort, she pried open her eyes. Sonny was before her, tenderly pulling a plush cover over the filthy clothes she was still wearing. She wanted to protest. Dirt and debris would get all over the bedding. But her worn-out muscles and drowsiness won out. Plus, the sheets and cover smelled like vanilla pine.

"I'm sorry," said Amara, her voice sticking, coming out softer than she intended. He paused, looking at her. "I guess I was tired."

"You fell asleep on my shoulder. I was going to crash on the couch. Would you rather I take you home?"

She shook her head, too tired to move. Never before had she felt so at home. It was ridiculous, of course, but briefly she wondered if maybe she'd been here before, in a dream or something. Looking around the room through her tired eyes, she noticed the pictures hung on the walls, again appearing to have been taken on the ranch. It was clear that the entire family lived and breathed their home and their way of life. It was extremely tasteful and genuine.

"I'm quite comfortable," Amara answered, yawning. "If it's not too creepy."

Sonny laughed. "Since when is it creepy to have a beautiful girl in my bed? If anyone is creepy, it's me. I invited you."

"Then there's Charleston," Amara suggested, "convinced I've applied for a job and want to stay forever."

They both chuckled, then fell silent.

"I've enjoyed having you here," said Sonny.

"I've enjoyed being here. Thank you for inviting me. It's been a dream come true. My mother, she has all these grand plans for my future. None of which I'm too excited about."

"You're not obligated to them. It's *your* future."

"I know. I'm not obligated to them." She said the words easily enough, but they weren't true. She *was* obligated to them. Her dad was paying for this future, and her mom was insistent on it, always knowing best and demanding what she wanted.

"Do you?" Sonny asked, unable to hide his doubt. And he was right. Swallowing, she suppressed her own feelings and nodded. He seemed to accept the answer and settled into a look of forced contentment.

Unsure whether it was safe to speak without giving away the truth, Amara nibbled on her lip. With him, she still felt like a child, but not in the same way as she did with her parents. With her parents, she felt a thumb over her, squashing her dreams and suffocating her with judgment and unattainable directives. With Sonny, she felt borrowed strength when she hadn't thought she had any, patient coaching when she was laughably daft, and compassion when she was wild and reckless. *Calamity-ish*, she thought, happily.

Able to tell that Sonny was about to politely leave so she could rest, she quickly had to think of something to buy her more time with him. Her fuzzy mind struggled. She was terribly tired and needed to rest, however; she could sense time was running out. She had assumed Jeanie and Rosalynn would have called already. To her knowledge, they had not, but they should any day now.

"Would you tell me a story?" Amara asked, patting the bed next to her, inviting him to sit.

He laughed. "Alright."

Amara wiggled on the mattress, scooting over, making room for him on his own bed. He accepted the invitation and laid down next to her, propping himself up on a pillow.

With Amara by his side, snuggled under the covers, her small face and dark hazel eyes trained on him, Sonny felt as if the entire world was at his fingertips. The beautiful woman next to him appeared to be buried in her own mass of cascading hair, like a princess in a fairy tale. She looked so adorably innocent, peering up at him, waiting for a story. For a moment, he envisioned a child laying there instead of a woman—his child, enchanted and spellbound. The image jarred him. For the first time in his life, he felt a yearning for something more than just the ranch and the animals. He could see himself as a father and a husband. And he liked it.

Clearing his throat, Sonny began, "Did you see the grave at the front gate when you arrived, resting beneath the tree?"

"Yes."

"That's Grandma Lizzy's grave. She would rock me in her arms when I was small and whisper tales in my ear as I fell asleep. This is her story.

"Once upon a time, there lived an eagle. His great white head and tail crowned his enormous majestic brown body with glory and pride. He would call to the creatures of the land, summoning them to take notice and acknowledge his grand splendor. He was so fervent that his calls could be heard for miles. After elevating himself to the sky and satisfying himself at the river's edge, he always returned to a single tree, next to the front gate of the forest, to sleep.

"One bleak, forbidding winter, the snows fell so deeply that Eagle's tree was nearly buried. He sat at the top, exposed to the harsh, cold winds, too proud to leave his splendid home overlooking the world. Slowly, his regal yellow beak dropped, lower and lower and lower. His ice-covered feathers and hard frosted talons were no match for the inhospitable, biting season of death. Bowing his head, bending to his fate, Eagle closed his eyes for what he thought would be the last time.

"When the sun finally broke through the clouds, Eagle was surprised to find he was warm. He lifted his beak and opened one eye. He had made it, though none to his own credit. An incredible eagle, larger than himself, had wrapped herself around him, as if he had been her young. It was she who had weathered the storm. It was she who had saved him.

"After that night, every flap of his wings and cry of his voice was for her liking and her ever-continuing love. He fancied her more than the wind that held him above the clouds or the fish which filled his belly. If she called, he came. If she flew, he followed.

"Together, they located a kingly tree amongst a thick grove within the forest to become their sheltered home. The eagles brought every meager stick and scanty twig to build the strongest nest which had ever been assembled. It would protect their adored chicks and withstand bitter winter after bitter winter.

"Every day following, after hard work and hunting, Eagle would meet his love at the top of the single tree upon which he had nearly died, next to the front gate of the forest, and they would soar home, to their nest, together.

"But one day, Eagle's love did not come. He searched and searched for her, until his wings could search no more. At a loss for what to do, he landed at the top of the single tree and cried weak, flat, chirping whistles over and over until the sun slid from the sky and darkness covered his heart.

"That night, he stayed on the tree next to the gate of the forest. As he waited and waited through the night to be reunited with his love, the Great Spirit took pity on his broken heart and granted his unspoken request.

"The next morning, Eagle awoke to a world brighter than the world he had previously known. The colors were deeper and richer. The wind was louder. The rivers were fuller. At long last, the majestic sound of his love's flapping wings ruffled his feathers, and her weight joined him on the strong branch of the single tree, next to the front gate of the other side. Touching beaks, the two eagles reunited their souls in eternity, and flew home together."

Tears streamed down Amara's cheeks. "That's a terrible story!"

Sonny gazed down at her in remorse. He hadn't intended to make her cry. He hadn't cried as a boy when he'd heard it. He only felt the warmth of his grandma's arms and the love in her voice. Perhaps he hadn't told it as well as she did.

"What happened to the girl eagle?" Amara asked, wiping her tears with her forearm.

Sonny wrapped a consoling arm around her, drawing her near, the way his grandma had drawn him near when he was sad. "The story doesn't say. All we know is she died."

Amara huffed and crossed her arms in bed. "I don't like it."

"But they ended up together."

"They ended up dead!"

Sonny laughed, earning him a glare. Unable to hold his gaze, Amara broke into adorably silly laughter. It was the tiniest straw of hay that finally broke the camel's back of Sonny's resolve. He turned and took her face between his hands. The size of his hands compared to her clear, petite face made him feel both impressive and uneasy. Despite all her splendid independence, he could see how extremely delicate she really was. He loved both her independence and her vulnerability. It made him want to hold her close, to protect her. Yet at the same time, he wanted to set her free so she could soar in celebrated flight. It was a confusing reaction, one he didn't know how to handle. So instead of coming to a decision, he kissed her.

When she responded with equal enthusiasm, his every cell ignited as if thrown into a sweltering furnace. Her body was arched, her hands hungry. Her passion both stunned and delighted him. It took all of his determination—and frustration—to lessen the intensity. Willing himself to steer the boat into less rocky waters, he slowly, and with great aching agony, pulled away.

"Where are you going?" Amara asked.

"I'm going to let you get some rest. Gramps will be in here soon enough to wake you for chores, I'm sure," he said, winking. Still breathless when he stood up, his head spun a little. Everything in him wanted to stay.

"You don't have to go," she said, flush from contact with his coarse skin.

He touched his fingertips to her flawless forehead, where concerned wrinkles had appeared, and felt a sting in his chest. "Neither do you."

Before he could start begging like a vagabond, he turned and walked out of the room.

## CHAPTER ELEVEN

The next morning, before the crack of dawn, Sonny took a pickup load of salt to distribute among hefty, nearly indestructible bowls scattered throughout the ranch. He hadn't been able to sleep anyway with Amara just a few feet away, so he decided to get feeding, and the day, underway. With constant darkness as company, Sonny filled each tub with an eagerness he hadn't experienced since he was a boy on his way to the county fair. He wanted to be done with chores early so he could spend his time with Amara. Like the rides at the fair, thinking about Amara sent a huge grin across his face, and just thinking about her sent his stomach spinning in circles.

Heaving a heavy salt bag from the bed of the pickup, he cut open the bag and began pouring the granules into the tub. The bag became lighter with each passing second, and eventually the gritty sound ceased. Wadding the bag up and throwing it in the bed, Sonny jumped back into the pickup, going over his great plan again.

Today, he hoped to make a good impression and double his unlikely chances at swaying her to stay longer. He'd barely gotten to know her, and he wasn't ready for her to leave his life—certainly not for good. Even if it was just a promise to visit again.

First, he would take her to breakfast. No peanuts. Then, it went without saying, he would take her on a horseback ride. However, when the sun went down, right before touching the earth, he would take her to the meadow: a very special meadow he had seen only once and had never forgotten. On occasion, he nursed the thought about going back, but had never felt there was truly a sufficient reason to revisit—until now.

A couple years had passed since he'd stumbled across the meadow. No, strike that. It wasn't that he'd stumbled across it, he'd been led to it. Miraculously, even now, he still remembered the route, the incident etched in his mind as if he'd been there yesterday—as if he were meant to return.

\*\*

A .223-caliber rifle strapped to the saddle, Sonny and Nick were on the dodgy trail of a mountain lion. The skilled hunter had been troubling the ranch endlessly, killing and burying calves to eat later. Diligently Sonny studied the ground, always in search of the uncommon soft tracks, bent grass, or little dog-like piles of partially uncovered scat. When tracking a cat, luck played a bigger part than actual hard evidence. Sonny searched the trees almost as often as he searched the ground, while Nick executed his part of the job without ceasing, picking his way through the rocky ground as he saw fit, with only a lifted rein from Sonny every now and again when a direction change was needed—or gambled on. One carefully placed hoof after another, on the tail of an uneasy hunter. That was when they found it.

Suddenly, he found himself in a circular meadow bordered by trees, an empty flattened, grassy bed nestled there, peaceful and secluded on the top of a bluff with an overlook for a view. The hair on Sonny's neck stood on end, as stiff as wire brush, upon the *realization the cat had only just left. Looking up into the trees, he witnessed the beauty around him, realizing how mysteriously spectacular life could be.*

*Fortunately, the hunted detected its hunter and opted to withdraw from the easy pickings of the ranch to the outer edges, where smaller prey remained numerous. Despite the unwritten agreement between Sonny and the lion, he speculated that she poked around every now and again from time to time. But on the whole, she remained on the borders of the ranch, well away from the interior, where Gramps kept the young on close watch. A small part of Sonny was grateful that he didn't have to shoot her. Without her intimately guided tour, he never would have come across the meadow and what he discovered there.*

\*\*

About the time Sonny had completed all of his morning chores, the sun broke over the horizon and cast yellow light across the cool, shadowed earth. Sonny blew his breath into his hands and regripped the steering wheel, thankful that his chilled insides would soon begin to thaw with the heater on. His jacket hadn't been thick enough for such a long stint on this particularly unsympathetic Montana morning. Removing his boot from the gas pedal, Sonny turned the wheel and directed his pickup off the dirt road.

The pickup bounced and jerked over rocky terrain as treacherous as it was protected—or was he just imagining it? Stealing a quick peek over his shoulder, he checked on the cardboard box rattling and jumping just behind him. It seemed to be staying intact as he jostled along. Sonny cringed as it took air over and over, no matter how slowly the tires crawled.

After a painful, time-consuming voyage, Sonny rolled up to a wall of trees clustered together. He didn't dare try to push through. Both him and his horse had barely made it through last time before the branches had enfolded upon each other, blocking their way. Furthermore, even if he could get through, he wouldn't attempt it for fear it would utterly destroy the location's sanctity, so perfectly sheltered and hallowed. Instead, he cut the engine, stepped out and prepared to walk in.

\*\*

*Amara clung to Moses' soft, sparkly mane as the wind whipped her hair behind her like a cape. She couldn't hold back her smile as Moses' wings lifted her higher and higher. Beneath them, a rainbow sea of wildflowers danced and sang a song of glory. Moses' powerful wings carried them effortlessly, slicing through the sky like a knife through pudding pie. Amara knew where they had been going. Just like the story of the two eagles, she could just see the front gate to the forest. She knew Sonny would be there, waiting for her.*

One of the great mysteries of life was how easily a person could wake from a dream before the reason was even revealed. Amara's eyes opened, excitement fluttering in her chest. She was in Sonny's room. As she was just about to fling the covers off yesterday's clothes, there was a soft knocking on the bedroom door.

"Come in," Amara called. The doorknob clicked and slowly turned.

\*\*

Sonny's hands firmly gripped the cardboard box he had stowed, so riskily, at the front of his pickup bed all morning during chores. One carefully placed boot at a time, he made his way, box in arms, across the rocky path of uncertainty and began pushing back through the thick, prickly branches towards the hidden meadow. Catching his toe on a rock, he leaned heavily this way and that, trying to keep his balance. He couldn't drop it now after he had successfully come so far.

\*\*

The recognizable brim of Charleston's white cowboy hat poked through first, followed by his gray mustache and a dark blue striped western work shirt. Amara sat up in bed, tossing the covers aside. "Is it time to go to work?" she asked excitedly. "Did you bring my coffee?"

Charleston's normally proud head dropped. "I'm afraid not. There's someone here to see you."

\*\*

The fragile dishware felt foreign in Sonny's large, callused hands. With a finger, he delicately tapped an edge of a thin plate here, scooted a crystal glass there, adjusting each piece until it looked just right. After he had set two perfect placings, he picked up what was to be Amara's glass and wiped away any trace of a dingy fingerprint he may have left. When the candles were placed just so in the center of the table, Sonny stood back. Wrapping his thumbs around his waist, he looked around, taking it all in, and smiled. A small, round wooden table and the dusty brown-and-blue-striped rug he had borrowed from the front porch made for a nice, homey setting in the middle of the meadow. It looked just how he had remembered it, trees lining the edges of his flawless patch of protected grass, the only open side facing west towards the setting sun. The rocky bluff overlooked a small fork in the river—full of fish, he assumed.

\*\*

Back at the house, Charleston stood at the front door, staring into the faces of an apologetic sheriff's deputy and a shocked woman who looked like an older Amara. The only differences were that her blonde hair had grayed around the temple, accented by how tightly she had pulled it into a stiff bun, and her ever-present scowl. Charleston couldn't help but cringe at her cold demeanor; while quite effectively refrigerating the air around her, she also wore a dreary, gray-colored business dress, the skirt hugging her knees. The shocked woman had just heard Amara's voice request coffee through the open bedroom door into which Charleston was speaking.

Swiftly outraged, she shoved past Charleston to look in the room for herself. Her eyes bulged, as did Amara's. The woman's face turned from pretty to ugly. "This man kidnapped my daughter!" she screamed at the deputy. "I want him arrested!"

"Mom!" Amara gasped. "What are you doing here?"

Mrs. Duncan ignored her daughter and screamed at the poor sheriff's deputy, "Arrest him! The sick perverted bastard!"

"Mom, stop it! No one kidnapped me!"

"I'm not here to arrest anyone, Mrs. Duncan, I'm just here to…"

"What are you wearing?" Mrs. Duncan asked, turning to her daughter, her face showing complete disgust.

Amara looked down at yesterday's wrinkled clothes. "I…"

Mrs. Duncan didn't wait for the answer. She stomped over to Amara and grabbed her wrist. "We're leaving," she interrupted, and began tugging on Amara's arm.

Charleston moved into the room. "Now wait one minute," he said. "Amara is here on her own accord. And a grown woman, at that."

Mrs. Duncan approached him, her face within inches of his. "No. You wait one minute. Go ahead, stand in my way. The sheriff is right here to witness you attempting to trap us." She glanced over Charleston's shoulder and glared. "Damn it, Deputy Dirk, stop hiding behind the door!"

Charleston stood tall. "This is my house, Mrs. Duncan. You barged in. You are free to leave. In fact, I *encourage* you to leave. Amara can decide for herself whether she stays or goes."

"You are in no position to tell me…"

"I'm sorry," Amara interrupted. "I should have told you, Mom." For the first time since her room had been bombarded, she had her mom's attention. "I hadn't planned to come here, but I *had* intended to keep it from you."

Charleston left the room and found himself in the kitchen, missing Lizzy terribly. His coffee stared up at him from where he had left it on the counter to grow cold when he had gone to welcome the deputy. Now it sat next to a pad of paper and pen Sonny had apparently left out—but nothing was written on it. Reaching down for the comfort of his caffeine, he grabbed the pen and paper instead and began scrawling on it as he overheard the voices in the other room.

"If you don't come home with me right now, I *will* press charges. Is that what you want, Amara?" Mrs. Duncan asked.

As the two women emerged from the bedroom, the deputy on their heels, Charleston's eyes met Amara's. He could see it in her expression, her heart was aching something fierce. "Please tell Sonny I'm sorry," she said sadly as she passed him. "I wish he was here so I could say goodbye properly."

Charleston nodded, falling in line behind Amara as Mrs. Duncan led the parade quickly out the front door. "The position is still open," he reminded her.

Amara turned and gave him a half-hearted grin as she slowly descended the stairs into the crunchy gravel. "Thank you, Charleston."

"That's quite enough," Mrs. Duncan ordered, glaring at Charleston. "Amara is not job hunting. Don't take her presence here personally. This was just childish rebellion. She won't be returning."

Ignoring Mrs. Duncan's statement, Charleston called after Amara, "Don't forget to empty the hay from your pockets!" right before her head ducked into the back of the patrol car. Mrs. Duncan halted, irritated that Charleston was still speaking without her permission. He lifted a shoulder nonchalantly.

Sneering, Mrs. Duncan lowered herself into the passenger side of the patrol car.

The sheriff's deputy breathed a sigh of relief and climbed in behind the wheel.

Charleston leaned against the gigantic log holding up the porch and watched as Amara's pretty face, peeking over the back seat of the cop car, faded into a blur and disappeared past the barn. For a brief moment, Charleston saw his wife, young and beautiful, a baby boy on her hip. She was leaning against the barn wall, her face to the morning sun, looking out over the pasture. God, he missed Lizzy. She would have handled this so much better. She probably would have had them all sitting around the breakfast table laughing and tasting her homemade jellies. When Charleston couldn't hear the patrol car tires crunching in the gravel anymore, Lizzy's memory disappeared into the blazing glare of the sun. He stared at the barn, not really feeling like doing anything else.

\*\*

Content, Sonny began trekking back to the pickup, mindful not to disturb the way the grass blades lay. He wanted to make as little human impact as possible, as if the dinner table had simply floated down from the sky. At the edge of the trees, he proudly allowed himself one last glance at his meadow before turning away and ducking through nature's endorsed barrier.

When Sonny returned to the main house, hungry for coffee and grits, he pulled the pickup straight up to the porch. Charleston could lecture him later. Only Charleston was already there, leaning against the porch's log post. His shoulders were slumped more than usual, his face matching his blue button-up shirt. His hands were empty. No coffee. No boots. No toast for the go. He was just standing there, arms crossed, looking past Sonny towards the direction of the barn. Sonny felt a tight pinch in his gut. Gramps only took an irritable stance when John "visited"—begging for money.

Stepping from his pickup, Sonny glanced around, seeing the place void of company. But there, in the gravel, sweeping into the grass, were fresh tire marks. "Where is he?" Sonny demanded, stomping quickly towards Charleston with an angry vengeance. The venom burning in his veins made him almost crazy. "Where is he?!"

Charleston shook his head.

Sonny stopped, looking over his shoulder at the tire marks. "Was he here?" he asked. Charleston hesitated, causing worry to creep into his veins. "I'm not blind, Gramps. Who was here?"

Charleston's heart broke as he studied Sonny's worried face. Sonny may have been his grandson, but in Charleston's eyes, Sonny was truly his son. With Lizzy gone, Sonny was the only person he had left, and next to the ranch's success, all Charleston wanted in life was for Sonny to have a good future. It's why he worked. It's why he rested. It's why he breathed, when all he really wanted was to join his sweet Lizzy. But Lizzy wouldn't have any of his moaning or pity-party throwing. She would have insisted he take care of Sonny, and make sure he was happy and taken care of. That's where Amara had come in—or so Charleston had figured.

It was clear that Sonny thought his rocking chair was rocking a little sideways in his old age, acting confused about Amara's presence on the ranch, pretending she had come for a job application and all. Charleston wasn't confused. He had seen something in the fragile-looking girl; appearances were deceiving. Her hazel eyes bore the softness of a rancher's wife and the strength of a cowgirl. She didn't believe in herself just yet, but Charleston did. And he imagined Sonny did as well.

Sonny's eyes were trained on him, waiting for an answer. Charleston wanted to look away from the pain he knew his news was going to cause, but he wouldn't. No, they would face the disappointment together.

"Amara wanted me to tell you she's sorry, Sonny. She's gone."

## CHAPTER TWELVE

Amara felt like a prisoner. With such a mighty fine view from the backseat of a smelly cop car, how could she not? Between the bars on the windows, the hard plastic seats, and the slow, depressing way the back of her mother's tight graying bun swayed back and forth, how could she not feel as if she had just received a life sentence? To top it off, she didn't have her stuffed horse to lay her head on. It had been left sitting on the couch, in the lower house, along with all of her things.

Though everything in her screamed she was going the wrong direction, she reasoned that this had always been the end scenario. Her friends would have shown up if they hadn't accidentally told her mom. Or if they hadn't come, the University of Denver would have started hounding her dad about failed attendance and lack of accordance. Shortly after, the credit card in her wallet—with her father's name on it—would have begun to decline purchases. Her entire world would have started to cave in around her as her parent's expectations were left unfulfilled. She owed it to her parents to finish what had been started after all they had done. They wanted the best for her, she knew, and were financing the path to get there. All she had to do was keep her head down, hair pulled back, face wiped. When she was successful, they would finally ease off. They would be satisfied, and she would be free of her obligations.

Sonny's words flooded back into her mind. *You're not obligated to them.* She had assured him she knew it. Of course she wasn't obligated, she reminded herself. Obeying her parents' wishes was her choice. As their daughter, it was only natural that she wanted them to bless her with their approval, to be proud of her. Her chin dipped. Except it seemed every time a piece of who she really was—or wanted to be—emerged, they disapproved, forced to reprimand her childish ways and bring her back to the path of unlimited success. Peering out from behind an unopenable door, where criminals sat detained in handcuffs, she wondered if it was indeed a choice.

"Amara," her mom snapped over her shoulder without turning around. "What were you thinking, leaving your friends and running off with some man? You could have been hurt!"

"I wasn't..."

"Or worse." Mrs. Duncan shivered visibly. "No one knows those people. You were very irresponsible disappearing to some dirty backwoods house, not telling anyone."

"Jeanie and Rosalynn knew where I was." Even as she said it, the logic sounded ridiculous. "I didn't want to go to the casino with..."

"Oh, that's just wonderful, Amara. You put your life in Jeanie and Rosalynn's hands. They're *such* responsible citizens, letting you get in a car with a perfect stranger."

"I didn't get in the car with a stranger, Mom. I took a..."

Mrs. Duncan threw her head back. "Stop! Just stop. I'm in no mood to listen to your irrationality right now. Deputy Dirk, can you not drive with more urgency than a worm?"

"Is the worm on a fishing hook or underground?" asked the deputy.

"What?" Mrs. Duncan asked, a look of exasperation mixed with barely contained madness crossing her face. The deputy looked at her as if he were awaiting a serious answer, and finally looked back at the road when none was offered.

Amara stifled a giggle. Deputy Dirk wasn't so bad. The poor guy was just another one of Mom's pawns in a battle to conquer all that was against her superior judgment. Amara wished she shared her mom's clarity. Her mom seemed to always know which direction she was headed and when she ought to arrive. In her spare time, she could articulate the same for everyone around her. Amara, on the other hand, couldn't form even a simple diagram—not to her mom's standards, anyway. It was actually quite difficult to draw a diagram of her goal: hair flowing in the breeze, on the road to freedom. Not exactly what Mom had in mind.

On the ranch, under the kind gaze of Sonny and Charleston, everything had seemed crystal clear. She knew where she wanted to be, who she wanted to be, and who she wanted to be with...on the ranch, she knew not who she was expected to be, nor who she ought to be, or could attempt to be with enough time and work, but who she really *was*. The knowledge of who she was inside had hit her smack dab in the middle of her forehead. And like the wind, the knowledge was freeing and exhilarating. Unlike the back of the patrol car carrying her away to imprisonment, away from Sonny, away from Charleston, away from Moses.

Away from herself.

Remembering what Charleston had said to her when she was leaving, she decided to check her pockets for hay. She had never bought into Charleston's rocker being off. He just cleverly used his crusty cowboy guise to get away with saying exactly what he wanted to say—which she liked about him. One day, she mused, she intended to use the same strategy.

Shoving her fingers down into her front pockets, she felt nothing, not even hay. She checked her back left pocket. Nothing. Feeling her way into her back right pocket, she felt a piece of paper. Pinching a corner, she quietly pulled it out. It crinkled, but she was fairly certain that the voices on the little black speaker muttering some sort of numbered code, and the rumbling of the patrol tires, were enough to cover the sound. No one paid her any attention. Carefully unfolding the creases, she found inside what had to be Charleston's handwriting; she almost needed a magnifying glass and a chicken to decipher the pen scratches. But when she squinted, she believed she could make out all ten digits of a phone number, and her heart skipped a beat.

"Mom," she said, "we left all my stuff, including my phone, at the ranch. May I borrow yours?"

"To call who?"

"You do realize I'm not actually a prisoner back here, right?" Amara asked snidely. That got her attention. Mrs. Duncan turned in her seat and glared. "Does it matter who I call? May I borrow your phone?" Amara asked again.

"Yes, it *does* matter," replied Mrs. Duncan. "You may not use my phone unless I know who you're calling." She swiveled around, facing the front again. "Your dad will be furious when he learns what you have done. Why don't you call him?"

"He doesn't know?"

Her mom did not reply.

"You came all this way with an armed officer, threatening to press charges, which by the way, you have no grounds to do. I don't know why I listened to you in the first place."

"Push me, Amara. I *will* press charges on that dirty old man."

"First of all, Charleston is not a dirty old man..."

"Oh yes he is! Inviting you to his..."

"*He* didn't invite me! His grandson invited me, and only for the most harmless of reasons..."

"Oh, pray thee!" Mrs. Duncan interrupted. "What blameless reason would a young man have?! You sleeping in his room, nonetheless!"

Amara could feel Deputy Dirk tensing. It was bad for a man to be in such close proximity to two females in an argument. "I admit that looked bad," she said. "But nothing happened. He invited me to the ranch to allow me to see the horses." As she spoke, her mom's bun shook side to side, disregarding anything she said. "For the first time in my entire life someone understood it was a dream I had to achieve! He—"

Mrs. Duncan spun in her seat. Her hair may as well have been on fire, and her eyes were burning. "All this over your damn horse dream?! Enough of your juvenile obsessions, Amara!"

"It's not juvenile! Did you know people breed and train horses for a living? I could—"

"Stop! Just stop! I won't hear it! You're not throwing away everything to run away and chase a—"

"I thought it was a choice," Amara said, cutting in. The car fell silent. For a moment, she feared she was still young enough to be whipped. Her mom's frozen face verified she was not. She was a grown woman, old enough to make her own decisions, if she could just step up to the plate. "Would you support your daughter in doing something rash, even if it seemed a little silly to you? I'm asking for your blessing to allow me to make my own decisions. Please." She was determined to be bold, though she felt like a bowl of Jell-o. "I want your approval. But I don't need it."

When Mrs. Duncan turned away, Amara feared her heart was going to break, but surprisingly, it didn't. It was stronger than she had thought. "Deputy Dirk," Amara said, taking a dangerous risk. His face tilted back slightly, signaling she had his attention. Committed now, her nervous heart stilled. This was the right decision. "Could you please stop the car?"

\*\*

"Charleston?"

"Amara?" Charleston's voice answered through Deputy Dirk's cell phone. He was surprised to hear from her.

"I checked my pockets for hay, Charleston," Amara said.

"So you did," he replied. She could tell he had been caught off guard, his mind slow to catch up. "So you did," he repeated, more pleased this time.

"Is the position still open?"

There was a stillness on the other end of the line, worrying Amara. She was sticking her neck out, well below the wobbly guillotine threatening to fall and swiftly behead the condemned. Had defying her parents been the right move?

Charleston cleared his throat. "You're late," he said gruffly.

"I know, I'm sorry. I'll start as soon as I can get there, if it's alright."

"No, you can start tomorrow," he said, his voice softer now. "What can I do to help?"

Even as her mom looked on, arms crossed, Amara couldn't help but experience a sense of relief. "Could you please give a message to Sonny?"

There was a rustling on the other end of the phone, then, "Go ahead, he can hear you."

Amara's heart started pounding. He was there. This was it. This was the moment of truth. An annoying trembling began in her hands, a wetness gathering in her eyes. When she spoke, it felt like someone had wedged a rock down her throat. "Sonny, do you remember the story you told me last night, about the eagles?"

"Yes." His voice felt like a soothing salve over her injured nerves.

"Would you be willing to meet me at the front gate?" she asked, her voice cracking. "Can we fly home together?"

There was no answer, and Amara pressed Deputy Dirk's phone to her ear more firmly, as if it would help her hear the silence better. "Sonny?" she asked, her heart simultaneously hammering and sinking.

"Amara?" Charleston's voice finally came through.

She nodded, unable to speak.

"Amara, he's on a horse, but he's coming."

Her heart leapt in her chest. "He's coming?" she croaked.

"Yeah." Charleston sounded irritated. "He's coming. If he doesn't break his neck before he gets there. All I can make out of him now is a trail of dust."

As the patrol car approached the front gate of the Morris Ranch, Amara could see that Sonny was already there, sitting on his gray horse, dripping sweat and waiting for her. A definite sight for sore eyes in his dusty white long-sleeve work shirt, blue jeans, and cowboy hat. Amara was fairly certain she heard her mom suck in a breath. In Sonny's hand, he held the reins to a second gray horse, its sides heaving.

The moment Sonny realized the patrol car was slowing down and Amara was inside, he shifted off the horse and stepped down. He stood next to the open gate, grinning, glad to see her. Amara's body tingled from head to toe.

Deputy Dirk kindly opened the car door for her from the outside. Feeling rather self-conscious, she slid out, banging her knees against the hard barrier separating the prisoner cage from the front. Automatically, the deputy shielded the top of her head with his hand, so she didn't hit her head on the door jamb as well.

Amara walked to the passenger side front window and peered in at her mom, anticipating that she might want to say goodbye. Mrs. Duncan's arms were crossed rigidly across her chest, and she stared straight ahead. Without a word, Deputy Dirk pressed a button on his door, and Mrs. Duncan's window slid down. Agitated, she squeezed her arms more tightly.

"Mom, all I want is to decide for myself," said Amara. "Please grant me this much."

"Granted," Mrs. Duncan said coldly, without even a glance. "But don't expect me to support you. This is, by far, the most childish, rebellious gesture you've ever committed. I don't know if I'll be capable of forgiving it."

Amara glanced at the toes of her red boots. "Tell Dad thank you."

Mrs. Duncan's head snapped, her eyes cold as ice. "What for?"

Amara pursed her lips. "For supporting me."

"He will not support this, Amara."

Amara nodded. "I know. But he already has. I'll cut up the credit card he gave me tonight."

Spying the small grave next to the front gate, Mrs. Duncan said, "You'll regret this, Amara. Staying in a place like this, your future will end right there, in the ground. Just like whoever that was, out in the middle of nowhere."

Glancing over her shoulder at the grave, a tiny smile crossed Amara's lips. "That's Grandma Lizzy," she said reverently. "I could only hope to be loved as much as she is."

Mrs. Duncan jerked her head away. "Don't call me when you realize you've made a mistake. Let's go, Deputy."

Amara stepped away and watched her mom's profile lurch forward. Expecting to feel some sort of regret, as her mom had suggested, she lingered a moment—but regret didn't come. Sad at how easily her mom had dismissed her, yes, but not regret. In fact, the blatant rejection only substantiated that she'd made the right choice. Amara turned around and faced Sonny. He had patiently waited for the mother-daughter exchange. The gentleness in his eyes suggested that he understood the gravity of the situation from which Amara had just unbound herself. A sensation of fresh freedom entered Amara's lungs.

Sonny held his arm out and extended a hand for her to take, welcoming her home. "Come on," he said. "I didn't bring you wings, but I brought you a horse."

"Even better," said Amara, grabbing his hand. Approaching the second gray horse, she asked, "Isn't this JoJo?"

A mischievous look crossed Sonny's face. No wonder Charleston had sounded irritated—Sonny had taken his horse!

"Should we go find him?" Amara asked, concerned.

"Nah, he knows where he is," Sonny answered, patting the empty saddle seat.

## CHAPTER THIRTEEN

The next morning, Charleston insisted on taking Amara with him on her first day of official work as a ranch hand. At first Sonny felt spurned, but after his initial anger, he decided that his grandfather's insistence had provided him with the necessary opportunity to try out yesterday's spoiled dinner plans again.

He had heavily debated whether or not he should take Amara to the surprise candlelit dinner in the meadow so soon after the situation with her mother, or wait until the timing was right. The romantic gesture was meant to highlight his feelings for her, and it didn't have anything to do with her sudden employment or her finally established freedom. Although he was proud of her for both, Sonny wanted dinner in the meadow to mean just as much to her now as he had hoped it would before she decided to stay on at the ranch. So he had opted to wait—and an entire day was as long as he could manage.

Once again, Sonny rushed through his daily chores of feeding, checking water sources, and testing and fixing another section in the long line of waiting fences. If he addressed a section of fence every week, he still wouldn't get to all of it in a year. The sheer quantity left room for failure to ensure the livestock were safely encompassed at all times. They did their best.

Pushing his thoughts aside, Sonny prepared a spread of food that could be kept cold in a cooler and packed it up. He poured ice into the cooler, draped a blanket over the top, and carried it to his pickup. Then he retrieved a small propane stove and a book of matches from the kitchen's emergency stockpile and slid those into the pickup as well. Lastly, he peeked into the pantry at the line of glass wine bottles. He and Charleston never bothered to get into them, and he didn't know one from another. Grandma had loved wine, not he and Gramps. Sonny wasn't sure how Amara felt about wine, but grabbed a pretty burgundy bottle with a picture of grapes on the label and took it out to the pickup with him.

Once he reached the edge of the meadow, he gazed inside, and the setting was just as perfect as he remembered it. Nothing had been touched or windblown. If anything, the hint of light dust gathered on the surfaces of the plates and silverware added to the mystery of how it had all gotten there. There was no trace of a fingerprint in the dust. The only suggestion he had been there was the breath of his footprints upon the grass, and nothing could be done about that. Hoping it was the last thing she noticed, and feeling the temptation to tiptoe, he headed to a tree in the meadow and hid the dinner preparations in its shade, then made his way back to the pickup to rejoin Amara and Charleston at the house.

About a half hour after Sonny arrived back at the house, the two rolled up on the tractor while he was sitting on the steps of the front porch and sipping on a mug of coffee. Amara's skin was darker from the days she had been spending in the sun; at least the skin he could easily see was darker. In addition to her tight jeans and tank top, she wore a smile, suiting her like birds suit a tree. She jumped from the seat as Charleston hobbled down the step, clutching the large wheel for balance. When her eyes landed on him, her smile widened, and she trotted over to meet him.

"What did you do today?" he asked.

Her eyes fell to his hot coffee mug in distraction, so he offered it to her, and she gleefully took it and started gulping. "Whoa, it's hot!" She shook her head and kept drinking.

"Thirsty? Or tired?" he asked.

She took a breath and lowered the mug, handing it back to him empty. "Both," she said, but she was smiling.

Sonny laughed as Charleston hobbled past them into the house, obviously thirsty and tired too. "Who tired out who?"

Amara took a seat next to him on the porch. "Well, Gramps works twice as hard as any young man, but I think I may have mentally tired him out with all my questions."

"What did you learn?"

"I drove the tractor!" She beamed. "At first, I just drove and moved the hydraulics. Then he had me move the manure pile behind the barn out into the field and spread it. Then I loaded the metal panels and moved them out," she said, pointing towards the distance, "and made a...uh..."

"Catch pen?"

"Yes! Then Gramps showed me how to switch the attachments...that took me a while. Then I grated the drive!"

Sonny couldn't stop from smiling at her.

"What?" she asked, her forehead wrinkling.

"You've never called him Gramps before, and now you've said it twice."

"Hmm, so I have," she said thoughtfully. "I suppose it's because it's what *you* call him. Is it disrespectful?"

"Not at all."

Amara wrapped her hands around her head, still smiling. "Geez, I feel like my brain is still bouncing along on the tractor."

"Want to go on an evening ride?" Sonny asked, crossing his fingers that she wasn't too plum worn out to go. Her dinner and candles awaited her, deep amongst the hills.

"On horseback?" she asked.

"Yes," Sonny answered, trying not to hold his breath.

"Then absolutely! Just no more tractors," she said, clutching her fingers together as if in prayer.

"Deal," he said, laughing, and pulled her to her feet. "No more tractors."

An hour into the ride, he had Amara riding Moses beside him down a long dirt road. Not only did they need to make up some time to get to the meadow before sunset, he loved watching her lope along. The wind blew her hair behind her like a golden cape and brushed pink into her cheeks. Her hips moved forward and back with each thrust of Moses' strong stride. Watching her floating above all the cares of the world inspired him to let go of some of his own cares, relax into the ride, and breathe a little easier.

When she turned her head to smile at him, he wondered how she'd stolen his heart so quickly. No one had ever been able to steal his heart before. His affections, maybe even his lust, but never his heart. Her eyes were like windows into a world to which he had never been. A world he wanted to know, only with her. Unlike any of the other girls he had met, or even dated, there was something about Amara that had seized him at first sight. She was different. She was small and petite, yet feisty and tough. Compassionate yet resilient. She was very much like the land Sonny loved so much—enigmatically beautiful, and as wild as the horses roaming upon it.

Amara spurred Moses to run faster, and Sonny followed after her, laughing. He knew then that he would always follow her. He would always protect her. He would always love her.

About the time that their horses began to tire, Sonny led the way off the main road, where the ground turned to rock, hidden boulders, and dangerous fractures and gaps. They gave the horses their heads so the treacherous terrain could be negotiated warily and instinctively.

"Oh, dear," said Amara. "This doesn't seem suitable for horses."

"It's not suitable for anything," Sonny agreed, but continued to lead the way. Credit to Amara, she followed, trusting him. Her absolute faith in him made him conscious that he was not only a man, but a man worthy of confidence: Amara's confidence. It was not something he shouldered blithely.

He pulled Nick up at the edge of the thick grove of trees. "Here we are," he said, stepping down from the saddle.

"Where are we?" Amara asked, looking around. It appeared they had come to a dead end.

Sonny held his hand out to her, offering to help her down. "I'll show you."

"Alright," she said, swinging her leg over Moses' back, patting Sonny's hand, and stepping down by herself. Her ankle twisted on the uneven rocky ground, and she fell straight into his arms. "Aw," she said, looking up at him endearingly, "thanks for catching me."

"Any time," he answered, balancing her on her feet. "Care for a piggyback ride?"

"Would I!" she declared, surprising him.

After securing the horses to a sturdy branch, he squatted down low enough that she could bound onto his strong back. When her weight hit him full force, he braced, and was pleasantly surprised at how incredibly light she was. He boosted her up a little higher, and she giggled in his ear. Both her legs and her long hair wrapped around him, swathing him with warmth against the cool of the evening. Distracted by her inviting, heated body, and the complete knowledge that he had wrapped his forearms behind his back and tucked them under her rear, he tried with great difficulty to focus on his footing. The last thing he wanted to do was trip or drop her. Her warm breath, exhaling down his collar, caused his cheeks to turn redder than the small amount of exertion it took to carry her the short way. As he pushed through the tree branches, she hunched closer and tucked her chin down into his shoulder. The smell of her filled his nose. As the branches opened up into the meadow, she sat up and gasped.

"Wow!" she cried out, unintentionally squeezing his waist with her thighs to get a better look. "Just wow!"

"You like it?"

"Yes!" she answered, planting a kiss on his cheek, then letting go of his shoulders and sliding down his back until her feet hit the earth.

He stepped out of the way so she could get a clear view, pleased to see that her eyes were wide and appreciative. At first they were fixed on the mysteriously placed table, set for two. Then she looked around at the circle of trees, surely wondering the same thing he always had. How had they gotten there?

"What is this?"

"I have my theories," Sonny answered. "But for tonight, it's dinner out." He opened his arms, indicating the obvious.

"You did this? For me? I just don't believe it!" she said, as she walked in circles, examining the simple but strange meadow. "How did you know this was here?"

Sonny laughed as he approached the table and scooted out a chair for her. "You're right, you *do* ask a lot of questions." As Amara sat, pretending to be dressed in something far more elegant than blue jeans, he fetched his supplies from the trees.

"I'm astonished at this view," Amara admitted, looking out at the sunset. Vivid hues of pink and orange bridged the heavens from the south to the north. They would provide just enough light to enjoy a romantic dinner, with the assistance of two glowing candles, before night overtook the sky and the sun sank over the distant horizon.

Returning, Sonny removed the cork from the wine bottle and poured them both a glass. "I couldn't believe it either, the first time I was here," he said, and opened the parmesan chicken and buttered asparagus to warm on the stove.

"This is amazing," Amara said, as she ran her fingers through her tangled hair. Finally giving up, she looked strangely bashful. "Do you bring many girls here?"

"Sure, tons," Sonny answered.

Amara frowned.

"No, none!" he added seriously. "Only you." Her expression revealed her skepticism. "Come on," he coaxed, "what's so hard about believing you're the only girl I've ever…" He was thinking, "wanted in my life the way I want you," but that sort of declaration would be unquestionably too sober and too soon. So instead, he finished the question with, "taken here? Surely you've had countless boys trying to impress you."

"Sure, tons," Amara admitted, laughing. "No. None."

"I can't believe that."

"Look who doesn't believe who now," she teased, crossing her arms over her chest.

"You must have been blind to their ways of trying to impress you," he suggested. "The possibility of no boys having shown interest in you is absolutely ludicrous."

"Pish posh."

"Well," he said, looking into her stormy hazel eyes—damn, he was drowning in them. "I, for one, am glad you were blind."

"I wasn't blind," Amara argued defensively, then quickly snapped her mouth shut. The corners of her lips turned up and she reached for her wine, taking a sip. "How did you know this place even existed?"

"I was following a mountain lion. It appeared she lived here, protected and unbothered. She had a great view, didn't she?"

"Oh!" Amara's eyes bulged. "Is she dead?"

"No. Not that I know of. Why? Have I frightened you? Would you like me to take you home?"

"It's just…" Amara's eyes were large as she leaned forward, as if to reveal a secret. "So far, all the animals in your stories end up dead," she said, smiling and proud of herself.

"Very funny," Sonny said, actually chuckling, as he began to dish both plates with chicken and asparagus.

"Thank you," Amara said, grinning at her plate of food, not specifying if she was thanking him for the compliment or the dinner. Picking up her fork, she started digging in like a ravenous spring bear.

Sonny looked at her, amused. He liked that she wasn't a bashful eater. He laughed, despite possible wrath. It appeared that she was very hungry.

Glancing at him, her closed-mouth smile revealed her feelings. "Are you eating?" she asked around a bite of chicken, eyeing the food on his plate. Before he could answer, she nodded, saying, "This is good."

"Yes, I'm eating." He held his hands over his food, protecting his ration. "Doesn't anyone feed you?"

"No, not really," she answered, giggling.

He knew she wasn't much of a cook, but dang. He was going to have to intervene, or else she'd starve. "Would you like to go to the store?" he asked. "I can take you tomorrow. You need groceries."

"Sure!" she said, stuffing in another bite. "This is really good!"

Sonny couldn't help himself from laughing, despite her honest hunger. "Here," he said, forking his chicken and placing it on her plate. "I'm not hungry. To tell you the truth, I'm going to go home and slash open a frozen pie and stuff it in the oven. How does that sound?"

"Good!" she answered happily, still digging in.

Sonny ate his asparagus and a roll from the baggie he had brought, not wanting her to feel self-conscious about eating alone. He sipped at his wine, disgruntled that it didn't taste at all like the grape juice it resembled. He was not a big fan of wine; it looked delicious, with its dark, deep color, but didn't taste at all like what he was always looking for. As a boy, and still, as a matter of fact, he loved grape juice. He'd grown up simple, with simple tastes. So he sipped tiny, dissatisfied sips as he watched her ravenous eating gradually slow down. It brought an unexpected satisfaction to him, seeing her grow stronger and more content.

Wiping her mouth with her napkin, she said, "You know, at first I considered this to be the perfect place to put a house, so secluded and remote. But I'm having second thoughts."

"Why's that?" Sonny asked, crossing his arms thoughtfully across his chest.

"Call me crazy, but I'm not keen on Mrs. Mountain Lion showing up asking for a cup of sugar—or a slab of meat." She threw her napkin on her plate, leaning back in her chair. "Particularly mine."

"Well, someone disagrees with you," Sonny said matter-of-factly.

"Oh really, who?" she asked. "You?"

"No, I'm on the same page as you, knowing what I know. Someone else."

Amara looked around for any sign of a previous structure. Finding none, she looked back at him, shrugging.

"Besides having dinner with you without Gramps' meddling, it's who I brought you here to see."

She leaned forward, squinting. "Sonny Morris, what are you talking about? There's no one here. I hope…"

Impulsively, he took a sip of his wine. "Look up, Amara."

She did, her eyes searching the fading blue sky, drawn to the softly tinted pinks and oranges of the sunset that had been magnificently sprawling across the horizon only moments ago. Now they were subdued. After a brief interlude admiring the changing tones of the sun, Amara's eyes came back to his. She retrieved her wine, taking a sip in obvious skepticism, then without reason, she looked straight up at the tree behind him, as if it had waved at her to catch her attention. She froze with her wine glass still at her lips, her breath catching in her throat.

Nestled in the top quarter of the furthest pine tree above the bluff, with the best view of the river in three directions, was a meticulously arranged nest. It dominated the branches near the trunk at a stunning eight-foot width. The interwoven sticks the bird couple had gathered were stuffed with clumps of grass and moss, filling in the holes and insulating their home from Montana's harsh elements.

Aimlessly, Amara's wine glass sank to the table. "That's the largest nest I have ever seen!"

Sonny nodded, pleased at her reaction. Looking up as well, he told her, "It's an eagle's nest."

Feeling her eyes upon him, he knew she understood now what he had brought her here to see. This nest either was, or represented, Eagle's nest from Grandma Lizzy's story. As a boy, he had assumed the story had been a fable for years. But ever since he had found the nest, he couldn't help but feel that the myth had been more than legend, and that Grandma Lizzy had known. At least here the story she had told him all those nights as a boy was real, even verifiable. Here was where love existed. Here was what he wanted to share with Amara.

Amara leaned forward across the little table he had set up for her and touched her fingers softly to his cheek. He felt his stomach shudder as she studied his face intently, first touching his rough jaw, then his temple and the hair above his ear. Her thin lips parted as if she had something to say, but no words escaped. There was desire in her dark hazel eyes, and it matched his own.

With a sweep of his hand, he shoved the table aside.

Everything on the table flew crashing to the ground, with the dull thud of the table following. He didn't care, and he didn't pay it any attention. The only thing caught in his sights was Amara sitting across from him, perfectly unfazed by the sudden crashing of dishes. He hit his knees, landing right where the table had been moments ago, and grabbed her by the shoulders, pulling her to himself, her rear sliding across the chair, her chest falling against his. She landed softly in his arms, and he pressed his mouth to her lips.

As they met together, having her sensual body against his wasn't enough for Sonny. He was greedy for her, and she was starved for him. He thrust his tongue into her open mouth, exploring, taking what she offered and giving what she took. He wanted to taste her soul, and she welcomed the endeavor. She pushed herself into his firmly tugging arms. They couldn't get close enough; they wanted to be firmer, tighter, nearer. He brushed her hair behind her, where it cascaded all the way to the cool grass.

Kissing her neck, he unfastened her shirt and yanked it from her shoulders. Bare and exposed, he wanted her more than anything he had ever wanted before. Laying her back, he kissed and tasted every square inch of her flesh and curves as her body bucked in appreciation. Purposely tangling his hand in her hair, he held her head right where he wanted it, back, so he could hear her moan in pleasure as he nipped her bra strap to the side and stole the flavor from between her breasts. Neither of them noticed the darkness slinking over them as the stars peeked out, lulling them into the embrace of furiously eager passion and abandoned restraint.

Feeling Amara's fiery fingers tugging and grasping beneath his shirt sent sensations rushing through him, unlocking bolted doors. Sonny trembled as he let his hips drop between hers. The fact they were wearing jeans did nothing to hinder the hot need. Using his left hand, he unbuttoned her waistband and slid his hand inside. She gasped and arched in indulgence as his fingers penetrated her.

"Sonny," she said, so delightfully and breathlessly that he nearly decided to strip her of her clothing right then and there and take what he knew she was offering, and keep taking her until tomorrow turned into next year.

"I know," he whispered, kissing her neck and sucking on the vein swelling there. He felt the muscles inside her clench and throb, massaging his fingers in a way which made him swell and ache, and adding to the undeniable temptation to start again. Not succumbing to his own desire was the hardest thing he had ever done. But he managed to do it, for her, and for everything he had hope in.

After he had redressed Amara, he held her curled up in his arms, her head on his chest, content as a baby. He had never felt more complete. Together, they were free from every worldly concern, every drop of loneliness, every loss of love. Together, they had everything they ever needed.

"I've never seen so many stars," she whispered.

"Hard to imagine they're always there, isn't it?"

Her little chin dug into his sternum as she nodded. "Harder to believe how many people never get to see them."

"Most of the time, it's by their own choice. The stars are there for the seeking."

"True," Amara admitted. "For example, I've never seen the top of Mount Everest, but I'm surprisingly at peace with that."

Sonny laughed and her head bounced, causing her to laugh with him. "Not a fan of adventuring, huh?"

"No, I am. I'm just not a fan of a slow, unnecessary death. Did you know climbers literally slowly die while climbing the last leg of Mount Everest?"

"Is that a fact?"

"Yes," whispered Amara. "I wrote a paper on it. A climber, should they make it to the top of the world, doesn't get to enjoy it for more than a few minutes." She was quiet for a moment, and then she asked, "Do you think it would even be worth it?"

Sonny stared at the uncountable, twinkling stars and unfathomable flashes of light until they blurred a little. Suddenly he felt as if they were all looking up at him, edging closer, like little committed climbers trying to reach the top. "Yeah, it's worth it."

"How do you know?"

"Because I'm at the top of the world right now," Sonny said, kissing the top of her head.

## CHAPTER FOURTEEN

The duties Amara took on at the ranch were tough and demanding. Sanding the fence around the ranch houses so they could be resealed made her arms ache. Scrubbing down the horse stall walls made her shoulders scream. Lifting hay bale after hay bale from the conveyer and stacking them side by side, lengthwise and then widthwise, made sweat slide down her forehead and into her eyes. Moving irrigation pipe one section at a time, keeping the line obsessively straight, was tedious. Dawn's bitter cold bit at her fingertips as she worked to untangle horse tack and wash the steel bits to go in the horses' mouths. But none of that could strip away the exhilarating happiness burning in her soul.

The rough work, the persistent purpose, the untamed freedom—all of it only multiplied her delight. With every grunt, she could feel herself growing stronger, closer to the woman she recognized in her soul. And at the end of the day, no amount of fatigue could wane the pounding in her heart when Sonny's hands landed upon her.

Charleston had insisted she stay in the small house she had already taken when she first arrived, allowing her privacy and independence, despite her and Sonny's obvious feelings for one another. He had a knack for providing structure, and weaved graciously in his own gruff way between being a boss and being a beloved Gramps. Every evening when she first stepped into the main house for supper, Charleston welcomed her as a working hand. But as the evening wore on, with her and Sonny sitting side by side, Sonny's hand resting on her leg, Charleston slowly merged into Gramps. A little warmer. A little more easygoing. A little twinkle in his eye.

One morning, Amara was perched on the top rail, next to the gate to which Charleston had assigned her. A newbie to branding calves, she watched the hurried morning prep from well out of the way. Her right leg was draped over the top rail, and she had wrapped her boot around the post, leaving her hands free to operate the gate latch with ease. Now she waited.

Rod Sandgren and his family had showed up to help with the chore. Amara watched as Rod hunkered over the fire he had started inside a large, pot-bellied portable stove and bedded a couple of branding irons deep inside. His horse stood tied to the corral railing, already saddled up and ready to work. Anita set a series of buckets next to him, touched his back gently, and went on her way. "Want to help me prepare meals in the kitchen, Amara?" she called.

Amara opened her mouth as she glanced at Charleston, preparing to ask for his approval, although she really didn't want to be stuck in the kitchen. Charleston had left her at the gate with specific instructions to open it when he called—let the calf through and promptly shut it. As simple as that sounded, she'd rather do it than be trapped in a kitchen. Either way, she couldn't leave without his consent. Anita understood and waited.

Charleston didn't even look up from where he was preparing a large syringe for vaccinations. "Don't you dare let Amara in the kitchen, Anita!" he bellowed.

"She's better off out here, working the gate. She needs to learn how this works."

"We're *all* better off," Sonny called from the back of a red horse Amara didn't recognize, as he let himself into the cattle pen.

Anita looked at Amara questioningly, and Amara shrugged. "They haven't forgiven me for setting the stove on fire."

"And the oven mitts!" Sonny added, around a mouthful of white roping gloves hanging from his teeth, swinging a large, stiff loop of rope next to his horse.

"Don't worry about it, dear," Anita said to Amara, heading towards the house. "I don't think I need help anyway."

"You don't," said Charleston.

William laughed as he entered the branding pen, stomping his boots heavily across the compact dirt. "Still living up to your name, huh, Calamity?" He threw an arm over the railing and looked up at her. "So you're still here."

"Surprised?" Amara asked.

"Honestly, I *am* a little surprised. I thought you were a short-term guest." He studied her plain working attire.

"Charleston hired me on."

William cocked his head. "So you're staying? How long?"

Amara shrugged.

William glanced at Charleston and began rolling up his sleeves. "Well, good luck," he said, spinning around and walking off.

"Gate!" Charleston bellowed.

Jumping, Amara flipped the latch and swung open the gate. Rod pushed a calf through, tight on its heels, his rope around its squarish head. The calf bucked and spun, Rod adjusting the angle of his horse in order not to become entangled. Sonny tracked in behind the calf on his jigging, nervous red horse, and with what seemed a soft and effortless move, picked up its little squirming back heels with the loop of his rope. Both men spread away, stretching the calf until it tumbled and fell belly down, legs out to the front and the back, as if they were going to roast him like a pig. Together, they pulled the calf right to Charleston's feet.

Quickly, Charleston and William took turns injecting the sprawled calf with different vaccination guns, which looked an awful lot like ordinary household caulking guns to Amara. Then Charleston pulled a knife from the side of his belt, and with a swift cut, the calf's balls were severed and thrown into an empty blue bucket. Almost immediately William was back, sticking his boot against the calf and pressing the hot branding iron into its velvety red hide. Smoke filled the air, along with the sound of sizzling. Charleston followed up with a quick notch to the calf's ear, and signaled to release it as he dipped his knife in a bucket of solution. William ensured that the ropes fell away, and the calf scrambled to his unbalanced feet and trotted off, his pride departed—abandoned—in a blue bucket.

Slightly shocked at the speed with which the men worked, and slightly revolted at the solution dripping from the tip of Charleston's knife, Amara found her hand clasped against her mouth. Then the nauseating smell of burnt hair hit her nostrils. The scent was pungent, and put a spicy taste on the back of her tongue. To say the least, she was impressed.

The little calf meandered to the far side of the corral, finding a safe corner away from the smell of his own burnt flesh. He didn't bawl or lay down. To Amara's surprise, he stood there, head up, watching, as if he were curious about what had just happened. With all the grace he had showed, one wondered if he could possibly comprehend that he now could withstand deadly diseases and infections.

Amara imagined that he could. Accepting circumstances and overcoming pain made him stronger. No different from how she had felt when she watched her mom turn away and disappear down the desolate road. She recognized then that she was stronger than anyone had given her credit for. She knew she would make it, just like this calf would.

"Gate!" Charleston's voice boomed, yanking her from her daydream.

Flinching, she jerked open the gate and watched as the same procedure was performed over and over for hours. Like an orchestra, they each played their part in the musical ritual. Soon barely even a word was uttered. Charleston quit bellowing for Amara to open the gate, because she knew and paid attention. William stopped cracking jokes. Sonny's horse stopped jigging when pulling the calf. The jobs were clear and everyone kept at it, until Charleston finally stood, stretched his back, and said what everyone had been aching to hear: "Let's take a lunch."

That was when they all turned towards the house; Anita was ringing the dinner bell. Somehow, as if in a trance, they hadn't heard the bell through their concentration until Charleston had freed them from it.

Amara's stomach growled, and she could tell everyone else was feeling the sudden hunger too. Dirty hands brushed against filthy pant legs. Charleston and William dipped their hands in a bucket of disinfectant mixed with water. Sonny and Rod stepped from their horses' backs and led them to bags of hay tied to the posts.

As Amara made her way to meet Sonny and William at the start of the road towards the house, her ankle rolled as she thoughtlessly stepped on a large dirt clod. She winced, rebalanced herself, and met them in a few steps.

William slapped a hand across her back like a pal, sending her tumbling another step. "How is it you manage to ride a horse so well when you can't even walk across flat ground?"

"I think God made me the wrong creature. I wasn't supposed to have feet of my own."

"So you were meant to be a snake? Poisonous or non-poisonous?" William asked, taking a step away.

"No, not a snake," Amara laughed. "Like a centaur, from Greek mythology."

Sonny laughed and grabbed her by the shoulders, pulling her into his arms. "You're perfect just the way you are. I much prefer you to remain fully woman." Then he placed a deep kiss upon her mouth, making her wish she was somewhere else, anywhere else.

"Yeah, yeah," William interrupted. "You're going to ruin my appetite, and I, for one, plan to eat an entire pie by myself."

"His mom makes the meanest apple pie in the county," Sonny told Amara.

William cleared his throat. "Excuse me? Try the country."

"How many did she make?" Amara asked.

William grinned. "Only two."

Without warning, Amara took off for the house at a dead run. "I call the biggest one!" she hollered back at the boys' stunned expressions. Their faces broke out in smiles, and Sonny gave William a stiff shove and burst into a run first.

"Hey!" William called in a complaining tone, tickling Amara's funny bone as she pumped her arms and laughed.

Sonny won the foot race, but in all of his charm, he decided to share the pie with William and Amara. Besides, after the fresh hamburgers, potato salad, and homemade buttermilk rolls, no one had room for an entire pie anyway. Or so they had agreed. After the first bite, Amara was fairly certain she could still put one of Anita's entire pies down. The flavors of cinnamon, nutmeg, and brown sugar hit her tongue, soaked into her bones, and made her want to beg for more.

After lunch, the crew went back to work while Anita stayed at the house to clean up and start again on preparation for dinner. Amara was grateful that Anita was so skilled and talented. She had no intention of being cooped up in a kitchen all day; it was said that the kitchen is where the heart is, but to Amara, the kitchen was a jail where she managed to destroy things, no matter how hard she tried to behave as a civilized woman.

She had her foot on the bottom rail, preparing to situate herself at the gate again, when Charleston called to her. "Amara, let William work the gate this time." Stunned, she paused. If William worked the gate, what would she do? "Come on," Charleston beckoned, impatiently.

She crawled through the rail and joined him, waiting for instruction. Surely he wasn't going to throw her in the deep end and have her take William's position? Sonny looped his rope and rocked it gently next to his horse's side. She looked up at him, but he just shrugged and smiled.

"Gate!" Charleston bellowed at William, who was still climbing the rail.

William jumped the last two rungs and busted the gate open. Rod and the calf trotted through. Sonny nudged his horse forward and swooped the loop under the calf's heels just as they kicked up. Everything was moving forward as it had all morning—except Amara, who stood frozen. She was being thrown into the deep end. Nervously she racked her mind; what exactly was the process she had watched so many times? What exactly had William done, and in what order? Her hands began to shake. The calf appeared at her and Charleston's feet. She stared at it, stuck.

"Gramps," Sonny said, backing up his horse, tightening the rope as Charleston tied up the calf's legs. "I think this is too much for Amara right after lunch."

Charleston glanced up at Amara, and bobbed his head towards the bucket where William had left the vaccinations he was using. "A sick calf is a dead calf," he told her, holding the calf still. "The longer you take, the harder it is on him."

"Alright," Amara said, more for her own benefit than Charleston's, and grabbed the gun she had watched William use. Taking a deep breath, she approached the calf and cringed as she stuck the needle in; his hide was thicker than she had expected. The liquid injected into the calf's neck. When she yanked it back out, she felt kind of proud, but Charleston didn't hesitate or congratulate her, just went straight to work. Fresh blood squirted onto the ground, joining the dark red dirt where it had squirted out before. The calf's balls were again tossed into the blue bucket.

Again Charleston glanced up at her. William was up next with the branding iron. She was behind the process. "Shit, I'm sorry," she said quickly, and turned to grab the iron from the fire. Charleston grabbed her arm tightly with his leather gloved hand, stopping her, his knife in his other hand. "You don't want me to?" she asked. He answered by hastily yanking off his own glove, stuffing it into her palm. "Oh," she said, quickly stuffing her hand inside, every passing moment making it harder on the calf.

Glove on, she grabbed the hot iron and approached the calf again. She didn't want to see its pain or smell its burning flesh, but she had already been the reason this calf had suffered twice as long as any of the others, so she pressed the iron into its red marbled hide, hard, and held it there for as long as she felt William had as the stench of the smoke floated up into her nostrils. When she released, the mark was dark, the hair around it singed.

Charleston's heavy hand slapped her on the back, and he signaled to the ropers that the job was done and to release the calf. As the calf trotted off, slightly shocked and wounded, to join the others, there was a cheer from everyone. Amara glanced up to see their uplifting smiles. Her own smile felt like it was beaming from her toes. She had done it. She was stronger than she thought. She was one of the boys, a ranch hand.

Everyone turned back to their jobs. Rod's horse wandered through the dwindling herd to fetch another calf and feed it through the gate where William was waiting. Sonny swung his rope, ready. Charleston nudged her. "Next," he said, implying that she get ready.

She nodded and grabbed the next vaccination. Ready.

## CHAPTER FIFTEEN

Towards the second half of September, it became evident to everyone that no piece of Amara wanted to leave the ranch and go back to college. No one wanted her to, yet they all wondered whether she would. Everyone maintained an unspoken yet universally understood pact not to talk about it, and no one so much as uttered the word "college," for fear that an unassuming conversation might spark a flame on a candle everyone assumed stay unlit and buried six feet beneath a mound of wet soil.

The three of them, Sonny, Amara, and Charleston, were fast becoming much more than a ranch crew or a group of working hands; they were becoming a family. In Sonny's opinion, the log walls of his and Charleston's bachelor home had been undomesticated for far too long. Indisputably, they had been good company for each other, but it was no match to the life and soul Amara had brought with her arrival. She had changed everything, and Sonny didn't want it to change back.

Pushing his thoughts aside, Sonny maneuvered the drip pan he was holding in his hand underneath the barn's utility tractor and crawled in after it. Looking out, he saw a pair of attractive legs and red boots. "Come on!" he coaxed.

"You're just trying to get me to do your job," Amara said, as she squatted down and peeked under. When Sonny offered no reply, she laid down on the hard concrete pad and joined him on the underside of the tractor.

"It's important to know how to change your own oil," Sonny replied, handing her a five-eighths ratchet. She looked at him, skeptically. "It's not hard," he said.

"That's beside the point," she replied, taking the ratchet.

"What if I'm sick and can't do it?"

She placed a sweet kiss on his cheek. "I'm sure you'll recover from your life-threatening cold or cough by the time the tractor needs service."

"Maybe," Sonny said, smiling. "Now slip the ratchet over the drain plug and loosen it. When it comes off, the oil will pour out into the pan by your ear. Theoretically."

"Theoretically?" Amara asked, as she put muscle into getting the bolt to crack open. With a grunt, it loosened, and she began spinning it off by hand.

The warm oil spluttered, dropping a few drips into her face, and then began pouring into the pan in which it was meant. Amara ducked away, grimacing. "You did that on purpose, didn't you?" she accused, glaring at Sonny from her oil-splattered face. He lifted a hand to block her from wiping her oily fingers on his rough jaw.

"You lined your face up where you wanted to. I put the pan right where it belonged." Pressing a hand to her shoulder, he pushed her body away and quickly retreated from under the belly of the tractor. "Come on, crawl on out of there."

Slinking like a caterpillar until her body was clear of the tractor, Amara stood and wiped the oil from her hand with the towel Sonny had hung on the fender, while he retrieved a second drain pan and an oil filter wrench. He threw the drain pan under the oil filter and handed her the circular wrench.

"Alright, slip this over the oil filter," he said, pointing to the black cylinder, "and twist her loose."

Amara did as instructed, then unscrewed it the rest of the way by hand and passed it over to him. "Easy," she said, with a smug smile.

"I told you it would be. I think you know where this goes," he said, handing her the new filter on which he had already rubbed a little oil. "Just twist it on and give it one more twist with the wrench."

Again, Amara did exactly as she was told, and looked to him expectantly. "You do realize showing me all of this is a mistake, don't you?" she asked, her fists on her shapely hips.

"Is it? Why?"

"Because I just lost all my admiration for how handy you…were."

Sonny laughed. "Oh, you're right, it may very well have been a mistake. Well… since you've got this covered, go ahead and duck your cute behind under the tractor and put the plug back on."

"You bet your dirty britches I can," she replied, ducking under the tractor momentarily and coming up with a broad, boasting grin.

"Alright, smarty-pants, fill her up." Sonny handed her a long funnel and a gallon of oil.

She took the funnel and oil, turned, and stared at the tractor for a good minute before asking, "Where?"

"Not ready to dismiss *all* your admiration for me just yet, are you?"

"Not all," she said.

Sonny crossed his arms and smiled.

"I still greatly esteem your body," she added.

Sonny frowned, then pursed his lips thoughtfully and nodded. "Alright, I can live with that. Right there," he said, pointing to the oil cap. Step by step, he walked Amara through the process of changing the hydraulic filter, changing the fuel filter, and filling the hydraulic fluid at the back of the tractor. She took blowing the dust out of the air filters all in graceful stride. The girl couldn't be taught too much; like a sponge, she soaked up everything he and Charleston threw at her. "Squeeze twice for each one," he coached, guiding her through oiling each joint nubbin.

"You would like that," Amara teased, glancing over her shoulder. Sonny smiled, about ready to reply, when a loud truck rumbled into the drive behind them.

"William," Sonny said in greeting, turning towards the truck as it stopped next to them. William's elbow protruded out the rolled-down window. "What brings you by?"

William waved at Amara and turned his gaze to Sonny. "We're picking McIntosh next week. You available?"

"Absolutely," Sonny answered. "Wouldn't miss it."

"McIntosh?" Amara asked curiously, as she joined Sonny at William's window.

"William's folks have one of the most successful fruit orchards in Montana. They have the perfect property for it, with large southern-facing slopes."

"More importantly," said William, "if you help pick, you get invited to the party."

"Party?" Amara asked.

"It's not the kind of party you want to miss," said William. "It lasts days, every evening after the work is done. My parents love music and food, and sharing too." He dangled his arm out the window, staring thoughtfully at her. "Weren't you going back to college?"

And there it was. Sonny could have strangled his friend. As it was, he glared at him over Amara's head. William caught Sonny's less-than-affectionate scowl. Amara was wordless. It seemed she wasn't quite sure what to say.

"Not that I'm complaining," William added quickly, trying to smooth over the ruffle he had caused. "We certainly would be glad to have another pair of hands. Will you come?" he asked, extending an invitation to her personally, and taking a crack at redirecting the conversation.

For a brief moment, which seemed like forever to Sonny, Amara hesitated in uncertainty. He knew she was fighting an inner battle with herself, and the ever-present voice of her disapproving mom. Sonny wanted more than anything to supply the answer for her—the answer he wanted—but he couldn't. It was her choice, and she had to live with her choices. It was no matter; he had to live with them, too.

"Of course," she finally answered. "I'll be there. Wouldn't miss it," she added, deliberately stealing Sonny's line.

"Super!" William slammed his heavy palm against the outside of his truck door. "Besides," he continued, lowering his voice and glancing around to make sure no eavesdroppers were listening, "there's someone coming I want you two to meet." His warm brown eyes lit up like fireworks on the Fourth of July—all excitement, color, and sparks.

"A girl?" Amara asked knowingly, captivated by William's enthusiasm.

William rolled his head around his neck, pretending to ignore the prodding question. Then he dropped his face back to the open window, widened his unblinking eyes, and allowed a smile to burst over his entire smitten face.

A hearty laugh erupted from Sonny's chest, and a giggle spouted from Amara. They understood completely, and were both thrilled for their friend and eager to meet this special someone. So much so that Sonny allowed himself to temporarily put his worries about it being halfway through September—and late for classes, if someone were to be taking them—out of his mind.

\*\*

The next week proved to be more backbreaking than Amara had expected. Box after box of aromatic, deep red apples filled every aisle, stacked beneath every ladder, collected and situated onto every flatbed. They roamed in Amara's every thought, frequenting the back of her eyelids every time they closed.

After she passed yet another box up to the flatbed to be arranged, it occurred to her just how much friends depended on friends in family-owned and operated agriculture businesses. It was no wonder the Sandgren family had helped hour after hour branding Charleston's calves. In a very short time, the favor would be returned when the Morris family helped the Sandgrens bring in their crop of apples.

"Montana is a hard place to grow fruit," said a tired young lady by the name of Nuna later, over a steaming cup of homemade apple cider.

Nuna displayed the beauty of the Blackfoot tribe located in northern Montana, with her long dark hair, dark brown eyes, and womanly curves. The Blackfoot tribe were known as hunters and gatherers, called "blackfoot" because of their dark moccasins. Nuna's mannerisms were guarded in this new place, but genuinely thoughtful. This was the young woman with whom William was smitten. She was sitting with Amara and Anita by a large bonfire while the majority of young men and boys played a game of flag football in the dark. There was a second bonfire about a hundred feet away, near the live music, where most of the workers and their families and friends had gathered, munching on treats and pies. Although Anita was the hostess, and could have been with the larger crowd, she preferred the softer atmosphere, relaxing into the evening with the two young ladies she desired to get to know better.

"Yes, Montana is hard on everyone," she said. "Our crops have been damaged a time or two, but McIntosh is robust and grows well in cold climates. Moreover, Rod and I have felt called to help with the fresh food supply. There's just so little, and not all of Montana is as capable of growing food as we are. We can't turn our back on the blessings the land provides here."

Nuna nodded, allowing her gentle eyes to fall upon William, who was currently inventing a peculiar dance of victory for having caught the ball. There was amusement in her expression. Both Anita and Amara caught it, but pretended not to have noticed when Nuna's eyes darted back to the small group huddled by the fire. Anita's right leg was draped across her left, and she swung it casually, sipping her cider.

"Sonny mentioned something about your southern-facing slopes playing a role in your orchard's success," said Amara.

"He's right," Anita replied. "Facing the south situates the fruit in the direct warmth of the sun, and the slope captures it there, blocking the harsh winds. The miracle part is that the slopes are not perfectly southern-facing, but also face ever so slightly to the east. It is as if God had scooped up the land, twisted it like a potter, and delicately created the perfect microclimate."

"East?" Amara asked. "Why is facing east good?"

"It faces the morning light," Nuna answered.

Anita smiled at Nuna, appreciating her youthful wisdom. "That's right. As the old saying goes, it's the coldest—"

"Right after dawn," Amara finished for her, understanding. "So facing east allows the most warmth from the sunlight, right when the fruit needs it most."

"Precisely!" said Anita. "There are other small microclimates, of course. It's not just us. There are microclimates everywhere, but they can be very tiny, or even if they are appropriate enough in size, tending them may prove too difficult or even dangerous. That's why Rod and I surrender the blessing of our land to provide for others. After all, we're only borrowing it. Isn't that right, Nuna?"

Again, Nuna nodded. Her Blackfoot name meant "Land," which Amara greatly admired.

"What are we talking about, ladies?" William asked, as he, Sonny, and Rod strode up to the fire to warm themselves. "Rooting for the winning team?"

"Yes," Anita said, smiling warmly. "The Grizzlies."

"Very funny," William declared, and dropped down next to a bashful Nuna. "But commendable."

Sonny held a hand out to Amara. "Care to dance?"

Amara slunk down in her chair. "I don't dance."

"That's a lie," said Sonny, raising his eyebrows.

"What?" Amara asked, taken back. "It is not."

"Hairbrush? Mirror? You've never done that?" Sonny asked. "I thought every teenage girl danced in front of a mirror, singing into a hairbrush."

"I wasn't your typical teenage girl."

"I'll give you that."

"Well, I have!" William announced, bounding excitedly to his feet. He grabbed Nuna's hand and pulled her, giggling, into his arms. "Let's show these two how to hairbrush dance!"

When Sonny's imploring eyes refused to abandon hope, Amara laughed. "I'm afraid of falling," she said, nearly pleading.

Amara was easily sidetracked when Nuna's face lit up, as William spun her around and around in the grass on their way toward the music booming out of guitars and speakers. William skipped and Nuna spun across the dark, grassy floor, towards the light of the other bonfire. Amara was taken by surprise when Sonny took her hand, and she was hoisted from her chair and met by his handsome face inches from hers.

"You're not afraid of falling," he whispered, wrapping her in his arms and holding her tightly against his chest. Her face flushed as heat trickled down her neck, all the way to her toes.

Returning his soulful gaze, Amara wondered how it was he understood her. No one else ever had. He was right, she wasn't afraid of falling; not from a horse, not from a mountain, not from the sky. But she was afraid she'd fallen for him. There was no standing back up. There was no brushing off the dust and trying again. There was no turning back.

"Please dance with me," Sonny asked, as he brushed her hair from her shoulder. He began gently rocking her side to side, dancing right where they were,

Rod and Anita watching on as approving witnesses. Placing his warm lips against her soft neck, he murmured against her skin, "I know you're scared, in your brave disguise. I can't promise you won't fall, but if you do fall, I can promise I'll be there. I will protect you, and I won't leave you." His blue eyes matched the twinkling stars of the night sky. Amara believed him and followed him.

The music suddenly changed from the quick strum of guitars, booming bass, and drums to a melodious string of velvety chords that swept Amara's feet out from under her. She didn't recognize the words, but she was becoming increasingly acquainted with the emotions they stirred. Every note illuminated her feelings for the man whose hand twirled her around his arm and drew her against his chest. She was no starry-eyed fella hunter like most of the girls she knew, but Sonny was a plunging romantic, and he had her pitching in after him, praying they never hit bottom.

Sonny held Amara as closely as he could, but it still felt like miles and miles of empty space. Close wasn't close enough. He pressed his nose into her fragrant hair, closing his eyes and breathing in the scent of lavender and honey. Finally, he understood why Amara was always closing her eyes. Even though his eyes were closed, he saw it all. He saw the music floating like colorful leaves in the breeze. He saw the sweet scent of apples and cider drifting through the crowd, circulating warmth and geniality. He saw, above it all, Amara: in his arms, in his heart, and in his future.

Along with the affection, sentiment, and instinctive hunger he felt from Amara's supple body pressed against him, he felt something else too: a little lump in his pocket where he had tucked the ring Charleston had offered him earlier. A single ring from Grandma Lizzy's treasure box. It was a simple gold band with a single red ruby heart planted in the center, the promise ring Charleston had given to her when she was a young girl, barely a woman. Here it was again, preparing to offer another girl another promise.

## CHAPTER SIXTEEN

It was autumn, and Amara's second approaching winter on the ranch kept nipping at the end of her nose and the tips of her ears every morning during chores, announcing its impending arrival. She was leaning against the kitchen counter, gearing up for this morning's trek into the biting air, carefully sipping the steaming hot coffee, and Sonny was doing the same, leaning against the kitchen sink and angling his body so he could see both her and out the window, the same way Charleston always did. It was as if those two men were always expecting something to happen out there—either that, or they just liked the view that much.

"We're doing what?" Amara asked Sonny, surprised. Surprise was a strange sensation to wake up to. It was still yet five o'clock in the morning, too early for surprises.

"Dinner," Sonny grinned at her. "In town. This evening. Gramps' treat."

"Huh," Amara half grunted. Charleston hated going to town. He hated going out to eat. He hated making a fuss over a holiday, let alone an average, nothing spectacular, zero to celebrate, typical Tuesday.

"Don't forget to put on your wedding ring," said Sonny with a wink, tapping his own gold band against the ceramic mug so it clinked melodiously. "I don't want any cowboys thinking you're up for grabs."

Amara lifted a hand away from the glorious warmth of her mug and studied her short but grimy fingernails, and empty left ring finger, grinning as she remembered their private winter wedding. The church may have been rundown from years of blistering weather, but the pews were lined with deep red roses and white baby's breath that had been shipped in, and filled with the faces of smiling friends. Not that she'd expected them to, but her parents were not among those faces.

Her empty finger stared up at her. She never wore her wedding ring at the ranch, which pretty much meant she almost never wore it. The ruby ring Sonny had given her was far too valuable and sentimental for her to simply lose it over the course of miles and miles of land—or over a steaming pile of manure, for that matter. Sonny had wanted to replace his grandmother's ring with one of diamonds, especially for her, but she had insisted she wanted to keep the family ring. Nothing could symbolize their love better.

"Did we miss something?" Amara asked, racking her brain. "It's not his birthday, or yours…or mine…or Grandma's…what are we missing?"

Sonny threw back his last swig and set his mug in the sink. "Not a clue," he answered, amused at her obsessing. He placed a kiss on her head. "Meet you at the barn," he said affectionately.

He was out the front door before Amara answered. "Uh-huh."

As she sipped her coffee, the knuckles on her hands hinted at how hard she had worked them. They weren't dirty, they were stained. If going to town meant she had to scrub six layers off her skin with a wire bristle brush, well then, she was inclined to put her vote in with Charleston; they shouldn't go to town. The exception being, this time, that it was his idea.

Squinting her eyes against the heat and bitterness, Amara hurriedly downed the rest of her coffee. A plan was brewing. She would work extra hard today, finish up early, and use the awful wire bristle brush if she had to. But preferably, she just wanted a good soak in a hot bubble bath, with sweet, seductive, scented oil. Then, and only then, would she feel like a girl again. If they absolutely *had* to go out.

By the time Amara jogged into the barn, Charleston had already scooped all of the manure out of the stalls and brought in fresh wood shavings. Sonny had already thrown hay into each stall's hay box, and was measuring out each of the horses' individual grain mixture and portion, according to size, workload, athleticism, and metabolism. It was her job to brush their coats until they shined, pick the old shavings and compacted manure out of their hooves, paint the white and black hooves with gloss, then wipe down their faces with baby oil. Today, four of their best two-year-old ranch horses were being picked up by their new, exceedingly enthusiastic owner. In fact, they were *all* pretty excited about it.

Perhaps selling the horses was what Charleston wanted to celebrate, assuming the sale was successfully finalized. Still, Amara thought, retrieving her box of grooming supplies, it was entirely unlike him to celebrate normal ranch affairs. Celebrating a common occurrence was ludicrous. Charleston woke up to work yesterday, he woke up to work today, and he would wake up to work tomorrow and every day following. No fluff and no fuss was his motto. So if he wanted to treat the family to dinner, there had to be a reason other than ranch business; it had to be personal. Whatever the motive for having dinner in town was, it couldn't trump today's highlight: a successful sale. Amara was no fool. They needed the sale.

The horse market being in a bit of a slump, folks just didn't have the money to pay for the type of breeding and training they actually desired and needed. Most ranchers, and even hobbyists, were having to cut corners and allow slack where normally they wouldn't just to get by. Charleston Morris wouldn't sacrifice his quality, nor his training agenda, to cut the cost down for the consumer. The benefit was that his horses still held a highly esteemed value, and proven promise and talent. The downside was, they weren't selling fast enough.

So when the Wyoming woman of newly acquired money called, wanting horses she could depend on—that wouldn't break down and could actually do the job proposed, unlike the flea-bitten, hairy scoundrels the other trainers were trying to sell her—Charleston and Sonny introduced her to their best. The best was what she wanted, and the best was what they delivered. She arranged to meet them, and hopefully pick them up—paid for in full.

When the cleanest blue Dodge rumbled down the drive, pulling an equally spotless matching blue, live-in, four-horse trailer, Amara held her breath. She had to wonder if the woman, new to the ranching world, had enough experience and insight to appreciate their fine animals, despite having driven so far. As the woman stepped from the driver-side door, neither Charleston nor Sonny ran to meet her. Indeed, they were nowhere to be seen.

Amara looked around, searching for them. How could they have disappeared, knowing the woman who was apt to purchase four of their best stock was coming in this morning? Having no clue where they had gone, and feeling irritated, she decided *someone* better make an introduction. Amara briskly walked up to the woman, who had her hand above her brows, also in search of any sign of life.

The woman appeared to be roughly in her fifties, but Amara guessed her age based only on the light gray streaks in her dark brown, wavy, waist-length hair. Her skin was brown but healthy, not brown and weathered like most women her age that had worked their lives out of doors. Her eyes were brown and gentle, and she offered a beautiful white smile. Suddenly, Amara felt self-consciously simple and unattractive in comparison. Her jeans were already soiled from where she had wiped horse eye and nose boogers, and she had systematically removed the dust and dander off the grooming brushes by scrubbing them against her jeans' seamline. She felt lowly, unappealing, and insignificant. Regardless, she straightened her back and shoved out her small, greasy hand. Whether or not the woman took it spoke to her own character, not Amara's. To her surprise, the woman eagerly grabbed her grimy hand and wrapped it with both of hers.

"Hello! I'm Elenore King. I've been corresponding with Charleston and Sonny Morris. I'm so pleased to have finally arrived. Please tell me my GPS didn't send me down the wrong rabbit hole."

"No, you're at the right place," Amara said, smiling sincerely. "I'm Amara Morris."

"Daughter?" Elenore asked.

"Daughter-in-law and wife. Not to the same man, obviously."

Elenore laughed. "Pleased to meet you, Amara. May I see your horses?"

"Certainly," Amara answered, and began to show the way, although inwardly she wavered uneasily on the edge of undecided. Ought she really to be showing Elenore to the horses? They were not, in fact, her horses to show. She was the one person on the ranch who knew the least about them. Uncertain, Amara kept walking, Elenore tight on her heels.

"I believe Charleston and Sonny intended to demonstrate the horses to you themselves, but I can show you to them while we wait," Amara said, glancing around. Where were they? With her back turned to Elenore, she rubbed her lips together nervously. "Something must have come up," she added, her voice full of confidence, but her stomach was tied in worried knots.

"Oh, it's fine," Elenore replied. "I'm beginning to understand ranching tells you what you are to be doing that day, not the other way around. My husband and I thought it was such a romantic idea, thinking we would see each other so often, spend quality time together. Not the case. Here I am in Montana. He's probably got his head stuck in some hole, grabbing a critter by its heels."

Amara chuckled, but was cut off by Elenore's elegant sigh of sudden admiration when she saw the horses. Her hand covered her perfect white smile, a habit she must have picked up before her teeth were perfect and white. "They are so much more beautiful in person!" she exclaimed.

"Charleston chose only the best for you and your husband, Mrs. King."

"May I?" Elenore asked, reaching for a latch, her eyes wide with the anticipation of Christmas morning.

"Certainly," Amara answered.

Elenore entered the stall of the first horse, a dark chestnut mare. When she offered her hand, the mare smelled it for treats, and finding none, blew gently. "She's positively divine! And so soft," she said, running her fingers over the horse's jaw and up to her mane. "Which one is this?"

"I'm glad you like her," Amara said, nodding her head at the chestnut, "this is your horse. She is by far the softest, both to touch and in the bridle. I've been watching my husband ride her for months, and she has always behaved as nothing less than a perfect lady. The gelding next door will likely be your husband's roping horse. He's a gentle giant, quick, athletic, and strong as an ox. But he'll lick your face like a dog, so watch out."

Elenore came out of the stall, glanced in at her husband's tall brown gelding, and followed Amara to the third stall.

"This," Amara said, putting her palm against the large white blaze, which seemed to drizzle down the head of the creamy palomino, "is the sweetest of them all. Charleston selected her specifically to safely carry any guest you may wish to entertain. Like the others, she's only two, but acts as if she's thirty and mothers everything. She won't drive a cow, but she'll gently lull it to where you want it to go, and then softly nuzzle it good night. She'll make a great mother, if you ever have it in mind. And the last one," Amara said, leaning into the stall of a short, gleaming buckskin, "he'll be three next week. He's your all-around, as they call the mounts who can and will do anything you ask, in any weather, any day of the year. Sonny calls him David."

"As in David and Goliath?" Elenore asked. "From the Bible?"

"That's the one," Amara said, smiling proudly. She hadn't realized how much pride she herself had taken in these horses until this moment.

Charleston ambled in, the clanking of his spurs following him at each step. He removed his hat from his head as Sonny followed him inside. "Appears Amara has covered everything, Mrs. King. Shall we saddle a horse for you to ride? Say, the mare in the first stall?"

Elenore's face lit up. "I'd like that very much."

After Elenore had ridden both her horse and the palomino meant for guests, Charleston and Sonny rode the other two, demonstrating everything the horses could do and what should be asked of them. Hours of fun later, everyone sat down to a cup of hot peppermint tea. Amara figured Sonny was happy that the sale was going swimmingly when he kept smiling at her, but later, after Elenore had left, with her four new horses in tow, he grabbed her and hugged her tightly.

"I'm so proud of you," he declared.

"You are?" Amara asked, her face feeling a bit like a lightbulb about ready to pop.

"You were amazing!" He set her securely on her feet.

"I just told Elenore what I knew," she admitted. "It wasn't much. Where the heck were you and Gramps?" she demanded, placing her fists on her hips.

Sonny scratched his neck and pursed his lips thoughtfully. "Just around the corner, listening..."

"What?!"

"It was Gramps' idea!" Sonny laughed and pointed at Charleston, who was attempting to slither into the house unnoticed. "He grabbed me by the arm and told me to wait and watch."

"Gramps," Amara growled, but he ignored her, no doubt pretending to be hard of hearing, and continued on into the house, shutting the door behind him. There was an unmistakable, muffled chortling from behind that same door. "I can hear you!" Amara called.

Sonny grabbed and kissed her. "I love you," he said, and then heaved her over his shoulder like a sack of potatoes, kicking and screaming. "You need a cold bath, I think," he said, as he started up the hill towards the barn.

"No!" she screamed. "Hot! I want a hot bath!"

"That I can do," he said sexily, and turned back towards the house. "One bath, with a hot cowboy in it, coming right up."

Amara laughed, and kept laughing, even when it hurt, as he bounded up the stairs.

Dinner at the Texas Roadhouse in Billings consisted of steak and potatoes with steamed broccoli, green beans, a side of coleslaw, and a basket of fresh baked rolls. It was heaven, and Amara decided dinner out was going to happen more often—pre-dinner spicy cowboy bath included. She had blushed for nearly half an hour after Charleston had asked, "How was the bath?" and Sonny responded with, "Hot."

They enjoyed their dinner, talking as they ate about the fantastic horses Mrs. King had driven away with, how the vibrant autumn colors were beginning to darken, and how the water troughs needed their heaters tested and reinstalled because it had frozen last night and would start snowing any day. After Charleston insisted on ordering everyone a slice of chocolate pie, he revealed a small paper bag he had hidden under the table.

## Holder of the Horses

"I have something very important I need to discuss with you, Sonny," he said, looking solemn. He pulled a pair of handmade horsehair reins from the bag. "I made these reins myself."

Sonny nodded, knowing full well he had. When Charleston offered the reins to him, he refused to take them from his hand. He glanced at Amara for a hint; maybe she knew what was going on. But she was completely unaware of what Charleston wanted to discuss as well, and returned his puzzled expression.

Holding the reins out to Sonny, Charleston said, "These reins symbolize the ranch. I want you to take the reins, son."

Sonny stared, mouth agape, shaking his head. "I can't, Gramps."

Undeterred, Charleston continued holding up the reins. A woman from the next table over looked at them, studying the dilemma, then nudged her husband to peek as well. He glanced over, adjusting his glasses, and smiled as she whispered to him.

"You are more than capable," Charleston said. "If you want the ranch, take the reins."

Sonny looked at Amara. They hadn't talked about it. They hadn't even thought of it. His searching, apprehensive eyes exposed everything she would ever need to know in order to confidently make her part of the decision. He wanted the ranch more than anything. He also wanted her, and wouldn't take something she couldn't see herself being part of—*wanted* to be part of. She supposed he couldn't possibly grasp the fact that she loved the ranch as much as he did. A part of him always had continually questioned her happiness when faced with perpetual isolation and merciless, grueling work.

Laying her fingers over his thick, blond-haired forearm, Amara smiled up at him. "I don't want anything in this world more than I want to be on the ranch with you."

The corners of his lips gradually turned up as the truth settled in, and he began to accept and believe it. His eyes shone as if they would burst as he touched her face. They had found their place in the world, and it was together, on the ranch. It was a liberating relief to acknowledge that their future was clear, undeniable, and definite. And, Amara thought, it would be full of love and life.

Sonny accepted the reins from his grandfather's outstretched fingers.

"The reins are yours," Charleston said, "as is Morris Ranch."

"Thank you," Sonny said, scooting his chair back and embracing Charleston. "You can still live there, though," he added, provoking the group into laughter.

"I think we can finally fill the loft room, too," Charleston said, looking at Amara. "Wouldn't you say?"

"What?" said Amara. She felt her face flush with embarrassment. How did he know? Even she had only speculated. One thing was certain; she needed to stop at a store and pick up a test to be positive.

## CHAPTER SEVENTEEN

Eight Years Later

In the wee hours of the morning, Barley Benson navigated his growling four-wheeler carefully through the bone-chilling darkness. His tires crunched over the frozen ground as he followed the soft glow of dim headlights. There had been snow on the mountains since September, but none any lower so far. October had brought the cold air down from Canada to refrigerate eastern Montana, but now it was officially November. All that was required for their winter blanket to arrive was a little precipitation. Benson shivered.

Not bothering to stifle his sleepy yawn, his drowsy eyes sweeping along the bumpy terrain, he fixed his attention on anything which happened to glow or move. He was a man on a mission. His old woman thought he had lost his grip on his last marble, but damn it, he was sure that if he stayed out, stalking the night and shadowing all its nocturnal critters, he would find the culprit. He would uncover the ghastly little beast that kept plucking away his chickens.

Desperate for something to show to his skeptical wife as the result of his determination, he swooped away from the farm and the coop he had prowled around all night towards the fence line. Truly, he expected to find just what he had been finding all night: nothing. This didn't end up being the case.

\*\*

The harsh ring of the telephone interrupted Charleston's sweet, thoughtless slumber. Squinting into the dark room, which was illuminated only by the soft green numbers on his alarm clock, he fumbled to locate the exact location of the phone's cradle on his bedside table. It continued to scream its annoying high-pitched bells on steroids until he picked it up.

"For Lord of almighty Montana, make it stop. What?" he said into the receiver. "It's four o'clock in the morning." He immediately regretted it. Whoever was calling at this hour, it had to be an emergency. He didn't sleep much as it was, but apparently a couple hours were a couple too many.

"Charleston, it's Benson, your neighbor."

"I know who you are, Benson." Barely, but still. Benson was an acquaintance from a smaller neighboring farm to the west, and he usually kept to himself.

"I'm sorry for calling so early, I wanted to catch you before you left the house."

"You caught me."

"We have a problem. You've got to come take a look at something. And bring your Black-eyed Susan."

Charleston sat up in bed, hurling off the covers. "I'm on my way." Tossing the phone in the direction of the cradle, he propelled himself towards the chair holding yesterday's discarded clothes, and grabbed the holster containing his pistol.

Benson wasn't the type of man to call and meddle in anyone's business, and he expected the same respect of his own privacy. The fact that he had called Charleston all bothered, and so early—or had called at all—had Charleston unsettled. Whether a man was a friend, a foe, or even a stranger, if he called for reinforcements, that's what he was going to get. This was the type of man Charleston was.

\*\*

Amara swung her sweet, lovely, blonde, eight-year-old daughter around and around in the crisp morning air, pieces of hay flying all around them. They were dancing atop the hay pile after climbing to the very top of their own private, pretend Mount Everest. They had made it! Charlie and Amara stood at the top of the mountain of hay, side by side, looking out over the rugged mountains and clouds, which oddly enough looked a lot like a row of horse stalls.

"The top of the world," Amara whispered reverently into make-believe thin air. "We made it, Charlie."

Wrapping an arm around Amara's waist, Charlie laughed. "Yup!"

"You running out of air up there, girls?" Sonny called as he strolled by, his horse's halter hooked on his elbow.

Charlie gasped and hit her knees, clutching her chest. "Daddy, my oxygen canister is empty! I don't think I can make it…" Dramatically, she put her tiny hand over her forehead and fell over into the pokey hay, her bent knee falling limp.

"I think I have to take drastic measures!" Amara called down to her husband. Scooping up Charlie into her arms, she signaled Sonny. "I'm going to throw her down the mountain!"

Charlie's eyes popped open. "What?!"

Sonny's bright blue eyes glistened as he held out his arms expectantly. "I'll catch you, Charlie! Throw her, Mommy!"

Amara began swinging her arms, working up the power to launch her baby girl past the edge of the hay and into her daddy's waiting arms.

"I'm breathing!" Charlie declared, squirming and loosening Amara's firm grip. "You can't throw me off the mountain!"

Amara set Charlie down. "Oh, good! Then we can parachute!"

"Parachute?" Charlie asked. "Off of Mount Everest?"

"Sure, it's our story, isn't it? We can do anything we want."

Charlie's face lit up. "I'll go first! Catch me, Daddy!" With this, she turned towards Sonny, spread her arms out like wings, and jumped.

Amara felt her heart soar with happiness as her small daughter's body launched and flew through the air, nothing but trust between her and the ground. Into the strong, dependable arms of her daddy she plummeted. He caught her with more ease than a receiver catches a perfectly placed football during practice, and squeezed her tight. They giggled.

Never a doubt, Amara thought, as she decided to descend the mountain one foothold at a time, saving her make-believe chute for another day. Besides, she didn't need it anyway; Sonny was there to catch her too if the need arose.

"You jumped in just the nick of time, my little one," Sonny commended his daring daughter as he set her down.

"Daddy! I'm not little anymore!"

"You are compared to me."

"I'm the tallest in my class."

"Is that so? Should I quit calling you my little one, then?"

Charlie wrapped her arms around his waist and smiled up at him apologetically. "No, you can still call me your little one if you want to, Daddy."

Sonny bent down and placed a soft kiss on her forehead. "I love you. Now go load Pops into the horse trailer." Though she turned to do as she was told, she did so while dragging her feet. Sonny called after her, "Get a wiggle on!"

Amara paused to watch Charlie release her pony, Pops, from his stall and skip out of the barn and out of sight, towing Pops behind. Those two had come a long way. It wouldn't be long until her daughter outgrew the deft and dogged pony who had taught her the valuable lessons of patience and persistence. However, since the time hadn't arrived yet, Amara brushed away the thought of losing Pops and commenced to lending Sonny a hand in loading their horses.

Inside the trailer, Pops stood alone, looking at them over his shoulder and stamping his hoof as if to say, "Hurry up, slowpokes." Obediently, they stuffed in two already-saddled young horses. Today's plan was to pitch the young horses, muzzle first, into the workings of the ranch. Young horses benefit greatly through exerting themselves over long stretches of vigorous ground covering work—as was the plan.

After loading the working horses, Sonny and Amara affectionately loaded Nick and Moses, then added Pops' tack to the bed of the pickup. Jumping into the cab of the pickup, arm to coat-covered arm, they fastened their seatbelts, and headed out to meet the school bus. If they didn't meet the bus in time, it would only slow slightly and continue on down the road to the next stop miles away. Amara glanced at the dashboard clock and pressed her lips together firmly. It took roughly five minutes to reach the highway. According to the pickup clock, they had four. She felt Sonny feather the gas pedal in an attempt to make up the time without sloshing the horses around in the aluminum box attached to their hitch.

After they offered their only child up to the big yellow Twinkie, they would drop off the three horses, Pops, Nick, and Moses, and then head off to Benson's place. They would mount up from there on the young horses, meet Gramps, and move the herd of imperiled fillies.

Apparently, Barley Benson had called early this morning, reporting visits by an unseen predator on several recent occasions. It started as mostly small attacks, a few chickens, which Benson assumed had been coyotes or raccoons. But patrolling his fence line adjacent to the Morris Ranch, he'd stumbled across a fresh carcass, the scattered bones and freshly ripped flesh of an adolescent filly. The fact that the ground around it had numerous scratch marks, both large and small, and that the remains were partly buried, possibly having been interrupted by Benson's patrol, was an unnerving warning. The predator was no small raccoon, and it had a hungry litter. If the partly buried meal was any indication, she and her cubs would be coming back.

## CHAPTER EIGHTEEN

To move the herd straightaway and investigate later was a knee-jerk reaction, but time was of the essence. Understandably, moving the herd had Benson clutching his hands together. His grandkids visited him every weekend. If the horses disappeared, what would be next? Naturally, the Morrises sympathized with his apprehensions, but an unlimited supply of unprotected meat would only keep the lion family in dangerously close proximity to Benson's home. It wasn't a question. The horses had to be moved.

They pulled up to the front gate of the ranch just as the long school bus crept into view. Thankfully, it had been ever so slightly behind this morning. Every school-age parent knows the feeling that erupted in the cab of the pickup: a strange mixture of flooding relief with a rush of sadness as the child dashed away and up to the bus, a pink unicorn backpack in hand, the scampering of two tiny feet.

"Meet you right here!" Sonny called after her eagerly.

A bright smile spread across Charlie's face. She waved hurriedly over her adorable shoulder, then climbed the steep stairs onto the bus. The double doors swung shut, swallowing her up.

"We didn't get our hugs," Amara complained, as she waved to all the dark windows, wondering which one Charlie was behind waving back at them.

"We'll get double hugs when she gets home," Sonny said, as he began to back the horse trailer into the stretch of grass he had graveled on the side of the drive, opposite the small family cemetery Amara had taken upon herself to improve.

With permission, and a great deal of respect, she had spent a considerable amount of time judiciously cultivating the barren ground surrounding Grandma Lizzy's grave, and added an abundant, healthy supply of small shrubs and flowers, regularly hauling water to the site herself. She left plenty of space to be later taken up by loved ones to follow, like herself one day—as her mom had predicted. Still sheltered by the old orange-barked ponderosa pine, she had added a round pole wooden fence and wire mesh to safeguard against deer and wild rabbits. She felt deep pride and desire to honor the woman who had planted the seed of love into this family. Unlike her own mom, who had turned her back on Amara when she had strayed from the inflexible mold of who she was supposed to become.

It was a rotten concept, placing one's own ideas above the happiness of one's daughter; a concept her dad had come and freed her from months after she arrived at the ranch.

"*Amara,*" *Mr. Duncan had said, looking down at his lap.*

*He was sitting knee to knee with her. His legs were covered in thin gray slacks, which had cost more than the entire wardrobe she had bothered to pack at the start of this adventure. She remembered thinking how handsomely they broadcasted his long legs and thick, bony knees. The toes of his shiny black shoes touched the toes of her filthy, scuffed red boots, which she had still refused to replace. His face was a mere* two feet away; she could smell the peppermint he had undoubtedly popped into his mouth before exiting his car and approaching the house.

"I love your mother, I do," he managed to convince himself, for who knows what millionth time. His eyes rose, pale green with brown and gold flecks, and she felt a jolt of unease in her stomach as they met hers in a straightforward stare. "My wife, your mom, she's a narcissist."

Amara was nodding her head.

"Not theoretically—literally," he added. "I have learned to cope, and in some ways, she has too. But it's obvious that the template she wants to cram you into, though it may seem like a generous gift to some, is a death trap to a girl whose soul needs to be blown by the wind. Don't be shamed, or hold yourself responsible for her dissatisfaction." He grabbed her fingers, squeezing them so tightly she bit her lip. "Chase your dream, Amara."

Amara tugged her fingers away and wrapped her arms around his skinny neck. "I will." Releasing her was the best thing he had ever done for her, after all those years of allowing her mom's strict and misguided expectations to control her. "Thank you."

His next words shook the ground under her feet. "Don't come back, though. Ever."

Years later, a shiver still ran down her arms, standing the hairs on end, when she thought about it. She hadn't planned to go back to her parents' home, but the finality in her father's voice that day had made it perfectly clear there would be no long-awaited reconciliation, no ceasefire, no stitching of a hem where it had once been ripped away. It was as if the clock had been opened, and the ticking hands had been halted. She was dead to them.

Apart from the chocolate chip pancakes drenched in whipped cream she had devoured in the kitchen with the nanny on Saturdays, and the pink color she had painted on her bedroom walls that her mom had fiercely despised, she was glad to never enter their house again. It seemed like a rotten thing to feel, but nonetheless, it was true.

Sweeping the past back into the past, where dust bunnies fed on memories best forgotten, Amara admired her husband from behind, so strong in the shoulders and perfectly tucked at the hips. He unlatched the horse trailer door, swinging it open and passing her Moses' lead. Moses stood in the center of the opening, he and Nick keeping the younger, more eager horses trapped inside.

"Come on, big guy," Amara clucked at Moses as he stepped down from the wobbly floor to the sharp rocks. She fussed over a few straws of hay in his hair as she escorted him to the corral. "There you go," she said, opening the corral gate for him, gesturing to his clean quarters as though she were his personal butler.

After Moses turned and faced her, she removed the halter from his big head and hung it on the rail. Sonny did the same with Nick, then ushered two rather rambunctious geldings to the side of the trailer and tied them with a quick-release knot. They both gawked around, bumping their big bellies into one another and neighing their apprehensions to anyone listening. No one was. Amara took Pops into the second corral while Sonny retrieved hay bales from the bed of the pickup for all three of them, then loaded the geldings back into the trailer. Their travels weren't over just yet.

Sonny pulled the long aluminum horse trailer onto Benson's lot and parked right next to Gramps' much older, three-horse, bumper-pulled trailer. No telling how long he had been there. He was nowhere in sight, so Sonny and Amara went to work, quickly unloading their mounts, sliding headstalls over the horses' foreheads and long ears, and throwing reins around their necks. They wanted to be back before the school bus dropped Charlie off at the end of her school day, so she didn't have to stand next to the highway alone or walk down a long, empty gravel road past angry cows and hungry coyotes.

The plan was, when the hurried moving of the fillies was done, that Amara and Sonny would trade out the exhausted geldings—which Charleston had agreed to pick up—for their steady steeds, and wait for Charlie to get off the bus. Then the three of them would ride home together: a family date.

Amara's gelding tossed his head like a baby getting its face wiped when Sonny checked the cinch around his belly for the fourth time, ensuring it was good and tight. The saddle wouldn't be rolling off to one side with his wife dangling precariously within striking distance of four powerful hooves.

"I can do that," said Amara, rather defensively.

"I just want to be sure. These two youngsters act as though they've got beehives hanging from their tails."

Amara bent over, pretending to take a peek under the gelding's tail, and he swished it in her face. "He very well may," she said.

Always the worrywart, Sonny was not impressed.

"He'll be fine," Amara promised.

Sonny glanced around, unconvinced, clearly second-guessing his silly idea of taking two green horses. Mostly, he was second-guessing his idea of having Amara on one of them. He trusted her, of course—it was the horse he didn't trust. The poor guy agonized endlessly over the safety of his girls, leaving them free to enjoy life, knowing he always had their back. His first-choice worry was over being a better father than Charlie's so-called Grandpa John, who Charlie had only met once.

The day before Charlie's introduction to her Grandpa John had been dreadful. A spring windstorm had dropped in upon them as sudden and upsetting as a drunken thief—knocking loudly against the walls, wiggling the door handles. The wind had whipped the thinning snow around like egg whites. The following day had been committed to cleaning up the mess.

Amara and Charlie were hunting roofing tiles like Easter eggs in the slushy snow, collecting them in tin pails and hoisting them up to the ravaged roof, where Sonny was tacking them back into place before the spring rains could cause more damage. Charleston was retrieving the back door to the barn from the pasture, where it had landed after being accidentally left open a crack and subsequently ripped from the structure, when John's car sputtered into the drive. It sounded like the poor metal beast of a car was choking on an engine full of rocks.

John stepped from the driver door, wearing a wrinkled pair of blue jeans and burgundy shirt, dirty not from work but from lack of washing. Slicking his thinning hair back with a bony hand, he looked Amara up and down. A smirk spread across his face like dark molasses over an uncooked white muffin—the plain kind, with no chocolate chips, berries, or frosting on top. But when his eyes landed on Charlie, only three years old at the time, he froze. Charlie was buttoned up in a light pink jacket, with multi-colored fuzzy cuffs and a hood. With a little pink mitten, she lifted a wet tile from its hiding spot in a patch of snow-covered grass, bursting with glee, as if she had found a secret stash of mint chocolate cookies.

"Who is this?" John asked.

Sonny was halfway down the ladder when he jumped down, before Amara even registered his sudden agitation. "Stay away from her."

"Your old man would never hurt his granddaughter," John reassured the protective parents now closing in on him, still not daring to take a step towards Charlie. She had looked up at him, confused over the unusual fuss.

"What are you doing here?" Sonny asked.

John opened his arms, palms up, adding a shrug. "To visit."

Amara remembered glancing at Sonny as she scooped Charlie into her arms, trying very hard to read the situation. She knew Sonny didn't have a lick of care for his father, but she hadn't known John to be a physical threat.

"What do you want? Whatever it is, you're not getting it."

"You're a hard son of a bitch—"

"You wouldn't know," Sonny interrupted. "You left her, and me." He took two solid steps in John's direction. "And you're going to leave again. Right now."

John hesitated, then scowled. "Where's the old man? Is he dead yet?"

"Nope," Charleston's gruff voice answered, from where he had leaned a shoulder into the side of the storm-beaten barn.

Caught off guard, a bizarre daze fluttered across John's face, like when a puff of steam escapes from a lifted lid. He turned to Charleston, recovering quickly and turning his palms up.

"Did you come for money?" Charleston asked straight out.

"I...I..." John stammered, evidently not sure how to say no when it *was* money he had come for. "I need—"

"No," Sonny cut in.

John sent him a scalding glare that could have singed the devil's cloak. Sonny didn't so much as blink; he clearly had been boiling for a chance to stand up to the man who had abandoned him, and in Sonny's opinion, had been abandoning him every day since. John was at fault for every moment Sonny had spent blinking tears away from his eyes as a disheartened little boy. The transgression could not be forgiven.

"What do you need, son?" Charleston asked.

Amara detected the softness still lingering there, even after all these years of wayward desertion. She supposed a loving father never completely loses a certain amount of softness for his own child, despite the cost of disappointment after disappointment. Her own father's face appeared at the back of her mind. There was softness there too, despite the cost. Unlike John, her father had deserted her so she could be freed. Was there a remote possibility John had done the same? Freed Sonny from a road of recklessness? It gave her cause to wonder.

"I need to get to Chicago," John answered. "There's an opportunity waiting there. I'm sure it can turn my life around. I'm sure of it."

"What's in Chicago?" Charleston asked.

John's mouth parted as he considered his reply. "An opportunity," he repeated. Charleston nodded once, unable or unwilling to respond. John lowered his head. "I got in some trouble, but I can get out of it by…" He glanced at each of them individually. They were judging him. Amara felt a nudge of guilt for doing so. "Well, never mind. I know what it sounds like. It's not like that. It's on the up and up. I just have to get there, and it'll straighten itself out."

Charleston crossed his arms over his chest. "What's stopping you?"

John rubbed his hands together. "I've got nothing to get there. Not so much as a penny or a peanut to eat."

Charleston nodded to Amara, and she knew exactly what she was supposed to do. Disappearing into the house, she quickly packed a lunch from the simple contents of the refrigerator: pickles, grapes, lunch meat, cheddar cheese, a Tupperware dish of leftover macaroni salad. It was large enough that John could eat on it for days, if he chose to be frugal. She threw it all in a Styrofoam box, adding ice packs from the freezer to the top. When she carried it to the door, Charleston met her there, retrieving his truck keys. Was he going to take John to Chicago?

She stood, stunned, as he turned to her, relieving her of the cumbersome box and placing a kiss on her cheek. "He's my son," he explained humbly, though he didn't have to. She nodded and stepped out onto the front porch after him, Charlie wrapping an arm around her leg.

"Say goodbye to Grandpa John," Charleston instructed Charlie.

Amara felt Charlie's little hand lift, shyly, from her leg. She assumed that Charlie had waved, but she really didn't know because she never took her eyes off Charleston and John. Charleston placed the Styrofoam box onto the bench seat of his pickup. Everyone watched him, perplexed. He circled the pickup, methodically removing his tools as he went. When he was done, he tossed John the keys.

"Say goodbye to your granddaughter, John," he said.

John stared at the keys in his hand, and then looked at the little girl clutching her mother's leg. "What's her name?" he asked. Sonny was visibly blistering under his searing anger.

"Charlie," Amara answered. "After Charleston."

John nodded, and stared at the ground for almost a minute before climbing into Charleston's pickup, behind the wheel.

"Return it when everything is straightened out," was all Charleston said.

And then John was gone, again.

Neither Sonny nor Amara had the perfect parental examples to be followed in life, yet they had made it through the torrential rains of youth, hormones, and the disenchantments of life. Surely, with parents who would always love and care for her, Charlie would come sloshing out on the other side of the torrent as well: soaked through, but blooming with freshly watered aspirations. They would see to it she had plenty of floaties to keep her treading water. Which was a parent's job after all, wasn't it? Keep the floaties inflated. And that was what Charleston had done.

## CHAPTER NINETEEN

After checking that his wife's saddle was on as tight as an arm wrestler's grip, Sonny stuck his boot into the stirrup and swung his leg over the anxious gelding's back. The gelding danced lightly in place, attempting to walk forward, until Sonny took the reins up with his right hand, clutching them with his left as if choking a man's throat and pulling firmly towards his waist. The gelding softly tucked his entire front end and began walking vigorously backward with all four hooves. At this point, Sonny released the animal and waited for Amara to settle onto her own mount.

"Ready," Amara said, as she shoved her cowgirl hat down tightly, nodding to him, a smile touching her lips. Her smiles, whether big and bright or small and fleeting, were the reason why he had been placed under this expansive sky. He hadn't known any purpose other than the ranch until the sweet day he had seen Amara step from the back of her college friend's car in her lacy white dress in Lovell. He had purposely stepped into her path, allowing her to collide into him. He found her to be attractively amusing. And she found him to be appealingly annoying.

Grinning at the memory, Sonny led the way, pointing their path away from the horse trailer, over the pea-graveled lot, and towards the Bensons' green house with cream trim. As the horses stepped onto the narrow concrete walk, which paralleled the front of the house and circled the entire well-kept yard, their hooves clip-clopped along. If they remained on the walkway, the concrete path would take them on a small tour around the entire house, turning a plain yard into a racetrack for laps with bikes still in training wheels. Instead, Sonny and Amara followed the miniature racetrack past the small, clean house and the homemade swing-set in the middle of the side yard—the kind of swing-set built to withstand generations of fun—and headed for the gate at the back right corner.

Sonny listened to the clip-clop of eight medium-sized hooves, filling the early morning air with restrained power and vivacity. The sound, as familiar to him as the thud of his own heart, summoned a sweet nostalgia. It floated across his soul, whispering a longing to stay in this moment.

*Don't let it pass. Don't let it fade.*

Only it did fade. At the small wooden back gate, Sonny stooped and lifted the latch, and they walked through, careful to not bump the fence with their horses or stirrups. The sound, and the sweet nostalgia, diminished. The hard-packed dirt on the other side of the gate turned the clip-clop into a light, deep thud, barely more audible than a scuff here and a thump there.

The sun was giving birth to a new day, melting away the night's freeze, and slowly diffusing the darkness of night with a soft feathery blue like the eastern bluebird—a common visitor to Sandgren's apple orchard. This morning, very few birds could be heard chirping in the distance, calling elegantly, giving sweet farewells to a season passed.

For a moment, Sonny felt a longing whisper on the tip of his tongue, but it evaporated as quickly as his breath. Thinking nothing more of it, he started off at a decently paced trot—a two-beat gait which a horse can maintain for hours. After all, they didn't have forever. The school bus would be on their heels before they knew it. Feeling the sudden pressure of time, he pushed his gelding to lengthen the stride of his trot even more. He and Amara began posting—methodically rising from the saddle when the horse's gait pushed them upward on beat one, and sitting quietly on beat two. Easily they kept pace with the horses' movements, reducing their weight on the youthful, still-strengthening backs.

Sonny felt Amara slide up next to him. Feeling her presence, close and passionate, he fixed his eyes on her. Her attractive, easy way in a saddle distracted him, stimulating his thoughts to flow through his veins in directions best postponed for a hot bath for two and an early bedtime. Her long blonde hair, poured down the back of her jacket, rushed and surged with life like a wild river.

"Amara."

Her serious eyes landed on him as her body lifted and rested with the fast two-beat rhythm of her gelding. "Yes?"

"Stop for a minute."

She lifted a hand immediately, her horse slowed, and she glanced around questioningly. Then she looked back at him, expecting an explanation.

After his horse stopped, he dismounted, wrapped his arms around his wife's waist, and pulled her off her horse. She gasped as she fell into his arms. He lowered her until her feet met the ground, then swathed a hand around and around in her hair and drew her to him. He kissed her, hard, as if it had been years since he had last seen her and would be years until he saw her again. Her surprise disintegrated into hunger, and she returned his sudden need.

In an outburst of aching lust and tender love, he pushed her hat backwards, out of the way, unzipped her jacket, and laid his hands upon her. Cradling her breasts, he embellished her neck with a fury of kisses. Softly, from the back of her throat, a moan escaped and formed into a single word: his name. Luring him and tempting him to take what was his. And he did. Right there, standing between the watchful eyes of two indifferent geldings, until they both lost themselves in marvelous waves of pleasure.

\*\*

Sonny spotted Charleston first, at about a hundred yards off, perched on top of JoJo's back. His gaunt rear rested on the cantle of his saddle, one leg pushed further forward than the other, tilting his entire body. If Sonny had to guess, he was attempting to find a point of release for his aching bones and joints. Sonny had sat like that from time to time after a long day in the saddle, too. Charleston was peering off over the herd of uneasy fillies, giving them roughly another hundred yards of calming space between them.

Despite having pulled up their horses to nearly a crawling pace, the closer Sonny and Amara got, the more uneasy the fillies became. The fillies had been eating, keeping a watchful eye on the lone horse with a human upon its back, apparently sensing no harm but still wary of the man. Now their heads lifted to full attention, all together, as if on the cue of an orchestra director.

It came as no surprise when Sonny's own young gelding's legs began quivering in excitement at meeting his stable buddy, JoJo, here of all places—and even more motivated by the herd of fillies staring up at them, tails raised high. The neighing began. A shrill call from the herd. A return call from the ribs quivering beneath him. Again, from the herd, lower this time, sounding like a chopped chortle. Amara's gelding danced next to him, and she laughed.

"Should we tell him now or later that he's..." She cupped her hand around her mouth, as if he wouldn't be able to hear her that way, "...a gelding?"

"Later." Sonny winked.

"Well, they're not going to settle," Charleston grumbled, "with your two boys hollering like a couple of idiots."

"Considering what they've just been through," Sonny said, knocking his legs against his horse's sides, "I doubt they'll settle any better than you already have them. Let's take advantage of their attention." He spurred his horse ahead.

And that was that—as black and white as newspapers, zebras, and movies from the 1920s. There was no need for snappy memos, brisk briefings, or lengthy meetings. Each of them knew their job. They'd been moving the herds, just the three of them, for years now. Charleston and Amara spurred their horses forward after him, spreading out to their positions.

Sonny felt better on the move, taking action. He couldn't stop taking it personally that his fillies had been targeted. Mother mountain lion knew them for their weakness and lack of experience. His chin dropped, thinking of the poor, dead, half-eaten filly. She had been his responsibility. Her last memory had been one of fright, running as fast as her little spindly legs could carry her, falling further and further behind, as the lead mares took the rest of the young away. Her lungs and hooves growing too tired to keep up...damn it!

His frustration traveled down his body, puzzling the inexperienced gelding he was sitting on. The gelding jigged sideways, wondering what kind of message Sonny was relaying. "Sorry, sorry," Sonny said, as he forced himself to relax, in turn relaxing his partner. Patting the side of the horse's neck, the two took off to get ahead of the herd, in position to lead them away to a recovering pasture.

Sonny had strategically picked a pasture to the northeast, since it was fully swathed by two other pastures. Both encircling pastures were occupied by veteran mother cows—which have a tendency to be hostile and protective. And in the pasture, shacking up with the cows, was their most aggressive bull, Phoenix, named after the mythological bird. "Phoenix" meant born from its own ashes—a symbol of renewal. A perfect symbol in a breeding program.

In any case, a small lion family would have to make it through the cows, and Phoenix as well, to get to the equine youth. And with cubs, they would be far less stealthy and far more easily disrupted, if not outright injured. In addition to the ungulate—hoofed mammal—bodyguards, there would be extra human patrols with daily hay being brought in, so the already-eaten pasture could sustain the horses. It would use up more hay than they had bargained for, but then again, they hadn't bargained on losing their livestock, either. Adjustments had to be made. Hopefully there wouldn't be many further unforeseen setbacks.

Sonny stuck two fingers in his mouth and blew hard, just as Gramps had taught him to do when he was a boy. Spit still came out, but a whole lot less than before. The no-nonsense work of getting the nervous fillies out of the pasture began with the penetrating sound of this high-pitched whistle, and the signal: fingers reaching toward the sky, drawing a large circle over the head. Round 'em up.

Next year's mares began fidgeting, sidestepping, and swishing their tails: what do you want from us? Charleston and Amara replied by quietly pushing, only on the outer edges, careful to not push harder than the band of flighty fillies could tolerate. Sonny slowly, steadily showed them an open door—a way out—a pre-blazed path to safely follow. The three Cs were the important ingredients: calm, cool, and collected. Raging hormones caused raging scattering, all-out sprinting, and in a brave moment, charging. All of which was more likely to go, and end, in pieces, than to be salvaged into order and composure.

The two mature mares, one fat and black with a white stripe down her forehead, and the other copper-colored like a penny, mingled, hidden within the crowd. Sonny could tell Charleston and Amara were keeping an eye on them, waiting on them. The mares would catch on to what was expected first, and then begin assisting with the procedure.

Sure enough, the black one, Mary, started the leading, while the copper one, Tooth (affectionately nicknamed for her abnormally long front tooth) began pinning her ears and imparting silent orders. Mary and Tooth had been chosen as Nanny One and Nanny Two of the adolescents because of their commanding, motherly traits. They had a strong sense of authority and conviction, yet they also possessed a gentle desire to protect and nurture, showing extreme sensitivity to the adolescents' needs. They had done a beautiful job caring for their young, equine bachelorettes. No one blamed them for the death of the filly. If it hadn't been for their guidance, surely the entire herd would have run itself to death, or impaled itself—one right on top of the other—on a fence line or a rocky bluff.

As they started tiptoeing his direction, Sonny lowered his rein hand, granting the inexperienced gelding under him the responsibility of serving as a quiet and focused leader. The assignment would allow the gelding to bud wings of confidence, much like the last little nudge of a parent bird sending its baby over the edge of the outgrown nest. At first, it's scary as hell. But then the little bird realizes it has wings!

Wings! Oh, sweet tender wings! Sonny watched Amara moving with her horse, guiding an entire herd of all different colors and sizes. He could watch her forever. He would never grow weary, never grow hungry, so long as he had her heart. There was no doubt she had his. No doubt whatsoever.

Like the swiftness of a Kansas blue sky transforming to tornado green, there was a stirring in the herd. A shift in the air, so small that a less experienced cowboy would never have felt it. Sonny turned his head, first glancing at the herd. They were walking briskly, trailing behind him in good faith, but their heads had come up. The heads no longer bobbed evenly with their withers, but rather floated above, as if just having received a telegraph. *Ladies, may I have your attention? A handsome stallion just walked into the room.*

Sonny glanced at Charleston next. The more experienced cowboy had undoubtedly noticed the change in the filly's disposition as well and was clearly scanning the surroundings. Something was awry, and with this particular herd's frightful, near-death experience last night still fresh in the breeze, they were not going to think before taking action. The ranchers had only moments to attempt to neutralize the anxiety growing in the herd before some sticky shit hit the fan.

"Hold 'em!" Charleston hollered over all the nervous heads.

At once, Sonny turned his gelding to face the herd, and both Amara and Charleston spread out from each other, each taking a corner. The intention was to hold the herd together, in place, in an effort to create a safe haven in which the horses could settle before moving on. The attempt may have worked had the disturbance not intensified.

Sonny heard the crackling of sticks breaking under a padded foot over the heads of the herd, from Amara's direction. One quick glimpse revealed that her horse was responding nervously, stomping and flinging his head violently when she pulled on his mouth. Commendably, she was still in position to hold the herd, while at the same time requesting the gelding stay with her—under her. The gelding was having none of it.

Damn it. Sonny knew he should have listened to his instinct, instead of her overoptimistic, unflappable faith. So much was riding on this decision—his decision—to move the herd. The decision determined what was to be won or lost. He never should have put his wife's safety in the balance by allowing her to ride an unfinished horse, no matter how confident or stubbornly persuasive she was.

Apparently, there was another soft crackling; Sonny didn't hear it, but the gelding he was riding did, as did all the fillies. They began spinning, wide-eyed, searching for a direction to flee, a horse and rider to challenge. The black nanny mare, Mary, made her way to the outer fringe and stood with her head in the air, like a magnificent statue, facing off with something that had yet to present itself behind Amara. Mary extended her neck and blew through her nostrils with such an enormous force that her entire body pitched forward, then back again. The sound was like a wheezing gust of wind, short and forced, and powerful enough to evoke a vision of an age-old dinosaur issuing a warning or invitation to battle. The fillies all froze. Listening. Waiting.

## CHAPTER TWENTY

As the seconds ticked by, holding the herd was fast becoming impossible. The attention of the fillies was fixed on Mary and her brave stand, blind to the presence of the humans. Upon Mary's very next move, they would all react in unison, without hesitation. Likely in a rush of panic, they would turn and flee like a forceful tidal wave, mercilessly crashing in on whichever rider was in the line of flight. They would either engulf the rider with crushing force like a wall of water, or sweep them up, taking them as a hostage.

"Wake 'em up!" Sonny called, meaning to get the horses' attention back where it belonged, on the riders, as long as they meant to not be flattened.

Working together, and off of each other, all three riders began trotting their horses back and forth. Stop and turn. Stop and turn. The aim wasn't to move the herd, or further irritate them, but to gain their attention. The fillies regarded them with a mere echo of an expression, once bound and yoked, now unrestricted and free. Mary mirrored Amara, back and forth, back and forth—only in reverse—so as to not have her view inhibited. She was spun as tight as a tire swing, ready to be released.

Sonny frowned. It wasn't working. "Whoa!" he called to Amara and Charleston. Halting at once, Charleston met his exasperated gaze, at about the same time Mary reared back onto her hind hooves. In the following seconds, shit was going to fly. Oh boy, was it going to fly.

Like a top, Mary spun around and raced straight at her herd, every thick muscle on her body flexing and thrusting her forward, her stout legs exploding beneath her, giving her a burst of uncontrolled momentum. Run! she commanded her young, innocent, equine bachelorettes. Run! Don't look back!

"Sonny!" Amara screamed, fear lacing her voice. "Look out!" Her horse reared.

The fillies whirled around, hurling themselves forward, not bothering to pick up their skirts first. Bursting from their frozen stances with all the grace and beauty of a terrified victim fleeing from a murderer, they tripped and stumbled along. As Sonny's adrenaline slowed their frantic sprint towards him to a crawl, he could hear their big hearts pounding over the sound of thundering hooves, see their worried-brown eyes turn to petrified white.

"Hold 'em!" he heard Charleston holler, breaking him free from his adrenaline-induced slow-motion picture. "Sonny! Hold the horses!"

They were headed for him all right. A part of him rejoiced; better him than Amara. Squaring off with them—they were still coming on fast. Turning broadside to them, they came faster. He loped, hoping to pull them back around, but they charged on. They weren't slowing, and they weren't going to be swayed.

"Damn it!" This situation was way over the head of the gelding beneath him, but the gelding was heroically defying his inexperience with courage, so Sonny spurred him on.

His valiant gelding quickly rolled around, facing the same direction as the oncoming torrent of hooves just as a crowd of thrashing bodies overtook them. Facing the same direction very well could have saved their lives, yanking them along in the frenzy rather than pummeling them into unrecognizable pieces.

Right as they turned, Sonny caught a glimpse of Amara's horse rearing again. Torn from her horse's back, she sailed backwards. The world around Sonny ceased to make sense as he watched his wife's body disappear beneath the thick cloud of horses and dust. He couldn't see how she'd landed. Couldn't see if she'd hit her head, broken an arm. He tried unsuccessfully to spot her over his shoulder as his horse lurched again and again, trying to stay upright and accelerate to a speed that would keep them from being trampled.

Charleston was riding behind the herd, pacing them, unwilling to lose the horses or Sonny. He hadn't seen Amara's fall. He didn't know she wasn't pacing behind too.

"Go back!" Sonny yelled. "Gramps! Go back!"

It was no use. The rumbling of hard hooves on the ground was too loud. Charleston pushed JoJo harder and harder, and she reached with her neck and pulled with her legs like the warrior mare she was. *Damn it, Gramps. Go back!*

Sonny studied the horses around him, their individual tracks, their dominant leads, for an available hole he could squeeze through. He had to get out. Carrying the additional weight of a man, his horse would tire before the fillies did, causing them to falter and be trampled. A larger concern was getting to Amara. Every ragged breath and beat of his heart ached as he agonized over his inability to reach her. He knew she needed him. He couldn't explain how he knew, he just did. They say people experience premonitions in a moment of life and death, and every cell in his body was screeching like a barn owl in the deepest, darkest corner: *wrong way! Go back!* He had to get back to her.

Before Sonny could make a move within the walloping bodies bashing into one another, a strapping mountain lion leapt stealthily from a tree where it had been crouching, unnoticed, only breaths before. Landing on the withers of the smallest, fatiguing, yellow buckskin on the outside edge of the group, the lion wrapped her enormous paws around the horse's thick neck, sinking her claws and teeth deep into her flesh. A noise like a high-pitched scream escaped the filly's tiny muzzle as her small body collapsed to the ground.

The herd veered left, away from her, unwilling or unable to assist her. A thick grove of trees forced them to halt, triggering a spin. All together, they swirled around like water in a flushing toilet, knocking against Sonny's gelding again. Sonny felt the plucky horse under him stagger and thrash with the fight of a bear. He needed not only solid footing, but a space within the mess to call his own: a place he could drift safely inside the current, unencumbered. What little strength the young gelding had left was certainly burning off—how much could not be determined. Sonny hoped it would be enough. As a complete herd—minus one—they were heading back the way they had come, in a straight line towards where Sonny had last seen Amara.

Her body came into view. She was crumpled on the ground, hugging herself, her horse bolting for the hills in the distance. When her face lifted, Sonny not only saw but felt the fear in her eyes.

*Hang in there*, he sent silently.

"Come on," he encouraged, as he spurred his horse through the exhaustion they were both feeling, their racing hearts petitioning for more oxygen. "I just need one more thing from you. One...more...thing... Bear..." Should this horse's heart not explode and live to see tomorrow, his name would be Bear, and he would never be sold.

"Pull, Bear. Pull!" Sonny pleaded for the horse's legs to run with a force stronger than the wind, stronger than the wave in which they were caught, stronger than all that death stole from life.

Bear did. Bear pulled. And wheezed. White froth escaped his mouth and floated in the breeze like soft feathers until it landed against his slick, sweaty hide. Bear continued pulling, again and again. He pulled for the man who had raised him with a tender touch and a kind word. He pulled for no other reason than he was asked to. Heart thundering above the cloud of dust, he pulled.

Bear pulled Sonny nearly to the front of the rushing herd, but they weren't going to make it. The head horses, including Mary, were going to reach Amara seconds before Bear would. Any one of them could crush Amara's lungs, or kick a hole in her head, before Sonny could get to her.

Instinctively, Amara threw her arms over her head, tucking her chin tight against her chest, hiding her wide, terrified eyes. Sonny could only watch as he waited for Bear to deliver his opportunity. He couldn't allow himself to be caught up in the dread of failing, the horror of missing, the terror of hearing the crack of a hoof against his wife's skull.

*Focus.* He blinked away his sweat, and the doubt. He couldn't fail. He couldn't miss. He couldn't afford to flinch too soon, or allow himself to pause too long.

*Ready.* He had one chance. It was going to be close. He kicked his feet from his stirrups. Bear saw the body on the ground and drifted to the side, disinclined to trample on it and risk falling. *Now!* Sonny sprang from Bear's back, fixing his eyes on his curled-up wife. With a solid thwack, Sonny's brawny frame landed on Amara's trembling, delicate body. Nearly simultaneously, a shot rang out. He had never been so happy to hear her startled whimper and feel her fear under him. It meant she was alive. To him, this was all that mattered. All he was called to do was protect her with his life. He would rise to the call every time. And every time again.

\*\*

It took Amara a moment to realize that it was not a horse which had just fallen on her, but the perfect protective weight, and even the sweet pine scent, of her husband. Nothing could have given her more relief. Sonny was here.

His body pressed down hard, forcing her to flatten herself against the ground, face down. Pain shot through her hip and right arm as he positioned himself so his body covered every inch of her, his chest over her head, pressing her cheek into the dirt, his legs over her legs, his boots cradling hers. He left no part of her uncovered. She was safe now. Nothing could come between them. His warmth pressed closely against her. She could feel his breath inhaling and exhaling heavily into her hair. He was so heavy, and there was a hot, burning sensation in her right hip, but she didn't dare move.

Hooves pounded the earth around them, setting her hair on end like lightning had struck too close. She felt tiny pebbles of dirt in her mouth, grinding between her clenched teeth. Sonny's body jerked. Something had clipped him.

"Sonny!" she tried to call out, but her voice was muffled.

"I'm here," he answered. "I've got you."

Amara felt an enormous amount of pressure bear down on her leg for an instant, then magically it lifted and pressed down on her back. The heaviness disappeared before a shout of pain escaped her lungs. Sonny stifled his shout, growling instead, but he didn't move; he didn't leave her.

Amara squeezed her eyes shut, not wanting to see through the tiny slit between the dirty ground and Sonny's underarm. Frantic hooves hit and struck the ground around her like bombs. Her chest burst with pain. Was it a heart attack, the bloody overworked muscle unable to take anymore? Or was it just pain?

Just pain. What an abnormal thought. Pain was always a part of life, it seemed. It was present during the worst of times, ripping at one's body or soul—in sickness and in health. It was present during the best of times, motivating one to persist, to last, to grow and cultivate, despite the sting.

Amara felt the sudden twitches of Sonny's body taking the brunt of every nudge, bump, and knock. Over and over, she tried to push her body further into the ground, absorbing Sonny into herself so he wouldn't protrude so far above. The horses stomped on him, tripped on him. Even when they jumped, they clipped him hard, and there was a sharp pain on the top of her head where Sonny's chin smashed into it.

Her eyes popped open. Little black dots floated in the way. "Sonny!" she called again over the roar, still muffled by his chest pushing into her ear. Dust had collected against her nostrils and lips, and she could taste it on the back of her tongue.

"I'm...here," he answered.

Amara had to concentrate on sucking in enough air to inflate her lungs. Their legs were bumped, and Sonny's leg fell away from hers. She felt the coolness of the air, another bump, and then Sonny's leg lifted slowly, like it was a great burden, and nestled back on top of hers. The thunder was easing, rolling away. The hair on her arms lay back down where it belonged. The burning in her hip increased as the shaking of the earth slowly faded away.

"Sonny?" Amara whispered, finally able to hear her own voice. He didn't respond. He didn't move. Amara's heart pumped, faster than it had even moments before. "Sonny?" She felt herself begin to panic. "Sonny?"

"I'm...here," he finally answered weakly, still not moving, his weight bearing down on her.

There was a faint pounding of four hooves approaching: just one horse.

"Sonny..." Her voice cracked. "Are you alright?" He didn't answer. Tears swelled up, washing the grit from her eyes. "Gramps is coming. I can hear JoJo's feet. Sonny? Talk to me."

"I...love...you," he managed, his breath ragged.

She didn't know why, but she began sobbing. She couldn't stop, her lips quivering against the sticky ground where her tears were wetting the earth. "I love you too. Hang on, we'll get you help."

Lying there, very still, Amara concentrated on the feel of his beautiful body against hers. The warmth he created. The sweet scent of horse and pine as it drifted into her nose, past the dirt and grime of this awful moment, plastered like wet concrete, still yet to dry, in her nostrils.

"I'm sorry, Sonny…I'm so sorry," she cried. It was her fault he had come back. She had fallen from her horse. With her broken hip and arm, she had failed to move out of the way of the runaway herd.

"Don't…be…" Sonny's voice sounded distant, like his mouth was too slow to shape the words his mind was reluctantly offering. "I'm…not."

JoJo slid to a stop from a dead run, less than twenty feet away from their piled-up bodies. Amara could feel the horse's presence, and could hear her hooves softly tap the ground right before the sound of Charleston's boots began rushing towards them.

"Amara…" Sonny's voice was weak, but she thanked God he was still with her. "It…was…worth…it."

Tears slipped from her eyes like lines of silver. "What was? Please, tell me everything is going to be okay."

"Being…at…the…" his whisper trailed off.

"Sonny?" Amara cried. "Sonny! Please!" Amara wanted to flail, to panic, to run him to a hospital in her arms. Afraid to move him, she didn't so much as flinch. Charleston was almost on them. He would know what to do. "Sonny, answer me!"

"…top…of…the…world," he said slowly, "…with… you."

A great wave of sorrow sucked the breath from her lungs. It may have sounded like gibberish to anyone else, but Amara remembered their conversation under the stars all those years ago. He was talking about Mount Everest. He had told her then that, just like those climbers, he was at the top of the world. She had asked him if he thought the long, death-defying journey up the mountain would be worth it for only a few moments of the spectacular view. However, just like the climbers, Sonny's time at the top of the world wasn't to last. Amara's grief exploded from her heart. A great wail escaped her, burning her throat, scorching her eyes.

"Sonny…" she sobbed. "Please hold on!"

In the very next instant, Charleston was at their side. Amara could see his knees touching the ground, just outside the little slit between the ground and the underside of Sonny's arm. "Oh, God," he muttered. He sounded sick. "Sonny, my son. Oh no."

Sonny groaned as his grandfather gently, so gently, rolled him off Amara onto his back. Charleston had his jacket in his hand already, tucking it under his head.

"No," Amara whimpered. She didn't want him moved. She didn't want him taken away. She wanted to stay with him, like he had done for her.

"Take…care…of…" Sonny struggled, breathing so shallowly that Amara hadn't been sure he was still breathing at all until he spoke. "…them…Gramps."

"I will, son. I promise." Charleston touched Sonny's lifeless arm, more lightly than a butterfly.

"Catch…Bear…"

Charleston squinted in confusion. The attack had been a cougar. Sonny was delusional. He shuffled away quickly, snatching his cell phone and cussing under his breath in frustration. The familiar tone of numbers being pressed softly sounded as he punched them in with his shaky fingers. For the first time since Amara had met Charleston, his gruff voice revealed a boundless pang of distress, as he begged for help from some person miles and miles away, a person who didn't know Sonny, and didn't care—not really.

Wiggling awkwardly, Amara scooted inch by inch until the tip of her chin just touched Sonny's shoulder. With what appeared to be the most immense agony Sonny had ever endured, he rolled his head, little by little, until he was face to face with her. His stare was nearly empty, his eyelids blinking slower than a drippy faucet. Amara couldn't help but notice the dark red wetness seeping into Charleston's shirt.

"No," she whispered, shaking her head from side to side, unable to accept what was before her eyes. "Please don't leave me, Sonny. Please hold on. I love you so much." She reached up with her right hand and touched her fingers to his cheek. It was pale and cold. "Please, Sonny. Please..." His eyelashes fell closed. "Open your eyes, Sonny. Stay with me, baby."

When he didn't, she began praying, *please take me too. Please take me too.*

Amara felt Charleston touch her arm tentatively and she jumped, wincing.

"Amara?"

She looked up at him, her vision blurry. She didn't care if her vision was blurry. She didn't care if her face was covered in mud. She didn't care if she died, right here, next to Sonny's side. She was where she belonged.

"Are you hurt?" Charleston asked, sounding exhausted.

There was no doubt that her hip was broken, as was her arm. But it didn't matter. Amara shook her head, placing her chin back against Sonny's shoulder. Feeling his fingers twitch against her stomach, she carefully picked up his heavy arm, bent the elbow, and placed her face in the palm of his hand.

"Meet...me..." Sonny's faint voice murmured, "...at...the..."

Amara waited patiently as he struggled, trying to snag and hold each word as they vanished like sparks falling from the sky.

"...front..."

She yearned to tell him to reserve his strength, but she didn't. Instead, she listened, hanging onto every word.

"...gate. We'll...ride...home...together."

There was nothing she wanted more. But even amidst her shock, she knew that he was not referring to meeting her today. Nor the simple, childlike family date they had made with Charlie this morning. Oh, Charlie... how would she tell Charlie?

"I'll be there," she wept, placing a kiss on his dry lips. "I'll be there." Her tears slipped down her cheeks and dripped on his face. "I love you."

His lips formed the warmest weak smile she had ever seen. Then his eyes closed and his smile slowly slipped away, like a magnificent rainbow slowly disappearing as the sun's light creeps behind the clouds. And he was gone.

# CHAPTER TWENTY-ONE

Amara's anguished sobs pierced plum through Charleston's heart. His phone slipped from his grasp, his mouth gaping. Benson knew where they were, more or less. He would be here any minute. The plan was to get Sonny to the ambulance. But it didn't matter now. They were too late. His grandson lay dead on the ground, his granddaughter lying next to him, yearning to die along with him.

A part of him wanted to just lay down with them, close his eyes, and finally give it all up. Let the ground soak them up like it had soaked up Sonny's spilled blood. Just like the saying "No use crying over spilt perfume", once blood is spilt, you can't put it back. Only there were plenty of reasons to cry. Of course, he had grieved for Lizzy with every breath since the moment she died, but this was different. He had known she was dying. Sonny hadn't been dying. He wasn't supposed to die. He'd just taken over the ranch and started a family. This wasn't supposed to be happening. Charleston covered his face with his callused hands.

It seemed like hours, kneeling there, face in his hands. It could have been a minute. It could have been an hour. He didn't know, didn't care. Like Amara, who was still clinging to Sonny's body, sobbing, he really didn't have anywhere else he wanted to be. Nothing in this world would convince an old man that he could tolerate losing his son, even if that son was a grandson. He felt gutted, like a living fish. All of the important things that kept him going had been taken away. Charleston felt his fist pound the ground in anger.

At the purr of an approaching engine, Charleston knew what he had to do. Like an empty corpse, he rose on his shaky legs and stood there, tottering, wondering if he could do what he needed to do. When the truck veered sharply, having spotted them, he knew there was no choice. A single tear spilled over onto his leathery, wrinkled face before he swallowed the rest back. He wasn't done being strong. He had someone else to take care of. Two, in fact.

Crouching behind his granddaughter and wrapping his arms around her, he whispered, "Amara, it's time to let him go."

Her head shook from side to side, her body stiffening. "No."

Benson and his wife, Sarah, stepped from their pickup, and Sarah's hand went straight to her mouth. Barley looked over his shoulder, and for the first time, Charleston remembered the mountain lion and her cubs. If they didn't move quickly, there would be the horrible tragedy of unwanted company to add to the nightmare. Steeling himself, Charleston began pulling Amara's shoulders away from Sonny. At first, when she screamed, he believed it to be the pain from her heart surging uncontrollably, and it had been at first, until his moving her caused an entirely different scream to begin heaving in and out.

"Stop, Charleston!" Sarah called, her hand reaching out towards him, looking like a victim with a gun being pointed at her. Under the elbow of her other arm, she squeezed a thick blanket. "She's hurt!"

Charleston immediately stopped, glancing first at Sarah then back at Amara. Those sad hazel eyes looked at him, full of pain of all sorts. "Where are you hurt?" he asked, supporting her weight on his arm, afraid and unwilling to lay her back on the ground.

"My hip, it's broke," said Amara with a grimace, "and my arm." She moaned, the pain clearly building.

Studying her face, streaked with dirt and tears, Charleston's mind spun. The loss of Sonny had him reeling. Now Amara lay next to him, hurt herself, having not said as much. He felt crushed by guilt for having not tended to her sooner. Dear God, what other injuries might she had sustained?

Sarah had picked up her pace, reaching them in a few strides, distracted from the horror of the situation by her old instincts as a nurse. A nurse's instinct never retires. "Don't move her!" she ordered. Charleston nodded, but refused to scoot aside. Sarah stooped down, checking Sonny first.

"He's gone," said Charleston. His firm, angry tone surprised him. It wasn't Sarah's fault. She had come, on her own accord, to help. Though he knew Sarah wasn't to blame for Sonny's death, that didn't make it any easier to accept.

Sarah's eyes turned downcast, unfairly taking the guilt of a failure that wasn't hers to take. Charleston should have apologized. He *wanted* to apologize—really—but he couldn't suppress the neverending merry-go-round of dizzying emotions enough to practice civility.

Sarah shifted her attention to Amara, and performed the world's quickest look-over while opening and spreading the blanket over her. Without permission, she began transferring Amara's weight from Charleston's tired arm. "I've got her," she said, jerking her head in Sonny's direction, silently indicating that Charleston had another job to do right now.

In a way, Charleston was relieved that Sarah had made the call. He was feeling more torn between his grandson's empty body and his granddaughter's hysterical shock than he could have ever plausibly expected. He supposed it made sense. Sonny's dying words had been, "Take care of them, Gramps." Since Sarah was here, he was afforded the opportunity to also take care of his grandson properly. After that, he would honor his grandson's request. He would take care of them. Amara and Charlie were just as much his family as Sonny had been when he was just a wee boy. This time, however, he was all alone.

Charleston shook his head, weighed down by immeasurable regret. Regret born of lost days, lost moments. He lifted his stiff, weary bones off the hard ground. Barley Benson was standing at his side, looking mournfully at the entire scene. Charleston hated subjecting an acquaintance to this, but he was grateful to Barley nonetheless. Someday he would tell him as much, but today, he just accepted Barley's gentle back pat with a single grim nod.

Amara curled into a ball and cried as if her soul was being ripped from her as Charleston and Barley lifted Sonny's lifeless body. With all of the grace that one would use to fold an American flag and hand it to the outstretched hands of the spouse left behind, the two older gentlemen loaded Sonny into the back of the pickup, carefully laying the body of the boy Charleston had raised onto a thick pile of blankets Sarah had prepared there. A bucket of clean towels stood next to him, no longer needed, but there just the same.

Charleston couldn't help but notice how strangely peaceful Sonny's face appeared amongst the chaos. Grieving was always assigned to those who were left behind, as it was for Amara. But in this moment, looking down at Sonny's serene expression, Charleston felt Sonny's consent to forgo this time of mourning for now. Rather than fall into a pit of darkness, he had to accept that Sonny was where he was—safely on the other side. It was Charleston's job to take care of his girls, and the business of hunting down the hunter.

"Alright, Sonny," he agreed, placing the backs of his cool hands against his own hot, upset cheeks. As if on cue, he heard Amara call for him and hurried to her side, helping to lift her and carry her to the cab.

"I'm sorry, Gramps! I'm sorry! I'm sorry!" she said over and over again, in between grimaces.

He frowned down at her. "It's not your fault. It's no one's fault." He slammed the pickup passenger door, leaving Sarah to care for his granddaughter for now. Climbing into the back of the pickup, Charleston took one last ride with his grandson.

**

Apart from all the horror that had transpired over the course of this awful day, Charleston felt an odd sensation of comfort. Perhaps it was the unmistakably serene expression on Sonny's face, or the consoling knowledge that Amara was in surgery and being cared for. Or maybe it was the presence of his great-granddaughter, Charlie, asleep on his lap.

He was sitting on a mildly comfortable couch, with a mildly annoying fabric pattern of zigs and zags, in the waiting room of the hospital. Charlie had cried nearly as hard as her mother when he delivered the awful news. He hadn't wanted her to make a spectacle and embarrass herself at school, and he hadn't wanted to tell her while he was driving. So he chose to tell her once he was parked in the hospital parking lot. She had scanned around inquisitively, but being the clever girl that she was, she glanced at him once, then anxiously reached for the door handle. He had stopped her by grabbing her by the elbow.

"Hang on there, Charlie." Where was he supposed to start? Was there an appropriate sentiment that could have made it easier? The imprinted image of Sonny's face, set so still, had covered his eyes so he could barely see through it to Charlie, sitting only a couple of feet away. He wasn't good with words. He was good with work. Work had always been enough to explain just about anything. Not this time. Not for this. "Your daddy is gone," he said, as gently as his coarse voice could muster.

Lack of comprehension, or disbelief, froze Charlie's young face. Saying nothing, she waited for an explanation, or the punch line. Her eyes flicked quickly at the hospital, surely wondering why they were here, and clinging to a sliver of hope that Daddy was only gone to the hospital. Not dead gone.

"He's not here." Charleston wrapped his callused hand around her tiny, trembling chin. "Mommy is. Your daddy saved her so you would never be alone." He had never seen a small body rock with such sadness in all of his days.

Now he sat on the mildly comfortable couch, desperately trying not to think about the itch on his ankle, afraid to disturb Charlie. He watched over her while she slept, hoping she was finding a place of calm within herself so her tender heart could rest, away from the world crumbling down over the top of her innocent, blonde head. Tomorrow she would wake to an entirely different way of life; a life in which neither she nor Amara had Sonny to make the world feel lighter and brighter. Besides him, they were alone now. And he was an old man with joints grinding when he moved, a tired back, and a dwindling amount of days left.

Charlie flinched, drawing his attention back to what mattered. Well, it wasn't his time to go yet. Sonny's girls needed him. Lizzy would just have to wait a little longer. She would understand. In his mind, he and Lizzy were both staring down at Charlie's face, still rounded at the edges like the child she was. Her flawless skin and rosy cheeks appeared to be crafted of innocence, if innocence were a tangible fabric that could be woven into perfection. He was reminded of the serenity surrounding Sonny, too.

Charleston sighed. It would be too much to hope a calm like that would find him in his sleep, so he resisted the urge to rest his heavy eyelids and lifted his paper coffee cup to his lips. The bitter, black liquid had grown too cold for his liking, but he sipped anyway. Better to endure the bitter cold in the cup than the bitter cold of an unrestrained mind. Nightmares, daymares… weren't they all sides of the same hull?

He sincerely hoped Amara wasn't having to relive the day over and over while in her anesthesiologist-induced slumber.

## CHAPTER TWENTY-TWO

Amara barely remembered anything about her hospital stay, other than two very specific things.

The first was that she was continuously plagued by vivid dreams and graphic flashbacks, all painfully hammering home that Sonny was gone. Each time she fell asleep, her dreams harshly brought back the sensation of Sonny's warmth protectively enveloping her, followed by crushing pain and death. There was no escape, for every time she woke, the devastation of reality would press down upon her, squeezing every single sensitive nerve until she exploded. Her brain having disassociated her from any embarrassment, she thrashed and screamed in complete and overwhelming fits of grief. The nurse would come quickly to her aid, bend over her, cooing and shushing, and the raw stabbing would succumb to a deep sleep, where it started all over again. There was absolutely no release, anywhere.

The second thing she remembered was that Gramps and Charlie had visited every day. At the time, she had vaguely presumed their visits were happening after school, but she knew now that Charleston had kept Charlie home to allow her to grieve in private. Of course, that made sense. Sadly, the precious times they were there by her bedside were blurred and indistinguishable through a thick haze of medication and unhappiness. Able to hang onto only a few fleeting seconds from each visit, she barely registered they were there before Charleston quietly escorted his granddaughter out again.

Out to where? To rest? To play? To eat? She didn't know, she hadn't asked. Had she been more aware, she may have wondered how Charlie was coping, what she was doing during the day, how she was sleeping at night, what Charleston was feeding her. Had she been more aware, she may have been concerned that Charlie might have been living on coffee and peanuts. However, the medications easing the ache of her broken bones and lessening the sharp, piercing hole where Sonny had been worked feverishly to block thoughts and emotions. The idea was to facilitate her ability to cope and sleep. As it was, the medication successfully brought her to sleep—through nearly everything, apparently—but failed in providing comfort, either for her or her tiny, neglected family. It had briefly occurred to Amara, once, that Charleston may have felt the need to contact her parents. She hoped not.

\*\*

Standing in the kitchen, staring up at the barn from his favorite window, Charleston dialed the number to reach Amara's parents and pressed the phone to his ear. He regretted having snooped through her things to find it, but he was desperate. She was struggling to cope and he didn't know what else to do. After the third ring a hopeful voice answered.

"Amara?" Mrs. Duncan's voice answered on the other end of the phone.

"No, this is Charleston Morris."

There was a dissatisfied grunt. "Mr. Morris. What has your son done now?"

"Died."

There was a short silence.

"I assume Amara wants me to come and rescue her now, does she?" Mrs. Duncan asked. "I warned her about this."

Charleston ground his teeth, working his jaw.

"Tell her I won't come. She can ride a bus if she likes, but I will not roll a car tire across your scheming pile of dirt. When she gets home—"

"She's *already* home," Charleston interrupted. "And she's not yet asked for me to even speak to you. I'm only calling out of...well, I called. Let's leave it at that."

"Your meaning, Mr. Morris?"

"I figured you ought to know, Amara fell from her horse. She's in the hospital. She's alright, but she's extremely upset about losing Sonny."

"This is the first I have heard from any of you. She chose him over me."

Charleston hesitated, taking time to breathe. "You're her mother. I think she, and Charlie, may need a mother's comfort to get through this."

"*Was* her mother," Mrs. Duncan corrected. "Amara's a grown woman now, making her own choices. I told her I would not support this. And I won't." She must have heard the faint rustle of him lowering the phone, preparing to disconnect the line. "Wait," she said. "Who's Charlie?"

He raised the phone back to his ear and tentatively scratched his chin. "Your granddaughter. Her name is Charlie."

"Charlie?" Her voice raised an octave. "And it's a girl?" she asked, conveying deep dissatisfaction. "Please tell me it's short for Charlotte."

"Charleston, actually."

"Oh God! How hideous. Well," she huffed, "tell Amara to take a bus, but leave the child. I don't want any part of you or your manipulative son in our lives. It's a clean break or—"

Charleston slammed the phone down so hard the thin black casing shattered, tiny pieces scattering across the countertop. A few pieces tumbled to the floor with a quiet tinkling. Standing motionless, he wiggled his mustache, waiting for composure to return. Charlie would come down from her room if he made a ruckus, and Lizzy would have insisted he not act on a fit of rage in front of a child—not in front of anyone, preferably, but at least not a child. So he stood there, desperately clinging to the soothing memory of Lizzy's gentle face, and hoping Charlie didn't come down in search of a snack and find Gramps frozen in the kitchen.

It took nearly ten minutes before he was cool enough to move. Ten well-spent minutes. For a second later, he walked into the living room and found Charlie already sitting there, flipping through a picture book of *The Runaway Bunny* by Margaret Wise Brown.

The entire family knew the story, and could all damn near recite it flawlessly. Amara used to read it to Charlie all the time. It was a sweet story of a little bunny who imagined running off to all sorts of places, and embarking on all sorts of made-up adventures, in search of the limits of his mother's reliability. With each testing scheme, his mother assures him, she would run after him. No matter where he went, or who he wanted to be, she would be there. He would never be alone. It was a lesson both Amara and Sonny felt was important.

\*\*

The day the hospital released Amara, the nurse dressed her in a navy blue, ankle-length polyester dress with long sleeves. She had never seen it before. Charleston pushed her in a wheelchair down a series of long, boring halls, while Charlie tailed behind, carrying a vase of flowers from the hospital room Amara hadn't recalled seeing before. Out in the cold air, she found herself grateful for the new, scratchy dress. It was warm. Luckily, Charleston's pickup was already waiting for them, as if by some sort of hospital magic. For the life of her, Amara couldn't wrap her foggy mind around how it had gotten there. Hadn't she come in Benson's truck?

Charleston wrapped his thin, plaid-covered arms around her weak and tender torso, gently lifting her from the wheelchair. She felt her feet brush the ground, and she pointed her toes to help lighten the load of her weight pulling against his grasp. The smell of his aftershave reminded her of Sonny, but Charleston was not Sonny. She felt his arms quiver as he set her on the passenger seat and fastened the seatbelt around her.

Once he closed the door, her heart felt like it was bleeding. She imagined it bleeding all over the seat, onto the floorboard, seeping out of the doors, and dripping onto the concrete. That was how it felt, anyway.

Vaguely, she registered Charleston and Charlie climbing in the driver-side door, fastening seatbelts, and sitting in silence as they drove for a long time. Despondently, she stared at her lap, not bothering to look out the window. She didn't want to appreciate the beautiful view, and she sure as heck didn't want to realize they were passing by something she recognized, tormenting her with memories of what had been.

Back at the ranch, she was woken by Charleston's arm once again gently sliding around her waist. She flinched. She felt as though she had been trampled; a full comprehension of what Sonny had done for her cut through her like a knife. The love of her life had taken the brunt of that trampling. The trampling had been hers to bear, yet he had run to her, willing and eager. He became her shield, taking the punishment of her fall. He fervently forfeited whatever cost was required so she could go on. So she could live.

"Amara," said Charleston's affectionate, gruff voice. "We're here." She looked, blinking, trying to focus on where "here" was.

Outside her window, she saw the little fenced area of the pretty, well-tended bushes she had worked so hard to plant and water to honor Grandma Lizzy, and the family to follow. The flowers were gone now, it being too cold. She saw Grandma Lizzy's grassy grave, and next to it, a large pile of fresh dirt had been patted with care until it was smooth.

As if they were being painted on the scene, one by one, Amara began to notice other people there, sitting in white plastic chairs. A preacher. Mr. and Mrs. Benson. Rod and Anita Sandgren. And Charlie, whom made her way over, still holding the vase of flowers.

"Come," Charleston whispered hoarsely as he pulled her to himself. "I'll carry you to your chair. I'm sorry I didn't think to pick up a wheelchair."

Once they were situated, the preacher began speaking. "Greater love hath no man than this, that one lay down his life for his friends. John 15:13," was the only line of the entire sermon Amara heard.

Pain burst like a spike through her soul and impaled her heart. She had known that kind of love. She had its sweet freedom. She had its burning and inextinguishable flame. She had happiness. She had Sonny. Now he was gone. He had left her behind. He left her to live in his place, he taking her place in death.

Their few friends there walked by her, touching her softly with a hand, expressing brief, apologetic words of sympathy. But she neither felt nor heard any of them. Her focus was set on the pile of fresh dirt where Sonny had been laid. Her heart yearned to be there, beside him. As their guests disappeared, one after another, erasing themselves from the painting in the same way they had come, Amara sat, staring. When at last they were gone, she slipped from her chair and crawled to Sonny's grave.

"Amara," Charleston began, but he must have changed his mind, or she had blocked him out, like she had everyone else, because he let her be.

She lay down on the edge of the dirt, curling up next to the place Sonny was buried like an abandoned seed—helpless, fruitless. Closing her eyes, she forgot to care about anything else in the world except Sonny and her promise to meet him. He had said he would meet her here, at the front gate, and they would ride home together. Well, she had come. She was here.

It was a tug on her shoulder that woke her. Charlie was standing at her feet, dusting off her matching blue dress, and Charleston was above her, drawing her body upright. She spotted Charlie's flowers resting over Sonny's grave. Charleston slid his arm under hers.

"No!" she cried. She didn't want to leave Sonny. She didn't want to go on living without him. She wanted to stay.

"Come on," Charleston said, as hushed and soft as a light breeze. "It's time to go home. I've got you."

"No..." But her body was heaved from the ground, with or without her willingness. She wasn't strong enough to put up a fight.

"Is Mommy okay?" Charlie asked, worry in her voice. "Should we take her back to the hospital?"

"No," Charleston answered. "She needs to be home, with us."

Close to Charleston's chest, Amara felt the tears break. They soaked her cheeks and ran into her gaping mouth. Why wouldn't they leave her be? Couldn't they just let her curl up in her sorrow until it ate her away?

Inside the pickup cab, Amara and Charlie rested their heads together. Once at the ranch house, Amara couldn't bear seeing it. "He's not here. He's not here," she couldn't stop herself from muttering. The words just kept spilling from her mouth as she shook her head from side to side.

"*We're* here," she heard Charlie whimper. "*I'm* here, Mommy."

At Charleston's touch, Amara instinctively draped her arm around his neck and rested her heavy head against his bony shoulder. She could feel his chest heaving, and hear his breath whooshing out of his nostrils as it blew across her bare arm. But his legs felt strong, and never wobbled as he carried her up the creaky wooden porch stairs.

As he softly placed her onto her familiar bed, she pried her eyes open enough to see his gray mustache twitching as he adjusted the pillows beneath her head. The smell of Sonny floated up from the sheets and blankets, filling her nostrils with sweetness and sorrow. Soon Sonny's scent would fade, and the last trace of him would be gone forever. Charleston's rough hand wiped her hair from her face, tucked the fragrant covers around her. When their eyes met, she felt the sting of shared sadness. Had he caught a whiff of Sonny too?

Turning away before Amara could see a glaze form over his eyes, Charleston guided Charlie from the room, placing a single aged hand with bulging knuckles from too many years of overuse upon her small shoulder. There they left her, to sob it out or soak it in. She wasn't sure which. Maybe both.

In all honesty, Amara would never remember how many days she spent in her and Sonny's bed, sobbing it out or soaking it up. From time to time, Charleston came in and sat on the edge of the bed, forcing her to sit up and take bites of sandwiches or soup and sip on some sort of salty-flavored water. She had hated both. But mostly, she just hated sitting up, which she felt whispered of an unspoken pressure for her to move forward. Her nighttime wailing made it clear that wasn't going to happen yet.

As she cried uncontrollably one morning after waking from a dream where Sonny's face was as fresh and real as a pinch, Charleston appeared with a small glass of water and her pills. Perched on the edge of the bed, with his scrawny legs crossed, he picked up one of the books he had left there—always of the Western variety—and begin reading to her by the glow of the bedside lamp. His calm, rugged reading voice placated her anxiety, and both of their nerves.

Lying there, listening, she had a feeling of being imprecisely stuck, somewhere between what she had known to be the perfect past and what was now the ever-painful present—staying in neither. Rather, she floated back and forth at the whim of some unseen force. She imagined it was her and Sonny's love. But if their love was strong enough to traverse worlds, then why did she feel so weak?

In the days to follow, Charleston dragged her out of bed and shepherded her to doctor's appointments, which she attended physically but blanked out mentally—even when the stitches were removed—until he lay her back in bed again. Irritatingly, he also began bringing only one pill at about just the time the bones in her arm started to throb under the cast. Without sedatives and anti-depressants, her anxiety spiked higher, and her depression sunk lower than she thought she could bear. She would waver between hyperventilating restlessly and sobbing wearily—and, she suspected, in and out of sanity. But by the force of her and Sonny's love, not for each other but for Charleston and Charlie, she began to survive, one ragged breath at a time.

One morning, Amara woke to the sunshine shining through the blinds, at last able to think clearly. Charlie had woken her, having crawled into bed with her. Her blonde head plopped down onto Sonny's pillow, evidently unafraid that using his pillow might wear the scent of sweet pine away. Amara feared it would, but didn't say anything.

Charlie's solemn face mirrored her own: tired and sad. She missed Daddy, there was no doubt, but she also missed Mommy. Both of them not quite sure what to do, they laid together, staring, allowing their tears to quietly slip from the corners of their eyes and soak tiny spots onto their pillows.

"I love you, Mommy," Charlie said at last.

"I love you too, Charlie," Amara whispered. It was the first thing she had muttered in possibly weeks.

Suddenly feeling the emptiness between them, Amara pulled her daughter close and held her tightly. Charlie quivered as she cried, letting everything she had dammed up finally flow out in gushing streams like melting snow in the spring.

"I was alone," Charlie sniffed. "Gramps said Daddy saved you so I would never be alone."

Charlie's words were a stab to Amara's heart. She had allowed herself to be so selfish, so consumed with her own mourning, that she had left her baby girl all alone. "I'm so sorry, baby."

"Please stay with us, Mommy," Charlie said, pulling away, looking straight into her eyes. "Me and Gramps need you."

"Gramps and I," Amara corrected, grinning softly. Then she pulled Charlie back to her bosom and closed her eyes. "I will, baby. I need you too."

After a few minutes, they heard Charleston calling for Charlie to wash for breakfast. Her body wiggled, legs flopping like a fish, until she slipped off the bed. Her bare feet pitter-pattered across the wood floor. As she cracked the bedroom door, she gave her mother a shaky but relieved smile and slipped out. It was the first time Amara could remember feeling something other than hurt. It may have been weak, but like a muscle, weak was something to build on.

## CHAPTER TWENTY-THREE

When Amara came tottering lopsidedly into the living room with the use of the wooden cane she had found propped up against her bedside table, Charleston looked up at her from the counter where he was dishing plates without even a hint of surprise. Charlie, perched on the bar stool, appeared optimistically startled.

"Called your rehabilitation therapist. You start tomorrow morning."

"Great," Amara groaned. "Good morning to you too."

"Morning started four hours ago," he said in his customary gruff voice. "You're—"

"Late," Amara finished for him. "I know," she said, carefully lowering herself onto the couch.

"Here, Charlie," Charleston said, holding a plate of eggs and toast out to her. "Take this to your mom."

"Yes, Gramps."

In addition to Charleston's traditional gruffness and Charlie's unquestioning obedience, the vibe in the air was one of notable gloom, with a thin and brittle lining of mild gladness. Amara presumed the perceived gladness was due to her reemergence. They were daring to hope, like an unholstered pistol—with the trigger guard meticulously locked to be safe. Then again, perhaps she was assuming too much. She had only just recovered even a marginal capability to reason with the pain of her loss—their loss—reflecting on the way things were without completely crumbling to pieces. Even so, she could feel even this feeble capability beginning to disappear. She could feel her heart beginning to bleed again, saturating and disintegrating the paper-thin layer of fragile strength between her heart and the rest of the world.

Amara looked at her lap as Charlie set the plate of plain scrambled eggs on her thighs. Her stomach turned, twisting round and round like a silkworm hanging in the wind. The acid inside her was bad enough without adding eggs. Guiltily wondering if Gramps was making more, she stared at them. It wasn't that she didn't like eggs, or her stomach wasn't empty; in fact, she had never remembered a time it had been so empty, and her ribs and hip bones were almost sticking out.

But unlike ribs and bones, the heart was harder to find. A broken heart is veiled from the knowledge of those passing by. Though shattered like glass into a million fragmented pieces, those shards and splinters stayed concealed. But still, it nicked at the innards of grief-stricken Amara until she barely felt hunger anymore.

Charlie retrieved her plate from the kitchen and returned to climb up on the couch next to her. "They aren't as bad as they look," she whispered. "Except for the mushrooms. Those are bad. Aren't you hungry, Mommy?"

"Not really."

"Try a bite," Charlie coaxed, turning the roles of parent and child around.

"I can't."

"Is it too hard, Mommy?" Charlie asked, dropping her own fork. "I can help you."

"No, it's not too hard. I'm just not hungry, baby."

Charleston appeared in the kitchen archway, with his infamous coffee cup in hand. Leaning against the wooden arch, he took a sip. "Headed to town today."

"For what?" Amara asked, willing to talk about anything other than eggs.

"Been looking into hiring some help."

Amara dropped her fork. She didn't want it anyway. "We don't need help. I know everything that needs to be—"

"You're in no shape."

"I *can*," Amara replied. She knew it wasn't fair to Charleston to argue the point. He had been, and would continue to be, working twice as hard, even if she had been helping—which she hadn't been, she regretted. But if they hired someone to do Sonny's job, wouldn't that person be taking Sonny's place? No one could take Sonny's place. She wouldn't have it. She couldn't bear it. She'd rather do the work alone.

"Amara, you're in a cast."

She moved the plate off her lap and set it aside. "It'll heal."

"Until then?"

"I can be Mommy's arm," said Charlie. "I'm not strong, but I'm tough."

"And smart," Amara added.

"Damn right." Charleston raised his mug proudly towards his littlest cowgirl. Charlie's face beamed, lighting up the living room with the flush of youth.

"Gramps, language," Amara reminded him, with less zeal than she would have normally. She was pretty sure he cussed every now and again just so she would correct him. There was a part of him that liked having women around to correct him.

"But you have school to tend to. That's your job," Charleston said gruffly.

Charlie's chin dropped to her chest. Something Amara knew about her daughter was her incredible sense of adventure and responsibility. Although Charlie had never been the one magnetized towards hard work and chores, Amara understood that she needed to help. She needed something to focus on besides Daddy's absence. She needed to test her bravery and toughness. That much, Amara understood. It was the same hurdle she was going to have to face.

"It's true, school comes first," Amara said. "But I *could* use your help." Charlie's eyes flitted up at her. "I need someone to keep the barn clean. Stalls mucked, aisles raked, and water buckets full. Every day. It's hard work. But a smart and tough girl can do it. Are you interested?"

Charlie nodded. "Yes, Mommy. I'll do it."

Amara smiled at her sacrificing daughter, with a faint sense that they might be able to make it through this awful time together. There was a flicker on Charleston's face too, but it was only his gray mustache dancing over his pursed lips. The conversation may have been pinned for later, but the puzzle of who was going to work the ranch was still unsolved. Hope had never kept the ranch afloat before, and it sure wasn't going to keep it afloat now. Charleston set his empty coffee cup on the counter behind him, then grabbed his keys and headed out.

A sick feeling swished inside Amara's stomach. They needed Sonny, but he wasn't coming back. Swallowing hard, she handed Charlie her plate of eggs. "You can have these. I'm done." Then she hobbled to her room to dress. Gramps was right. Only work was going to keep them afloat. Distraction and work.

Taking one look into her closet, Amara realized there was no way she would be squeezing into a pair of her own jeans with a bruised and swollen hip, so she grabbed a pair of Sonny's. They would be more than loose enough to accommodate for soreness and swelling. Not to mention, she would feel better having a piece of him keeping her company. She pressed the jeans to her nose and inhaled. *Sonny.* Hugging them close, she considered returning them to the closet where she wouldn't wear the scent away. Pausing, she considered that if she didn't put the jeans on, she would be going pantless. So she struggled into them, fastening them around her waist with a belt. Standing in front of the mirror, she looked absolutely ridiculous in baggy pants extending two feet past her toes. But who cared? She had no one to impress.

Wincing, she sat down and carefully rolled the hems of the legs over and over, one-handed, until they were thick wads at her ankles. At least she wouldn't trip on them. Falling certainly didn't seem like a good idea. Then she hobbled into the bathroom, where she toiled at removing the toothpaste lid and squeezing the blue goo onto her toothbrush head. She managed. Spat. And pulled a brush through her hair, growling in frustration at the awkwardness of having only one good arm.

"Charlie," she called through the open door.

Charlie appeared.

"Would you please put Mommy's hair into a braid?"

"Okay," Charlie answered, somewhat hesitant. "I don't know how to braid."

"I'll teach you. Fetch me your white pony from your room. The big one with the long pink tail."

Charlie did, and the lesson moved to the couch, where Amara sat and showed Charlie how the hair was split into three long sections. Then, taking turns, the outside strands were crossed one at a time over the inside strand, each becoming the new inside strand. And so on. Charlie fussed over Amara's long hair for a few minutes, partly practicing, partly playing, until a very loose but woven braid formed. Charlie wrapped a tiny black rubber band limply around the bottom. Amara wasn't sure how long it would stay, but she pulled her daughter in close for a hug.

"Thank you," she said sincerely. Charlie grinned. "Want to help Mommy totter up to the barn?"

"Okay," Charlie agreed, handing her the wooden cane.

By the time Amara and Charlie heard Charleston return, Charlie had picked the stalls, scrubbed and refilled the water buckets, raked the aisles, and brushed and fed the horses an early dinner. Charlie had done it all for the sake of practice—and because Amara couldn't stand looking Nick, nor the gelding that had carried Sonny to her rescue, in the eye. Nick surely wondered why neither she nor Sonny ever came, but she couldn't explain it to him. She was scared he would see through her, see it was her fault. And as for the horse who had carried Sonny on the day he had died... well, he already knew the truth.

From inside the barn, they could hear Charleston slam his pickup door. Then another door slammed. Charlie looked up from battling with the heavy water hose, trying to coil it back up against the wall the way

## Holder of the Horses

it had been before she filled all the buckets. "Someone is here."

"Sounds so," Amara said, uninterested, from where she sat on a short stool, massaging oil into the leather headstall she had gripped between her knees.

"He's tall."

"Humph."

Less than thirty seconds later, Charleston appeared in the open doorway with a rather young man on his heels. Charlie was right. The man was taller than Charleston, and built like a pole—a scrawny pole. Thick brown hair seemed almost piled on his head, like someone had glued it there. Apparently the brown mop did not allow for a hat, as he wore none. He had brown eyes and a pointy chin. The most noticeable thing, however, was his pair of perfectly clean Wrangler jeans and spanking new burgundy shirt, still creased from manufacturing. He was a greenie.

"This is where we keep the working horses," Charleston explained. "Anything you touch, you keep clean. You ride a horse, you clean it. You use a saddle, you clean it."

Charlie stopped winding up the hose and stared up at the burgundy-creased giant. Amara paused, staring too, but with a lot less awe.

"Tom, this scowling young woman is my granddaughter, Amara."

Tom's head bobbed once. She hadn't realized she was scowling, but once she knew, a polite woman would have made an attempt to smile instead. She didn't. Charleston moved on.

"And this pretty young lady," he said, grinning, as Charlie bowed like a princess, "is my great-granddaughter, Charlie. Newly appointed barn manager."

"He always calls me the *great*-granddaughter," Charlie boasted.

"Pleased to meet you," Tom replied stiffly, his head doing the single bob thing again.

Charleston led Tom past them, past the stalls, and walked him straight through the barn. Tom looked around, unaffected, as if he had seen a thousand barns, but Amara couldn't help but notice that the bottoms of his boots were as clean as his hands. When they stepped out the back door, Amara looked at Charlie and stuck her finger in her mouth, pretending to gag.

Charlie giggled. "That's not nice, Mommy."

Amara sighed. Charlie was right. It wasn't nice—to gag.

When the barn chores had been finished and all the tools were back in their proper places, Amara felt drained. It wasn't the house tugging at her tired bones, though. She felt pulled in the opposite direction. She wanted to visit Sonny.

"Would you like to go see Daddy with me?" she asked Charlie, as they tottered towards the barn door and switched the light off.

"Okay," Charlie agreed.

The girl fetched the keys to Sonny's pickup from inside the house, and with a great struggling effort, climbed into the pickup, finally managing to get the door shut. Then she waited patiently, already buckled in. From behind the wheel, Amara closed her eyes against the pain, taking a few steadying breaths before inserting the key into the ignition.

"Are you okay, Mommy?"

Returning her attention to the task at hand, Amara turned the key, and the truck rumbled to life. "Yes."

The drive from the house to the front gate had never seemed so long or agonizing. Every bump seemed to jolt every fiber of her body, causing her to realize she was probably due for pain medication. However, since she was transporting her most precious cargo, Charlie, she wouldn't have taken it anyway. Pain was better than grogginess, as far as alertness and motor skills were concerned.

When they arrived at the cemetery, Amara pulled the pickup right up next to the little wooden gate, saving herself steps, rather than across the drive in the pullout next to the empty corrals. This way, she only had to hobble a few feet and through the gate. Getting down from the pickup proved harder than climbing up, but she made it. Side by side, she and Charlie entered the small family cemetery, holding hands.

At Sonny's dirt plot, Charlie released her hand and commenced to removing the dead flowers she had placed there before, and traded them for a small, stuffed white rabbit she pulled from her pocket. Sonny had given Charlie the stuffed animal when she had been sick with the flu. He had made a trip to town for something—probably Sprite and crackers—and had returned with the only thing that would make his daughter feel better.

Tired, Amara laid down next to Sonny on the cold dirt, as she had before on the day of his funeral. The last thing she remembered was seeing the tiny little sprouts of grass beginning to poke through the settled soil. When her eyes fell closed, she saw him.

It was the day Charlie had been sick with the flu. And there was Sonny, squatting next to her. She was laying on the couch with a washrag draped over her forehead. In Sonny's hand, hiding behind his back, was the tiny white rabbit.

"*Charlie,*" *Sonny said. "I found something I think will make you feel better."*

"*What, Daddy?*" *Charlie whispered sadly, not believing anything could make her feel better. He revealed the little white rabbit, with a pink nose and long ears. Amara felt her heart flutter when a sparkle of light appeared in Charlie's eyes.* "*He looks just like Little Bunny, from the story!*" *Gently, she took the rabbit as if he were real.*

"*That's just what I thought,*" *Sonny replied.* "*Now, hold him close, so he doesn't run away.*"

*Charlie obeyed, cradling the little bunny close to her chest. Grinning, she closed her eyes, and after a long night's battle with fever, she finally rested.*

*Sonny stood up, turned around, and smiled at Amara.* "*The hero,*" *he said silently, moving only his lips, while pushing his chest out.*

"*Yes, you are,*" *Amara whispered, smiling. She reached for him, wrapping her arms around his waist, the warmth of his body seeping into hers.* "*Our hero.*"

\*\*

"How long have you been here?" Charleston asked Charlie, bending down. Charlie was sitting cross-legged on a bench in the cemetery, with a gray wool blanket from behind the seat of Sonny's pickup wrapped around her.

"I don't know," she answered, shrugging.

"Are you cold? Why don't you go jump in my pickup with Tom?"

"I'm not cold." She glanced at his pickup. "What about Mommy?"

"I'll get her."

"What about Daddy's truck?"

"Are you old enough to drive?"

"Not yet, Gramps."

He scratched his chin thoughtfully. "I suppose Tom could bring it back for us. You think?" Charlie nodded. "Alright then. Go get in, and tell Tom to get out."

Charlie giggled and trotted off toward his pickup, the bottom of her blanket flapping at the backs of her ankles. As gently as he could, Charleston walked over to Amara and began gathering her into his old arms.

Tom materialized behind him. "Need help?"

"No," Charleston answered gruffly. He didn't need to be treated like an incapable old fart—even if he was old, and farted on occasion. Looking after Sonny's girls was *his* job. Not to mention, Amara didn't think too highly of Tom, and would be fit to be tied if she woke up to his face inches from hers. "Take the other truck back, would ya?"

"Yes sir." Tom retreated and jumped into Sonny's pickup. Soon it started up and began backing into a place where Tom could turn it around.

Lifting Amara, Charleston grunted. Good thing she was a tiny thing. He carried her to his pickup, where it sat idling with Charlie waiting inside. Her body may have slowly been healing, but her heart was as broken as ever. Both of their hearts were. He only hid it better. For the girl's sake.

## CHAPTER TWENTY-FOUR

The following morning, Amara woke up early, as she always had. The first thing on today's list was a bath. From the feel of her hair, she hadn't had one since...gawd, did she really want to know the answer? Deciding she didn't, she began filling the bathtub with water hot enough to turn her skin rosy red, then climbed in. Leaving her casted arm stretched out, resting on the side of the tub to keep it dry, she washed her hair and body with her left arm and hand. Nothing had ever been so uncooperative as her left hand attempting the particulars.

The whole time she squeezed drops of shampoo into her hair and lathered it up, she couldn't help but center her thoughts on the diminished memory of Sonny's shape and features across from her. He was lounging against the other side of the tub, his long legs straddling her. Water drops dripped off the short facial stubble he never allowed to completely grow out. His smile, capturing her heart—and breaking it, simultaneously.

Tears slipped down her cheeks and dropped onto her breasts unnoticed. The only thing she was aware of was Sonny's expression. It was changing from happy to sad. He did not like to see her cry. In life, he seldom had a chance; she never had cause to cry. Closing her eyes, she imagined his face above hers—so close, so warm, so real. She could feel the roughness of his cheek against hers. The softness of his lips. His comforting words—although she couldn't make them out. It was no matter, it was his voice murmuring in her ear. Through closed eyes, Amara's tears flowed, unable to stop, until the temperature of the water cooled and drove Sonny's image away.

Shivering, Amara opened her eyes. Sonny was gone, of course, but the day had only just arrived, and she was already tired. Sighing, she leaned on her left side and pushed with her left arm and leg. It was quite the labor just getting out of the tub without slipping. When she was finally dry, she labored again to dress, and at long last, she hobbled into the kitchen. Charlie was there on a stool at the counter, nibbling at a bacon-and-toast sandwich.

"Mommy, your hair," she said, her eyes round and unblinking.

Amara touched her left hand to her head. "Oh yeah. That."

"Do you need help again?"

Grinning weakly, Amara removed a brush from her back pocket and handed it to her. "Please?"

Trading places, Charlie hopped off the stool, Amara taking her spot. "Gramps is making me go to school today," the girl explained, as she ran the brush through Amara's hair.

"That's good, baby. That will make Daddy very happy."

Charlie set the brush down, separated the hair into three long sections, and began crossing section over section. Amara waited patiently. She waited, not only for her hair to be done, but for her daughter to confide in her. Even without being able to see her daughter's face, Amara could sense Charlie's heavy thoughts hanging over them. Charlie was an innate thinker—a worrier—just like her daddy. Also like her daddy, unburdening on a loved one—or anyone—was something she did *not* do.

"I'm sorry," Amara said, turning in her seat slightly. "I know it's hard to talk about Daddy." She took Charlie's hand, stopping her from braiding. "He's watching over us still, don't you know?"

Charlie nodded. "I know, Mommy. It's not that."

"What is it then?"

"You call me baby."

Caught off guard, Amara quickly attempted to change her line of thought. "Yes, does it bother you?"

"No." Charlie's head dropped, her eyes scanning the kitchen floor, refusing to make contact.

"Then what is it?"

Her little chin wobbled. "Daddy called me 'my little one,'" she finally answered, a slight quiver in her voice. "He won't call me that anymore." Immediately, Amara wrapped her arms around her daughter and pulled her close. Charlie cried into her shoulder, letting go of the sadness in her young, but big, heart.

Something powerful must have been floating around in the air this morning. Amara understood just how Charlie was feeling. Overwhelmed. Tired. Sad. However, now was not the time for that. Now was the time for the strength they both so desperately needed. "Daddy will still call you his little one," Amara said soothingly.

"How?"

"When he talks to you."

"Talks to me?" said Charlie, clearly both wounded and frustrated. "He can't talk to me anymore."

Amara ran her good hand through Charlie's baby-soft hair. "He can, baby. And he will. In your heart. In all your memories. And again, when we meet him on the other side."

Charlie's shoulders began to shake with sobs. If losing Sonny hadn't completely shattered Amara's heart, her broken-hearted little girl was doing a fine job of finishing it off. They clung to each other tightly, as if a tornado was threatening to rip them apart.

The front door slammed, a cold rush of air followed. Charleston cleared his throat a moment later. "Time to catch the bus, Charlie."

"Yes, Gramps," Charlie muttered, sniffing and wiping at her nose and eyes with her sleeve. "I have to put this in Mommy's hair," she said, as she quickly wrapped a rubber band in what she had completed of Amara's braid. Then she grabbed her unicorn backpack off the floor by the foot of the stool and turned to follow Charleston.

Gramps' expression looked apologetic, but he said nothing.

"Here," Amara said, holding out the half-eaten bacon and toast sandwich. "You can finish this on the drive up to the road."

Charlie took it. "Thank you."

"Daddy and I love you, baby."

Another tear dripped from Charlie's eye, and she quickly brushed it away. "I love you too."

Gramps led the way out the front door. Amara wondered how it was that he was so much stronger than they were. Out the frosty window, she watched him open the passenger door for Charlie, hoist her into the warm cab, and close it again. Briefly he hesitated, studying the frozen dirt pasted on the side of the pickup. Something clicked, and he ambled over to the driver-side door, stepped in—the same long-legged way Sonny used to—and drove her little girl away to be swallowed up by the yellow bus.

By the time Amara tottered like a penguin to the cold outside world, Tom was pulling into the yard with the tractor and long bed. Piles of loose, grassy alfalfa hay stuck in the cracks of the wood, having been left behind instead of swept off, signified that Tom had just returned from feeding Sonny's morning route of hungry, anxious mouths. But unlike Tom, Sonny had always swept the extra hay off, especially in the winter months when it would freeze and become a thicker and thicker pile of icy leaves and stems to slip on. A pang of resentment spiked through Amara's chest.

Tom parked the tractor and long bed on the concrete pad, jumped out, and dusted off his jeans. They appeared to be the same clean pair from yesterday, but the shirt was different. She could tell from where his jacket was unzipped that today he was wearing a green button-up shirt with creases, also straight out of the package. Tom saw her and waved.

It wasn't one of those friendly-type waves, though, it was more of a, "I see you staring rudely at me, fuck off" wave. Amara glared at his backside as he disappeared into the barn. What did he need? There was nothing but horses in there. He didn't look like the riding type. She decided to follow him to supervise. In fact, if he was riding, she might just want to see this.

The trek up to the barn seemed even longer than yesterday's, maybe because Charlie wasn't here chattering at her. Or maybe it was because Charlie wasn't here to lean on for breaks. Huffing and puffing, she wondered: who said she needed to start physical therapy? She was doing it right now. A few steps, and rest. A few steps, and rest. An unknown number of exhausting minutes later, she arrived at the wide-open barn door, grimacing and wondering if she should be pushing it quite this hard.

"Pish posh," she muttered under her breath. There was work to be done. "A little pain never hurt anyone." Well, considering her current state, that was an inaccurate and ridiculous philosophy. Nevertheless, on the other hand—and there is always the other hand—pain reveals strength, courage, and perseverance like nothing else. That was what she had to focus on.

"What?" Tom asked, looking up from where he was attempting to fasten a girth around a horse.

Startled, Amara looked up from carefully watching where she placed her feet and cane. The horse Tom had out was Nick, Sonny's horse. "What're you doing?" asked Amara.

Tom froze. Clearly, he really *didn't* know what the heck he was doing. His mouth opened, and she knew he was about to mutter "I don't know" when he shut it again, just as quickly, swallowing the nasty words down like a puke burp.

"I'm saddling Mr. Morris' horse. He expects me to ride an hour a day until he clears me to go out alone," Tom replied, in a tone suggesting that Gramps' good judgment had stepped upon his fragile pride. "Which I think is pretty stupid."

Leaning heavily on her cane, Amara set her jaw. "My husband was a phenomenal rider, and he just died. The back of his head was kicked in by a horse. It's not stupid."

"Sorry," Tom said, but neither his expression nor his arrogant manner softened. Instead, he began fiddling with the girth again.

He wasn't ready to ride a horse. Both his attitude and his competence stunk. One whiff of him, and any horse was bound to trouble itself with deflating his high-flying balloon of an ego. Maybe that was precisely what Gramps had in mind, since he hadn't bothered to be present to coach Tom properly. Certainly he had figured just as easily as she that Tom was not prone to learning any other way than by self-discovery. Except Amara had a firm line she wouldn't allow him to cross. And that was Nick. Nick belonged to Sonny.

"Put that horse away," Amara ordered.

"What?"

"You heard me. Put that horse away. It's my husband's horse."

A smirk played on Tom's lips, not reaching his eyes. "I don't work for you."

"No?"

Tom shook his head, challenging her.

"What if I told you, you *do* work for me, Tom?"

"Why don't I just finish what I'm doing here?" Tom replied. "I'll do my job. You do yours." He gawked at her cast and cane, silently suggesting there wasn't much she would be doing.

"Last chance, Tom. Put my husband's horse away. Take any other. Then feel free to ride until you fall off." Amara checked the imaginary watch on her wrist. "I give you thirty seconds. I'll even stay and watch."

"Yeah…no thank you. Mr. Morris said I could ride any horse in here. No offense to your husband, but I've already got this one out, and she's the tallest. I need a tall horse."

"Apparently being tall doesn't make you smart. It's a gelding."

"What's a gelding?"

"The horse you're about to put away, *he's* a gelding. As in male."

Tom inhaled impatiently. "I'm not putting *him* away. I'm going riding. If you don't like it, take it up with Mr. Morris."

"I won't be taking it up with anyone, Tom. You're fired. Put the horse away. Pack up your things and go home."

The stunned look on his face was all the insincere gratitude she needed. She didn't need an, "I apologize for misjudging you as a useless cripple," or a, "Thank you for the opportunity that I squandered." Just the stupid look on his face, which portrayed a long-overdue realization that he had lipped off to the wrong cowgirl, was more than enough to lift her spirits.

How was that, Sonny? she wondered. She imagined Sonny nodding, kicked back on a haybale, sucking on a hollow hay shaft. *Well done*, he might have said.

"You've got to be kidding!" Tom exploded, ripping the saddle off Nick's back and tossing it to the ground.

Nick turned towards him with a big, wrinkly eye, begging the question, "What turned over your grain bucket?"

Not long after Tom's departure, Charleston came in the house to find Amara sitting in his chair, feet propped up, an icepack on her hip, going through the ranch's books and receipts.

"Where's Tom?" he asked, already knowing the answer. Tom had flagged him down on the way out, fussing and carrying on like a spoiled schoolgirl.

She looked up at him with eyes as innocent as a fawn's. "Tom?"

"Yes. Tom."

"Oh, him. He's fired," she said simply, and then went back to working the books.

Exhaling, Charleston pursed his lips thoughtfully, wiggling his mustache side to side. A wise man knows not to stick his finger into a hot socket. "You have an appointment," he said. "Let's get it over with."

Amara growled like a child who didn't want to get out of bed for school. A remix of Charlie's exact behavior this morning, in fact.

\*\*

"Can I help you?" asked a short, plump receptionist at the physical therapy office. She pulled a pencil from the knot of brown hair tied up in a bun on her head.

Charleston nodded to Amara, standing at his side and leaning on a cane. The wooden cane had been Lizzy's after she had become so weak that she lost her balance if she so much as turned her head. Worrying constantly she would fall, the doctor had suggested she use a cane, sort of as a third leg. It had helped—for a while.

"I have an appointment," said Amara, peeking over the tall counter separating the short receptionist from the equally short client. "Amara Morris."

Charleston studied the design of the thick, wall-like barrier, thumping it to see if it was hollow. It was a wonder any official business could be successfully communicated with such a barricade. The women could barely stick their noses over it.

"Sir," the receptionist said, grabbing his attention. "Is there a problem?"

"No," he said, thumping it again, this time with the toe of his boot. "You seem to have a wall of china here.

What's on the other side?" He leaned over the counter to take a look.

"Sir," said the woman, holding her palms over the paperwork like a magician about to cast a spell. "This is confidential. Please return to your full and upright position."

He did as she requested with a chuckle.

"What are you laughing at?" she asked, obviously bothered. "This is no laughing matter. Patient confidentiality is very important."

"Are you new?" Charleston asked. The receptionist faltered. Clearly, she *was* new, but thorough. He nodded at her approvingly. He glanced over the counter, resting his arm on the top and dangling his hand over the other side. "That one," he said, poking a file. "That's hers."

The receptionist's eyes widened in alarm. "Sir!"

Charleston glanced at Amara, giving his best impression of innocence.

"Sir, I'm going to have to ask you to leave."

"How long will this take?" said Charleston. "I need her help at the ranch this afternoon."

"Most definitely not," the hassled receptionist replied with a huff. "She cannot be helping you on a ranch. Physical therapy is a process, not a Band-Aid."

"Gramps, can you possibly wait in the pickup?" Amara asked.

"Do you have coffee?" said Charleston.

The receptionist glared, refusing to answer, but her eyes flicked to the corner of the waiting room.

"Thank you," he said, accepting her accidental assistance.

"Take it outside with you, please," Amara said in her motherly tone.

"Humph." The air was stuffy in here.

As the receptionist guided Amara towards the large room full of unnamed gadgets and yoga balls, Charleston introduced himself to the coffeepot. Whoever had decided the office counter ought to loom over the lobby must have been the same person who decided finding the paper coffee cups ought to be a scavenger hunt. Rooting around for a decent mug, he found only children-sized cups. Checking the supply cupboard beneath the coffee machine marked "Employees Only," he found sugar and creamer refills and napkins, but no adult cups. Disenchanted, he filled three diminutive children-sized cups. A full cup in one hand, and two full cups squeezed between the fingers of his other, he opened the swinging glass door using his back, allowing a gust of chilly wind to blow into the lobby, and headed toward his pickup to take sanctuary.

He could see through the window that a young, attractive male therapist had met Amara at the seat in which she had been placed. The therapist knelt down at her feet on the floor and took one of her legs in his hands, talking to her. By Amara's uncharacteristic stiffness, Charleston could tell she was uncomfortable. A moment later, she dismissed the well-meaning fellow. A female therapist took his place, and this time Amara went through all the correct motions without a fuss. Charleston chuckled, sipping his coffee.

When it was done, he could see Amara making her way slowly to the wall of china to make another appointment, or so he figured. Stiffly, he set the last child's cup on the dashboard in line with the first two he had drained, opened the door, and stepped out. By the time her figure appeared in the swinging glass door, he was there waiting, holding it open for her. She thanked him with a thin grin and the brief brush of her fingertips across his forearm.

"Shall we?" he asked.

She nodded, pulling her sweater around her tightly.

At the passenger door, Charleston took her cane, slid it under the seat, and lifted her in. Her quiet gloom had him worried. She was tired, and no doubt missing Sonny. They all were. But he couldn't fix her loneliness the way he could fix a broken fence. He couldn't bring Sonny back with all the wishing in the world. What if Amara decided she couldn't bear it at the ranch without Sonny, and she and Charlie up and left? Amara had family she could go back to if she felt the absolute need. Surely Mrs. Duncan wouldn't actually turn away her own granddaughter. But what would *he* do without them?

Starting up the pickup, he tried to push the thoughts aside. It was Amara's prerogative—her future. His only choice in the matter was to let them decide and then carry on. Alone. That is, if he didn't count the five-minute visit from John every seven years. And he didn't. But try as he may, he couldn't drop the notion. It clung to him like a tick, sucking out his peace. The entire way home, the same silence Charleston normally found soothing and companionable ate at his insides like indigestion. This silence wasn't peaceful, it was contemplative, like the quiet before a storm. He wasn't sure what sort of storm was headed their way, but it had his nerves on edge.

## CHAPTER TWENTY-FIVE

The following week, the sky turned gray and snow began falling. The wind wiped across yards, fields, and roads. Only against houses, barns, and fences did the snow rest from its vengeance, and once it found a place to rest against a structure too big to move, it slowly piled up. If it was to be a heavy snow year, those piles would soon turn into walls and mounded hills large enough to comfortably lodge an entire family. Nonetheless, the weather wasn't the trouble.

One day, in the distance beyond the horse pasture, Amara noted Francis Shultz: a gentleman of nearly sixty years with the belly of a pork pig, thin gray hair, and a tobacco-swollen bottom lip. He had taken up residence in the lower house, along with his Australian shepherd Doozie, two days after she had fired Tom.

Francis was clearing the manure out of the corner of the pasture on their barn utility tractor from where they'd dumped it after cleaning the stalls, spreading it further away to rejuvenate the grass that would sprout up come spring. As winter waged war, spreading manure would become impossible. It would be buried by snow, frozen, and buried again. Doozie was stalking the tractor, convinced he was herding it from the paddock to the field and back again. Trip after trip. Amara had never seen such a hardworking, useless dog.

Turning her back, she retreated into the house to fetch the last bag of Christmas decorations she was donating to the secondhand store in town. She intended to have the decorations out of the house before Charlie returned from school. Not all of them, of course, just the excess. They didn't need as many as they currently had. Not one of them—her, Gramps, or Charlie—aimed to hang lights outside on the house or the barn. That had always been Sonny's job. Inside, the Christmas tree would be put up, a garland hung here and there. It would be enough. The remaining decorations would be saved for another year—or for another donation next year—stored away, back where they had come from.

On her last trip from the house to the pickup, with a bag in her good hand, Francis wobbled up. Tipping his hat, he asked, "Coffee hot?"

"No, not since this morning," Amara answered, tossing the bag in the pickup and shutting the door.

"Humph," he grunted, and disappeared into the house.

A few minutes later, he emerged from the kitchen with a steaming mug for drinking, and an empty mug for spitting. He stood in the living room, watching her, as she stuffed decorations she meant to keep into a large green plastic box marked "Christmas." As she sat on the lid, it clicked into place. She sighed, satisfied at last. Francis looked about at the strands of silver, gold, and red garlands she had left strewn across the couch.

"Putting them up?" he asked, taking a sip from his mug. He exhaled. "It's November."

Amara nodded. "Yes, I'll let Charlie put them up when she returns home from school."

"Why don't you put them up? Why wait for someone else to do what you could do yourself? It's not so hard, now, is it?"

Irritated, Amara began slamming her cane into the box, scooting it slowly towards Gramps' bedroom. She may or may not have been imagining Francis' face on the outside of the plastic box. "I'm not *saving the job* for someone else, Mr. Shultz. Charlie enjoys decorating for Christmas. Don't you have children?"

Francis spat a stream of black tobacco into the empty mug. "Two. Can't call them children anymore, though. One's thirty and the other's thirty-six."

Amara stopped just before disappearing into Charleston's bedroom. Maybe Francis was part human after all. "Did they used to enjoy decorating for Christmas?"

He shrugged and spat again. "I don't know. That was the wife."

Rolling her eyes, she knocked the box the rest of the way into Charleston's room and jammed it back into the depths of his closet.

\*\*

After dinner that evening, Charleston lay back in his favorite chair, wiggling his toes and staring dreamily into the crackling fire. Francis had poured himself a third cup of hot coffee. There was no way the man was going to fall asleep. Apparently, though, he felt the call to hold up the wall between the living room and Amara's room. He looked awkward and out of place, but seemingly didn't notice Amara glowering at him.

They had watched Charlie carefully hang the red garland around the fireplace, the gold garland around the archway. Over the past few months, her shaky disposition had slowly begun to heal. Like her daddy, she worried about her family and now she was climbing onto a stool from the kitchen with the silver garland to hang over the front door to brighten the holidays. She glanced at Charleston over her shoulder.

"Gramps," Charlie said, blinking innocently.

"Yes, darling?"

Stacking everyone's dishes one on top of the other to carry them to the kitchen sink, Amara froze. "Charlie, pay attention to what you're doing up there so you don't fall."

"Aw, leave her be," Francis said, earning himself a sharp glare from Amara.

"Yes, Mommy," Charlie answered, ignoring Francis' unnecessary support and averting a war between him and her mother at the same time. Unwrapping the garland from around herself, she began draping it over the tiny nails left from last year.

"Gramps," she began again, as she started climbing down off the stool. "Can we go look for a Christmas tree tomorrow? I don't have school."

"Once the tree is cut, it begins to die," Charleston explained. Then he immediately regretted it.

Everyone except Francis just kind of stopped whatever it was they were doing and quietly went into themselves. It was like a disco ball was reflecting the word "die" all over every surface of the room. It could not be ignored. It had been heard, and understood on levels an eight-year-old girl shouldn't have to understand.

Charleston rubbed his chin. Charlie needed some life in the house. Even if it was just a tree. If it began to die, he would sneak it away and replace it with another. "Saturday doesn't mean animals don't eat," he warned.

"I'll feed the horses, bright and early. I promise." Charlie crossed her arms over her chest and hugged herself, holding her hopes tightly.

"Francis, can you feed the cattle in the morning?" Charleston asked. Normally he gave his help the weekend off, making his all the longer.

Francis nodded.

"Charlie, if you could get them barn chores done, and Amara, if you can handle feeding the horses?"

Amara nodded.

"I saw the line on the eastern most side leaning. The posts can't take any more rot. I'll take new posts out there, but after that, we'll use the rest of daylight to hunt up a tree."

Charlie grinned, not showing her teeth. Her expression was easy to read. She wanted to be excited, but even excitement wasn't quite the same anymore. So she held back.

Francis cleared his throat. "Sending Amara to feed...is this such a good idea?"

Charleston hesitated before answering. The man presumably meant well. Before Amara could spit in Francis' face, though, he quickly asked, "Well, can you, Amara?"

"Yes," she snapped, glaring at them both. "I can."

Charleston nodded, satisfied. There she was, the fiery cowgirl Sonny had fallen in love with. The one who tried to climb fences to touch wild horses and took a job on a Montana ranch without so much as a minute of experience. But she had made up for it by being a hard worker, a bright beacon of light in a monotonous world, and then she brought Charlie into the world. After the accident, Charleston had hoped she would return, but didn't know if she could. Now she had showed up temporarily, and it gave him hope.

**

The next morning, Amara hobbled out to Sonny's old pickup and backed it up to the second long bed, which was sitting next to the tractor Francis would be taking to feed the cows. Positioning the ball of her hitch below the coupler, she gingerly lowered herself down from the seat where her husband had sat so many times, and then sunk the coupler down over the ball, switched the lever—locking the underjaw into place—and plugged in the electrical wire. Francis looked over her shoulder.

"Need help, little lady?"

Finished, and ready to move to the hay barn, Amara straightened her back. "None whatsoever." She grabbed her cane off the bumper and hobbled past him, back towards the driver door.

"Hang on there," he called to her. "Don't drive off just yet. I'll check it to be sure."

He started to bend over to inspect her work, so before she even shut the door, she began pulling away. Not so fast as to rip off his face. Just fast enough that he pulled back and stepped away, gawking at her in the rearview mirror with a stunned expression.

At the hay barn, he growled up next to her in the tractor. He cut the diesel engine, and it puffed a cloud of exhaust. She had already climbed into the forklift, and had her trailer half loaded by the time he clambered down.

"I suppose you didn't hear me back there," he hollered at her, staying well out of the way. Driving a forklift is different from driving other equipment. Clearly he didn't trust either her ability or her spite. Well, he was right about the latter.

Continuing to load the last few bales, Amara refused to give him the satisfaction of looking at him. "I heard you," she mumbled, doubting he'd heard *her*.

Judging from the way he angrily crossed his jacket-covered arms, he might have read her lips. She couldn't help but smile. "Want me to load you up?" she asked cheerily. "Forklifts can be tricky."

"No," he growled. "I don't need help from a–" He stopped short of saying "a girl."

"Suit yourself," Amara said, as she swung the forklift's rear around, barely missing his toes and parking as close to her pickup door as she could. Then she carefully stepped out. Ending her gloating with a nasty slip on the cold metal wouldn't feel too good—to her body or her ego.

As if reading her mind, Francis warned, "Pride comes before the fall!"

"Pride *goeth* before the fall," Amara muttered, having studied the expression.

Waving, she hoisted herself back into the warm cab, silently celebrating having not fallen on her face. Starting up the engine, she shoved it into four-wheel drive and hit the lights. She would need both to pierce through the heavy falling snow. It felt good to be working again. But the good feeling didn't last long.

Driving over the cattle guard, Amara entered the first pasture. She swung the rig around to the right and pointed it due north, and watched happily as the yearling figures seemed to almost pop out of a winter painting, galloping towards her. Out of old habit, she revved the engine and opened the door. That's when she remembered just what it was she had forgotten. She had to bail out of the pickup while it was moving.

As the cold breeze hit her face, she looked down at the snowy ground going idly by. She had never had two thoughts about jumping from a slowly moving pickup before. It was an everyday thing, multiple times a day. The pickup drove itself while the feeder threw off hay, making a nice neat little line that stretched for about fifty yards. That way every horse got a helping of food. Yet what had seemed so easy every other day was not so easy today. She hated to admit it, but Francis may have been right. Readying herself, she sucked in a breath of wintry air. She had spent her pride; here came the fall. She jumped.

Snow hit her in the face, and the ground smacked against her good hip and shoulder. Quickly assessing, she found nothing hurt. But the truck was on the move, so she groped in the snow until she found hard ground and pushed herself to her knees, and then her feet. The flatbed had met her. It was time to get on. How could she have forgotten about this? What had she been thinking? What had Gramps been thinking? How was it only Francis had been thinking?

No—she did *not* just give Francis credit for thinking. She could do this. Growling under her breath, she threw her torso onto the flatbed before the back half slipped by her and she would have to chase it on foot, alongside all the hungry yearlings. Hanging there for a moment, she breathed hard, her heart pumping. When had she gotten so out of shape? Grasping the strings of the large hay bale, she pulled and dug her elbow in until she could grab the wooden surface with her good knee. It hurt like the hot place people tend to tell other people to go. Once she was up, she felt a surge of success. She would have liked to sit there, enjoying the moment, thinking about Sonny clapping her on the back, but this stretch of ground only lasted so long, then there were scattered trees and small ravines formed by melting snow.

Breaking away the thick flakes with a heave and a ho, she tossed them overboard. The yearlings had caught her, following behind at a walk. A few of them took a flake straight in the face, while other, more patient yearlings waited for it to hit the ground before commencing to eat breakfast. One by one, the yearlings all found a place in the line of strewn-out hay and began nibbling contentedly, tails swishing almost in unison.

It was time to bail again, before she reached the tree line.

"Fine," Amara grumbled, wishing she hadn't agreed to this chore. Physically, she wasn't ready. Yet here she was, her good old stubborn bones to thank. Sitting with her legs dangling over the edge, all she wanted to do was hesitate—to rethink what she was about to do. But peeking into the distance, with the trees getting bigger and bigger, the ground growing bumpier, she knew there was no time for that. She jumped again.

For less than a second, she flew like an eagle, belly down. She didn't want to hit knees first and jar her hip. At the last moment, she turned and aimed her good side at the ground. With a wham, snow hit her face and embedded into her ear. The sensation of biting cold combined with the stopping force of the ground knocked her breath out.

Blinking, she looked up. The pickup and long bed were crawling away; the weight of the load dragging through the snow slowed the pickup's pace. Finally, something was working for her instead of against her. Wiping the snow off her face using her wet jacket sleeve, she sighed. With every drop, there would be less hay and less weight. It was going to get harder before it got easier.

Who was she kidding? It wasn't going to get easier. Not today. But it was going to get done, she thought determinedly.

Back at the house, Amara climbed stiffly from the cab of Sonny's pickup. It had taken her twice as long as it should have. Every muscle ached. She was tired. She was thirsty. Most of all, she was cold.

"You look wet, little lady," Francis noted, walking up and joining her. He swung a chainsaw he had fetched from the tool shed by its front handle.

"Master of the obvious, are you?" Amara asked grouchily. All she wanted was a hot bath. The thought kept her shuffling towards the house, inch by inch.

Charlie came running outside to greet her in blue winter pants and a short-sleeved pink t-shirt.

"Where's your coat?" Amara asked loudly.

Grabbing onto Amara's good elbow and placing it over her shoulders, Charlie snuggled close. Amara knew the girl was trying to take some of her weight. God had never made a gentler, more selfless young girl.

"It's hanging in the house by the door," Charlie answered plainly, thinking nothing of the implications as to the coat's whereabouts. "Ew, you're wet."

Amara sighed. It was no use. "I take it Gramps isn't back yet?"

Charlie shook her head. "He's here. Loaded up posts, but never left."

"Well, are you excited to go looking for a tree?"

"I don't think we're going," Charlie answered sadly.

"What makes you say that?"

"Gramps got a phone call after you left. Now he seems sad. I asked him if we were still hunting for a Christmas tree. He didn't answer."

"What do you know about this?" Amara asked Francis, finding herself suddenly in a worse mood then she was already.

Spitting a stream of dark tobacco into the pure white snow, leaving an ugly brown splatter mark, Francis answered, "Nothing."

If it wasn't already bad enough, the sound of a car crunching over snow-packed gravel reached their ears, and the three of them turned at once. Recognizing not the car, but the style, quality, and price of said car, Amara halted.

A black metallic Volvo with aluminum wheels, chrome trim around the windows, and studded performance tires slowly crept down the slight slope. The three of them stood staring: Charlie and Francis in awe, and Amara stuck somewhere between shock and disgust. Something like the feeling of holding a friend's snoozing, elderly lap dog when it coughs and farts, and out the rear explodes a wet pile of lumpy orange diarrhea. After the morning she'd just had, this was the last thing she needed.

*No, it can't be them*, she thought—not the people she'd once called parents.

## CHAPTER TWENTY-SIX

Amara watched the two strangers she'd once called her parents step from their car, almost in unison. Mr. Duncan was dressed casually, in gray slacks and a matching polyester jacket. To the rest of the world, he would appear prepared to go run off to some meeting. Mrs. Duncan was a different story. She hadn't made any attempt to dress casually, and she was wearing a pair of white, flowing slacks, a pale peach-colored knit sweater accented by a white fur shawl draped around her shoulders, and a broad golden belt with matching thick necklace. Her hair was wound tight in her typical migraine-causing bun. Amara wasn't sure how she would appear to the rest of the world. Nor did she care.

Biting her tongue, she managed to swallow the questions she wanted to ask. Instead, she just thought them, while watching her parents approach through narrowed eyes. *What are you doing here?*

If she waited, the governing Mrs. Duncan would supply all the questions, followed up by all the answers. Mr. Duncan probably had the script she'd written for him tucked in his back pocket. For a fleeting moment, Amara pitied him; returning to such a woman, day after day. What kind of life had he resigned himself to? Indeed, the very life he had warned Amara not to come back to—but *he* did. Why? Then he smiled—a big and genuine smile—and began rushing at her like a linebacker, only his arms were outstretched. Unable to help herself, she forgave him instantly. She didn't even know what he was forgiven for. Working too much? Always being gone? Forgetting that a daughter needed motherly love, not just calculating directives? Not standing up for her? Then again, he had, in a way, when he told her to never come back.

"Don't tackle her, you fool!" Mrs. Duncan snapped. "Look at her."

Mr. Duncan stopped and stood up straight, the excitement draining out into the snow under his feet. "I'm sorry," he said. "I forgot." Then, with all of the delicacy of a clown perched on wooden stilts, he bent over and wrapped his arms around her, barely touching her, tapping the palms of his hands on her back. "You're wet."

"Yeah, I fell in the snow."

"How many times?" he asked, standing up and examining her.

A small laugh escaped her. "A few," she admitted. Biting her tongue again, she suppressed the temptation to ask him why they had come. Having lost her husband was simply not the sort of reason capable of prompting a visit from this particular manipulative woman and her disciple. Then again, here they were. Which sparked a rather curious follow-up question. How had they even known?

Turning away from Mr. Duncan, standing before her, and Mrs. Duncan, still tiptoeing through the snow in her unpractical white dress shoes, Amara scanned the kitchen window. There, peering from his favorite spot, was the suspected culprit. The stoic expression on the old leathery face hiding beneath the cowboy hat did not appear to be at all knocked for six at the arrival of their guests. Amara didn't wonder why.

"Gramps!" Amara called to him. "Why don't you come and greet your guests?"

Charleston lifted his coffee mug up, as if toasting her. Francis spat, deposited the chainsaw on the porch, and disappeared into the house, evidently convinced the guests were none of his concern. Charlie shivered, not uttering a complaint or even an inquiring word—which Amara found unusual.

"This is Mr. and Mrs. Duncan," said Amara.

In return, Mr. Duncan glanced at Amara, looking for the reason for such a proper introduction. When none was provided, he simply smiled at Charlie, offering his hand warmly. Bashfully, Charlie accepted the handshake.

Mrs. Duncan scowled. "I'm Grandma Duncan," she told Charlie, not offering a warm hand or a warm greeting. She clucked her tongue. "No coat in weather like this will cause you to catch pneumonia, not admiration," she told the shivering child.

"She wouldn't be out here if not for your arrival," said Amara, hugging Charlie close. Charlie didn't speak or budge, but kept hugging Amara's waist tightly as though she were only three years old.

Charleston opened the front door. "Come on in and get warmed up. Hurry, Charlie."

"Go, baby." Amara tried to push Charlie towards the house, but she clung, refusing to run ahead.

It was clear that Charleston had been referring to his girls, but of course it came as no surprise that Mrs. Duncan was the first to make a quick dash for the door, while Mr. Duncan gestured that he would follow behind the ladies. Once on the porch, with Charlie under her wing, Amara glared at Charleston as she hobbled by. "I know this was you."

The puppy-dog look he gave her begged for either naiveté or forgiveness. It was difficult to decipher which. The only thing she was certain of was that he was not innocent. After she and Charlie passed by, Mr. Duncan grasped Charleston's arm and thanked him for extending the invitation. Once more, Charleston's eyes flicked to Amara sadly, and she shook her head. An invitation, indeed. Charleston's head twitched subtly from side to side, either denying having sent an invitation or imploring her to behave. The latter seemed more accurate.

Once he shut the front door, Amara felt like all the fresh air had just been sucked out of the room. The normal warmth of the log home suddenly felt tight and pinched. Everyone gawked at each other uncomfortably, wondering what could be said that would ease the awkwardness. All Amara wanted was a bath. All Charlie wanted was to go Christmas tree hunting. All Francis wanted was more coffee. The question was, what did Gramps and Mr. and Mrs. Duncan want? She looked at each of them, one after the other, until someone finally spoke.

"Francis, call it a day," said Charleston.

Francis grunted, deposited his coffee cup in the kitchen, and walked out the front door, pouting.

"Take a seat," Charleston said, although he didn't specify to whom he was speaking.

Amara leaned longingly towards her bedroom, as Mr. and Mrs. Duncan sat next to each other on the leather couch and Charlie took a spot on the floor in front of the fire. At the first chance, Amara tried to sneak away; if not quickly, then quietly.

"Amara!" Mrs. Duncan called. Amara could feel the hook, like a fisherman's hook, catch the back of her neck. Of course, there wasn't actually a hook, but her shoulders went up protectively anyway. "Where are you going? Join us."

It may have been presented as though it were a well-mannered offer, but Amara knew better. Mrs. Duncan didn't offer anything. She decided, commanded, and reinforced. Feeling like a child, Amara turned around and faced the group. Everyone was staring at her expectantly. What were they expecting?

"Is this some sort of intervention?" she asked.

"Goodness, no," said Mrs. Duncan with a laugh. It sounded forced, and fake.

"We just wanted to visit our daughter," Mr. Duncan volunteered.

"And your granddaughter," Gramps added purposefully. He began helping Amara scramble out of her jacket and rainproof pants.

"Yes, of course," said Mrs. Duncan, glancing at Charlie, feigning a look of affection. "Charlie, I can't say I've heard very much about you. Why don't you tell us about yourself?"

As Charlie played with her fingers in her lap, she answered. "I...I like to write."

"Write? Write what exactly? The letters of the alphabet, I assume?"

"I like to write stories," Charlie answered.

"For as much as she's being unusually bashful," Amara said, "Charlie is extremely talented. Charlie, why don't you go get your blue box?"

"Stories?" Mrs. Duncan asked skeptically, stopping Charlie before she could agree to fetch the box that would bore her to no end.

Charlie nodded shyly.

"You're awfully young," Mrs. Duncan retorted, somewhat snootily. "What sort of stories could such a young child actually write?"

"Little stories," Charlie answered, as though their being little explained everything. She, of course, didn't know Mrs. Duncan the way Amara did. The woman despised all things she considered to be a waste of time. Drawing and writing for enjoyment, and not advancement, was at the top of the list. Charlie continued proudly, surely believing Mrs. Duncan had an actual interest, "I write stories about animals that go on adventures in Montana."

Mrs. Duncan's nose lifted slightly. "I see. How truly enthralling."

"Would you like to read one?" Charlie asked hopefully. She was about to rise and go fetch her beloved blue box, packed full of notebooks, drawing books, and colored pencils, when Mrs. Duncan answered.

"No. Very generous of you. But no. I'm fine. I think I'll visit with the adults."

Charlie sunk back down, disappointed.

Before Amara could pluck a word from the boiling water of her anger, Gramps beat her to it, surprising her by picking her up. He was taking her to his leather chair. "Easy," he whispered.

In Gramps' calming tone, Amara heard the reflection of Sonny. He would have said the same thing. Her heart sank. If only he were here. Sonny was a peacemaker, but when the time called for it—such as now—he would demand that the two intruders leave immediately. Where he was a peacemaker, he was doubly protective.

Amara wasn't the only one who was surprised. Mrs. Duncan's mouth dropped in an expression of absolute horror, a gasp escaping her. It appeared as though she had just been slapped. Of course, this pleased Amara. Undoubtedly, the woman had plenty to say about Gramps carrying her around like a child, or a wife, but she managed to snap her mouth shut. A person could practically see the steam seeping out of her ears, as she sat in silence like a baking potato.

The entire exchange between the members of the group for the rest of the afternoon was disgustingly superficial. It reminded Amara of when her mom had house guests. None of her guests could have actually been friends. The dialogue was always too proper, too showy. In general, too repulsively fake. The same could be said about today.

Mrs. Duncan droned on and on about how wonderful the years had been to them, and how wonderful it could have been for Amara, had she been there to enjoy it. But all Amara could think about was how sore Gramps' legs must be getting. He'd been leaning against the side of the fireplace, behind Charlie, for hours. Charlie kept yawning, looking out the windows, the sky outside growing darker and darker. All her hopes for hunting a tree were melting before her eyes, like the snow on the bottom of her boots.

Even after hours of Mrs. Duncan's droning, Amara still had no idea why they had come here. She accidentally fell asleep, leaving Mrs. Duncan gaping at her rudeness. When Gramps touched her forearm gently, she woke with a jerk.

"You're tired," Gramps said. "I'll help you to bed. Come on." He leaned over her, encouraging her to lean forward.

"You're going to bed? It's only three o'clock," Amara heard Mrs. Duncan object. She had barely heard Mr. Duncan utter a word. "We came all this way to see you."

"You'll see her tomorrow," Gramps said, lifting her from the chair. He was right, she was tired. Resting her head on his shoulder, she closed her eyes. Gramps could handle the guests without her. He had invited them, after all.

Mrs. Duncan huffed, unable to suppress her valuable opinion any longer. "I find all of this *highly* inappropriate."

"What?" Gramps demanded. Amara felt him inhale, corralling his anger with composure.

"You, Mr. Morris!" she snapped. "Carrying her like that. It's far too intimate for a man your age. Of anyone."

"Why don't you come carry your daughter?" Gramps suggested, hesitating long enough to prove that the woman had no intention of rising to the occasion or putting a wrinkle in her sweater. "Amara is tired and sore. Whether you find it inappropriate or not, I'm taking her to her room to rest."

Mrs. Duncan huffed and poked an elbow into her husband's arm. He got up obediently and offered to take Amara from Gramps. For a second, Amara's instinct was to cling to Gramps like a child, afraid of being ripped away. But she allowed herself to be given to her father. Mr. Duncan's arms trembled as he tried to support her weight, as little as it was. Her dad's arms had never lifted her from a fall, carried her up the stairs to bed, or held her in his lap to read a story. Rightly so, his arms felt as foreign as a palm tree on the North Pole.

As Mr. Duncan placed her on her bed, she noticed tiny beads of sweat forming along the edge of his hairline. An athletic man he was not, and neither was his wife. Where had she gotten her desire to be outdoors with horses, cows, and chores? Certainly not from the perspiring man before her. Composing himself, and unsure what to do next, Mr. Duncan looked around her room.

"This is nice," he said breathlessly. "Different, but nice." They were finally alone. The man may not have acted like a dad should, but he was one thing for certain: honest. So she asked what she'd been wanting to ask.

"Why are you here?"

"To visit."

Amara gave him a firm look. "After all these years? No phone calls. No letters. Why now?"

He sat on the edge of the bed, folding his hands nervously. He had no right to be here, Amara thought, after he had told her to never come back and then never called, never wrote, never visited. Not even when she had sent a picture of Charlie as a newborn baby.

"Mr. Morris called us," he said. "He explained to your mom what had happened."

*What had happened* was such a formal phrase. Amara wanted to hear him say it. "Which part?"

Wringing his hands, Mr. Duncan's thin lips parted, but nothing came out.

"Do you mean the fact that I nearly died, at a place—" Amara stopped short of saying the word *Mom*. "—*she* abhorred, and predicted I would die at? Or was it the fact she was wrong? That I didn't die? Or did she come to gloat that it was my husband who died? How could she hate a good man she'd never said even a word to? You know he died saving my life, don't you?"

Mr. Duncan nodded. "I'm sorry, Amara." After clearing his throat, he continued. "Mr. Morris explained there had been a terrible accident. He thought you might need a mother's care."

"Then you brought the wrong woman. She's not my mother, and I don't believe she cares."

Refusing to meet her eyes, Mr. Duncan glanced at the open bedroom door. "Of course she cares about you." He wrung his hands. "And she wants to take you home. *We* want to take you home. That's why we're here."

Amara felt the sting of tears beginning to form in her eyes. Unfortunately, no amount of blinking could chase them away. She hated how weak they made her look. She hated how weak losing Sonny made her. More than that, she hated how unsure her future felt. Her entire world had been doing nothing but collapsing around her.

"Please leave me," Amara said, turning her face away. For a moment, he hesitated. Then obliging—relieved, really—he quietly walked out of the room, clicking the door shut behind him.

As tired as Amara felt, sleep would not find her. Even after the tears died away and she could no longer hear the low muttering of voices drifting from the other room. A single thought kept running around and around in her head, riotous, like an abandoned yearling. Stirring up the peace, stomping and screaming in anguish.

*Gramps wanted me to leave?*

\*\*

On Sunday, Amara woke in time to help with the morning chores. After awkwardly bathing, blotting herself dry, and clumsily climbing into clothes that didn't fit, she planned to tiptoe to the kitchen and dig up a granola bar—something fast that didn't require cooking. The last thing she wanted to do was tip off her parents that she was attempting to sneak out. She knew Gramps would have put them up in Charlie's room—he was a good man. But now, thanks to him, she felt like a teenager again. Desperate for freedom.

Just as she was about to exit her bedroom, from the corner of her eye, she saw an old friend: little glass brown eyes staring out at her from beneath the clothes hanging in the closet. Her stuffed black horse must have been buried under something she had moved while dressing, for now he was revealed and half-fallen over. Her spirits low, she went to him, hungry for anything providing even the smallest trace of comfort.

She held him up so they were eye to eye. "Hi there."

The black horse stared, unblinking.

"It's alright, I know," she said, and hugged the fluffy stuffed body to her chest. "I miss him too. What are you doing hiding in there?"

There was no reply.

"I wish I could hide too," she admitted. "Well, I'm afraid if I have to go out there, you ought to as well. It's only fair."

Horse tucked under her arm, she cracked her bedroom door, and like a stealthy soldier, she peeked out the tiny opening to the right and then to the left. Charlie was sound asleep, buried under a mountain of blankets on the couch. Other than Charlie, she didn't see or hear anyone, so she quietly slipped out. Setting the horse on the counter, she dug in the cupboard until she located a cherry-flavored package of Pop-Tarts. Her nose wrinkled in displeasure as the foil wrapping crinkled loudly in her hand. She'd wait to open it outside.

"Morning," she heard Gramps greet her from behind. "Where are you off to?"

Amara jumped. "Geez, Gramps!" she stage-whispered. "You scared me. I'm running away from home."

Both sides of Gramps' gray mustache bent upwards.

"I'm feeding the horses," she confessed.

"First," Gramps grumbled quietly, "having you feed the horses was a mistake. Francis was right. I thought you might try to take another crack at it, so he's already feeding them as we speak."

Amara rolled her eyes. How she hated hearing the words "Francis was right."

"And second, you're spending the day with your folks." Sensing her growing agitation, he whispered, "They only requested one day, Amara. They leave tomorrow."

"No!" Amara whispered harshly. "They showed up yesterday unannounced. That was their *one* day, their chance to do whatever it was they came for." She intentionally failed to mention that she knew what they had come for, and why. To take her away. Gramps wanted her to go. With the pain of this knowledge, Amara added, "They discarded me as their daughter the moment I embarrassed them. I chose here over the life of a wealthy prisoner. Then my dad warned me to never come back. What kind of man says something like that? What kind of woman instigates such a deep-seeded fear of revenge? I'll tell you. The two people upstairs, sleeping in my daughter's room. They don't deserve our hospitality."

"They're your parents."

"No. They're not." Amara could feel tears beginning to form out of pure frustration—and hurt. Determined not to allow Gramps into her world, she turned away and started hobbling for the front door.

"Amara..." Gramps called in a loud whisper. "Where are you going?"

"To do my job," she answered, shutting the door firmly behind her.

"You're going to leave Charlie here?" Gramps called out, but the door was already shut firmly behind her. Only the stuffed black horse remained. His chin dropped to his chest.

Why had her parents showed up? He knew very well from the conversation on the phone with Mrs. Duncan that they didn't want a single thing to do with Charlie. He comforted himself with the knowledge: Amara would never leave without her daughter. So what good could possibly come from all this? Of course, he knew the answer. None.

## CHAPTER TWENTY-SEVEN

Amara had the hood up on the barn's utility tractor, preparing it to be stored for the winter, just the way Sonny had taught her. Using a tester to check the antifreeze was good for Montana's cold winter temperatures. Then she completely drained the fuel out of the gas tank, replacing it with about half a gallon of high-octane fuel. After carefully ascending the tractor, she started it up and ran it, letting the fuel run through the system.

While she waited, she glimpsed Francis pulling into the lot and parking Sonny's pickup and long bed. She could tell he'd spotted her, too. Though she tried to ignore his presence, he walked over anyway. *Oh joy,* she thought.

"What are you doing playing around with this here tractor, little lady?" he called up to her, then spat on the ground in his typical fashion.

She could smell the unique odor that high-octane fuel produces, which meant it had made its way through the tractor's system and out the exhaust. She cut the engine and began her slow, careful descent. "Readying her for winter."

"Uh-huh." The disbelief in his voice was thick as mud after a winter thaw. "You shouldn't be playing around with the equipment. It's none of your business, anyway."

Narrowing her eyes, she asked, "How do you figure?" When she put a wrench over the transmission fluid cap, Francis put his gloved hand over hers, causing her to cringe.

"Whoa, whoa, whoa," he said. "Do you know what you're doing before taking a wrench and prying things open? Does Mr. Morris know what you're doing?"

Amara resisted the temptation to deck him. Elder or not, she didn't like being touched—or disbelieved. "Taking care of the equipment has been my job, Mr. Shultz, for years. I take great pride in it. If you must know, I'm checking the transmission fluid for condensation."

Francis removed his hand. His blank expression made it obvious that he knew nothing about tractors. He wasn't about to admit it, of course. Instead, he simply nodded, a disgruntled pout on his face.

To make the point that she knew what she was doing, whether he did or not, she continued to explain. "Not only does water separate from oil, it freezes."

Francis nodded knowingly, so Amara waited for him to finish her statement for her with the reason why this was relevant. When he didn't—or couldn't—she resumed. "If there's any condensation in the transmission oil, and someone were to start it up, it could freeze the gears."

Francis nodded again, approvingly this time, as if it had all just been a little test. Without another word, he turned and stalked away. Curious, she watched him. Was he off to accomplish a chore, making his snarky attitude worth having around? Or was he headed off to take another long coffee break? The man consumed his wages in coffee—and that's saying something, considering the price of coffee. Sure enough, he waved off and headed straight towards the house, spitting as he went. She was rewarded for not firing him on the spot when she saw Charlie barreling up the hill toward her.

"Mommy!" She lifted her gloved hand weakly as she flew past Francis, who paid her no mind. "Mommy!" she called again.

"Good morning, baby." Amara mustered up a smile for her beautiful blonde daughter.

"Mr. and Mrs. Duncan are wondering when breakfast will be," Charlie said, out of breath from the short sprint up the hill.

"Beats me. What are they making?"

A playful smile crossed Charlie's lips. "I don't think they're making anything."

"And what about you?" Amara said, wrapping her glove around Charlie's sweet face. "What did you have?"

"Toast and peanut butter," she replied, grinning.

"Good for you." Amara glanced at the house and then back at her daughter. "Want to help me with the tractor?"

"I haven't cleaned the stalls yet," she admitted.

"Tell you what, I'll help you. Then you can help me. Then neither of us will have to go back into the house."

Charlie grinned, showing no teeth. The deal was accepted.

Inside the barn, Amara stopped at the first stall where Moses was, still refusing to go any closer to Nick or the other gelding. "I can muck one-handed. I'll get started on Moses' stall. Would you turn them all out into the paddock?"

"Sure," said Charlie. She retrieved the rope fastened to the wall of the tack room and stretched it across the hay area, which would keep the horses from buffeting on the hay after she let them out. After snapping it onto the eye hook on the opposite wall, all was ready.

Amara rolled the wheelbarrow over to Moses' stall and grabbed a pick while Charlie opened the back door, which led directly to the large paddock. Once the door was open, she helped Charlie by letting Moses out, who stepped forward, dropped his head, and used the fat muscly nub on the tip of his muzzle to sift and sort the dirt for bits of hay left scattered on the floor. Before Charlie had the chance to let out the rest of the horses, Amara ducked into the stall, pulled the wheelbarrow into the stall door, and applied all of her concentration to the job of picking up Moses' blobs of manure and wet sawdust, then dropping them into the wagon.

She could hear the sound of hooves thudding over the hard-packed dirt floor, and Charlie's voice speaking encouragingly as they exited. Assuming all the horses had left, she was startled when a long brown face appeared in the doorway, hanging over her wheelbarrow and smelling its contents. It was the gelding Sonny had ridden the day he died.

Amara felt her heart stop, like the hands of a clock after it had ticked its last tock. The gelding stared at her with its big, brown, knowing eyes as she stood there, nearly suffocating. If she didn't know better, she would have thought he was reading words written on her soul: *It's my fault.*

It was true. It was her fault Sonny had died. It was her fault the ranch was void of life. Everyone missed him. Everyone needed him. Gramps, Charlie, her, the horses, the cows, even the birds. There was a great emptiness within the soul of the ranch. It had known it belonged to Sonny. And now Sonny was gone. Neither Amara nor even Gramps could heal the land. Therefore, it was right the gelding blamed her, as she had known he would. The sadness in his face was unmistakable. Unbearable. It was why she had been avoiding him. All of them, really.

"I'm sorry," she said at last, tears streaming down her face. She was still holding the pick in her left hand like a frozen statue. "I lost him too," she said, the tears silently rolling without an end in sight. "I'm sorry." She meant it. "Do you think I should leave?"

"Bear, what are you doing?" Charlie asked, throwing her arm over his neck and giving him a squeeze. "Why aren't you going outside with everyone else?" Then she glanced up and saw Amara, suspended in time, a river of tears flooding down her cheeks. "Mommy? Are you okay?"

Amara nodded. The motion helped her head clear, and she started wiping the wetness from her face. She reminded herself that it was she who had decided she needed to focus on what pain revealed—strength, courage, and perseverance, not pain itself.

Charlie pulled on the gelding's long, thin neck, and with a blink, he started to follow her.

"Wait," Amara said, sniffing. "What did you call him?"

"Call him?" Charlie looked at her, confused. "You mean Bear?"

"Yes," Amara confirmed, giving her best attempt at a thin smile. "Did you give him that name?"

"No. Gramps said Daddy gave Bear his name."

Amara swallowed hard. "When? Daddy never told me that." She could see Charlie hesitating, holding something back. "Do you know, baby?"

Charlie nodded, then looked at Bear, intently studying his mane. Absently, her small fingers stroked the soft brown hair on his jaw on the other side of his long face.

For a moment, Amara was distracted by the realization of just how calm Bear was. He wasn't the same jittery, excitable horse she had mounted up next to the day she and Sonny had taken off to relocate the fillies. She realized that she hadn't asked Gramps about anything since that awful day. She hadn't asked him how *he* was. She hadn't asked him what had become of the fillies. She hadn't asked how he had gotten the geldings back home. And she hadn't asked about the cougar. Was it alive? Was it still causing problems? Clearly, her singlemindedness knew no boundaries.

Bear blinked. He was enjoying the sweet fingers stroking his face, but his eyes were fixed on Amara. "I'm sorry I hadn't bothered to learn your name," she told him.

Charlie looked up. "You couldn't have, Mommy."

"Why's that, baby?"

Suddenly, Charlie appeared bashful. "Gramps said Daddy told him Bear's name in a dream."

Amara felt like someone had just punched her in the throat. "Oh?"

"Do you dream about Daddy?" Charlie asked.

"Yes..."

"Me too." Her lips barely curved up before falling again. At that, she began walking Bear towards the back door. Amara stood there, still holding the pick in her left hand, listening to Charlie visiting with Bear as she escorted him outside. "When I find you a Christmas tree," she heard Charlie saying, "I'll ask Gramps to put it in the big window. That way, you and Daddy can see it glowing when you look down."

Amara's hand flew to her mouth. There had never been a more selfless child. She hadn't wanted a Christmas tree for herself. She'd wanted a glowing tree for Bear and Sonny. For Bear to see from the barn on the hill, and for Sonny to see from the sky, where eagles soared.

\*\*

"Charlie," said Gramps, as he entered the house. "Where's your mom?"

Charlie shrugged. She was sitting at the counter on her favorite stool, surrounded by piles of notebooks, papers, drawings, and colored pencils, her blue box sitting on the floor at her feet. The pencil in her hand was carefully forming word after word in one of her many notebooks—she loved notebooks the way most children her age love Barbies and dolls. She was writing another one of her stories. When she finished the word "squirrel," she looked up at him proudly.

"I helped Mommy work on the tractor today," she boasted in a hushed voice.

"Good job!"

Mrs. Duncan was sitting in the living room, a laptop open next to her on the couch. She stared at it for a while, jotted something down on the paperwork she held in her lap, then stuck the pen in her mouth and stared at the laptop again. When she looked at him, she glared. If she was upset that he had disturbed her peace, well, so be it. That particular wind blew in both directions.

"Where's your..." he trailed off. It hadn't escaped his notice that Charlie hadn't referred to Amara's parents as Grandma and Grandpa, any more than

Amara referred to them as Mom and Dad. Charlie was a very perceptive young lady. "Where's Mr. Duncan?" he amended.

Charlie shrugged again. "He was upstairs for a while. Then he went outside. On a walk, I guess."

"What's for dinner?" Charleston asked. "I'm peckish." He put both his elbows on the counter next to her, and his cowboy hat bumped her head. She looked up, giggling softly.

"I don't know," she replied. "What are you making?"

"No one has made anything all day," Mrs. Duncan complained from across the room, throwing her paperwork and pen down.

Charleston looked at her as though she were an afterthought. "Well, why didn't you?"

Mrs. Duncan huffed. "This is not my house, Mr. Morris. I do not presume to stick my nose into cupboards that don't belong to me."

"That's a pity. A person could starve that way." Charlie started to giggle, but Charleston touched her arm lightly, and she stopped.

"I can't say how rude you have all been," said Mrs. Duncan. "All three of you left my husband and I here alone, all day. It's a horrible way to treat guests." Now she was pushing herself to her feet, still wearing dress shoes, despite having never gone outside.

"I didn't invite you to be my guest," Charleston said, turning to face the woman whom he had never known to say a kind word to anyone, least of all her own daughter.

"You called *me*."

"Yes, I made a call to you in good faith."

His anger lit a fire in his gut at the memory of that particular phone call. The disrespect she had for every member of his family was enough to make him throw her out on her ear. But with Charlie sitting right behind him, listening in on every word, he had to be civil. The last thing he wanted was for her to blame him for whatever transpired during this visit. Because whatever it was wasn't going to be good. This was the storm he had felt coming.

"I came here to see Amara," Mrs. Duncan snapped. "Produce her."

Charleston stood up straight. "Listen," he said, running his fingers over his mustache. "This is a working ranch. Amara is working."

As true as it was, he withheld the fact that he knew she was also hiding. On his way back to the house from replacing those rotten posts he hadn't gotten to yet, he had run into her driving Sonny's pickup. She rolled her window down, explaining to him that she was making rounds and checking livestock. They both knew she wasn't likely to see much livestock from the roads.

Mrs. Duncan huffed, crossing her arms across her chest and scowling. Briefly, Charleston thought about telling her that she would look more attractive without the scowl, but thought better of it and said nothing. "I regret having come here. I vowed never to set even a tire on this dreadful property. I sincerely wish I hadn't. Does that make you feel better, Mr. Morris?"

"No, not really."

"Amara has run off from me again," she confessed. A far-off look of hurt crossed her face, but it quickly vanished. As much as he hated having anything in common with this woman, he understood this one certain sentiment. She quickly replaced the hurt with resentment. "I would have left hours ago without her," she acknowledged bitterly. "Except my husband seems to have run off too!"

Charleston's phone rang in his pocket. "Hello?" he answered, his voice thick with thankfulness for having been rescued, at least temporarily.

"This is Henry," the voice on the other end said.

"Henry?"

"Clare's husband," the voice said.

"Who is Clare?" Charleston asked. "If this is a prank–"

"I'm Clare," Mrs. Duncan answered. "Who's asking? Who would be calling *you*, mentioning *me* by my first name?" Her arms were still firmly crossed over her chest.

"Your husband," Charleston answered over his shoulder.

"I went for a walk," Mr. Duncan was saying. "I needed some fresh air…"

"He's calling *you*?" Mrs. Duncan's voice squealed, displeased. "And he has his phone? I've called him ten times, and he didn't answer. I figured he left his phone up in the room…"

"Tell her I must have had the volume off," Mr. Duncan said.

"He said his volume was off," Charleston told Mrs. Duncan.

"I'm up at your family cemetery now, by the road."

"Tell *him* I want him here *now*!" said Mrs. Duncan. "I can't believe he…"

Charleston put his hand up to her, which did nothing to cut her off. He turned to her, frowning. "You walked all the way up to the cemetery?" he asked. "That's–"

"He shouldn't be out in the snow, having eaten nothing..."

"I wanted to pay my respects before we left," Mr. Duncan said, then sighed heavily into the receiver. "Tell her I ate three of those boiled eggs in the fridge."

"Is he listening to me?"

Charleston narrowed his eyes at Mrs. Duncan. "Unfortunately," he muttered, "he ate three of the boiled eggs." Turning his back to her, he walked to the refrigerator. Boiled eggs sounded good. "Amara will appreciate you having paid respects," Charleston said to Mr. Duncan. "When are you planning to leave?"

Mrs. Duncan followed him. "He ate boiled eggs? Just got into someone else's fridge and started eating boiled eggs?"

"Originally, we planned to leave tomorrow. However, after how today developed, we haven't had much of a chance to convince Amara to return with us, her being absent and all. Perhaps we'll stay a bit longer."

Charlie was staring at Mrs. Duncan in amusement. Never had they had such a demanding guest. "You can get into the fridge any time. Around here, you'll starve if you don't," she said, using Charleston's words.

Mrs. Duncan patted both sides of her head, pressing any stray hairs back into place. "You need a cook," she said to Charlie pointedly.

Charlie looked at her feet, dangling from the stool. "My daddy was the cook."

Charleston, meanwhile, was saying, "Stay a bit longer? I don't think that's a good–"

Mrs. Duncan's head snapped sharply. "Stay a bit longer?" she asked, her tone and expression soaked with displeasure. "I don't intend to stay on where I'm clearly not welcome."

"Mr. Morris, please understand," said Mr. Duncan. "My wife has her heart set on helping her daughter. So much so that she has agreed to come here. Even after everything."

"Even after everything?" Charleston echoed. "What everything? Amara hasn't so much as heard a word from either of you until yesterday."

"It certainly wasn't any fault of ours," Mrs. Duncan inserted arrogantly. "The girl chose to stay here, rebelliously, like the ungrateful schoolgirl she was. Still is, it seems."

"Which is why we have come," Mr. Duncan explained evenly, without the bitterness his wife had in tonnage. "To make things right for her."

Charleston knew making things right had nothing to do with Amara, and everything to do with Mrs. Duncan's manipulative scheme. "You mean to take her away from what she loves," he said. It wasn't a question, it was a fact. Nonetheless, he had a fleeting fear Mr. Duncan would take the fact and lash out at him. To Charleston's surprise, he didn't. He didn't even seem to register any particular meaning or emotion. Mrs. Duncan did, however.

"She loves us!" Mrs. Duncan yelled, standing behind Charleston with her hands propped firmly upon her hips, her body leaning towards him.

Charleston noted how hungry she looked, her eyes nearly colorless, like a crow hovering above a dying carcass. Charlie's eyes were as wide as saucers, never having witnessed such hostility.

"Yes, we want her to come back with us," Mr. Duncan answered, not at all aware of the drama on the other end of the phone—either that, or just ignoring it. "I believe there's much for her to learn to love. Now that she's made a few mistakes, and hopefully has grown up some, maybe she will finally be able to see things from an adult's perspective."

Charleston's rough hand went to his face and started massaging his clenched jaw. He should have shaved today. It was coarse, but he didn't care this morning and he didn't care now.

"Mrs. Duncan," Charlie spoke up. "I can make you a peanut butter and jelly sandwich. I heard you say you're hungry. I can find a Jell-O cup in the cupboard. There's cherry, strawberry—"

"No," Mrs. Duncan snapped, not removing her eyes from Charleston's tall back. "You ought to run along. I don't want Jell-O. This conversation is for adults, and does not involve you."

"I know it's not what you want to hear," Mr. Duncan said, "but we think it's what's best for her—after everything that's happened." There was a rustling on the other end, like he had switched the phone to his other ear. "I think you know it too. You called *us*."

Charleston felt like someone had just stapled his feet to the floor. He hadn't called them to take away what was left of his family. Amara wasn't coping after Sonny's death. She was failing, and he was scared she wasn't going to pull through. At his wits' end, he wondered if what she needed was a mother's love and comfort. However, after calling and speaking with Mrs. Duncan, he knew reaching out to her had been a mistake. Now he feared it had been much *more* than a mistake.

"You're talking about my mommy," Charlie said quietly, sure the conversation involved her. "I don't want to leave."

Mrs. Duncan turned to Charlie and said, her voice flowing slowly with sugary fakeness, "It's not your decision, now is it?"

"Anyway," Mr. Duncan continued, "I called because Amara is here."

"What?" Charleston croaked. Amara was listening to this entire conversation? Did that mean she agreed with leaving? He whirled around, not sure where to go. He needed a place to sit. Quickly, before he fell, his long legs carried him to a stool next to Charlie. He sat heavily, both Mrs. Duncan and Charlie staring at him.

"I found her lying next to your son's grave, wrapped in a blanket, asleep," said Mr. Duncan. "This is very dangerous behavior. She could have frozen to death out there, and no one even knew where she had gone. God only knows how long she's been lying here." There was a short pause as he made up his mind. Had to straighten his spine, perhaps. Then he said, with confidence, "She can't stay here with you anymore. Especially after stumbling across this, we won't allow it. This life isn't right for her. Clare is right, you're going to kill her, just like…"

"Gramps…" Charlie poked his shoulder with a slender finger.

Charleston's head had been in his hands, wondering what he had done, what this all had come to. Then Mr. Duncan's words trailed off. *Just like…* Charleston's head shot up so quickly the vertebrae in his neck popped, like someone had twisted a length of bubble wrap. "Just like what?"

"Gramps," Charlie said, looking up at him pleadingly, "I don't want…"

"Nothing. Nothing," said Mr. Duncan quickly. "Would you drive my wife up here to come get her?"

"Hush, child," Mrs. Duncan scolded. "You're interrupting." She stepped towards Charleston. "What's wrong? What's going on?" When she didn't receive so much as a glance, she demanded, "Answer me, Mr. Morris."

"You have my permission to bring her home using her pickup," Charleston said, feeling dizzy, and more tired than he had felt in his entire life—as if years of hard work had caught up to him all at once. He wasn't sure if he was even strong enough to move from the stool to his bed. His heart felt too weak to withstand the few extra pumps it would take to get there. Instead, it might just stop, right here and now, in front of Charlie. He couldn't have that, so he sat and concentrated on breathing. "May I speak to Amara?" he asked weakly.

"No," said Mrs. Duncan. "If Amara is there, *I* want to speak to her. I'm really quite upset she left me here all day, knowing full well..."

"She's still asleep," Mr. Duncan answered.

"You mean she's fallen *back* to sleep, after you put her in the warm pickup," Charleston told Mr. Duncan, hoping he was right.

"No, I mean, she's still asleep on the ground next to your son's grave. It's–"

Charleston stood up so quickly that the stool he had been resolved to die upon a moment ago flew backwards a good ten feet. Not bothering to disconnect the call, he dropped the phone into his pocket as he ran for the front door, grabbing his pickup keys on the way out, hoping, praying, he wouldn't need it to call an ambulance. Not for Amara, anyway. "Come on, Charlie," he called over his shoulder. "Unless you want to stay here."

"No," Charlie answered bluntly. He could hear a few of her colored pencils fall to the floor, and her tiny shoeless feet sprinting after him. Neither of them stopped for a coat.

## CHAPTER TWENTY-EIGHT

To Mr. Duncan's credit, at least he had woken Amara and had her sitting on the bench by the time Gramps and Charlie pulled up, the heater pumping viciously in preparation. She was sitting in the darkness amongst the snow-covered plants, which would bloom bright reds and pinks come spring, the sun having descending in the sky. Being outdoors after dark during the winter was not just a bad idea; it was unforgivable. The weather was unforgiving. People all over the world had been known to die from far less perilous conditions than Montana's plummeting temperatures.

As Charleston pushed his door open and stepped out, he couldn't help but notice that Mr. Duncan was sitting next to Amara, his jacket wrapped tightly around himself, hands in his lap. Looking in from the outside, Charleston reflected, the man looked more like a concerned stranger, waiting for the police to arrive so they could take over, than a father. Immediately his heart ached for Amara. She had been born into a world without a foundation of love, then after she had found it in Sonny, it had been ripped out from under her. Amara was broken, and Charleston didn't know if she could ever be whole again.

She was sitting on the bench, wrapped in the blanket from Sonny's pickup. When her tired eyes lifted and met Charleston's, Mr. Duncan looked over too. But Charleston was intensely locked on Amara. He didn't give a damn about her father.

"What are we doing sitting in the snow?" he asked as he approached. She didn't answer.

Commendably, Mr. Duncan stood, offering Charleston his seat. "She won't leave," he said, likely covering for having failed to get her somewhere warmer.

Charleston nodded, acknowledging the confession and dismissing him from the duty of watching over her in one fell swoop. Despite Charleston having dismissed him, it still came as a surprise when Mr. Duncan did the most unfatherly thing possible: he walked away. Sonny's keys dangling from his fingers, he retreated to Amara's pickup and left.

Sighing, Charleston plopped down next to Amara, lowering his chin to his chest. He felt for her, though he would never say as much. Amara wasn't the type of girl who wanted pity. If she was down, it was how she honestly felt. She wasn't looking for anyone's commiseration. She was just like him, in a way: a tough turkey.

Amara opened her blanket and wrapped it around him, laying her tired head on his shoulder. "I'm sorry I worried you," she whispered sadly. "I just...I just..."

"I know," Charleston said, patting her knee. "I know."

Almost as if on cue, Charlie crawled from the cab of the warm pickup, clutching the blanket from behind Charleston's pickup seat. Charleston and Amara made room for her between them, where it was most warm, and she snuggled in, throwing the second blanket over the three of them to share. They sat, staring at the mound of dirt, shivering. It was only Sonny's body, not Sonny. They understood. But where else were they supposed to go? This was where half the family was resting. It only made sense that the rest join them, if only for a while.

Somehow, as the three of them sat there trembling from the cold, something clicked. Charleston felt it jolt through him, as though a finger of lightning had tapped him on each shoulder. This was his family. These were *his* girls now. Sonny had entrusted him to look after them. No one else. Of course, that wasn't a new concept, but it was a renewed faith, a strengthened understanding of what he needed to do.

Placing a kiss on top of Charlie's head, Charleston said, "Let's go, girls. We're going to look like popsicles in another five minutes. Say good night."

"Good night, Daddy," Charlie said.

Amara said nothing, but began helping Charlie up. The girl, who was the fastest to recover from the cold, sprinted towards the idling pickup, eager to warm up. Charleston stifled a grunt as he forced his old joints to lift his weight from the low bench, then without waiting for the muscles and spine in his old back to agree to the terms, he bent over, bundled Amara into his arms, and carried her to his pickup. The strength of his youth long gone, all that was left now were stubborn bones and an even more stubborn determination.

"I can walk," Amara complained, feeling him stagger in the snow.

"You can walk tomorrow," Charleston maintained. "In fact, tomorrow, you can carry *me*."

Amara laughed, and for the first time since Sonny's death, he saw a light twinkle in her eyes.

When they arrived back at the house, Amara insisted on removing herself from the pickup and walking inside under her own power. "It's time to get stronger," she said. Charleston couldn't have agreed more. So, painfully, he stood by and watched her hobble slowly toward the house while Charlie ran ahead.

"I've been meaning to ask you something," Amara said over her shoulder. "Was it the mountain lion that spooked the horses?"

Charleston pursed his lips thoughtfully.

"I want to know, Gramps."

He nodded. She was right. She deserved to hear what had happened. "It wasn't the mountain lion that spooked the horses," he said. "It was her cubs. They were hiding in the brushes, still too inexperienced to hunt."

After swirling the information around in her head like wine in a glass, she asked, "What happened to the lion?"

"I shot her."

"And the filly?"

"She died. Suffocated by the bite."

"And you, Gramps?" Amara asked, turning to face him. "How are you?"

Charleston nodded, bowing his head so his hat prevented her from seeing his face. "Doing alright."

After peeking inside, Charlie hollered back to them. "They're still here!" she called, speaking of Mr. and Mrs. Duncan.

*So much for subtlety,* Charleston thought.

"Thank you," Amara said, rolling her eyes.

Inside, the smell of cooking food hit them in the face. Mrs. Duncan was in the kitchen, boiling spaghetti noodles and warming a loaf of buttered French bread in the oven. In a bowl, she had mixed together a salad and sprinkled it with Italian dressing and parmesan cheese.

Amara's jaw dropped. "I don't think I've ever seen you cook."

"My mother cooked," Mrs. Duncan replied flatly, as if the simple statement explained everything.

"I see you found what you needed," Charleston noted, and headed straight for his chair, as if a woman he didn't particularly care for cooked dinner in his kitchen every day.

Mr. Duncan was sitting on the couch, an ankle set upon his bony knee, a book in hand, glasses sliding down his nose. He stared over the top of his glasses for a minute, then finally said, "We're leaving in the morning."

Charleston nodded, straight-faced, pretending he didn't care one way or another.

Mrs. Duncan turned, checking that the bread wasn't burning, and for a moment Amara glimpsed what she had guessed other moms might have been like. But when she turned back towards Amara, there was a cold politeness in her hard, tight expression, and the vision of what might have been faded away.

"There's something I hoped to be able to talk to you about today, Amara," Mrs. Duncan said. "Thus far, you've successfully disrupted my plan, but now that you're here, let's get it over with. Have a seat."

Amara sat, feeling more like a child than ever.

Standing over Amara, Mrs. Duncan looked down her nose. "I don't want to get into an argument. Just know, I've made up my mind on this, and your father supports the idea. We're going home tomorrow." She paused. The woman had always known how to control a conversation. "We're taking you with us." She put up a hand, clearly expecting an argument.

Amara noticed that the hand had aged, the skin wrinkling even in the palm.

## Holder of the Horses

When Mrs. Duncan was met with silence, she continued, "As I'm certain you can now see, this place is unhealthy. Whatever dreams you have been trying to chase, it's time to let them go. It's time to move on. You can only move on if we take you away, give you a fresh start. Everything can get back on track. This can all be a bad dream. A lesson learned."

"Get back on what track?" Amara asked.

Mrs. Duncan smiled. "The track I set out for you. You can come home, put your head down, and find yourself amongst the best, on the path to success. We'll both finally feel we've been successful. It's not too late."

"*Why* do you want this so badly? What does your success have to do with me?"

Mrs. Duncan looked stumped. Buying herself time, she slipped an oven mitt over her hand and pulled the French bread from the oven, placing it on the counter. After having thought about it, she turned back and answered, "It's all I've ever wanted, a daughter I could show off and brag about. It's what every mother wants. To be proud of her daughter. To be proud she helped her daughter get there. It's a mother's legacy, I suppose." Amara was quiet, and Mrs. Duncan misinterpreted the calm as acceptance. She touched Amara's pale cheek with a finger, not recognizing Amara's rigid response. "I'll help you find another husband, help you start a new life. Then, in time, you'll have a successful child too, and I'll be a grandmother." She was glowing in the boasting she could already envision.

"Charlie–" Amara started.

"No," was all Mrs. Duncan said, deep lines forming between her eyebrows.

"No what?" Amara narrowed her eyes.

"Mr. Morris' grandchild stays here. She is *his* grandchild, not mine. You will undoubtedly have another."

There was a tiny gasp and a scuffle of movement. Amara turned and saw Charlie fleeing, upset.

"How can you say such a thing?" Amara yelled at the woman she refused to call Mom.

The front door slammed.

"Charlie!" Amara called. "Wait!" Getting to her feet, she met Gramps at the front door.

"Where's Charlie going?" Gramps asked her, holding up Charlie's empty jacket. She had left without it, again.

"She just ran outside! I don't know where she's going!" Amara grabbed Gramps' arm and squeezed. Alarm spread over his tired face like dark clouds. "We have to catch her."

Mrs. Duncan huffed. "Such a dramatic child. Let her go," she said flatly. "She'll be back as soon as she realizes what a dumb stunt she's pulled. Running off into the snow...not a bright child."

"Get out!" Amara screamed.

"How dare you speak to me that–"

The front door slammed again. Gramps was gone, as were his and Charlie's jackets. Amara reached for the door handle, prepared to stomp out into the cold darkness after them. She was terrified of what could happen to her baby. The handle twisted in her palm, and the latch withdrew from the strike plate, freeing the door to swing open without obstruction, when there was a breath across her neck. When she turned her head to glare at either Mrs. or Mr. Duncan, no one was there. Clare was a good six feet away, arms crossed, and Henry hadn't moved from his comfy spot on the couch—although he was staring. Shrugging away the sensation, she started to yank on the door.

A large, invisible hand covered hers and stopped her. It wasn't an aged, weak hand that had never known a day's hard work. It was a warm hand, one she recognized better than her own: Sonny. She stared in disbelief, seeing nothing, but afraid to look away for fear the warmth would vanish. But it did vanish, just as quickly as it had arrived. Reluctantly, she pulled her hand away from the doorknob, still feeling bizarrely warm.

Just then, a strong gust of wind hit the side of the log house. They all heard it. The windows rattled, and a tiny gust of air pushed under the door. Amara could have sworn it was warm, not cold. A natural curiosity taking over, she opened the door—though this time she had no intention of hobbling after Gramps. No, her going out there would only make matters worse, as hard as it was for her to do nothing. She told herself that she just needed to make sure. As insane as it sounded, she had to make sure Sonny wasn't standing out there.

Had she opened the door and found Sonny there, she would have undoubtedly fainted. Eyes straining into the bright snow and dark night, she searched for him just the same. She had felt him. Somehow, he had been here, right behind her. A faint movement at her feet caught her eye and seized her heart. A large white tail feather, from an eagle, drifted into the house, coming to a rest against the inside of Amara's right foot.

Bending carefully, she picked up the feather, staring at it. "Sonny," she whispered. In this moment, she knew—was comforted—that Charlie was alright, Sonny was with her, and Gramps would find her and bring her home.

\*\*

Hunkered down in Bear's stall, Charlie was crying. She had forgotten her jacket, and now as she shivered, she regretted it. Bear stood over her, blowing warm breath into her messy hair.

"I want my daddy," she cried.

Bear tickled her forehead with his whiskers, blowing his warm breath across her crumpled form and triggering goosebumps all over her body. She wrapped her tiny arms around herself, unable to stop the trembling. Bear dropped his muzzle into her lap and hung his head there. She reached up with both arms, pulling his head into her cold, trembling arms, snot and tears dripping into his mane.

Fifteen lengthy minutes later, Gramps found her sobbing at Bear's feet and carried her home, through the front door of the house. Mommy was there, and her worry quickly washed away with relief, arms open wide.

"Baby, don't ever do that again," Amara said, hugging her daughter tight.

"Found her in the barn, in Bear's stall," Gramps explained, "holding the damn horse in her arms."

Amara looked at her before hugging her again. "Don't ever do that again! You scared me. You could have been hurt."

"If he hadn't been keeping her warm..." Gramps trailed off, leaving the remainder of his thought unspoken.

"Bear wouldn't hurt me."

It was then that Charlie noticed the suitcases lined up, one right after the other, like the cars on a train. The suitcase train was waiting by the door to leave, Mr. and Mrs. Duncan standing possessively behind them.

Both of them looked down at her disapprovingly, if not a little arrogant.

Charlie pulled away. "Are you leaving me, Mommy?" Were Mr. and Mrs. Duncan taking her away? Scared, she glanced at Gramps for reassurance that he wouldn't let them. Gramps' hand froze on the hook where he had just hung his jacket. He was looking at Amara, waiting on an answer as well.

"No!" Amara declared emphatically, grabbing Charlie by the shoulders and glancing at the suitcases. "I would never leave you—or Gramps," she said, looking up at him.

His tired worried expression softened.

"Don't you remember?" Amara asked Charlie. "Wherever you go, I'll find you. I'll always be with you."

A tentative smile played on Charlie's lips. Little Bunny from her storybook. "I remember."

With a grimace and a grunt, Amara stood, grasping Charlie's hand firmly. "Our guests were just leaving, however. Say goodbye, Charlie."

"Goodbye," Charlie repeated obediently.

Neither of them replied. They simply retrieved their luggage and slipped out the door. At the last second, Mrs. Duncan turned, her face as expressionless as a stone—as cold, too. Charlie shivered. "You're a disappointment," she told Amara. "I should have had another child."

Gramps was next to Charlie in a heartbeat, throwing a casual arm over her head and around Amara's shoulders, linking them all together. Charlie was glad he did. For a second, she felt sad, like a broken toy. But Gramps' strong arm squeezed the pieces of the toy together in his vice grip, and she felt better—safer.

"One man's trash is another man's treasure," he declared, then kicked the door shut with his foot. The pretty wooden door slammed, concealing Mrs. Duncan's ugly scowl.

A small bubble of amusement gurgled up in Charlie's chest, trifling and insignificant at first. Then, like a Mentos plopped down inside a carbonated soft drink, the amusement fizzled and frothed, making its way further and further upward, growing in both size and intensity. A giggle escaped. Gramps' and Mommy's eyes turned upon her. In their serious faces, she saw a reflection—a reminder—of Mrs. Duncan's iron-clad scowl. Charlie imagined Mrs. Grumpy-Face stomping off in full tantrum. A laugh burst out, and in quick order, it became a string of unstoppable giggles and hoots.

There is very little else in this world which spreads as wildfire-fast as a child's laughter. In no time, the three of them were gasping for air in between fits and roars of merriment, grasping at their chests as though they were having simultaneous heart attacks. It was a much-needed moment of spontaneous re-balancing; the kind which can see a person through, however far away the next moment of laughter may be.

# CHAPTER TWENTY-NINE

"Looking good." Charleston nodded as Amara passed by him on a brown and white, four-year-old gelding.

Spring in the riding pen meant slop. Snow had fallen last night, but due to the warmer day temperatures, it quickly receded and turned to dirty slosh that splashed all over the legs of the gelding.

"Just rest your palm on the apple," he told her, referring to the saddle horn.

This was her first ride since...well, since. And she was trotting stiffly, as her injuries had understandably stripped her of her easy, naturally gliding hips. He had expected as much. What he hadn't expected was that her bravery had taken a massive hit. Charleston wasn't fooled; it wasn't the fall which had stolen her pluck, she'd fallen before. What had her paralyzed was Sonny's absence. A part of her spirit had died alongside him. Now the *fear* of a fall was real, and nine out of ten times, fear of a fall is a far greater danger than the fall itself.

Amara's pasty white hands gripped the horn and the reins—too hard. Charleston could see her thighs trembling from where he stood. Shaking his head, he sighed and adjusted his hat. "Relax," he said, wishing old Moses was still around.

Amara had trusted the old gelding since day one. Moses could have healed her, Charleston was sure. But Moses was gone. Passed away during the winter.

And with everyone still haunted at Sonny's passing, Charleston put Nick out to pasture to live his remaining days free as well: free as a domesticated, recently released horse without a partner and a purpose could be.

"I *am* relaxed," Amara snapped.

Charleston pursed his lips. "Uh-huh. You know," he said, rubbing his stubble-covered jaw, "I'll just hire back Francis, Smithy, or Darrel. Pretty sure one of them could get in shape faster than you."

"Don't you dare! Not one of them can train horses."

"How about what's his name? Tom. Maybe I could teach him to uncork a horse. He could probably learn to ride sooner than you could decide you still can."

"Tom was *insufferable*."

"Like someone else I know," Charleston muttered.

"What?"

"Nothing," Charleston mumbled. "You can't fire every man I try to take on. I need help, damn it."

"I'm sorry, Gramps, but I'll fire every last one if they're not worth a hill of beans."

"That's my phrase. You can't use it against me," said Charleston. "Besides, Smithy feeds twice as fast as you."

"*Fed* faster than me," Amara corrected him. "I fired him. Plus, it really isn't saying much, is it?"

Charleston shrugged. She had a point there, for sure.

Throwing her hands up, she added, "Plus, he was always late, *and* he couldn't even put on snow chains! Really, Gramps?" Knowing she was right, she lowered her hands again, taking a deep breath and lifting her chin. "Snow chains," she repeated, exasperated.

Charleston bobbed his head. "Well, I'll give ya, they're not Sonny."

"No one will ever be Sonny," Amara said quietly.

Charleston knew better than to keep pressing. "You know," he said, changing the subject, "how about we enlist you into therapy?"

"I already did physical therapy. I don't think it's going to help me ride."

"I'm not talking about physical therapy," Charleston remarked. "Besides, I didn't like them much."

Using the power of only one eye and a sideways glance, she sent him a death arrow. "Your point?"

He shrugged. "They thought I was a cowpoke." Calling a man "cowpoke" was an insult, and worth four knuckles to the jaw, if that were still permissible—which it wasn't.

"No one called you a cowpoke."

"They were *thinking* it," he said, tapping his hat.

Four tires of a pickup crept over the hill, interrupting Charleston's bantering. As it pulled alongside the riding pen, he noted the time on his wristwatch. The blue Ford was ten minutes early. Mentally, he added a point in favor of the new hand.

A thick, dark-skinned man stepped out of the Ford and landed in the snow with a wet, sloshy kerplunk. Charleston smiled, then glanced at Amara. She had halted her horse, eyes wide and mouth hanging open. When she recovered, a shining light almost seemed to burst forth from her.

"William!" she called. She began scrabbling to dismount, slowly, and with a certain amount of rigid discomfort. Still on the outside of the riding pen, Charleston fumbled to get in while William Sandgren—despite his sturdy build—leapt over the railing like a deer, and was by her side before Charleston could utter the words, "toss a copper, my bet's on the boy."

It was Charleston's turn to drag his chin off the ground when Amara allowed herself to slide into William's waiting arms. In the last six months, she hadn't wanted to be so much as addressed by the male gender—with the exception of him, of course. Carefully, William set her down in an inch worth of slop like one might set a china doll on a floating raft. Amara hugged him tightly.

"Miss Calamity Jane," he said, "I've got to say, you look scared shitless up there." He laughed over her head.

"I was not!" she replied, pulling away with a smile.

William lifted a single eyebrow.

"Okay, so I was a little nervous."

He nodded, satisfied, then sobered up. "I'm sorry I didn't stay and help out after Sonny's funeral."

Amara shook her head. "I heard about Nuna's battle with cancer. I'm so sorry I wasn't there for either of you."

"Looking back, I should have moved her home." He shook his head. "I thought it would be best if we stayed close to the hospital care. I thought we could beat it if we stayed and fought. Nuna had suggested going home to our family and friends time after time. She knew you needed help. I had been so determined, I didn't listen."

"William, don't kick yourself. You did what you had to live with, and that was doing absolutely everything you could, leaving no stone unturned for doubt to hide under. Besides, I wouldn't have noticed if you had. I didn't notice much."

William nodded his understanding. "It was amazing," he said, his face brightening with something indescribable. "Nuna's heart was at complete peace with everything. It's like she knew her future. No, it was more than that—it was like she knew *my* future. She wasn't physically strong, but she was strong. You know? So strong. Stronger than me, for sure."

"So was Sonny. It wasn't a long time, his knowing," Amara said, sadness threatening to overtake her. "But he knew. He was so..." Her voice trailed off. "...strong. I remember every word."

There was a long stretch of comfortable silence between the two of them as they stood toe to toe, each meditating on their own thoughts. After a bit, William began making good use of their shared time of necessary reflection, checking the tightness of the cinch around the pinto's belly. Then he pulled haphazard hairs of the horse's forelock out from where they were trapped under the leather piece going across its forehead, and smoothed them out between the ears.

"I'm doing better now," Amara said after a while.

"If you don't count her riding," Charleston grumbled, stepping up to lighten the mood. He knew how easily Amara could slip into a downward spiral if not regularly distracted.

William slapped the pinto, snapping himself out of his own familiar hole of despair. It's healthy to pay a visit to loved ones on the other side. It's unhealthy for the living to lose their spirit there. "Are you done for today?" he asked. "I think I may have seen a speck of potential intermixed with your terror."

Amara laughed. "I think I'm done. For today. I'll try again tomorrow, if Gramps has the time."

"I have the time," William offered.

She looked at him, unconvinced. "You can't drive all the way back out here. Are you staying with your parents?"

This time, William loosened the cinch around the pinto's belly. "Nope," he said with a smile, then took the reins from Amara's hands. For a moment, he looked at the leather split reins, frowning. Then he grunted and glanced at Charleston.

Charleston shook his head from side to side.

"Well," said William, meeting Amara's gaze this time. "I'll meet you here, tomorrow, same time."

"Bring your son tomorrow, will you?" Amara asked, looking around as if his son might have been hiding in plain sight the entire time.

A warm smile slowly spread across William's face, his white teeth glowing against his dark skin. Immediately, Charleston was reminded of Sonny's handsome smile. And judging by the look on Amara's face, she was remembering Sonny, too. "He's here, napping in the truck," William replied. "He was up at dawn helping Grandpa Sandgren lay down mulch before I stole him away. He was excited to come see the ranch, but he fell asleep on the way." William lifted his head, and bellowed over his shoulder. "Billy! Come meet my friends!"

The small, sleepy-eyed head of a nine-year-old boy appeared on the passenger side of the blue Ford. A moment later, the door creaked open, and out bounced a dark-skinned boy—the spitting image of a youthful William before he thickened. Dressed in his dirty farm clothes, heavy-soled miniature work boots, and a filthy cowboy hat two sizes too big, the boy stomped over, crushing the tallest mounds of snow which hadn't melted yet into smithereens as he approached.

## Holder of the Horses

"This is Mr. Charleston Morris and his daughter, Amara Morris," he told Billy. Billy extended his hand, and both Charleston and Amara took turns shaking it.

"How do you do?" Charleston asked.

Billy squinted, momentarily confused, but recovered quickly. "I do my chores pretty well without being asked. And homework sometimes, too," he replied seriously.

"Well, of course you do," Charleston replied with equal seriousness, slapping a hand on the boy's shoulder.

"It's nice to meet you, Billy," Amara said. "You know, we have all sorts of piles for you to tromp in." She gestured to the snow piles, the manure pile, and the wood shaving pile. "And there's a giant haystack called Mount Everest in the barn my daughter and I once climbed. She parachuted off the top."

Billy's eyes lit up.

"Whoa there." William put a hand on Billy's shoulder, but directed his attention to Amara. "Let's not encourage parachuting off haystacks."

"What happened to your sense of adventure?" Amara asked, but turned to Billy all the same. "It *was* pretend."

His head bobbed up and down, and his eyes began scanning the snow and wood shaving piles when a bundled-up girl emerged from the barn, pushing a wheelbarrow full of manure.

"That's my daughter, Charlie," Amara said. "She can play soon; she's nearly finished. Got a late start on her chores, it being Saturday."

Saying nothing further, Billy ran toward Charlie, a blurred tornado of arms and legs, as though he'd been drawn to her by a magnet. The stunned adults watched as he took his place by her side, enthusiastically offering to help push the cumbersome wheelbarrow. Charlie stood there, stunned in surprise, while Billy commenced to taking over the job, chattering like a squirrel just released from its cage. When she hesitated to join him, his skinny arm beckoned wildly.

"Huh," William grunted, observing his son's behavior. "That was odd."

Charleston and Amara laughed. Something they both had done more than once since William arrived. Charleston added another mental point to William's side of the imaginary scoreboard.

\*\*

Charlie watched as Billy drudged over the soft gravel path to the manure pile. The wheelbarrow was only half full, making it easier to push. When she cleaned the stalls, rather than making a couple heavy trips, she made numerous smaller ones. But for Billy, the job appeared effortless. She frowned, perturbed. Cleaning the barn was her responsibility, and she was proud of it—not because she enjoyed it, but because it was hard work. Billy was proving that notion incorrect.

After the manure slid out of the wagon, landing in a heap at the base of the manure pile, Charlie took the wheelbarrow back. "Thank you," she half-snapped, and took it back inside the barn, setting it up on end against the wall.

Billy followed her in, chatting on and on. "Grandpa Sandgren told me I'm a hard worker, and I am. I like chores. The harder, the better. My dad said he's going to teach me how to do ranch work and ride horses. I like Grandma and Grandpa's orchard, so I know I'll like ranching. Grandma Sandgren says I have a talent for being outside. Do you know what that means?" he asked, flopping down a hay bale.

Charlie shrugged. She had taken the rake off the wall and was raking the hard dirt floor, pulling all the little stems and seed tops, which had fallen from the hay when feeding into a pile. When she was done, she would pick them up and throw them into one of the stall's fresh shavings, so they could be found and nibbled on once the horse's hay bag was empty. Horses appreciated small deeds, Mommy said. It helped pass the time. Of course, Mommy had also said that throwing them into the field supplied little birds with things to insulate their nests with when there was little else to scavenge during the winter. So Monday through Friday, she took turns throwing them in a different horse stall, and Saturday and Sunday, she threw them into the field for the birds. A time or two, during the heavy snow, she had spotted a bird there sorting through the tidbits.

"Can I help?" Billy asked.

"No."

"Do you ride?"

"Yes," she answered, as she scooped up the small pile and tossed it out the back door.

"Which one?"

"Pops mostly, the hairy red pony outside. I'll outgrow him soon, though," she said proudly, hanging the pick on the wall where it belonged.

"My dad used to ride all the time. Grandma and Grandpa have horses."

"I know, they bring them when they come help us with branding."

"Oh," Billy remarked. "Maybe they'll get me one so *I* can help. Do you like animals?"

"Yes."

Noticing she was done with her chores, Billy leapt to his feet. "Want to play now?"

Sighing, Charlie agreed, "Okay."

Side by side, they walked towards the house. "What do you like to play?" Billy asked.

"I like to write stories. Would you like to see them?"

Billy's head bobbed happily. "Sure!"

Their jackets and boots flung on the floor by the front door, Charlie showed Billy her blue box and all the treasures inside. Sprawled out on the living room floor in front of the glow of a dying fire, Billy read each of the stories she had written, flipping through the notebook pages, one at a time. Drawings were sparse, but when he came upon one, he would stop and study it.

"I'm not a very good drawer," Charlie said. "You'll just have to use your imagination."

"I like them. You need more." Adjusting his elbows on the hard floor, Billy stuck his nose back into the notebook, a pink string hanging from its spine. When he finished, he handed her a heap of clean paper, dumped out her box of colored pencils, and picked up a green pencil. Holding it between two fingers and a thumb, he hovered it over his own stack of clean paper and said excitedly, "You write, I'll draw."

And thus began a production line of an afternoon's worth of illustrated short stories by Charlie Morris and Billy Sandgren. Neither noticed the hours ticking by. They didn't notice the adults returning to the house, or Gramps adding wood and stoking the fire. When dinner was done, they were called to the table.

"Where did they come from?" Billy asked, gaping at the sudden appearance of the room full of adults.

They glanced at each other, shrugged, and burst into giggles.

\*\*

It felt good to Amara to have the dinner table put to use again. It hadn't been touched for six months. Once the kids had been called and the adults had taken their place, every wooden chair was full except one. Even still, it felt nice. Honorary, in a way.

Gramps had opened and heated a can of pulled pork, defrosted a bag of hoagie rolls, and pulled the cork from a wine bottle. It wasn't fancy, but no one seemed to notice or care. The atmosphere was that of good company. Dishes clattering, chairs squelching, voices rising and falling like the tides of the ocean. Sacred is the easy manner in which conversation between those we hold dear swells and subsides.

Over food and drink, the table flowed with talk about the war the weather seemed to be waging against the fruit orchard, the price of cattle, the price of horses, land conservation, the increase of wild hooved animals carrying diseases—which experts feel preserving predators is the answer to, despite the concern of attacks on livestock. Through it all, Amara's mind was out of the reach of her incessant sorrow. To her surprise, she felt relieved—as if for the first time since Sonny had passed, she could feel a rush of fresh air, replacing the dark cloud of depression which had been choking her.

"I've got something I'd like to talk about," Amara said, raising her eyebrows at Gramps. He acknowledged her with his attention. "Let's talk about the empty house below us."

"It's not going to stay empty."

"I know. You're going to keep hiring help, and I'm going to keep firing them."

"Amara," Gramps started to growl, but he was cut off by William.

"Fire?" William asked with amusement. "Why do you keep firing them?"

Amara's lips puckered, as though she were thinking. Gramps lifted his hand and was ignored by the entire table; even the kids were waiting for Amara's answer. Charlie had her fork stuck in a pile of meat, and Billy's plate was empty, a red colored pencil tucked behind his ear.

"Well?" William pressed.

Taking a deep breath, she replied, "Because they're all useless and utterly incompetent." Everyone laughed.

"Really?" William asked, doubting her. "*All* of them? Surely not every single man was utterly incompetent."

Gramps grabbed his chin and squeezed. "She found a reason for every one of them."

"Yes!" Amara nodded vehemently. "They were! I swear Gramps was purposely hiring them just to infuriate me. He claims he needs help, but all these men were the opposite of help. Every last one of them."

William leaned forward, interested. "How so?"

She took another cleansing breath before she informed him, "Tom was disrespectful, didn't even know how to saddle a horse. Francis was vile, egotistical, knew nothing about the equipment other than the fact I shouldn't have been within spitting distance of it. You know, 'cause I'm a girl. Smithy knew *nothing* about cows, and when I say nothing, I'm not exaggerating. Plus, he was never on time—not an exaggeration.

## Holder of the Horses

Darrel...don't even get me started on Darrel. We'll just say he was too old.

"Anyway, stick them all together in a barrel and shake them like cream, and there's absolutely no way butter would come out, let alone a horse trainer. It would just never happen. We desperately need a younger man than Gramps for training the yearlings... no offense, Gramps..."

He shook his head, slow and deliberate. "None taken."

"But he's got to know horses and how to ride! *And*," she emphasized, "he's got to follow Gramps' training plan. People want Morris horses for a reason."

William nodded, probably assuming the bout was over.

"Tobacco spit," Amara added. Every eye was back on her, as if she were the star contestant on "Who's Lost Their Mind?" "I could trail every step Francis took. Most of them led directly back to the house, of course." She shook her head. "You've heard of yellow snow? Everywhere Francis went, black spit snow."

"I see," William said. "What would make good help? Someone you wouldn't fire?"

Gramps held his cheeks between his two leathery palms, Billy giggled, and Charlie just stared, only her eyes moving back and forth.

"Arrive on time," Amara said. Gramps and William nodded. "Know the job." Gramps and William nodded again. "Be respectful. Know how to ride. It would be particularly nice if he were good at it. Know the difference between a cow's tail and a cow's head..." Gramps and William were still nodding. "What are you doing?" she asked, annoyed. "You two look like a couple of bobbleheads going over a bumpy road."

Billy and Charlie both giggled, trying out bobbling for themselves.

"Just agreeing," William said, grinning.

Gramps sighed, apparently giving in. "You're right," he said. Amara shrunk back. Gramps didn't give in. What was he trying to pull? "That's why I hired William," he said, with his typical no-nonsense gruffness.

Amara looked at William, lips parted, but finding no words to say. Did she approve? Heck yeah, she approved. But those little players…

"I hope you don't mind," William said. "You're not going to fire me, are you?"

Amara glared and threw her spoon at him. William tried to dodge it, laughing, but it hit him smack in the chest. This got the kids excited. They started wiggling in their chairs, wanting feverishly to start a food fight, but refraining with only a mere cell of sense.

"Charleston had been asking if I'd be interested in a job since I was back. He had mentioned a rather challenging boss, but he hadn't warned me you'd been firing everyone," William goaded.

Picking up a bite of hoagie roll she hadn't eaten, she threatened to throw it at him. "It's never too early," she replied.

## CHAPTER THIRTY

At six o'clock in the morning, Amara was sitting at the desk in the corner of the living room. Though it seemed totally buried, it was strategically organized with ranch business papers and receipts. Amara had haphazardly plopped her hat at the top of the stack, like a topper on a leaning wedding cake. She was sipping her coffee and scrolling through the local news on the computer when Charlie came shuffling down the stairs in her pink knee-high cotton pajamas and slippers.

"It's Sunday," said Amara. "What are you doing up already?"

"I just woke up."

Setting her coffee mug down and swiveling to face her daughter, Amara smiled. "Well, in that case, how do you feel about putting one of your famous braids in my hair?"

"They're not famous," Charlie replied sleepily.

"But they should be. They're terrific. They never fall out, and they look amazing."

"Okay," said Charlie, momentarily disappearing into the bathroom and returning with a brush in her hand.

She began to pull a brush through Amara's hair, taking her time to get out every tangle. Then, in a flash, she bolted up the stairs, leaving Amara gaping after her. A moment later, Charlie advanced back down the stairs, backpack in hand.

"What's that for?"

"You'll see," Charlie said, setting the bag on the floor. She unzipped it, pulled out her purple school safety scissors, and held them up with a devious smile. Amara quickly grabbed her hair and flung it into her lap protectively. "Oh no you don't!"

Charlie gave her a look of disapproval, a motherly look Amara was sure she was already practicing for her future children. "Trust me," she said, lowering the scissors to a less threatening height. She sunk, clunking her bare knees on the hard floor. "Give me your hair."

Hesitantly—against her better judgement—Amara tossed her hair over her shoulder. It fell before Charlie, and her scary purple school scissors.

"You have stragglies," Charlie explained, as she snipped away the stray ends extending past the thick, beautiful blonde mass. "There," she said, "that's better."

"Maybe you'll be a hairdresser."

"Nah." Charlie stood, setting her scissors on the desk and trading them for a rubber band, which she wrapped around her finger like a ring. "I don't want to touch everyone's hair. Just yours."

"What then?" Amara asked.

Charlie shrugged. "I don't know."

"Want me to braid your hair today too?"

"No, it likes to be free."

Amara could sympathize, having felt the same way most of her life. But she had come to prize her morning moments with Charlie so much that she continued the routine of having Charlie braid her hair for her—even though they both knew she could do it herself now. That wasn't the point. It may have started out the point, but it was the point no longer.

Gramps appeared from around the log archway of the kitchen, coffee cup in hand. "Good sleep in?" he asked.

Charlie rolled her eyes, not considering getting up at five-forty in the morning to be sleeping in. Amara, on the other hand, usually got up at five o'clock, back on schedule—more or less—and rather enjoyed a lazy forty extra minutes.

"I did," she answered. "How about another forty?"

"You're up mighty early," Gramps said to Charlie, ignoring Amara completely. "Got big plans?"

Charlie blushed. "No. I just woke up."

"I see. You take after your Gramps. The more years you acquire, the worse it gets." Charlie nodded perceptively, agreeing with Gramps, though she had no idea as to what he meant. Just so long as no one mentioned the new kid, Billy. "Well, you best get dressed," Gramps suggested. "We're bound to have company in, say..." He glanced at his watch. "Thirty seconds."

Charlie's eyes widened, and with a high-pitched shriek, she disappeared up the stairs.

"Huh," Gramps grunted, as if he hadn't expected such a response, and took a sip of coffee. Turning on his heel, he disappeared into his bedroom.

"Huh," Amara repeated to an empty living room, gulping the remainder of her lukewarm coffee and retrieving her cowgirl hat from the tall pile of papers needing to be filed. No one wanted to file. It was a daunting task.

The eagle feather she had secured to her dirty hat gleamed pure white, like the snowy winter night it had fallen from Sonny's tail and blown up against her foot. She sighed, running her fingers across the soft vanes, pulling the barbs apart and smoothing them back together like nature's Velcro. Only at Sonny's grave did she feel as close to him as when she touched this feather.

The front door swung open, and heavy boots began stomping off the cold of the morning. Closing her eyes, she imagined it was Sonny. It felt like Sonny. The presence was strong and familiar. She smiled.

"Good morning," William said. "Cripes, I hope I didn't interrupt you praying or something."

Amara looked up. William—not Sonny, she thought, disappointed. "And if you *had* interrupted a prayer," she said, "you have this annoying knack for jabbering right through it."

"Sorry."

Running her fingers across the feather one last time, she added, "I wasn't praying. I don't think." Then she slapped the hat down on her head.

Gramps emerged from his bedroom, a stack of pictures protruding from an envelope in his hand. "Good, you're here. And on time." He turned to face Amara.

"Yes, very punctual," Amara agreed tartly.

William straightened his shoulders. "Yeah, that's what Nuna always said."

Amara's hands flew to cover her ears. Scowling from between her elbows, she hollered, "Criminy! Don't make me fire you, William!"

William laughed.

Gramps handed William the envelope. "Dug these up for you last night. When you both were boys."

"Thank you," William said, composing himself.

## Holder of the Horses

Amara removed her hands from her ears, which had William looking at her mischievously. She pointed a finger to his face. "I swear," she warned.

William drew a cross over his chest. "I'm going to get coffee," he said. When he turned with a smirk on his face, Amara saw his hand hiding behind his back, two fingers crossed.

"He's—"

"A big kid," Gramps interjected. "Always will be." He poked an elbow in her side and winked. "But he can ride." He took a swig of coffee.

"You better be referring to horses."

Choking, Gramps spewed coffee back into his cup, wiping his chin and trailing off after William without a word.

There was a knock on the front door, and when Amara answered it, she had to look down. There was Billy, all bundled up. Amara grabbed him by the sleeve and dragged him inside. "For crying out loud, you don't have to wait outside. Or knock. William!" she bellowed. "You left Billy outside!"

"In my truck, with the heater on," he defended, handing Billy his cup of coffee over the counter.

Before Amara could say "kids don't drink coffee," Billy took the cup, climbed onto a stool, and started drinking. She huffed, briefly reminding herself of her mom. Brushing away the awful association, she said, "You look bundled up to help this morning. Are you?"

Billy nodded, swallowing. "I want to help every day."

"Then we'll put you on the secret payroll for people under four feet tall," Gramps said.

Billy's face lit up.

"It's called an allowance," William said. "And only after your schoolwork is done."

"Yes sir," Billy replied, going back to guzzling his coffee. "Got any doughgods?" he asked, looking up at Amara.

Amara looked at him inquiringly.

"First off," William said to his son, as he filled a second mug with hot coffee, "Mrs. Morris is not the right person to ask. We don't let her cook. Secondly, a doughgod is actually a biscuit."

"Grandma Sandgren calls doughnuts doughgods," Billy countered.

"I can cook!" said Amara.

Gramps coughed.

"She's Grandma. She calls things whatever she likes," William said.

"I think doughgod is a very fitting name for a doughnut," Amara decided.

"They certainly sound good," said Gramps. "Wish we had us some doughgods right now."

Billy laughed.

"What's a doughgod?" Charlie asked curiously, walking in—dressed to work, Amara noted.

"It's a doughnut!" Billy answered excitedly, his voice raising an octave.

"Biscuit," William corrected.

Charlie's face lit up. "Do we have any?"

"No," everyone in the kitchen answered simultaneously, depression lingering in following silence.

"Oh," Charlie said sadly.

"We will by lunch, though," Gramps announced. "Amara, you and William feed. I'm headed to town. I'll be back by lunch with two boxes of doughgods."

"Yay!" Billy and Charlie cheered. Amara couldn't help but feel a rush of excitement herself. William smiled too, setting his second cup of unfinished coffee on the counter.

"Well, let's get to it," Amara said, ushering the kids and William towards the front door.

Amara liked this new troop. It was closer to how it used to be, and nothing like it had been lately. From the looks of Charlie bounding out the door, Billy on her heels, and William smiling ear to ear, she wasn't the only one. When she glanced over her shoulder, Gramps was following them out, keys in hand. For a split second, she glimpsed a misty image of Sonny's muscular body leaning against the log pillar, holding up the porch roof. Her heart fluttered...until she realized his face was blurry. Slightly panicked, she blinked, trying to bring him into focus. But he was gone, the image erased by reality.

"Amara," said Gramps, catching up to her. He didn't ask if she was alright, just laid his comforting hand upon her shoulder.

Feeling queasy, she ripped her eyes away from where Sonny had been so many times before. "Yes?"

"Is all of this too much?"

She shook her head. "No," she lied. "I just..."

Gramps grabbed her by her other shoulder and pulled her into his strong, scrawny arms. She felt the short whiskers he hadn't bothered to shave off this morning rub against the top of her head, where his chin rested. "I'm gonna go get you some doughgods," he whispered. "Okay?"

Swallowing the lump in her throat, she nodded. "Okay."

"Okay," he confirmed, and released her. "William!" he called up the hill.

William turned from where he was stuffing kids into Sonny's pickup, attached to the long bed. As he did, Amara realized what a tight squeeze they all were going to be.

"Give her hell!" Gramps ordered. "But don't get fired!"

## CHAPTER THIRTY-ONE

After every mouth had been fed—either hay or doughgod—Charlie and Billy ran out to the barn to clean the horse stalls, and Gramps took off on a three-year-old filly to check the first-calf heifers. Calves had begun dropping early this morning, and he wanted to be absolutely certain all was well. Which left William and Amara together, totally stuffed, over a box of crumbs and frosting smudges where doughgods had been only minutes before. Amara was preparing to excuse herself when William stopped her short.

"Ready to ride?" he asked.

Feeling gorged and tired, she faltered before answering. "No, I don't think so."

"The girl I used to know never turned down a chance to ride," he said skeptically.

"Well, now I do," she answered, glancing at her stuffed horse sitting on the counter by the door. She had adorned him with the homemade reins Gramps had given to Sonny the same day he gave him the ranch—the same damn reins he had been using the day he died.

"I thought we agreed to ride today. Same place. Same time. Ring a bell?"

"I don't feel like it today, William. Maybe tomorrow."

"No, there *is* no tomorrow," William insisted firmly. His boldness was admirable, but annoying.

She turned to him, returning the favor. "There is if I say there is."

"Is that so?"

"Yes!"

Although perturbed at his insistence, the fact she really didn't want to share was that she was scared. Plus, no one—least of all Sonny's best friend, William—wanted to hear how angry she felt at Sonny for leaving her. And no one wanted to hear how she wrestled with trying to be strong, or just giving up.

"Why?"

"Because I said so!" Amara snapped.

"Why is it because you say so?" William replied. "Do you own this ranch?"

"In fact, my husband does!" Amara slapped the palm of her good arm on the counter.

"Sonny is gone, Amara," he said, a little too coldly for her liking. He leaned into her space, and asked, "Who's running this ranch?"

Her lips parted, saying nothing.

"That's right. From where I stand, it doesn't look like it's *you.*"

His words stung her pride, what little she had left. "How dare you?"

"How dare *me*?" he said, leaning in further. "Who's outside checking the livestock?" Amara didn't give an answer, and William didn't require one. They both knew it was Gramps. "And who's standing in here claiming she runs this ranch, which *that man,*" he pointed vaguely in the direction they had seen Gramps trotting off in, "built with his two hands?" William looked deep in her eyes. "His grandson died for this place. One drip at a time. And in the end, he gave it to you. All of it. All at once. He didn't think it over. He didn't deliberate it. He knew exactly where he stood, Amara. And he was ready and willing to do it. That's more than I can say for where you stand right now."

Amara flinched.

William softened his voice and spoke more slowly, no longer baiting her. "Where's Calamity Jane?" he asked. "Where has she gone?"

Tears stung Amara's eyes. She swallowed and blinked. Damned if she would let them spill out. Not for him. Not for the pain he was purposely causing her. Not for his willingness to throw her off her own imaginary yacht of self-preservation into the storm. Suddenly she felt more lost than ever before. Mostly because he was right.

"I don't know," Amara answered, holding her trembling chin in the air.

Stealing a quick glance at the stupid stuffed horse she'd bought years ago, she imagined Sonny pressing its soft fur against his cheek. "Soft, it should do the trick," he had remarked once. Oh, how she yearned to hear his voice again. To feel his touch. Amara squeezed her eyes shut, holding the memory close to her heart. "I think she died," she admitted quietly, tears flooding her face.

"No," William insisted, his voice softening. "She didn't. Open your eyes, Amara." She did, and immediately felt William's deep brown eyes burning into hers. "Sonny did. But he chose to forfeit himself so you could take his place." His face was just inches from hers. "I know you miss him, and you're going to continue missing him. Do you understand?" Amara nodded, and William nearly pressed his nose to hers. He was so close, so intense. "Charleston is tired. I've never seen him so tired. It's time for you to stop dying with Sonny and start honoring him."

He pulled away, taking a large step backwards, standing before her like a mountain. With mountains, you don't have to be told they will always be there—you just know. They will be at your back, holding you up, pressing you forward.

A warmth surrounded her, just as it had the night Charlie had run off. Sonny wanted her to hear what William was saying: to listen. There was no mistake, he was here with her.

"Take the reins," William said confidently. "Run this ranch."

A chill crawled up Amara's legs and spread to her arms. Sonny had released her. And although William had purposely pitched her off the boat, he also pointed his long arm through the fog in the direction of the shore. It might be reachable, if she swam hard.

"Are you ready to ride?" William asked, repeating his first question.

"No," Amara replied honestly. She wasn't ready. "But I will."

This time, William nodded, pointing her to the front door. She grabbed her jacket and hat, walked outside, and stuffed her feet into her boots. William snatched the homemade reins off the neck of the stuffed black horse. "You don't mind if Amara borrows these, do you?" he asked the horse, and followed her out, shutting the door.

## CHAPTER THIRTY-TWO

Out of the corner of Charlie's eye, she noticed the relaxed way Billy sat, perched on a bale of hay, his knees spread wide as though he were sitting on a horse. At eighteen years old, it's just the sort of thing a girl notices. His dark hands hung between his knees, his fingers dangling like fishing lines in a pond. His dusky brown eyes observed her movements as she cleaned and organized all the gear hanging on the barn wall in alphabetical order, according to the horse who wore each piece. Every few months, the order had to be changed due to the sale of the horses William and Billy trained together, under Gramps' often unavailable supervision.

As Billy watched, his dark eyes felt like storm clouds. She liked storms. Storms made her creative mind spark with ideas, drawing her to hunker by a cold window. With lightning flashing in the distance, rain pelting upon the windowpane, she jotted down short stories. In her most recent one, a group of young, argumentative Bighorn rams take their adolescent quarrel to dangerously steep cliffs to test their bravery and battle for the best. As they encounter danger on those vertical rocks and sudden drops, they find the best in the least likely of the rams. And in the clutches of danger, they find friendship.

"Why do you do that?" Billy asked her, as he listened to her reciting the names of the horses in order.

"Do what?"

"Alphabetize everything. It's just going to change when we bring new horses in. Besides, Dad and I know what bit we want when we come looking."

"I'm sure you do," she replied. "I can't just throw them up here without rhyme or reason. Certain things need certain care."

"With you, *all* things need certain care."

Charlie grinned over her shoulder, hanging the last set on the wall. "There's nothing on Earth which doesn't require care."

"What about me?" Billy asked, a wide smile wrapping around his smooth face. "I require care."

Charlie laughed. "You most of all!"

Billy stuck a piece of hay in his mouth, like a cigarette. "How about I take you out to celebrate your graduation? A movie? Dinner?"

"Graduation was a week ago," Charlie answered, standing near his knees. "How many times are you going to use it as an excuse?"

"As many times as it works," he said, grinning.

Being a year older, Billy had graduated last year, and had made as little fuss over his graduation as humanly possible. Constantly ducking questions about moving out and leaving the ranch, he filled his extra time with chores. Working harder than he should, he made himself indispensable. Charlie knew why. In fact, everyone knew why.

Charlie grabbed his hand, pulling him to his feet. "One last time," she agreed. Then she let him go, adding a gentle push to his chest. He toppled backwards into the hay. "After you finish filling the hay boxes and bringing in the horses," she said, smirking as she walked away.

"That's your job!" he called after her.

"I have to get ready for a very important date," she replied, blissfully leaving her evening chores for Billy to do.

"Well, when you put it *that* way."

\*\*

"Wow!" Amara declared, looking Charlie up and down as she descended the stairs from her room. "Where are you headed?"

Charlie was wearing a black flowing skirt that swept back and forth across her kneecaps as she walked, and a red knit sweater hugging her thin arms and waist to accentuate her bosom and hips. She had stuck the little diamond studs Gramps had given her for her sixteenth birthday into her earlobes, and borrowed her mom's black high heels with silver studs across the toes. They were a little bit too big, leaving more room at her heel than necessary, but they weren't so big that her foot slipped around.

"Just going to a movie," Charlie answered.

"A movie." Amara's voice contained a knowing smile. "With Billy?"

Rolling her eyes, Charlie felt a tiny fire ignite below the surface of her cheeks. "Yes, Mom." Her answer was short and cool, but her mom wasn't buying her indifferent tone any more than the excited blue butterflies fluttering in her stomach did.

"What's the special occasion?" Amara asked. Code for "has he asked yet?"

Everyone knew Billy had always been head over heels for her, since he was nine and she was eight. Being the son of the Morrises' most trusted employee, and living in their ranch house, Billy stayed just clear of asking Charlie if she would be his girlfriend. No one had said he couldn't. No one made him feel as though he was unworthy. The opposite, in fact. Everyone loved him. So he respected that trust, flirting endlessly but never crossing the line. It wasn't until the last few years that Charlie started edging closer to the line, wondering what it would be like to...

"Charlie?" Amara asked, tugging at her sleeve. "You there?"

Charlie blinked. "We're just celebrating my graduation."

"Again?"

Charlie laughed. "This is the last time."

The thought of being driven all the way to town by Billy turned the blue butterflies in her stomach red with warmth. A knock at the door disrupted further interrogation from her mom.

"What are you knocking for?" Amara yelled at the door.

It opened, and Billy stepped in. Both girls stared at him, starting at his spotless, freshly polished brown cowboy boots clunking heavily on the floor. His legs looked longer than usual in a pair of dark blue jeans he had never worn before. On his waist was a brown belt with a shiny silver latch, accenting his long-sleeved button-up royal blue dress shirt.

"Damn, Billy," said Gramps from the background, as he stepped from his bedroom, dressed shamelessly in his two-piece white cotton pajamas. "Getting married, son?"

Billy laughed. "No sir. Just taking Charlie to a movie."

"Aw." Gramps' whisker covered wrinkled face registered a tender memory, one he didn't share with the room. "What's the occasion?"

"We're just celebrating her graduation," Billy answered, tucking four fingers into each front pocket.

"Again?" Gramps asked.

"If it's alright."

Amara's hand clasped down over Charlie's forearm, and before Charlie could prepare herself to walk gracefully in the high heels, she felt herself being dragged toward Billy, tripping and staggering awkwardly. "Of course it's alright," she volunteered.

Somehow she made it to Billy without completely disgracing herself by flying forward and sprawling out on the floor, her face hitting the hardwood at his feet—though she was blushing so badly it looked as though she had. She glared at her oblivious mom and straightened herself out. Billy was choking on a laugh, his lips curled against his teeth. In all fairness, she was glaring at him, too.

By the time they were sitting in the movie theater in Billings, Montana, staring up at previews and munching on shared popcorn, Charlie had recovered from her humiliation. It wasn't like it was the first time Billy had seen her do something stupid. Only she had hoped to make a slightly different impression this time. He was used to seeing her covered in horsehair and cow shit. This evening, she wanted to amaze him. It wasn't as if she expected his eyes to pop from their sockets or anything. She just wanted…what did she want?

In the soft glow of the theater lights Billy looked at her. His brown eyes looked like chocolate, sparkling against his smooth, dark skin. The corners of his mouth turned up. For a moment, that was all she saw: the corners of his mouth and chocolate.

"Are you excited?" he asked.

"What are we seeing, again?" she asked, earning her a chuckle from somewhere deep in his chest. It had a nice sound. So intimate, here in the near dark.

The lights started to dim. The romantic comedy Billy had picked out for was about to start.

Billy's eyes fixed on hers, his mouth no longer turned up in the corners but a straight, serious line. In the faint glimmer radiating from the movie screen, surrounded by loud music which drowned out the rest of the world, Charlie couldn't help but feel alone with him. The first time they had seen a movie together, they had focused on the movie, barely bumping fingers in the popcorn. This time was different. This time, she wanted to feel his fingers and his lips. She wanted to taste the salt lingering there. Based on his unbroken concentration, the way he brazenly sat there so calmly, he must know.

When the movie was over, Charlie and Billy sat side by side, as the glowing lights steadily returned. Billy's arm was draped over the armrest between them, the comforting weight of his hand on her leg, their fingers entwined. As the music played again, Charlie felt a longing for this moment never to end. Billy must have been following her thought process again, for he seemed quiet. When the theater was nearly empty, he finally spoke.

"When are you leaving?" he asked gloomily.

Charlie knew what he was asking. She had registered with the University of Montana to pursue her dream of writing children's storybooks. "In a month," she replied. Billy nodded. "What about you?" she asked. "What have *you* decided?"

His shoulders lifted and fell. "As long as I can remember, I've loved ranching with your family."

"Have you considered going to college?" she asked hopefully. "I know which one I would suggest."

There was an appreciative twinkle in his eyes, but it didn't last. Like the music blaring through the speakers, it faded, sending him back to the present.

"You're smart enough to do anything you want," said Charlie. "And the girls would flock to you like vultures."

His amusement showed in the corners of his mouth, and she realized how very much she wanted him to go with her.

"I've already found what I want," Billy replied. "But I'll think about it," he added, the twinkle returning to his eyes. She believed him.

As they walked towards Billy's new-to-him filthy white Toyota pickup in the cold night, Charlie shivered, and Billy wrapped his arm around her. It wasn't strange. She and Billy were best friends. So why did it feel different? At his pickup, he paused outside her door, his hand on the handle. Instead of opening it, he turned to her, released the handle, and placed it over her left ear, his long fingers wrapping around her head.

"I'm going to kiss you now," Billy said. "Speak now, or forever hold your peace." This is where he would normally smile and laugh at how he'd triggered her to recoil and run. But he didn't laugh. And she didn't speak, or run.

In an instant, Billy leaned down and placed his lips over hers. She felt his warmth cover her like melting chocolate. Slowly, it drizzled from her lips all the way to her toes, which tingled in response. She'd been kissed before, but never before had she felt this. Inside her jacket pocket, her cell phone began vibrating. Billy heard it too, pulling away from her and studying her expression.

"Are you going to answer that?" he asked, his voice husky in a way she'd never heard before. She liked it. The sound reignited the fire beneath the chocolate he'd drizzled over her.

"I don't think so," she replied, feeling stuck. The only thing she wanted was for Billy's mouth to touch her again. But the phone refused to stop. She was prepared to ignore it until Billy smiled.

"You better."

He opened the door for her and continued to his side. They slipped inside the cab at the same time, and Billy started the engine, adjusting the heater dials so they pointed hard right—deep into the red.

Recognizing the moment had passed—for now—she dug grumpily in her pocket and pulled it out. "Hello?"

"Charlie!" her mom's voice came through with piercing alarm. "Charlie, have you left Billings yet?"

Mid-reach for the seatbelt, Charlie froze. "Not yet, Mom. What's going on?"

"Don't," she warned. "Can you two meet us at St. Vincent's? We're headed there now…following the ambulance…" Amara's voice was choked with tears.

"Go to St. Vincent Hospital!" Charlie told Billy.

He didn't argue or ask questions. To his credit, he wasted no time putting the pickup into gear and leaving the parking lot.

"What happened, Mom? Who's in the ambulance?"

"Gramps..." Amara sobbed. "He...he collapsed..." William's voice said something in the background. "Which theater are you at?" she managed to ask.

"Oh no..." Charlie glanced at Billy, who stopped concentrating on the road long enough to lock eyes with her. At the intersection, he stopped and took a right. "AMC Classic," Charlie answered.

"Twenty minutes," Billy advised.

"We'll be there in twenty minutes," Charlie repeated to her mom. Her arms and legs no longer felt warm with chocolate; they felt brittle, and trembled with adrenaline. She was grateful Billy was next to her.

"William will meet you at the doors," Amara's shaken voice informed her.

"Mom?" Charlie said. She needed to know.

There was a large pause, filled with breathless anxiety on the other end. "I don't know..." her mom's unsure voice finally answered, revealing she did know and wasn't admitting it. A tear slid down Charlie's cheek.

Billy noticed, stepping on the gas and pushing the boundaries of reckless driving. Every minute counted, if it wasn't already too late. Charlie's only comfort was knowing that if Billy could help it, she would get there in less than twenty minutes. But he wasn't going to make her wait that long.

## CHAPTER THIRTY-THREE

Amara would have lost track of the cars littering the sides of the highway, their gravel drive, and all over the pasture—if she had been counting. But she wasn't. She was sitting on the bench in the family cemetery, staring at three graves: Lizzy's, Sonny's, and Gramps', surrounded by the green flowering shrubs she had tenderly loved into blossom. Directly next to her sat Charlie. On each side of them sat William and Billy in white plastic chairs.

John hadn't responded to her letter, the way he did when she sent Charlie's picture and birthday party invitations. But unlike with those invitations, he had shown up. To her pleased surprise, he had driven up in Gramps' old pickup. He still had it. Dressed in black slacks and a slightly wrinkled, but clean, white button-up shirt, he skulked in like a stray dog. William recognized him and acted first, whistling for someone to throw him another plastic chair. He squeezed John in between himself and Amara like the last pool ball being placed in the rack.

There was only enough room inside the wood-fenced cemetery for immediate family. The other hundred chairs were set up on the outside. It wasn't nearly enough. There's a phrase, "standing room only," that could have been applied to Gramps' funeral. However, there's a beautiful benefit of being under the wide-open sky of Montana: plenty of standing room.

## Holder of the Horses

Not everyone would be able to see the grave, but every ear would be able to hear, due to the fact that the preacher had wisely brought a small speaker which echoed his words. Amara had caught a glimpse of Sarah Benson (Barley Benson had passed away a few years ago), and her heart went out to the amazing woman who had come, despite danger, to help try to save Sonny on that dreadful day.

Many people were moved by the preacher's sermon dedicated to Charleston Morris. What moved Amara was the people's presence, some having traveled all day to commit this deserving man their time and prayers. A deserving husband, father, friend, and neighbor. But to Amara, he was so much more than any of those things. Charleston had taken her under his wing. He had lifted her up when she was sinking, taking on both her and Charlie as his own. This was the first time he had ever left her. But he had to go. It was time. Lizzy had been more than patient, and generous too.

"Isaiah, chapter forty, verse thirty-one," the preacher introduced the next verse to be read. Amara wasn't paying him much mind as she stared at Sonny's grave, remembering all those times Gramps had come and lifted her up into his arms, refusing to let her go. "But they who wait for the Lord shall renew their strength," the preacher said.

Amara closed her eyes, squeezing Charlie's hand. *Renew your strength, Gramps*, she prayed.

"They shall mount up with wings like eagles," the preacher continued.

Amara's eyes flicked open at the mention of eagles' wings and looked up at the early summer blue sky, searching. Sure enough, according to family legend, there, flying high above the forlorn crowd, was an exquisite eagle. Uninhibited by pain, soaring without growing weary, his wings spread wide and free as the wind itself.

"I love you, Gramps," Amara said.

Charlie and John peeked sideways at her first, joined by William and Billy. Following her gaze, they all looked up in unison and saw the eagle circling too. Huge smiles stretched across their faces. Studying the front row of grinning grievers, the preacher hesitated. Mid-sentence, he stole a curious glance at the sky. He stopped speaking. With the preacher staring off into the heavens, the crowd waited. When his sermon failed to resume, one by one, faces in the crowd began turning heavenward too. The eagle pumped his large feathered wings, waving. With intermittent gasps and pointing fingers from the assembly of people, the eagle slowly disappeared from sight.

"Go meet her," Amara whispered adoringly, a tear sliding down her face until it reached her smiling lips.

When the eagle did not return, the preacher whispered a single heartfelt prayer into the speakers and dismissed the congregation to enjoy the remainder of the God-gifted day. Gramps' life on this earth was over. They were all better for having known him, and had been gifted with—everyone in attendance agreed—his good-bye.

Over Gramps' lifetime, he had changed many lives. It was his death which changed Charlie's.

## CHAPTER THIRTY-FOUR

William slammed his fist into the hood of Gramps' broken-down truck. "Damn it!"

The truck had always started for Gramps. But it wouldn't start for William. It just groaned and gave up the ghost. To make matters worse, they wouldn't have the money to have it looked at until after the hay was cut...hopefully.

In the meantime, he was stranded on a dirt road instead of checking on the broodmares. The mares weren't as far out as other herds, and were easy to get to in a vehicle, so he had opted for the cushy seat over a hard saddle. He was kicking himself now. He should have chosen the saddle.

**

Amara was not having a leisurely morning. Next to her bent knee, the flat tire of the hay-piled long bed stared at her with its lifeless, straight-lined rubber mouth, smashed against the hard ground. "Great," she grumbled.

She glanced up at the tractor; she had killed its engine after she felt the trailer's wheel dragging. These days, the tractor was her first choice for feeding, since it putted along slowly in first gear, making it easier to scrabble from the cab to the trailer and back again than it would be in a pickup rolling in neutral down a hill. Unfortunately, the tractor didn't carry a spare.

**

Billy, meanwhile, was adding the last bit of body suppleness to a sleek, dappled gray mare with a jet-black mane and tail. She had already been bought and paid for, but riding her was something he looked forward to every day. He was sad to see her go. He wished she would be staying at the ranch, but Amara said that not only did they need the money, they also had too many mares. She had decided to bet on the two coming up that Gramps had his eyes on.

Therefore, it was decided. Billy was instructed to load the sleek mare up tomorrow morning, drive her two hundred miles, and deliver her to a sixteen-year-old buyer with big roping dreams. He didn't have the faintest clue if the guy could rope, but since he'd saved enough money to pay for the mare, he at least should be able to take care of her, and probably compete with the same determination.

Just as Billy was situating the mare's weight in the makeshift roping box, his cell phone rang. He rewarded the mare for her concentration and let her step calmly out of the box. They were done for the day. The roper had a perfect athlete in this young girl. She was patient to read the cow, and quick to break.

"Dad?" he asked, pressing the phone to his ear as he stepped off his horse, taking a long rein with him. The mare sighed, her job done for today, and followed dutifully.

"My truck died. Can you come and pull me back to the sheds?"

"Uh..." His phone beeped in his ear. "Wait a second." He pulled it from his ear and looked at the screen. "Amara's calling me too."

"What does she want?"

"Well, she wants a chocolate chip muffin and a manicure," Billy answered sarcastically. "I don't know!"

"Well, see what she wants," said William. "I'm not going anywhere."

Billy pressed the hold button. "Hello?"

"Billy," Amara's voice said. "I'm sorry, I tried to call William, but he's not answering. It went straight through to voicemail. The long bed has a flat. Could you bring me the spare from my pickup?"

"Funny, he's waiting on my other line. Sorry, but no, I can't bring you the spare."

"Why not?"

"Charlie has your pickup."

"Well, where is she?" Amara asked impatiently. "Go get her."

"Go get her," Billy repeated back to her, as if she could hear how ridiculous the suggestion was if it came from *his* mouth. "She went to town."

"She went to town? Why?"

"Uh..." He could hear her sighing impatiently. "She said something about there being nothing in the house to eat, and mailing back the books she had bought."

"Mailing back books? What books?"

"I don't know," he answered. Come to think of it, it was a darn good question. "I'll call you back," he said.

"Wait–"

Billy hung up on both his dad and Amara, and dialed Charlie's number.

"Hello?" Charlie answered, sounding out of breath.

"What are you doing?" Billy asked.

"Loading groceries into the pickup. What are you doing?"

He wanted to ask about the books, but there were more pressing matters. "Calling in a favor. I need your help."

After he explained what was going on, she calmly presented the game plan. "It's just a matter of organizing what you have," she advised him. "Have my mom disconnect from the flatbed, and use the tractor to go pull William's truck home. When I get back, I'll take a spare out to the trailer and bring it back myself."

"Huh," was all Billy could say in reply. "What do *I* do?" he asked, the emergency suddenly solved.

"Call Mom and William back, then go back to doing whatever it was you were doing."

"Okay then," he said, smiling. "That was easy! I knew you could help! Not how I figured you would, but still!"

"You're welcome. Bye, Billy."

By the time Charlie had returned to the ranch and packed all of the groceries inside the house, the others had figured out how to get the remaining chores done, and had borrowed the pickup with the spare in the back while she put the groceries away.

"Billy said you returned books today," Amara said to her, when she came inside later and sat down to watch Charlie boil noodles and chop tomatoes. "What books was he talking about?"

Wondering how to approach the subject, Charlie bought herself time, tossing handfuls of tomatoes into the pot and picking up every last little piece off the counter. She liked her work station clean. A person should never cook in a dirty kitchen.

"Charlie?"

Charlie grabbed a head of lettuce from the refrigerator and took it to the sink to be rinsed, turning her back to her mom. "Just a few college books I won't be needing after all."

"And why won't you be needing them?" Amara inquired.

Suddenly, William barged through the front door with a loud, manly sigh. Billy followed noisily, climbing the short stairs to the porch and stomping off his boots. It sounded like cattle being shoved up a wooden ramp into the stock trailer, bellowing and stamping protests.

"What do I smell?" William asked. "Something is speaking to my belly!"

"Smells good in here," said Billy as he hung his hat by the door.

Amara peeked over her shoulder, glaring at the annoying men in her life. Then she turned back to Charlie. "Tell me again why we continue the stupid old tradition of feeding employees supper?"

"Gramps said, 'It makes us family,'" Charlie answered, as she chopped through the lettuce head in one quick slash. Billy's eyes bulged.

William turned to his freshly traumatized son. "Do we want to be family?"

"I don't know anymore," Billy said, looking placidly disturbed. "It smells good though, Charlie," he complimented. "Really good."

"Suck up," Amara coughed into her hand.

"Really?" Charlie threw the cut lettuce into a large bowl. "It's just boiling water and simmering tomatoes, guys. You can't ruin spaghetti."

"Whoa!" William threw up a hand and grabbed Amara's shoulder with the other. "We have to get Amara out of the kitchen!" Everyone laughed—except Amara. "No, seriously," William said, pulling Amara off the stool on which she was perched. She tripped over her own feet as he dragged her in the living room. "Come away from the kitchen. We have to keep it sacred so you don't ruin supper."

"I wasn't even touching it!"

Billy chuckled as he took residence on the warm stool. "Can I help?"

Charlie lifted her eyes, meeting his concentrated gaze. "Sure. Will you open two cans of olives?"

"You don't trust me," he complained, as he stepped to the cupboards, swinging open a door. The olives weren't there. He tried the next door. Bingo.

"What do you mean?" Charlie asked, tossing chopped green onions and parmesan cheese into the lettuce.

Toting his two cans of olives, Billy nudged into her space and whispered, "Why were you returning books today? Were they your college textbooks?"

"Not you too!" Charlie muttered.

"You know I'm not going to let it rest. Something is going on. What's up?"

Charlie sighed. Her decision couldn't remain a secret. There was no way she would be able to hide it. It would, with absolute certainty, reveal itself in short time—which wasn't the worst part. The worst, and most uncomfortable, part was the motivation behind her decision. Not the obvious, short-sighted intention, but the naked truth.

"Are you staying on here?" she asked Billy point-blank.

"Yeah," he admitted, looking down. "They need my help, Charlie. I want to be with you. I wish I could go to college with you, I really do. But we both know I can't afford it, and I don't have a big career change in my future. The ranch is what I love. It's what I'm good at."

"I know." Charlie nodded. "I understand."

"You do?" Clearly he had been deliberating painfully over his own choices, like she had been over hers. And like her, he had come to a tough decision. When she nodded, he said, "I'm sorry I'm not going."

Charlie turned away from him to stir the simmering tomato sauce. "No, I'm sorry I asked. It was selfish. I've been doing a lot of thinking lately." She paused. She believed her decision felt right—it *was* right—but she couldn't help doubting, wondering what she would be sacrificing. She finally answered the question. "Yes, they were my college textbooks. I sent them back." She could feel Billy's eyes staring at the back of her head.

"Why?"

She turned around to face him, grasping the oven door's handle with both hands behind her back. "I'm not going."

"What?" Billy's eyes widened. She saw surprise there, for sure. Did she see relief? Happiness? Had he decided to stay at the ranch because he was ready to move on? Date other girls? Did he still want her? His chocolate eyes divulged too little. It was unnerving. How would she ever know if she didn't…

"I'm staying here…to be with you."

His face exploded into joy. First he crouched like a lion, and then he pounced on her, grabbing her into his arms and lifting her up, swinging her around and around right there in the kitchen.

"I'm sorry! I'm sorry, I'm so happy you're not going!" he said, spinning her until her stomach turned and her eyes started to blur. "I know you wanted to go to school for your writing, but…but…I'm just so happy! I'm sorry I'm so happy! You don't have to stop writing! I promise!"

On the verge of fainting, Charlie mustered up all the strength she could. "Please...stop...spinning..." she begged.

Billy did, and set her down on her unbalanced feet as William and Amara peeked their curious heads around the corner, each of them holding a handful of Uno cards.

"What on earth?" said Amara.

"She's not leaving!" Billy said happily.

Amara glanced at her daughter, her expression full of unspoken questions. Instead she smiled at Charlie's flushed, dizzy face. "Alright," she said. Then, turning to Billy, she added, "I intend to remind you to keep the promise you just made."

"I expect you to," Billy admitted wholeheartedly.

"What promise?" William asked, oblivious to the undercurrent hiding beneath the surface.

How Charlie had not seen the plot twist of her own choices barreling toward her like a stampede of angry African elephants was a ridiculous mystery. One would think she could have seen it coming years ago, but she hadn't. She just hadn't. It was as simple as that. Hindsight is twenty/twenty, they say. It must be true, because it was so very clear now in the aftermath of Gramps' passing.

As Charlie had driven back towards the ranch today, groceries rattling in the back of the pickup, she had thought once more about the dilemma which had kept her tossing and turning all night instead of sleeping. After being able to observe today's ranch struggles, and then provide a simple fix using nothing but her organizational skills, the answer to her dilemma was suddenly crystal clear. She was convinced.

She was going to stay on the ranch to help. Gramps had always been the staple holding the fragile seam of the ranch together. He was the rock in the middle of the raging creek, the safe and dry step to take to the other side of every difficult decision. With him gone, Amara and William, even Billy, threw themselves desperately into the creek, trying to fill the empty dimple where Gramps' rock had once sat. But no matter how hard they tried, they just couldn't fill his place.

Charlie may have envisioned her life turning in certain directions, but from the moment Billy trotted up to her on the first day and insisted on pushing the wheelbarrow full of pee-soaked manure, each turn brought her back to where she started, like a circle. The naked truth was that she loved him, and leaving him made her feel like a fish trying to breathe out of the water.

Her family had thrown their lives like rocks into this creek, and though it may have appeared chaotic, a pattern had emerged. It floated on the surface, unmoved by the current, and it snaked its way from one side of the creek to the other. But there was a missing piece in the pattern. The missing piece was her. Once she threw herself into the creek, a perfect, serpentine path of jumping rocks was revealed—completed, and ready for the future.

## CHAPTER THIRTY-FIVE

The next morning, Jonny woke up face down on the couch, his cheek stuck to the pages of Grams' blue, heavy book tied together with twine. Slowly lifting his head to look at the clock on the wall, the handwritten pages peeled away from his face one by one. The clock read four o'clock. No one would be up yet. He had a little more time.

He had spent most of the night reading Grams' notebook instead of sleeping. It had been enthralling to finally read the family's unspoken history, an intimate peek into nearly each person's perspective. No wonder Grams had waited so long to show it to him. It was very personal to all of them, but especially to her. When he dropped his head back down to get a few more z's, he regretted it immediately. Instead of his face falling into a soft pillow, it smashed hard onto Grams' blue book.

Grimacing, he grabbed the book by its cover and yanked it out. As he held it up to the faint light of approaching dawn, glaring at it for being so rude as to purposely slap him for falling on it, the last blank page fell open.

"What are you doing out here, Jonny?" Charlie asked from the doorway, surprised. "And already dressed?"

Jonny startled. "Geez, Mom! What are you doing up already?"

"I always get up early. How do you suppose the coffee is always made by the time you get up?"

Jonny sat up and stretched his stiff neck. "I don't know. I guess I've never thought about it. I never got undressed, actually," he admitted.

She squinted at him. "You slept in your clothes? Why?"

Jonny held up the blue book. "Doing some reading and fell asleep."

"So you slept on the couch?"

Jonny flung his legs over the edge and sat up, stretching his arms wide and yawning. "Yep."

"Alright, then," Charlie said, raising her eyebrows and walking off toward the kitchen to turn on the coffee. She was often left speechless with things he did. It tickled Jonny to know it.

Grinning, Jonny decided to go put a fresh pair of clothes on. There was to be no extra few minutes of sweet sleep. Besides, he was young. He could handle it. When he emerged, dressed and ready for the new day, he passed his dad groggily inching his way to the kitchen for some coffee.

"Morning, Dad," he said as he sped by. He had to grab the last package of Starburst from the freezer before his mom did. If she got to it first, he would be lucky if he got a square or two. If he got to it first, he would have the entire package to himself, and she would probably share a cookie or two from her stash of snacks.

"Morning…" Billy returned the reply, but with less gusto.

Jonny ripped the freezer door open, grabbed the frozen package of Starburst, and slammed it shut. Then, after retrieving a coffee mug from the cupboard, he splashed coffee into it. On his way out of the kitchen, he ran into Billy, coming in at the pace of a sleepwalking sloth.

"What's the plan for today?" Jonny asked energetically, following it up with a sip of hot coffee. It slid down his throat like lava. Sweet, black, caffeinated lava. He sighed, letting some of the extra heat escape and cooling down his tortured esophagus.

"Keep your voice down." Billy crept toward the coffeepot, hands out in anticipation like a zombie. "Grams is still sleeping."

Jonny rounded the corner to the living room and plopped down in Grams' favorite chair. Tossing a quick glance at her bedroom door, he froze, the smug only halfway to his mouth. Her door was usually closed when she was sleeping or resting. This morning, it was open. And not just a crack. It was wide open.

"Um...I don't think so," Jonny said. No one replied. He stood up, preparing to investigate.

"Jonny, pick up your book," Charlie lectured in her motherly tone as she swished by on her way to the kitchen. She would pour her coffee and then realize the last package of Starburst was gone. She'd have to pack cookies, which she hated to bring because they crumbled in her saddlebag.

Jonny grinned, feeling the package of Starburst tucked safely into his pocket. Then he obediently grabbed the blue book off the couch, stuffing it down the back of his pants to drop off in his room after he (quietly) peeked in Grams' open bedroom door. As he peered around her doorway, he saw her bed, empty and made. There was no Grams in sight. She had appeared so tired yesterday and eaten absolutely nothing. How could she have risen so early? Was she planning to ride again?

Jonny paused, considering his options. He could pretend he had seen nothing and see how it played out. Or he could speak up. After all, it was more than slightly concerning. After his ritual bedtime cookie meeting last night with Grams, he had decided to switch sides. Mom was right. She shouldn't have ridden the other day. It had been entirely too much, and had zapped the smallest reservoir of strength she might have had. It was gone now. He had seen as much with his own young eyes. He wouldn't make the same mistake again. And so it was decided.

"Mom," he called over his shoulder, before turning and making his way toward the kitchen. "Something's not right with Grams."

"What's wrong?" Charlie appeared quickly, worried, the empty cup in her hand suspended in midair.

"She's not here."

The hustle began. Even his dad came alive with worry. Where was she? Where could she have gone? The first realization was that all the vehicles were still parked outside. They weren't sure if the fact was a relief—though her driving license had been revoked about a year ago now—because the next thought hit them harder. Where was her horse? Together, the three of them sprinted up to the barn in the dark hours of the morning.

Jonny reached the barn door first, flicking the light switch and barreling down the aisle. There was no chestnut mare, and no Grams. He exploded out the back door. In the dark, he could barely make out the faces of the horses as they lifted their drowsy heads. He counted the eyes staring at him. He came up two eyes short, and he was willing to bet they were the eyes of Grams' chestnut mare. When he turned around, he spotted his mom touching the empty spot on the wall where the headstall Grams used the day before yesterday had hung. On the hook, above the empty space, Grams had slung her dirty cowgirl hat with the large white feather—either she had forgotten it or forsaken it. Billy stood by Charlie's side, a motionless popsicle stick. They were *all* standing there like motionless popsicle sticks. Grams had left, on horseback, alone.

At first no one moved, their minds spinning individually. Which way would she have ridden? There were hundreds of acres in every direction. Would she stick to the clearly marked roads with which she was familiar? Would she ride into the hills, which she had forgotten how to navigate? Did she just want to see her herds again? Had she thought she could go see them and get back before anyone was the wiser?

"Should we split up?" Jonny finally asked.

Charlie nodded.

"I'll take a couple horses and check the hills, south and west," Jonny volunteered. The hills would be the toughest track. There was so much ground to be covered which could only be reached by horse, and countless terrain dangers which made it exhausting. If Grams had headed out there, it would require a hard ride to find her. Thus, the extra horse. He would have to switch mounts more than once, and hope he didn't kill them both.

"I'll take two more horses and check North and East," Billy said. "Charlie," he directed, working on husband mode now, "you take the pickup and extra gas. Check every last road." He looked at her. Charlie was his wife to protect, and Jonny could see that Billy was

## Holder of the Horses

struggling with splitting up. "Don't forget the highway," he added somberly.

"Both of you, take your phones," Charlie instructed. "And if none of us find her within an hour, I'm calling for reinforcements." Everyone nodded in agreement.

"We'll find her," Jonny announced. At this, they broke off in separate directions. No one expressed the nightmare condition in which they feared they might find her.

Jonny pushed his horse, Nick, carefully, wanting to cover ground, but not wanting to stumble over anything in the grayish light of dawn. The saddleless spare horse galloped behind them, keeping pace, its neck stretched out. Nick went along with his long, powerful legs while Jonny scanned the horizon in every direction. He was purposely keeping a close watch on Nick's ears. His horse was likely to sense another horse in the vicinity long before Jonny could with just his eyes. His dad had taught him how to read a horse's ears. His dad had learned it from *his* dad, Grandpa Sandgren. All worthy lessons are learnt, and passed down.

If you learn a lesson, it is your obligation to pass it down, Billy had told him.

It was then that Jonny remembered Grams' blue book, and the story inside. Alarm coursed through him like a bolt of lightning. He must have lost it. He had tucked it in the back of his pants, and now it was gone.

Then there was a sudden change in the cool morning air. Strange as it was, it felt as though he was no longer riding alone. Someone—or several someones—was riding with him. Only there was no one there. The unexpected sensation resembled seeing colors, gliding in the wind, in and around him. Green, like the grass. Purple, like the flowers. Yellow, like the breast of the meadowlark. Brown, like the muskrat. Blue, like the Montana sky. The earth seemed to reach up and embrace Jonny and his two horses as their muscles burned with repetition. If they listened, they could hear the colors whispering. He was sure of it.

Nick's ears flicked an instant before he felt a slight tug on the rope of the horse following behind. The extra horse had not only heard something, but had looked at it.

Screech!

Jonny glanced at the dim sky. A giant bird—an eagle—was soaring over their heads, like a great majestic guide. Straightaway, he remembered the bedtime story Grams had told him when he was younger. *The Legend of Eagle's Love*. A smile stretched across his face. The eagle turned away, heading a different direction now. Jonny sat up hard in his saddle.

"Whoa!" he called to both horses. It took them a moment to collect their legs and slow down after pushing each other so hard only moments before. All three of them breathed in and out, their ribs contracting and expanding in quick rhythm. "I think I know where we need to check," he told the long fuzzy ears.

After calling his mom, he turned his mount in the direction in which the visiting eagle had flown off. Enthusiastically, he asked the horses to pick up another brisk gallop. If he was right, they wouldn't have far to go. Had he not read Grams' book, he wouldn't have thought of it, but he had, and now he was sure he was right.

As Jonny reached the family cemetery, he slowed his horses and stopped at the front gate where Great-Grandma and Great-Grandpa Morris were buried, and where Grams' husband, Sonny Morris, was buried.

Charlie had taken over the duty of bringing water to the shrubs and flowers so they looked nice, even though the flowers wouldn't open fully until they felt the warmth of the sun as it emerged from the other side of the world. The lonely, orange-barked ponderosa pine still leaned over the entry gate, gracing the cemetery with shade and shelter. Looking up, Jonny half expected to see the visiting eagle from the field sitting on top of the pine, waiting. The tree was empty, but there, by the little wooden gate, stood a tremendously patient chestnut mare.

In one fluid motion, Jonny stepped from Nick's tired back, the leather creaking with the pleasure of its usefulness. With his weight on his legs, they began to tremble beneath him. He supposed it could have been the hard ride, but he doubted it. He was used to riding. No, his legs shook because he was thankful to have found Grams. Yet he was afraid. He was afraid of the quiet surrounding the scene. Nothing had so much as flinched since his galloping arrival. The only exception being the mare's ears greeting them, comforted they had arrived. Even the needles on the tree resisted swaying. He was afraid of the sadness growing in his heart. It was too quiet. Stepping through the little wooden gate, Jonny saw her.

Grams was laying on the ground next to her husband's grave, curled up like an infant in the womb. In her arms was a well-loved black stuffed horse with brown glass eyes. Jonny immediately recognized the horse, which was typically adorned with Grams' horsehair reins—the ones she had bought in place of touching a real horse. Today, however, one of those reins hung on the neck of Grams' mare, and the other draped from the mare's bit to the wooden fence. The mare wasn't tied, but she assumed she ought to be, and that was good enough for her.

On shaky legs, Jonny approached her. "Grams," he whispered. She remained motionless. "It's Jonny. I'm here." She was so still. Something, a feeling—perhaps the colors which had ridden with him—stopped him.

*Don't come any closer,* the colors whispered. But there was no voice.

It wasn't that he was frightened of Grams. He couldn't be; he wasn't. But he could feel Grams' tired, fiery spirit lingering. Even without checking her body, he knew her spirit was no longer in her. It had left. But it was still here, in this place. He could sense her. She was waiting. So he waited with her, glancing up, his eyes searching the tops of the trees, expectant. He had seen an eagle heading this way, after all. Was he crazy to believe the legend was not a story, but history?

"Jonny!" Charlie's voice startled him, quietly approaching from behind. He hadn't even heard her pull up in the pickup. He glanced at her, but she forgot all about him the moment her eyes landed on Grams. "Oh, Mom," she said, and began to cry.

Like a child, Charlie raced to her mom, falling to her knees. With a shaking hand, she reached to feel a pulse in Grams' neck, but Jonny already knew there was none. Charlie's head dropped, and she began sobbing. Jonny didn't budge. Like Grams, he was waiting. He wasn't sure for what. And with every passing breath, he wondered if he was indeed crazy.

A warmth touched his cheek, right where Grams' ink-handwritten words had transferred to his face as he slept upon the pages of her storybook. He turned to look, and a ray of sunshine through the branches of the tree temporarily blinded him. The sun was creeping slowly over the land. It was a new day. It was then that the branches started to sway under the gentle push of a breeze. The rays of sunshine flickered. Inside the flickering rays, hidden behind the branches, there was a movement. Jonny squinted.

At the top of the pine, lit up like a fire from the sun's rays, something landed: a single eagle, shimmering with gold specks. When it called out, the sound nearly pierced Jonny's ears. From far off, on the back of the breeze, a second eagle approached. Its wings reflected the sun as if the feathers were made of mirrors. Landing softly on the branch with its majestic, flapping wings, the tree leaned under the eagle's burdensome weight. Touching beaks, the two eagles reunited their souls. At that moment, both eagles began changing, hazy forms beginning to materialize and slip lower and lower through the branches until the sparkling light touched the earth. Blinking, Jonny figured he had to be either hallucinating or dreaming. As true and genuine as it felt, he knew when he woke that the vision would waver and slip away.

"Mom..." he said nervously, afraid the mere sound of his voice would break the spell. "Look."

Charlie glanced up, and as if the vision had only just been revealed, Grams' chestnut mare lifted her head, alarmed, and began sidestepping away from the strange burst of moving light, pulling the reins free from the wooden fence.

*Take the reins.*

The bright haze fashioned itself into four separate forms. One was a gray dappled horse with a black mane and tail. The second form became a huge red horse with gentle brown eyes. The third form was Amara, young again, and the fourth form was a handsome man, who Jonny recognized instantly as a version of himself: Sonny. Sonny held his hand out to Amara, and she took it, smiling widely, her spirit finally whole again. In the time it took Jonny to blink, Sonny and Amara were sitting on the horses.

Charlie had made her way over and was standing next to him, mouth gaping. "Daddy?"

Sonny looked at her.

"I miss you. Will you wait for me on the other side, Daddy?" she asked in a shaky voice, sounding like a child, a tear running down her face.

He nodded and smiled at his daughter, leaving a shimmering path of brightness as he did. He held out a single translucent finger: his pinky.

Jonny felt a wet river slipping down his cheeks and neck. He hadn't even realized he was crying until then. Charlie was crying, and smiling as well. Amara's forsaken chestnut mare began spooking wildly.

*Take the reins.*

Without hesitation, Jonny reached up and took hold of the black and brown homemade horsehair reins, and the mare settled instantaneously. Sonny and Amara began fading, little by little, Grams' smile unmistakable. She was finally where she was meant to be, next to the front gate of the other side with her true love. And they rode home together—leaving Jonny holding the reins, and the colorful flowers stretching their petals open to a new day.

## EPILOGUE

On the raked dirt floor of a horse barn in eastern Montana laid a blue, heavy cardstock-covered journal, tied together with twine. It had fallen in a rush, unnoticed, for safekeeping. The wind had swept over the book, flipping page after page as the day wore on. At the end of the book was an empty page, signifying the end. But the wind swept the page one more time.

The large white eagle feather attached to Amara Morris' dirty cowgirl hat, hanging on the wall, fluttered down in the graceful way a dancing feather tends to do. Softly, it landed on the open book, marking the actual final page.

The final page read:
*Two years later, on July seventh, Jonny Sandgren was born to Billy and Charlie Sandgren. He was born with a mound of blond hair, squinty eyes, and a gummy smile which everyone claimed was gas but Amara knew was joy. By the way, she had been right.*

*Jonny was a joyous boy, untouched by the tragedies borne by the others. He was the hope, the life, and the love of the family, and Morris Ranch. He was destined to take the reins, and to be named Holder of the Horses.*

More books by Lisa Slater
 CHANCING HOPE
 A story of love and unpredictable suspense.

Kerwyn Bartel, a talented horse trainer, knows a thing or two about reading a horse's ability to confront fears and recognize a good partnership. If only Kerwyn could apply those same qualities to his relationship with the vibrant, carefree girl of his dreams, Mable Conners, who just happens to be his long-time childhood best friend.

Haunted by the loss of his mother, Kerwyn is determined to not compromise Mable's future. He is forced to make a big change. However, when a mysterious loner begins interfering, those changes may not by what he had expected. They both may just be left to Chancing Hope.

For reviews visit www.slaterlife.com

Made in the USA
Monee, IL
15 March 2021